Chapter 1 – Upper cut

Thursday 23rd June 1983

A figure dropped from the right and appe

yards ahead of us. It was a young black lad, wh glance in our direction, and was on his toes. Dawn responded instantly, throwing her hat off, and sprinting after him whilst she spoke in short rapid bursts into her radio.

"Chasing suspect, Belgrade Road, towards the High Road."

Instinctively, I began to run too, and, in a few paces, was into my stride and overtaking my instructor. As the lad neared the High Road, I knew I was closing on him.

At the junction he turned right and, no more than ten seconds later, I swept round the corner without breaking stride but, as I looked along the road and beyond a crowded bus stop, there was no sign of him. I slowed my pace but after a short distance knew there was no longer any point: my prey had disappeared into thin air. Not quite thirty seconds after it had started, the chase was over.

I stopped and turned around, frustrated that once again, I had let my instructor down.

As I strolled back slowly there was a sudden commotion amongst the crowd at the bus stop; people had formed a rough circle around some exciting but hidden event and were jostling for position. What I heard as I drew near, however, put urgency into my step.

"Leave him alone, he ain't done nothing."

"Fuck off, pig; he's been here all the time."

I pushed my way through the crowd and caught glimpses of Dawn, rolling around the floor, struggling with a black youth in his mid to late teens. The youth was trying to get to his feet but Dawn had wrapped herself around him and had her right arm around his chest, but his jacket was slowly coming off and, when it did, he would be able to escape. I had to get there; this was the opportunity I'd been waiting for to prove myself.

"Get out of the way, let me through," I growled.

Sensing freedom, the youth suddenly threw his head backwards and caught Dawn on the nose with a deep, bone-breaking crack. Stubbornly, she refused to let go. As I was clearing the crowd, a hand grabbed the tail of my tunic and checked my forward momentum.

"Fuck off," I spat.

I swung around looking for the hand's owner, but whoever it was had wisely decided to let go. As I turned back, I saw the youth had got to his feet. Dawn was on her knees, her arms now gripping around his shins in a poor imitation of a rugby tackle; her eyes were closed, blood poured from her nose and covered her face.

The youth was still looking down when my clenched fist met the underside of his jaw; there was a definite crack, followed by a collective gasp from the onlookers. At first, the youth went up, briefly, and then he fell like a stone, unconscious, directly on top of Dawn, who groaned under his weight, before quickly pushing him off.

Fifteen minutes later, those of us involved in this incident were making three very different journeys. Dawn was in an ambulance on her way to the London Hospital; the youth was in the rear of a police van; and I was being driven to the nick, by a grey-haired middle-aged PC in a panda car, by the most roundabout route imaginable.

I suspected I'd been deliberately separated from the youth and was worried someone else was going to claim my arrest. The delay did, however, give me time to think over the several matters which were troubling me. In no particular order these were – Was I going to get in trouble for punching the youth? Was I going to be blamed for what had happened to Dawn? Why had I been separated from the youth? Was the youth who'd been arrested the same lad who was running away? Even if Dawn had got the right person, what had he done wrong? It was no offence to run away from police, so what had he been arrested for? Policing, I decided, was a lot more complicated than I'd anticipated.

I had never met the driver before, but I needed his help.

"Listen, mate. Can I have some advice?"

"Yes, of course," he replied, but before I could ask anything he volunteered his own.

"Never get separated from your prisoner, son, especially not when he's punched a WPC. At this very moment the young man will be getting a very thorough lesson on why he shouldn't have done that. He'll be lucky to arrive in one piece but whatever happens to him, he'll be your prisoner."

"But he never really assaulted Dawn, their heads just knocked together. I'm not sure it was even deliberate; he was just trying to get away. Do you think we should tell them?"

"I think that's pretty academic, son. Dawn's face was a real mess; her colleagues will be seeking swift retribution. What's he nicked for anyway? I heard the chase but what's he done?"

"That's just it you see; I'm not sure."

"Are you serious?" the driver replied incredulously.

"He just climbed over a wall in Belgrade Road, saw us and ran. Before I had time to think, Dawn was after him and I just joined in too."

The driver had already heard enough and spoke into his radio.

"Golf November: can you get a unit to check for signs of a burglary near Belgrade Road and Wordsworth Road? The arresting officer says the suspect from the chase had climbed over a wall from the rear gardens."

Before the Reserve responded, a unit called up to say he was still at the scene and would have a look and, as we drove into the rear yard, the unit confirmed there appeared to have been a burglary because the back door of eighty-eight Wordsworth Road had been forced open and was now hanging by one hinge.

"There you go; arrest him for burglary and the assault on Dawn Matthews," the driver said.

I toyed with the thought of mentioning my next problem, which was that I wasn't at all sure we'd arrested the right man, but decided against it.

As I got out, the driver undid his window and called to a tall blond PC who was standing smoking by the stables.

"This is him, Pete."

Pete had apparently been waiting for the arresting officer and walked over to hand me a black bin liner.

"What's this?" I asked.

"This is your prisoner's. He dropped it when you were chasing him."

The PC spoke slowly as if he was talking to a child.

I knew I was being helped, so I took the bag. The blond PC stubbed his cigarette out under his Doc Marten and walked off. The bag was surprisingly heavy and jangled when I shook it.

I walked up the ramp, which led from the back yard and entered the charge room. The youth was sitting on a wooden bench, which was bolted to the floor against one wall. His head was in his hands, which were still handcuffed at the wrists. He looked up briefly as I entered, and I caught sight of a badly swollen left eye which had almost completely closed up. In front of the youth, at a desk, sat the sergeant. He was writing something on a large sheet of carbonated paper which was resting on a black plastic base.

"Are you the arresting officer?" the sergeant asked.

I nodded.

"Circumstances of arrest, please?"

I was meant to explain why the prisoner had been arrested, so the sergeant could be satisfied the arrest was lawful and that his continued detention was necessary, but I faltered, knowing I really couldn't say that this youth was the same lad I'd been chasing.

"We were walking down the road …" I hesitated.

The sergeant sensed my unease, lifted his head, and looked me up and down.

"Are you on Street Duties?"

"Yes, Sarge."

"Where's your instructor?"

"She's gone to hospital, Sarge; she was injured during the arrest."

The sergeant looked at the prisoner's face.

"That answers my next question."

"Name?"

"WPC Dawn Matthews, Sarge," I replied.

"I don't want her name, lad, not yet anyway."

"Oh, I haven't asked the prisoner yet?"

"I don't want his name either yet, I need yours," the sergeant said patiently.

"Oh sorry, PC Christopher Pritchard, four six six, Sergeant."

The sergeant wrote this information in a box on the form.

"What offence has the prisoner been arrested for?" the sergeant asked.

"Burglary, Sarge."

"Time of arrest?"

I glanced at my watch.

"Ten past one, Sarge."

"Thirteen ten, okay; location of arrest?"

"The High Road, Sarge, at the junction with Belgrade Road."

"And what makes you think he committed a burglary?"

"Because he climbed over a wall from a back garden in Belgrade Road and there's been a burglary at number eighty-eight."

I waited for the prisoner to deny climbing over the wall and to protest that he'd just been waiting for a bus, so when he didn't, I took this as a sign we'd arrested the right person.

"What's in the bag?"

I'd forgotten I was holding the bin liner.

"I don't know, Sarge, but he dropped it when we were chasing him."

"What's in the bag, young man?"

The youth shrugged his shoulders and sucked through his front teeth. Again, I was reassured that he didn't deny having possession of it.

"Empty the contents on the desk, please," the sergeant instructed.

I produced an assortment of obviously stolen goods, including a camera, several unspectacular watches, a clutter of cheap gold jewellery, a heavy money box in the shape of a pink pig and six packets of unopened cigarettes. The sergeant directed his next statement at the youth.

"Stand up and come here."

Slowly, grudgingly, the youth did as he was told. When he took his hands away from his face, I found it difficult not to stare at his damaged eye, and he kept opening and closing his mouth, as if he were checking whether his jaw was broken.

"You've heard the officer; what have you got to say?"

"I want my solicitor, Colin Stephens."

The youth rattled off a local telephone number, which he obviously knew by heart, and the sergeant scribbled it down on a notepad. I realised this was not the first time the youth had been arrested and took this as the final indication that we had arrested the right person.

The charge room door swung open and a short white man in his forties entered. I noticed straight away that he smelt of alcohol. As he was wearing a suit and tie, I guessed he was a company rep, who'd had a bit too much to drink over lunch with a client and been arrested for drink drive. The new prisoner sat quietly and patiently on the bench whilst the sergeant listed the property from the bin liner.

When this process was complete, the smartly dressed gentleman stood up and tapped the youth politely on the shoulder.

"What?" the youth said aggressively, without turning round.

He tapped him again; the youth turned round this time.

"What's your fucking problem?"

Without any warning the new prisoner swung a haymaker so wide that both my prisoner and I had to duck to avoid it. I moved quickly behind the suited gentleman and pulled him backwards.

Although intoxicated, he was strong and pulled violently against me, so hard, in fact, I had to slip my arms around his chest and physically lift him off the floor to hold him back.

"PC Pritchard," the sergeant shouted.

"What, Sarge?" I replied, as I struggled.

"Put the Chief Superintendent down, and that's an order!"

Chapter 2 – Selection day

My stuttering police career had started some ten months earlier, in the autumn of 1982, in a spectacularly dull classroom, illuminated by a dozen harsh strip lights, each filled with the bodies of a thousand dead flies, which was situated on the third floor of Paddington Green police station. There were forty of us, men of varying ages of whom I was definitely the youngest and we were all white, except one Asian chap, who was more my own age. We were seated in rows of five and addressed by a middle-aged man wearing a blue civilian jacket with two small silver pips on the lapel.

"This building is bombproof and fitted with metal shutters which will close over the windows should a threat be identified. There are no tests or drills scheduled for today so if they do come down and plunge the place into darkness, it's the real thing. Right, take a ten-minute break, gentleman; there's tea and coffee behind you. Then form yourself into the three groups as instructed and we'll get on with meds."

A few of the men pushed their chairs back and stood up but being less confident than the other candidates around me, I hesitated because something in the man's voice suggested he hadn't completely finished speaking. I was right.

"Oh, and one more thing." He paused, waiting until once again he had everyone's attention.

"If you're queer, now's your opportunity to leave. What sick acts you get up to in private is your business, but we definitely don't want you in the Metropolitan Police. So do yourself and us a favour and quietly slip out during the break; we won't ask any questions if you're not here when we resume."

The man waved his right hand in a gesture, which indicated the first part of our selection day was over. Everyone headed towards the refreshments at the back of the room and formed a polite, orderly queue.

In front of me was the Asian lad, with whom I was just about to spark up a conversation, when someone tapped me on the arm. I swung round to see a very smartly dressed older gentleman who was wearing a dark pin-striped suit.

"Can I ask you a question, old sport?" he said, with an impeccable public-school accent.

"Of course," I replied, curious to know what information I could possibly possess that he would require.

"Don't take this the wrong way but why the devil aren't you wearing a suit? Or at least a shirt and tie?"

I hadn't really thought about it but looking around the room, I noticed I was indeed the only person not wearing a collared shirt and tie. Instead, I had donned black cords, a white T-shirt, a black artificial leather jacket and an impressively long pair of winkle pickers. I had thought I looked quite smart; I didn't any longer.

"I don't have a suit," I answered, sheepishly.

"Listen. You had better make some excuse at the start of the interview otherwise you are bound to fail. I know, tell them you can't afford one. Go for the sympathy vote."

"I can't afford one," I replied, in complete honesty.

"That's the way, old sport," the gentleman said enthusiastically.

I hadn't been confident of success when I'd arrived. I was even less so now and put my chances of being selected for the Metropolitan Police at about one in a hundred.

The selection day was to be conducted in two distinct parts: meds – or to use the full title, medicals – in the morning and then an interview in the afternoon. Meds was split into four stages: an eyesight test and then a colour blindness test, a dental check-up and finally something called an inspection.

The first three I passed without trouble, but the final med was quite bizarre. For this, they got us to strip completely and queue in a corridor wearing only a towel and an uncomfortable smile. I had no idea what was coming when, without solicitation, the chap in front of me, who was covered in tattoos, offered an explanation.

"This is where they check if you're queer."

"Oh," I replied lamely.

I racked my brains but couldn't imagine how 'they' were going to discover such a personal thing; was there going to be some kind of examination? As I neared the front of the queue, curiosity got the better of me.

"Excuse me?"

"Yes, mate," the tattooed man replied pleasantly.

"How exactly are they going to do that?"

The man answered me in as matter of fact a way as if he'd just been asked directions.

"Well, I don't know how they do it here but, in the navy, they get you to bend over, and they examine your arse hole. Don't worry about it, mate, it's no sweat."

I thought this bloke might be winding me up but was soon to discover he was being completely serious.

The room I entered several minutes later was ridiculously cold but still warmer than the unfriendly stares of the three gentlemen seated behind a long mahogany desk. I assumed, I hoped, they were doctors. One pointed to a taped black cross on the floor, which was roughly in the middle of the room.

"Drop the towel on the chair, Pritchard, and stand there; put your hands on your head."

I felt very embarrassed and stared at a picture of Her Majesty the Queen which was hanging on the wall immediately behind the middle of the three doctors. Her Majesty held my stare with dignity.

"Stand on your toes."

"Open your legs slightly, with your knees straight, bend over and touch the floor."

"Now turn around and touch your toes again."

Immediately after each instruction, I did as I was told.

"Good. Now pull your cheeks apart."

My indignation and humiliation were tempered only by the knowledge that all forty applicants that morning had gone, or were going to go through, exactly the same procedure.

"Still tight, everything's all right, off you go," one of the other men said.

I assumed they had discovered nothing to suggest I was queer.

After lunch, which was a selection of sandwiches with very little filling, a packet of crisps and an apple, I and five other applicants sat quietly in a small room waiting for our interviews. I kept turning some answers over in my mind, like, why I wanted to join and what I had to offer the Met, but the more I did, the more my confidence shrank. The man sitting next to me was the Asian guy from the queue; although he was slightly older than me, we were similar ages. I gave up rehearsing my answers.

"Have you come far?" I asked.

"Not really, Manor Park," he replied.

I had no idea where Manor Park was. In fact, I'd only been to London twice and both occasions had been a school trip.

"Is it near the Science Museum?" I asked innocently.

"No."

The Asian man laughed, but not unkindly.

"You don't get many Indian police officers," I commented, keen to keep the conversation going, as it was easing my nerves.

"I'm not Indian, I was born here. My father was originally from Pakistan. I'm Rik by the way."

"Chris."

We shook hands.

"Actually, my father doesn't know I'm here today. I'm not sure he'd approve. My two older brothers are at medical school, but I was the thick one, so he wants me to work in the shop and carry on the family business. Then I saw the advert in the Telegraph, seven thousand a year, so I thought bugger selling cigarettes for three grand, I want to earn some real money."

"Seven thousand a year?" I said.

I had no idea how much the job paid.

"Don't tell me you didn't know?" Rik asked disbelievingly.

"Never gave it a thought. I haven't got a chance anyway. Most of these guys are ex-military and they're a lot older than us; loads of them were talking about their time in the Falklands and Northern Ireland. I mean, fuck me Rik, why are they going to pick us?"

"You never know, you might be just what they're looking for?" Rik said hopefully.

"Maybe," I said without conviction.

The door opened and the man in charge, the one with the two pips on his lapel, called out a name from a list on a clipboard.

"Patel."

Rik stood up.

"Good luck."

"Thanks. I'll catch you later," he replied.

I was the final candidate to be interviewed. I'd sat there patiently for two and a half hours when, at last, my name was called. I timidly entered the interview room and saw two solemn-looking, middle-aged men sitting behind a desk. They were marking some paperwork in front of them and didn't look up when I entered. A lonely chair had been placed in the middle of the room facing them. I sat down quietly trying not to disturb them.

"Who told you to sit down?" the slightly older of the two men asked curtly.

"Sorry," I said, quickly jumping up.

"Put the chair against the wall. For your interview you can stand in the middle of the room. After all, you're not going to be here long."

I stood in an awkward silence. Having put aside one piece of paper, they collected and studied another. I assumed it was my application form.

'You're not going to be here long,' he'd said; I turned the words over in my mind and decided they'd obviously already made their minds up not to take me.

"What's with the T-shirt and leather jacket?" the younger man said, eyeing me up and down, disdainfully.

Before I could launch into the answer I'd prepared, the man spoke again.

"You look like that guy out of that TV programme my kids are always watching, the Fonz."

"I don't have a suit, Sir, and the letter said smart, so I chose what I would wear if I was going out for the evening."

"And where would you be going if you were dressed like that?"

"One of the nightclubs in town, Sir."

The younger man raised his eyebrows and frowned.

"Perhaps if you had sacrificed a few nights out, you might have been able to afford a shirt and tie."

I didn't reply but looked to the floor submissively. Before I raised my stare, the other man, the slightly older one, asked:

"So, both your parents are dead, young man?"

"Yes, Sir. Mum died six months ago. I never knew my Dad."

"Is that why your A level results were so poor?"

I hesitated, even though it was the truth; I didn't want to sound like I was making excuses.

"No excuse, Sir, I should have worked harder."

Both men nodded; I just knew I'd said the right thing.

"No brothers or sisters?"

"No, Sir."

There was silence for what felt like a minute.

"You play rugby, then?" the same man asked.

I noticed a change in the intonation in the man's voice; I wasn't sure quite what to make of it.

"Yes, Sir. I played for the county last year and got through to the England final trial."

"What position?"

"Centre, Sir, outside preferably."

Again, both men nodded; suddenly, I got the distinct impression that despite my cock-up at the start and my massive clothing misjudgment, this might be going all right.

"A lot of coloured youths today complain about being repeatedly stopped by police. Do you think they might have a point?" the younger man asked.

"No, Sir. If they haven't done anything wrong, why should they be worried about being stopped?"

"Quite right," they both muttered almost simultaneously.

"Think very carefully, Pritchard; only one further question stands between you and thirty years in the Metropolitan Police."

I was amazed. The five men who had gone in before me had been in much longer than this; I'd only answered five or six questions and most of those were about my family and rugby.

"It's a year from now. You are on patrol and receive a call to help a WPC in a pub fight. How do you feel? I mean women shouldn't really be police officers, should they? And you're now expected to put your own life on the line because she's not physically strong enough to deal with a very common situation?"

I sensed a trap and took a deep breath, giving myself a few extra seconds to consider my answer.

"I wouldn't mind going to help the WPC, Sir. After all, the next day I might have to look after some children or even a baby and then I'd need *her* help, wouldn't I?"

The interviewers looked at one another. Then the older man stood up and walked around the side of the desk with an outstretched hand.

"Welcome aboard, Pritchard. I am Inspector Allan Franklin. I am confident we're going to be seeing a great deal of one another."

"Will I be working at your station?" I asked, as we shook hands.

"Good Lord, Pritchard; I very much doubt that. I work at the Yard."

"Then can I ask why we're going to see a lot of one another?"

"Because, young man, I'm the head coach of the Met Police Rugby Club and our current outside centre has just done his ankle ligaments and will be out for the rest of the season. We'll need to fast track your application but, with any luck, you'll be at Hendon by Christmas and available for selection in early January."

Rik had been right; I was just what they were looking for after all; well bugger me!

Chapter 3 – Service station advice

We had entered the outskirts of London on the M4 and, off to the right, a regularly spaced queue of coloured lights in the eastern sky waited for permission to land at Heathrow.

It was early January and a constant depressing drizzle fell; intermittent wiper blades swept the windscreen clear. We were listening to the top twenty on Radio One when Gerald, my next-door neighbour and long-retired Met Detective Inspector, turned a knob and silenced Phil Collins in mid-song.

"Let me ask you a question," he said, without taking his eyes off the road.

I turned to face the elderly driver, detecting a note of seriousness in his voice, and anticipating, quite correctly as it turned out, I was to be given some words of wisdom.

"You walk by a bus stop where a group of youths are loitering. As you pass them, one shouts *'cunt'* as loud as he can, the others laugh."

I was shocked to hear Gerald say the 'C' word, it was completely out of character. In the ten years I had known him, I'd never heard a curse or blasphemy pass his lips.

"The insult is clearly aimed at you. From everything you know about the British bobby, how are you going to respond, PC Pritchard?"

It was the first time anyone had addressed me by that title and the reality hit me; when I was attested tomorrow at the Police Training College at Hendon, that is exactly who I would become.

I was keen to impress Gerald; in fact, it had been him who'd encouraged me to join. I thought the question through. I had been brought up in a small village in Wiltshire where the police were respected and revered for their tolerance and impartiality.

"I'd just walk on. They're just trying to wind me up; if I respond that's just what they want. After all, a word can't hurt me, and they are entitled to their own opinion."

The old man nodded slowly, and I assumed my response had met with his approval. I relaxed into the comfortable leather seats of the big Ford.

Several silent miles on, I realised we were slowing down, and Gerald indicated to take the slip road into Heston Services. A quick glance at the petrol gauge showed we didn't need petrol, so I assumed Gerald wanted to use the toilet. The old man, however, pulled into the parking area, but well away from the main building, and applied the hand brake.

What was he doing? Why were we stopping here? Gerald undid his seat belt and turned to face me. All of a sudden there was the merest hint of tension in the air.

"Listen carefully, son; this is what you do. You walk *slowly* back to the group. Don't ask who said it, don't say a word, just identify the biggest, hardest-looking youth and, with one deft blow, you punch him into next week. Then you nick him for threatening behaviour. And if he fights back, you go toe to toe until one of you goes unconscious. When you wear that uniform you never, ever, ever, take a step back."

Gerald's eyes drilled deep into my soul and it took a gargantuan effort not to look away.

"You see, because if you don't, the little old lady who was watching and heard you called by that appalling word and saw you just walk on, will be frightened for the rest of her life. But if she sees you bravely challenge such behaviour, even when you are completely outnumbered, she will sleep feeling safe in the knowledge there are police out there who will put their lives on the line to protect her."

My first lesson over, our journey recommenced.

Chapter 4 – An alarming first assignment

Early one Monday morning in May 1983, I and twenty other classmates left Training School in a Green Goddess. We were then deposited at various police stations; in the same way a Spanish coach would deliver holidaymakers landing at Barcelona to their hotels on the Costa Brava.

At two o'clock, Police Constable four six six 'G' Christopher James Pritchard was officially welcomed by his new Commander at Divisional Headquarters, above City Road police station. The meeting lasted no more than thirty seconds and was spectacularly unremarkable. I would have instantly forgotten it, had it not been for the fact I recognised the Commander from a contemporary Met recruitment advertisement.

Afterwards, I sat in a tiny interview room with absolutely nothing to do but stare at a few benign posters. I waited and waited and waited. Just before five o'clock, the door burst open, and a policeman appeared.

"Pritchard?"

"Yes, Sir."

"Don't call me Sir. We're here to collect you, come this way. Sorry if you've had to wait but it's been one bloody call after another."

"Don't worry, I was fine. The Commander said it was a busy division," I replied.

"And what the fuck does he know? Some Bramshill public-school wanker in his ivory tower. Don't take any notice of him, mate, and you can forget that shit they taught you at Training School too."

His rebuke shook me, and I decided in future to keep my thoughts to myself and my mouth shut. We set off at pace and, carrying my heavy kit bag, I struggled to keep up. I followed as the officer led me quickly through ever-narrowing corridors and down several flights of stairs until we emerged into the back yard.

I was shepherded into the rear of a police transit van and sat on a thin uncomfortable bench. The engine was running and the driver, a PC in his early thirties, completely ignored me.

My guide jumped into the front passenger seat and slid the door closed with a clunk. He and the driver resumed what I assumed to be an earlier conversation.

"That story is bollocks, I'm telling you."

"It's what I've heard. He came home to find his wife in bed with another woman, and the other woman was his sergeant."

"Lucky bastard."

"No, seriously, the wanker is divorcing her."

"On what grounds?"

They laughed.

"I mean, wouldn't you just climb in bed with them?"

"You couldn't stop me."

"Him and the missus had had a big bust up the night before. He was on early turn the next day and asked his skipper if he could take half a day to go home and sort it all out. She'd said no, as they were down to minimum strength. He thinks *'fuck it, I'm going home anyway'* and when he gets home, he discovers his wife and the skipper naked and in bed together."

"The skipper's been suspended and the PC's getting divorced."

Their conversation started all over again with the driver declaring his disbelief and my mind wandered. I was a police officer. A real, fully fledged, warrant-card-carrying, police officer. I wished my mum could see me now, she would've been so very proud. And what about the teachers at school? Only last year I was getting in trouble for chewing gum in class and running in the corridors and yet, here I was, in full uniform, about to enforce the law on some of the toughest streets in the country.

The van was stuck in heavy rush hour traffic and making slow progress along a bustling high street. I stared through the darkened rear windows and watched everyone going about their business. I was amazed at how few white people there were, and those that were, were a generation or two older than everyone else. Compared with where I'd grown up, London was like a foreign country.

The RT set, the Radio Telephone, was affixed to the dashboard near the driver's left hand and I heard a constant stream of messages being transmitted. When the driver went to pick up the handset, I realised the vehicle we were in was being called.

"Golf November two?"

The driver depressed the transmit button.

"Go ahead, Golf November."

"Did you go back to 13 Tintagel Close?"

"Yes, yes."

"Did you inform the female occupier that her husband has died?"

"Yes, yes."

"Is she going to the hospital now?"

"No, no. She said, if she didn't want to see him at two o'clock when he was dying, why did the Metropolitan Police think she would want to see him at four o'clock now he's dead?"

"I'll let the hospital know. Golf November out."

The radio was silent for only a few moments before the van was being called again.

"Golf November two, are you making your way back from headquarters?"

"Yes, yes."

"Can you take a central station hold up alarm at the Abbey National Building Society please? One three two, one hundred and thirty-two, Kingsland Road."

"Yes, yes, show us in red."

For a minute or two we remained stationary in the traffic and then the operator turned and spoke to me.

"Listen, mate. It'll take ages for us to get through this traffic, so put your helmet on, get out and take a walk down to the Abbey National. Tell them their central station alarm's been activated and then hop back in. It's just up there on the left."

I glanced through the windscreen and saw, about fifty yards ahead on the left, the distinctive red and white logo of the Abbey National Building Society.

The driver flicked a switch on the dashboard and a weak light illuminated the rear of the van. The instruction was concise enough, the task simple, but its execution less so because I'd never before been in a public place in uniform and, although six months of training should have prepared me for this moment, all of a sudden, I felt terrified. I dithered.

"Get on with it, mate, what the fuck are you doing?" the driver asked impatiently.

I fiddled uncertainly with the rear door handle. Did it lift up or down? Was there a catch? Did the door push out, pull in or slide? I pushed, pulled, twisted, and eventually stepped out of the dimly lit interior and into the late afternoon sunshine; my eyes needed a few seconds to adjust. I paused and gathered myself, as I positioned my helmet carefully, using my right thumb to measure the correct distance between the dip at the front and the end of my nose.

Satisfied my titfer was in exactly the right place, I set off to deal with my very first assignment, a central station alarm at the Abbey National Building Society in Kingsland Road.

I walked smartly and found myself almost marching. I overtook the stationary queue of rush hour traffic and was immediately aware that I was being watched by just about everyone in the street. I felt extremely self-conscious.

The pavement was busy. I weaved my way politely through a bored crowd at a bus stop, sidestepped a pram being pushed without due care and attention and inadvertently kicked an empty coke can with such perfect timing that it shot like a bullet into the road where it was trapped and then flattened by the creeping wheel of a juggernaut.

My eyes focused on the red and white Abbey National sign that hung above a glass door now only thirty yards away. On the wall behind the sign, a small blue light was flashing on a white alarm box, but there was no audible indication of activation.

The front door of the building society opened, and a customer walked out. The man stopped momentarily, as if he was getting his bearings. I was relieved the building society was still open, as it would make my task easier; I would be able simply to pop my head in and let them know their alarm had gone off.

I checked my watch, one minute to five.

When I looked up, the man, the customer, was facing me and our eyes met. A grimace spread across the man's face, as if he had forgotten something really important, and I expected him to turn round and re-enter the Abbey National. Instead, he lifted his right arm. Whatever he was holding, perhaps an umbrella, glinted against the sun. I was about fifteen yards from the man when I identified the object as a double-barrelled sawn-off shotgun. As the realisation dawned, the man brought the weapon up to shoulder height and pointed it directly at my head.

Without a conscious effort to do so, I dropped face first to the pavement. On the way down, I heard two loud bangs in rapid succession and an instantaneous whoosh just above my head, accompanied by several almost delicate pings. I wasn't sure whether I'd been hit.

I heard the man's footsteps running away. A woman nearby screamed. I lay perfectly still, perhaps for a second or maybe a minute, as I had no concept of time, but when I looked up my helmet was still rocking from side to side several feet away.

I heard a bell and looked up to see the police van, its blue light flashing, desperately trying to find a way through the traffic. As it drew level with me, the van lurched to a brief undignified halt.

"You alright, mate?" the operator shouted through the open passenger door.

I nodded.

"Have you been shot?"

"No," I shouted back.

"Well! What the fuck are you doing? Taking a nap? Get the fuck up and give chase."

Chapter 5 – Tooling up

When I eventually arrived at the nick, late afternoon had succumbed to evening. I sat in the canteen and made a written statement about the shooting. Technically, I was the victim of an attempted murder. Curiously, I didn't feel like the victim of an attempted murder, it had all happened too quickly to be scared; by the time I'd realised what was going on, it was all over.

I did find it interesting that, even though I'd been shot at, I was still expected to get up and give chase. It was probably that which struck me more than anything else about the dramatic events that afternoon.

I was reminded of a lesson we'd had at Training School. I'm sure it wasn't part of the curriculum, but our wily old sergeant delivered it, nonetheless. One Friday towards the end of the course, we'd just come back from lunch and the afternoon session was underway when there was a knock at the door and another sergeant, who we assumed was also on the teaching staff, entered and began to discuss with our sergeant the booking of the Court Room for the following day. He suggested our sergeant had crossed out his booking and overwritten the entry with his own. An argument ensued and the visitor left slamming the door. It was all rather embarrassing, but our lesson continued until the smoke break.

Upon our return, the sergeant directed us to write out our recollection of the earlier argument, paying particular attention to the physical description of the other sergeant. Then twelve men came in, all numbered and lined up at the front of the room, and we each wrote down which we thought had been the sergeant. Of course, in all respects we failed abysmally, because all twenty-two of us had naturally looked away when the discussion had started to get heated. From now on, and for the rest of our service, the sergeant explained, when trouble started, we walk towards it with our eyes and ears open. Never in the six months I was at Training School was a point better made.

After I finished my statement, I sat in the canteen and watched the staff close up. They were two middle-aged black ladies who seemed to move at a slower pace than the world around them. They had a radio playing in the kitchen churning out reggae music, to which I paid little attention, until Bob Marley's *I Shot the Sheriff* came on and I allowed myself an ironic smile. For some reason, I noticed both canteen ladies left with bulging carrier bags.

"Goodnight, darling," they both called to me cheerfully, as they walked out of the door.

"Goodnight," I called back.

It was dark by the time a CID officer came to collect my statement. The man, a white chap in his early forties with tobacco-stained teeth and breath to match, sat himself down opposite me and carefully read through my two pages of handwritten script.

"Can't you give a better description, mate? White, about forty, brown hair, that narrows it down to about eight million people."

"Sorry, but I only saw him for a second."

"If we showed you some albums, do you think you'd be able to recognise him?"

"I'll try," I replied, grateful for any opportunity to do more but not wanting to ask what an album was.

The CID officer read on. As he came to the last sentence he laughed.

"Where you've written at the end *'I am willing to go to court and give evidence'*, cross that out, mate. I rather think that's why the Commissioner pays you."

At Hendon we'd practised taking statements from pretend victims and witnesses and all ended with a sentence indicating whether the person was willing to go to court. Of course, I shouldn't have written that on my own statement. I felt pretty stupid.

"And we'll need your helmet. I gather there's some shot in it?"

I picked it up from the next chair and handed it over. The CID officer examined it carefully.

"You were fucking lucky, mate; can't have missed your head by more than two inches."

"I know. I always wanted to be six foot, I'm rather glad I'm not, now. If you're taking my helmet, where do I get a new one?"

"You'll have to wear your cap for now. Speak to your Street Duties Sergeant; he'll sort it out. Who's your instructor, do you know yet?"

"No idea."

"Get Dawn Matthews, avoid Dean Campbell like you would a bad dose of the clap. Dawn may be a split purse but she's good old bill."

"Will I have a choice?"

"No."

I thought in that case, whilst his advice might be well intended, it was rather pointless.

It had been a long day, but I had one last thing to do: unpack my kit bag. To do so, I would need to locate my locker key. The admin girl I was meant to meet had long since gone home but fortunately, she'd been thoughtful enough to leave my key on the Station Officer's desk.

I found my locker in the basement next to an impressive and immaculate snooker table. Two plain-clothed officers were finishing a game; only a few colours remained. I was as quiet as I could be, so as not to disturb them.

"Are you the new guy that was shot at?" one enquired, as he was about to pot the black.

"Yes, that's me."

The black shot across the table and into the top right pocket without touching the sides.

"Thanks to you we're all on overtime trying to catch your man."

I didn't know what to say. Should I thank them? They didn't seem to be trying too hard, but I thought it better not to point that out. I smiled weakly and started to unpack my bag.

"Another game, Jim?"

"No, night duty will be in in a minute. Let's get a pint. I need a word with the guvnor about court next week."

I relaxed after they'd left but the task of emptying my kit bag into one small thin metal locker was going to prove challenging. At least I didn't have to fit a helmet in, too. The locker room was an untidy place. For a start there were far too many lockers for the available space and most had things on top and in front of them. Shoes, jackets, sports bags, helmets, overcoats, aftershave, deodorant, football boots, tennis rackets, cricket pads, cardboard boxes and a hundred other articles were scattered everywhere.

Damp towels hung over old iron radiators, which gave the place a musty atmosphere, but there was something else: a strange sickly-sweet smell in the air.

As I unpacked, other officers arrived and got ready for night duty. Most were wearing their uniform below a civilian jacket; others came in jeans and a T-shirt and had to get completely changed. Everyone acknowledged me as they came in.

"Hello, mate."

"Alright."

"Ain't seen you before, are you new?"

"Do you know what relief you're going on?"

"Did you hear about the PC that was shot at?"

"It was you? Fucking hell, my friend, you alright?"

I kept my answers short but was quietly impressed; I felt an easy friendship from these men, who ranged in age from twenty to fifty. I thought it was interesting that they spoke with such a variety of accents, surprisingly few of which were London. What was abundantly clear, and actually quite reassuring, was that being shot at was not an everyday event.

When I had just about finished unpacking, a large Welshman, who was nearly old enough to be my dad, opened the locker immediately to my right.

"Hello, boyo," he said pleasantly, holding out an enormous hand.

"Welcome to the Stokey. I am William, William Rees."

"Thank you."

"So, you're the laddie who tried to arrest an armed blagger on his very first day?"

"Not quite."

"You've got quite a reputation already, boyo."

William spoke slowly but he had an air about him, a charisma that was quite striking.

He took off a tweed jacket and started his well-practised ritual of dress. As we chatted about what had happened to me, William put his epaulettes on each shoulder, dropped a truncheon in his trouser pocket, clipped his tie into place, slid his belt through the loops in his trousers, fitting a handcuff pouch to one side, pulled his jacket on and before doing up the shining silver buttons, slipped several small clear plastic bags containing a green-brown substance into his inside left pocket and a flick knife and horrendous looking knuckle duster into his right.

I tried to ignore what William was doing but my eyes must have given my thoughts away because William said apologetically, “Sorry, it’s the first night duty so I’m probably going to need this lot. Tell you what, if I get some more, I’ll slip some through the vent into your locker.”

“That’s all right, I’ll be fine,” I replied quickly, but apparently unconvincingly because William was quick to explain, in his slow rolling Welsh accent, why I should accept his offer.

“Listen, boyo. Take some advice from someone who’s been doing this job since before you were born. Sometimes the wheels of justice need a little oiling, sometimes those bastards out there need to be reminded who’s boss. They’ll accuse you of it anyway, whether you fit them up or not. So, the way I sees it, you might as well get in there first.”

William nodded his head slowly, as if he was considering his own advice and then agreeing with it, and he put his hand on my shoulder, in a fatherly gesture.

“I’ll slip you a few packets of herbal later in the week.”

“Thanks,” I replied. What else could I say?

It was perhaps fortunate that I didn't know that, with that one word, I'd committed a criminal conspiracy and several offences under the Misuse of Drugs Act 1971.

Chapter 6 – Nostrils

I'd already had twenty weeks intensive training at Hendon but wouldn't be allowed to patrol alone for another three months. During this time, I would have to work alongside an experienced officer at all times. Officially, this period in one's career is known as Street Duties; unofficially, it is called being puppy-walked.

The following morning when I opened my locker, I was mightily relieved to discover William hadn't left me anything. I put my uniform on and asked directions to the Street Duties office, which I learnt was a weather-battered portacabin in the rear yard. I entered just before eight o'clock.

"Constable Pritchard? Or should I call you Nostrils?" the sergeant asked.

This man would be in charge of me for the next twelve weeks.

Nostrils? What did Sarge mean by that?

"How do you do, Sarge?"

"Don't shorten my rank, son, or I might choose to shorten yours, Cunt.....stable."

"Sorry, Sergeant."

"That's better. I am Sergeant Bellamy and it's my job to make sure you're fit to join your relief in twelve weeks' time. WPC Matthews will look after you; she's very thorough, very good. She'll report to me on your progress at the end of each week. If I don't see much of you, I'll consider it a good sign. I have an inspector's exam to pass, and I'll be unhappy if I have to divert any more than the odd minute or two from my studying. Do I make myself clear?"

"Yes, Sergeant."

"How old are you?" he asked.

"Nineteen."

"Were you a gadget, Nostrils?"

"A gadget, Sergeant?"

"A cadet, but if you have to ask, you obviously weren't. Nineteen. Christ! I must be getting old. You play rugby, don't you?"

"Yes, Sergeant, but the season's over until September."

"The Chief Super's very keen on it, so keep it up. It helps to be part of something in this job. Now go and find Dawn, she's probably in the canteen."

Sergeant Bellamy turned and waddled through a door at the far end of the portacabin and into what could only have been described as one of the smallest of offices, which was somewhat ironic really, as Sergeant Bellamy was about the fattest person I had ever seen. His belly was so large it hung over his waist in rolls completely obscuring his belt, his face was round and red, and his chin had chins. The man huffed and puffed with every step and the portacabin floor seemed to strain under his weight.

I remembered what the CID officer in the canteen had said the previous day and was pleased to have been allocated to Dawn and not the other guy, whose name I'd already forgotten.

I glanced about my new place of work; what a dump. Empty and half-empty paper cups were everywhere, including in the confidential waste sack, which seemed to have in it very little that was confidential, unless there were great state secrets written on sandwich wrappings, crisp packets, cigarette ends, tin cans and plastic bottles.

Forms, statements, report books were scattered untidily about the place. Some were blank, but many had clearly been started and discarded. A much-used kettle sat on a tray above a fridge; coffee, tea and milk stains had combined on the tray to form a brown gunge. From a circular coat rack hung at least thirty pieces of police uniform; some had been there so long they had gathered layers of dust, a few of such an age I didn't think they were still regulation issue. Everything at the training school had been so neat and tidy, nothing had ever been out of place and there was never any rubbish or litter anywhere. Was this what the Metropolitan Police was really like?

I suddenly remembered that I didn't have a helmet. I knocked quietly on the sergeant's office door, worried about disturbing him so soon after he had told me he wanted to be left alone. A few loud bangs later and his door opened, a gust of yellow cigarette smoke escaped, and the sergeant asked impatiently, "What?"

"I haven't got a helmet. I had to give mine to the CID 'cos they said it was evidence."

"Take one off the rack, Nostrils. Now leave me alone, I'm studying."

There was that word again, Nostrils; he was definitely using it in place of my name. Why would I be called by such a random word? I studied my nose in a small wall mirror; it looked as unremarkable as ever. I was perplexed.

Having found a helmet, which although nearer to my size than any of the other three, was definitely too big, I made my way over to the canteen. I was more than a little surprised that Sergeant Bellamy hadn't mentioned the shotgun incident; after all, surely such an event was rather unusual? Perhaps he hadn't heard about it? But then, if that was the case, wouldn't he have asked me why I had to give my helmet to the CID? I concluded that he knew but wasn't really that bothered or interested. I felt slightly disappointed; everything at Training School had prepared us for this day and we'd waited and counted down the weeks in heady anticipation. Now the day had arrived, I sort of expected the Metropolitan Police, in the guise of Sergeant Bellamy, to be just a little bit excited too; but it wasn't, it really wasn't the least bit interested in me. I hoped this Dawn Matthews would be a bit more enthusiastic.

The canteen was really busy. Nearly every table was taken, and a dozen or so administrative staff were queuing to buy tea and toast. A vociferous group of CID officers were sat on a large table discussing passionately and audibly the case of a colleague, who'd been arrested by a 'rat' for drink drive. After listening to their conversation for only a few moments, I gathered a 'rat' was a traffic officer.

Alone in a far corner, sat a uniformed WPC; she was thumbing through Woman magazine, a photograph of a smiling Princess Diana was on the front cover. The WPC was in her late twenties, had short black hair and noticeably protruding ears; her frame was small, and she looked as though a gust of wind blowing through a nearby open window might carry her away. She glanced up and caught my eye.

"Dawn?" I mouthed.

With both her forefingers she made a T and nodded towards the counter. Even I could work out what that meant. Five minutes later, and twenty-four pence poorer, I joined the WPC, who managed to ignore my arrival with disdain and contempt in equal measure. I sat immediately opposite her, unsure what I was expected to do or say. Awkward seconds ticked by until I could bear the silence no longer.

"Dawn?"

She looked up and slowly shook her head.

"No."

"Oh, I'm sorry; I thought you were my Street Duties instructor?"

"I don't think they'd let me anywhere near probationers, but thanks for the tea, is it sugared?"

"No."

"Two, please."

I thought her manner bordered on rudeness but felt obliged to return to the counter and collect two white square sachets and a plastic spoon, which I dropped next to her cup.

"Do you know where I might find WPC Dawn Matthews?" I asked.

Without acknowledging my question, she reached for her transmit button.

"One eight two, one eight two, you receiving, over?"

"Go ahead, Tommy," a female voice replied.

"Your new puppy is in the canteen and looking rather lost."

"Get him to sit and stay," one eight two replied, as if barking orders to a dog.

There were ripples of laugher about the room.

"Tell him if he's good, I'll take him for walkies."

The ripples of laughter rose briefly to a wave, which washed completely over me; I felt very small indeed.

Chapter 7 – Dawn patrol

Twenty minutes later Dawn Matthews and I were walking slowly along Stoke Newington High Street. Dawn was in her mid-twenties, 5'4" tall and very petite; her mousey-brown hair, tightly tied under her hat, was of indeterminate length and she wore no make-up, earrings or jewellery; her features were unremarkable, almost plain. She was wearing a long uniform skirt, black tights and flat, unflattering shoes.

I explained to Dawn how the WPC in the canteen had tricked me into buying her a tea.

"Classic Tommy."

"Tommy. Isn't that a bloke's name?"

"Her name's Sarah Thompson. She's lovely. If it's about to kick off, you want Sarah by your side, I'm telling you."

I genuinely thought she was joking and laughed before quickly realising she wasn't and trying to conceal my amusement, but it was too late. I didn't look at Dawn but could feel her displeasure. Was I being stupid? Tommy couldn't have weighed seven stone wet. What's more, a woman holding her own in a fight? Wasn't that a ridiculous concept? How was this Tommy, or Dawn for that matter, who shared both gender and stature, going to slog it out with some eighteen-stone drunk? For the next two hundred yards we walked through a thick, uncomfortable silence.

"The first thing you have to get used to is being stared at; everyone you pass watches every step you take," Dawn said.

"And they make no attempt to conceal their stares, as they might if you were disabled or disfigured, they just ogle shamelessly. You'll get used to it; all coppers do. If someone's not staring at you, you should be asking yourself why not. Stroll like you own the street, smile and nod to everyone as you pass, never walk by anyone without acknowledging them; oh, and in any situation, the more apprehensive you feel, the slower you walk."

I nodded.

"I gather you had a rather eventful trip from City Road yesterday?"

"Just a bit."

"Are you alright? I mean I know you weren't hit or anything but mentally are you okay?"

"Yeah, of course," I replied with confidence, but I knew the second the words had left my mouth, I'd sounded too arrogant, too cocky, too self-assured.

"Don't know why I asked," Dawn said, and I knew I'd made another gaffe.

The molasses silence returned. I wanted to say something, anything, to suggest to Dawn I wasn't the arrogant nineteen-year-old I'd somehow managed to portray, in the few minutes we'd known one another.

"How long have you been in the job?" I asked.

"Five years but I was a cadet for two years before that," she replied.

"Sergeant Bellamy asked me if I'd been a cadet, well he asked me if I'd been a gadget, is that the same thing?"

"Yes."

"The CID officer in the canteen yesterday, the one who read my statement about the shooting, he used a different expression."

"Did he, what was that?"

"Well, he said even though you were a split purse, you were good old bill."

"A split purse?"

"That's what he said, does that mean cadet, too?"

"No, the expression he was using was split arse, not split purse, Chris."

"Oh, that doesn't sound good."

"It's not, it's a very derogatory term for WPC and if I ever hear you using it again, we'll fall out."

Dawn had stopped walking and was looking me squarely in the face; for the briefest moment this seven-stone woman was quite intimidating.

"Sorry. The words will never pass my lips again."

I'd clearly touched a nerve but felt a little put out; after all, I had no idea the term was offensive.

The tension between us continued; this was not going well. I hoped the day would improve.

"We're going to do the bus lane this morning. It starts at seven and is very popular with the public."

"What? They like being done for driving in a bus lane?"

"No, you idiot. The public love to see those drivers trying to sneak along the bus lane getting caught. I'll do a couple, it's a simple process book, watch what I do and say, it's really just like they teach you at Training School. Whilst I'm sticking the driver on, you make sure you do a vehicle and name check. Then we'll swap and you can have your first process, okay?"

"Piece of cake," I replied.

I meant the comment as a joke, but Dawn took it completely the wrong way.

"Let's hope so," she replied seriously.

As we walked slowly up the slight incline, I tried to make conversation.

"Are you married?"

"No."

"Have you got a boyfriend?"

"No."

"Do you want to have children?"

"No."

"How long do you think you'll do this job?"

The last query didn't even solicit a response; it was almost as if Dawn was offended by my questions, even though I thought they were friendly enough.

Half a mile and one very one-sided conversation later, we came to a large oak tree growing out of a sea of concrete. Dawn explained we were to use the tree to hide behind to keep out of the view of oncoming traffic.

"This is the only tree for miles, so every dog uses it; be careful where you tread," she warned me.

Dawn had taken her hat off and every ten seconds she was glancing along the road. In no time at all we had our first customer. Mr Suited and Booted in his company Ford Cortina took it all with resignation, he even said thank you before recommencing his journey.

The local rabbi in his white Volvo, who was next, was less impressed and tried to suggest Dawn was being anti-Semitic, but his case was undermined when a motorist held in the long queue undid his passenger window and shouted, "Good for you, officers, he does that every bloody morning."

I couldn't help but notice the Volvo, which was less than a year old, was absolutely covered in dents and scratches.

"Did you see the state of his car?" I asked, as the man drove off.

"Orthodox Jews can't drive," Dawn replied, in a matter-of-fact way.

"Are you serious?"

"Oh God, yes. I mean they're no trouble to us at all. They're honest, non-violent people but by God, they're dreadful behind the wheel of a car. That's why they all drive Volvos, 'cos they're built for safety and as strong as tanks. Oh, and 'cos they won't buy German, obviously," she added, as an afterthought.

"Okay, it's your turn."

Dawn pointed to my helmet, indicating I should remove it; whilst peeping around the tree, I did.

It took an age for the next driver to decide to use the bus lane but eventually a red Ford Fiesta chose to take the risk. I waited. The vehicle drove by and then on.

"Why didn't you stop the Fiesta?" Dawn asked, with a hint of frustration in her voice.

"I wasn't sure, so I was waiting for you to tell me to," I replied.

"Oh, for goodness' sake, Chris. What more information do you need? It's a car driving down a bus lane. Wake up."

I could see her point; yes, I had been indecisive but wouldn't be next time.

"Okay, okay," I replied and we resumed our positions.

Next came a brown Austin Maxi but, just as I was about to step out, the driver signalled to turn left into the side road just behind us, which seemed fair enough to me, so I allowed it to drive past unhindered.

"Why didn't you stop the Maxi?" Dawn asked, with growing annoyance.

"It was signalling to turn left," I said defensively.

"And has it turned left?"

I didn't reply, a quick glance told me all I needed to know. The car hadn't turned left but gone straight on and was now trying to cut back into the queuing traffic.

"Oh."

"Listen, Christopher, what do you think these other poor drivers think of us now? They've sat patiently in the traffic and you've let two cars drive down the bus lane."

"Sorry, Dawn. I promise I'll stop the next vehicle that comes down the bus lane."

"That would be really good, Chris, as long as it's not a bus."

"Honest, I'm not that stupid."

"Really?" Dawn replied sarcastically.

Our vigil recommenced. I was grateful to see a small yellow Datsun van hurtling at pace towards me in the bus lane. My opportunity for redemption was immediately at hand. I stepped out boldly and held my right hand aloft, signalling to the driver to stop.

When the Datsun was fifty yards away, I interpreted the fact it had not slowed down at all as a challenge and I stepped forward in a dramatic gesture. When the car had still not eased up at thirty yards, the first element of doubt entered my mind. At twenty yards my nerves started to give as I realised, even if the driver stood on the brakes now, he wouldn't stop in time.

"Move!" Dawn screamed at me.

I threw myself to the pavement, falling in the most undignified way imaginable, and ending up on my back, with my head coming to rest firmly in the soft, muddy texture of a still warm dog turd. A yellow blur passed at some fifty miles an hour.

"Golf November. Failing to stop for police, a yellow Datsun van, part index WWS, Stamford Hill, south towards the one-way system," Dawn transmitted.

Almost instantaneously, I heard a police siren not far away and sat up to see the area car, a Rover SD1, with its blue lights on, coming down the bus lane towards us. It screeched to a halt as I was collecting my helmet. We jumped into the back and set off in pursuit.

"At least you managed to get one car to stop in the bus lane," Dawn said unkindly.

"What the fuck is that smell?" the driver asked, within seconds of us getting in.

"Dog shit," I replied. "It's in my hair."

"I've never fancied you more," Dawn replied, whilst holding her nose and simultaneously opening her window.

The chase was short. The yellow Datsun was no match for the 3.5 litre V8 engine and we overtook and boxed it in against the kerb. Dawn jumped out, closely followed by the operator and driver. I was desperately keen to do something right and tried to follow but my door wouldn't open. Momentarily confused, it took several seconds to realise the child lock was on. I located and then pushed the electric window switch, intending to reach through the open window and unlock the door from the outside, but as the ignition was off, the window wouldn't work.

In between the back seats were several kit bags and overcoats, which formed a barrier and made sliding across quite impossible. There was only one way to go. I climbed awkwardly through the gap between the front seats and went out of the passenger door, but just when I thought I was clear, my right foot caught in the seat belt and I tripped and fell, landing hard on all fours on the concrete pavement.

Despite my knees hurting like hell, I got up immediately and just hoped no one had noticed. My delayed exit meant I was noticeably late arriving at the Datsun which, I was surprised to learn, was being driven by a small, elderly Asian man and not the hardened criminal I'd assumed had tried to run me down. Also present was his wife, who was shouting at the driver in a foreign language, and two screaming children who were in the back on a mattress. To add to the symphony of confusion, from a small push-button radio in the dash loud Indian music was playing.

"Oh, nice of you to join us," Dawn said.

"I couldn't get out the car."

"Why? Didn't they teach you that at Training School?" she asked spitefully.

It soon became apparent we were not dealing with a case of attempted murder but a harangued husband who had been somewhat distracted by the chaos inside his van. The usual checks on the vehicle and its occupants all came back clear and I issued a producer to the driver, requiring him to attend a police station of his choice within five days with his driving documents.

WIth my hair still covered in shit, the area car driver refused Dawn's request to run us back to the nick, so we had to set off on foot. I was limping and my right knee was throbbing.

"When we get in, let me see your process book before you hand it to Sergeant Bellamy," Dawn instructed me.

"What process book?" I asked.

"The process book for driving in the bus lane. You did stick him on for that, didn't you?"

"No, in all the mayhem I forgot."

"Christopher?"

"Yes, Dawn?"

"You're absolutely useless."

Chapter 8 – Deaf and dumb

My first week being puppy-walked by Dawn started badly, got worse and then culminated in a gloriously awful Friday.

On one day I went on patrol without a pen, on the Wednesday I was an hour late when my old Ford Fiesta refused to start and the following day at the scene of a burglary I managed to knock over and smash the only valuable piece of antique pottery that the thieves hadn't stolen. Dawn rarely spoke to me and when she did, I detected nothing but scorn in her voice.

On Friday we were working with A relief who were early turn and so at just before six o'clock, Dawn and I were in the Collator's office with a dozen or so other officers; all were white males in their twenties or early thirties. There was a little conversation between them, but no one seemed to want to make too much effort to be social. The few who were smoking stubbed out their cigarettes as footsteps approached, and then a sergeant and inspector entered. Those who had been sitting stood up and those who were already on their feet stood up just that little straighter.

"Thank you, relax," the inspector said; he was a small serious-looking Scottish man in his late forties.

"Appointments," the sergeant said.

I had no idea what he meant but quickly copied the others as each produced a truncheon, whistle and pocket book. The sergeant then posted everyone to either a vehicle or a beat and gave us 'refs' time.

Dawn and I were posted to the beat which covered the streets immediately south of the nick.

The sergeant read out entries from the parade book, which contained snippets of information which we needed to know before going out on patrol; this morning's bulletin included the descriptions of a missing teenager, three recently stolen cars and an address where police had been called during the night to a domestic dispute and the officers who had attended were asking any other calls there to be treated as urgent. The parade ended with a piece of advice from the Scotsman.

"I want everyone out by six thirty. If you're in the nick and it's not your ref's time, you'd better have a damn good excuse."

A couple of officers said, "Yes, Sir", and the rest nodded.

I realised that refs must be your mealtime and guessed correctly it was short for refreshment.

As the parade broke up, the inspector took Dawn gently to one side.

"How are you, my dear?"

"I'm fine now; thank you for asking. How are you, more to the point?"

He shook his head slowly.

"I take a day at a time, you know," he replied pragmatically.

"How's the sprog getting on?" The inspector nodded towards me. I felt awkward.

"The jury's still out on that one, Sir," Dawn replied, as if I wasn't there.

I walked off and left them to chat as they clearly knew one another quite well. I went to book out a radio and use the toilet.

When I went to find Dawn, she was chatting to the crew of the night duty area car, which was parked up in the back yard. As I approached her from behind, I overheard the tail end of their conversation and instantly wished I hadn't.

"Seriously, Guy, he'll never make a policeman as long as he's got a hole in his backside."

I gave myself no points for guessing who she was talking about. When she saw me, Dawn didn't look the least bit concerned. With a curt wave she said goodbye and without a word to me, set off and out of the nick. I jogged a few paces to catch up with her.

"Parade was very formal," I commented as I joined her.

"That's 'cos Inspector Duff is really old school. He runs his team with a rod of iron, but they really respect him. In fact, they'd do anything for him. If I ever become an inspector, I want to be just like him."

"Do you think you'll ever take promotion?" I asked.

"I'm thinking about it, now I've got five in; you can't get promoted until you've done five years unless you're high potential."

"What do you mean high potential?" I asked.

"I wouldn't worry about that," Dawn replied, and the sides of her mouth almost curled up into a smile.

"Dawn, what did he mean when he said he takes one day at a time?" I asked, realising this was about the longest conversation we'd had all week and keen to keep it going.

"His wife died of cancer last year. Except for the funeral he didn't take a single day off work."

"That's incredible."

"I agree," Dawn replied.

"He couldn't have loved her that much then," I added.

Dawn stopped walking and I thought she'd seen something in the side street to our left.

"Chris?" she said.

"Yes," I replied eagerly whilst my eyes searched up and down the road to try to see what Dawn had seen.

"You're a real arse."

Dawn shook her head and walked off.

***

At refs, Dawn sat on a separate table with one of her old relief, deliberately leaving me to eat alone. I'd obviously really pissed her off but had no idea how or when.

I ate a cooked breakfast and then thumbed through a Sun newspaper; an article about the first American woman in space caught my eye. I wondered whether I should mention it to Dawn. Perhaps it would give us something to talk about? And demonstrate that I recognised women could do lots of things men could do these days.

When we'd been in about an hour, I looked across at my instructor. Only two people were now sitting at her table: Dawn and an older PC, who appeared to be doing most of the talking, and they were deep in whispered conversation. I formed the impression Dawn was seeking his counsel on a delicate personal matter and then the male officer must have said something significant, because Dawn suddenly looked really upset, on the verge of crying, but desperate to hold back her tears. She glanced up to see whether anyone was watching and caught me staring. I looked away guiltily.

As soon as we left the nick after refs, I could sense Dawn's unhappiness. She'd hardly been a barrel of laughs earlier and now she was even worse. To try to find some common ground, but even more because I couldn't stand the silence, several times in the afternoon, I tried hard to start up meaningful conversations.

"Are you doing anything this weekend?"

"Have you got lots of housework to do?"

"I don't 'spose you're into sport?"

I received one-word answers or sometimes just a grunt and eventually gave up.

On our return to the nick, Dawn stopped a white Ford Capri, which had pulled out from a side road, right in front of us, across give-way markings and nearly hitting a cyclist. As it slowed down and pulled to the side, she turned to me and said quickly.

"He's all yours. Stick him on for failing to give way."

I knew this was a test but also a chance to redeem myself. I opened the passenger door and told the driver to join me on the pavement. A dark-skinned good-looking male, in his mid-twenties, wearing designer sunglasses, got out.

"Do you know why we've stopped you?" I asked, with a pleasing hint of authority.

The male smiled, shook his head and pointed to his ears.

"Can you understand me?"

He shook his head and tapped his ears.

"Are you deaf?" I asked slowly, mouthing out the words to assist him to lip read.

He nodded in a much-exaggerated fashion and smiled.

"You failed to give way and nearly hit that bloke on a bike."

The man shook his head and pulled an expression, which indicated very clearly that he didn't understand.

"Driving licence?" I said, shouting and mouthing simultaneously.

Again, the man just smiled sweetly, his eyes showed no comprehension.

I looked across at Dawn who was standing with her arms crossed; she made no attempt to assist me.

"Slow down," I shouted.

I got no response. I gave up, despairing at my terribly bad luck; I mean, of all the cars to stop. The man went to walk away, but stopped, as if asking me whether he could go. I hesitated and then nodded; the man smiled and started to walk back around the front of the car.

"Is this your money on the floor, mate?" Dawn called.

Without a moment's hesitation the deaf driver turned round and looked down. The game was over, and he knew it. He suddenly found his voice.

"Can't blame me for trying, can you, mate?" the driver asked cheerily. "Your mucker there, she's on the ball though, 'cos I'd convinced you." He laughed.

I felt stupid enough and the last thing I needed was some smart-arsed cockney rubbing it in. Dawn was standing on the pavement with her arms folded and an expressionless look on her face.

"Oh, come on, darling, cheer up," the driver said to Dawn, who replied by pulling a smiley face and then dropping it an instant later.

"Tell you what, darling, how about I take you out for a drink tonight? Give me your number and I'll call you later when you're off duty."

I couldn't believe it. The driver was asking Dawn out.

"What do you say?" he asked, with a grin which stretched from ear to ear.

"I say no," Dawn replied.

The driver ignored her, reached into his back pocket, produced a short blue pen and a five-pound note from a bundle and leaning on the Capri's bonnet, got set to write her telephone number down.

Dawn kept her arms crossed and shook her head.

"No, thank you."

"Give me one good reason?" the driver demanded.

"I'll give you three," Dawn replied.

"One would have done," the driver replied.

I think he sensed he was beaten.

"I don't go out with blokes who've been inside; it, sort of, blemishes one's career. I don't go out with married men, and my mum told me to avoid gamblers like the plague."

The man looked genuinely unsettled before quickly regaining his confident cockney composure.

"How do you know so much about me? Have we met before, darling, or have you got a team up my arse?"

From the man's reaction it appeared Dawn had been spot on.

"No team, let's just call it woman's intuition."

"Come on, darling, you can't leave it at that."

"I can and I am."

Dawn put on the fake smile once again.

"Now stick him on, PC Pritchard."

I did as I was told and ten minutes later, we were walking back to the nick. I didn't want to ask but I just had to know.

"Dawn?"

"Yes?"

"How did you know all that about the driver of the Capri?"

"Don't you believe in woman's intuition?"

"No."

"It was all very obvious really. If he wasn't married, he'd have given me his telephone number, which is a much less forward approach; as it was, he couldn't because if I called, his wife might answer. Secondly, he had four blue dots amateurishly tattooed on the knuckles of his right hand. Prisoners do that to each other and themselves when inside: the four dots represent the words *'all coppers are bastards'* and are a sure sign the person's done time. Finally, the pen he took from his back pocket was one of those short cheap biros you only get in betting shops."

I was impressed; I felt like I'd just had a lesson on observation from Sherlock Holmes.

I just had to ask Dawn one last question, the most important one of all: how on earth she knew the driver wasn't deaf. She shook her head and replied, "Oh, that was the easiest observation of all."

"Go on?"

"Because when we stopped him his car radio was on."

Chapter 9 – Solace at the Elephant's Head

As I drove home through the slow Friday afternoon traffic I felt really fed up. I'd worked hard at Hendon and achieved impressive exam results, but when it mattered most, when I was on the street, I couldn't hack it. I felt young, stupid and if I was honest, completely out of my depth. In my first week I'd been shot at and nearly run over but, strangely, that didn't bother me anywhere near as much as the fact that I was hopeless at the job. I flirted briefly with the idea of throwing in the towel, but knew that was an overreaction; and anyway, in my financial position, that wasn't a viable option.

I lived in Hackney in a bedsit, two steep flights of stairs above a chemist, in a parade of shops about half a mile from the town centre. It wasn't much of a place: a single bed; a black and white TV which couldn't pick up BBC2; a double wardrobe; and a small kitchenette, consisting of a sink, a draining board, below which was a fridge, and a lethal two-ringed oven which gave a significant electrical shock to anyone who dared touch the base of a pan with a metal fork or other utensil. I was cooking a pork chop the first time it happened to me. I was knocked backwards against the wall and the chop ended up on top of the wardrobe. Thereafter, I used a wooden spoon. I'd mentioned the problem to the landlord, Perry, who'd promised to send someone round to earth it, whatever that meant. The wallpaper in the room was dated and faded, the carpet threadbare in places and the white net curtains were a nasty shade of dirty grey.

I hung up my uniform and having examined the shirt collar, decided it would last a third day. I took a brief glance in the mirror; my hair badly needed a cut. I slumped onto my bed in only pants and socks, lit a cigarette and drew deeply. When the smoke hit my lungs, everything was momentarily right with the world. I was a great cop with excellent career prospects, Dawn thought the world of me and had already told Sergeant Bellamy she believed I was high potential, and my beautiful girlfriend was, at that very second, donning sexy underwear and applying bright red lipstick to pouting lips.

Reality was very different. I was really quite alone in the world. My father had died before I was born. My mother had joined him on the day I'd taken my first A level exam. Incidentally, the day before my eighteenth birthday. Mum never managed to move on from Dad's death and, over the next nineteen years, slowly drank herself to death. Despite her illness, I had loved her unconditionally. After she had died, I had lost any motivation to go to university and wandered aimlessly through several dark months until my kind elderly neighbour, Gerald, handed me an advert for the Met Police cut out from a daily newspaper and suggested I apply. For several weeks, the advert sat on the kitchen worktop, until a letter arrived from the council informing me that in light of mum's death, I had three months to vacate the council house which had been my home all my life. I put the letter down, picked up the advert and made a decision. There was a part of me, a bigger part than I would ever like to admit, which hoped to find in the Met a new family. Much of my disappointment at the end of my first week emanated from the realisation that it would be a long, long time, if ever, before that was going to happen.

I got to my feet and pulled on a pair of jeans and an old T-shirt. When the TV had warmed up, I flicked between the three channels and briefly watched a new ITV police drama called *Woodentops*, but it just reminded me of the disastrous start to my own police career, so after a few minutes

I turned the set off. I felt unsettled, lonely and bored. The long empty weekend stretched before me. I gathered up half a dozen dirty shirts that were in a black bin liner, and headed off to the launderette, which was only fifty yards away. When my whites were starting the first of a thousand spins, I was sipping a pint of draught Fosters and lighting a Rothmans next door in the Elephant's Head.

Although the bedsit had been home for less than a fortnight, I was rapidly becoming a regular at this typical London pub. The clientele were a fascinating microcosm of local life: the owner was a Canadian called Red who'd settled in Hackney after the war; the rotund barman, Eddie, was a rosy-cheeked sixty-year-old, whose dodgy hip made every step an effort; twin sisters in their late eighties who could make their snowballs last all evening and tried to give away bags of mint which they claimed grew like a forest in their garden; a gentle seventy-something West Indian male whose grace of movement hinted of a youthful dancing spirit which age could not conceal; a young Asian couple, completely in love, who always squeezed into a corner and never took their eyes from one another; the Chinese man who owned the dry cleaners and poured his takings into the fruit machine; a cardinal drunken bore with a bright red nose whose name I fortunately had yet to learn; and now me, who sat quietly at the bar people-watching.

I decided that whilst in the Elephant's Head, I'd keep quiet about my occupation, mainly because I thought they would treat me differently if they knew I was a policeman, but also because it reinforced the pub as a place to escape the realities of my unsuccessful career.

Shortly after eleven, I was climbing the stairs to my room, my clean washing in one hand, a doner kebab in the other and four pints of lager swilling in between.

Chapter 10 – Disqualified policing

The following week, which was my second on Street Duties, I gave up trying to make any conversation with Dawn that wasn't job related. Even work questions seemed to aggravate her, but at least I got an answer. On one of the days, we did a visit to Old Street Magistrates Court, which was a cross between a busy railway station and an undisciplined school assembly and nothing like the calm subdued library-like atmosphere I'd imagined would prevail in a court of law. On another day we met representatives from the local Sikh community and on the Thursday, we did a round trip to the Old Bailey, Scotland Yard and an office building on the south bank opposite the Tate Gallery whose name now escapes me. The idea, said Dawn, was to familiarise me with important Met buildings, but I'd rather have been out on patrol. Personally, I thought Dawn just wanted a day out in London. Everywhere we went, Dawn bumped into people she knew and, when she met them, she was all smiles, hugs and kisses. The contrast to how she interacted with me couldn't have been starker.

On the last day of what had felt like an eternally long week, we were going to look for two drivers: they lived a stone's throw from one another and both had recently been disqualified for drink drive. Dawn showed me photographs of each of the men and I'd made a careful record of their descriptions in my pocket book. I wasn't sure recognising faces was a skill I possessed and could just imagine how stupid I'd look if I missed my man: a Mr David Petersen of 42c Cazenove Road, who had been driving a red VW Polo when he was arrested.

"If they're going to drive after a ban, they normally use a different car, they're not stupid. So, concentrate on the individual and his front door.

Your chap works at a bank so he's going to leave for work at a sensible time. Make sure he doesn't see you, lose your helmet and take the epaulettes off your jacket. Also turn your volume control on the Storno in between the settings, it dulls it right down, but you can still hear it. I'll be around the corner watching Mr Daniels, but as he's unemployed, you've probably got more chance with your disqual. If you spot him, call me up and I'll come straight round."

Cazenove Road had residential terraced houses on both sides of the street and cars were parked nose to bumper. I couldn't see the red VW Polo anywhere. Almost opposite forty-two, but at an angle, was an access path between the houses. It was an excellent spot to watch from and I settled down for a long wait. Dawn's tip about the volume switch on the personal radio worked perfectly and she was right, I could just hear the transmissions. I felt quite excited.

After about thirty minutes all hell broke loose on the radio. From what I could gather, the central station hold up alarm at the Tower of London had been activated and my division's part of the Met's response to a possible theft of the Crown Jewels was in full swing, with units being sent to specific locations to set up roadblocks on routes out of London.

I offered a quick prayer to the Almighty that Mr Petersen didn't choose this moment to leave because I knew communication with Dawn would be impossible. My lips had barely finished moving when the front door of number forty-two opened and a smartly dressed man walked out. I recognised him instantly and dropped quickly down behind a brick wall. I waited a few moments and glanced along the road. My mind was racing; calling Dawn was not an option, as the radio was really busy, but I knew I had to act fast and decisively. I was haunted by my poor performance so far and arresting Mr Petersen was a real opportunity to show Dawn I wasn't completely useless. If I could make the arrest without any help from her, my instructor might just start to take me a little bit more seriously. I held my nerve and didn't leave my hiding place until Mr Petersen was a good forty yards away. He was walking away from Dawn's location. I had taken off my helmet and had removed my epaulettes as instructed and hidden them in a bush, I stuffed my radio deep into my jacket pocket; and could now just about pass for a normal member of the public who was wearing black trousers and a long dark coat.

When I thought it was the right time, I left the alley and walked quickly, gaining on the man. As Mr Petersen rounded the first road junction, he glanced behind him towards me and, as he disappeared out of view to the right, I thought I saw him start to run. I responded instantly, but when I came around the corner, he'd disappeared.

I knew he must be hiding somewhere, as he couldn't have cleared the other end of the road that quickly. As I walked slowly along the pavement, I heard the slightest of rustling noises coming from a front garden and leaning over the waist-high wooden fence, saw a now dishevelled Mr Petersen squatting down trying to hide in some undergrowth. He was panting heavily.

"You are Mr Petersen, aren't you?" I said.

"Yes," he replied tentatively, standing up slowly.

"But who are you?" he asked nervously.

Got him, I've only fucking got him I thought, barely able to contain my excitement.

“You’re a disqualified driver,” I said, deliberately making the sentence a statement rather than a question, so he had no opportunity to deny the fact.

“Yes, I know. Are you a police officer?” Mr Petersen asked, sounding somewhat relieved.

I nodded and took a few deep breaths, in preparation for the diatribe I knew I was about to deliver.

“You are under arrest for disqualified driving. You do not have to say anything unless you wish to do so but if you do, anything you say may be given in evidence.”

Even though this was my first ever arrest, I’d got the caution word perfect.

I still had to wait several minutes to get in on the radio, but took the first gap in transmission.

“Golf November, four six six,” I said, with composure.

“Go ahead, four six six.”

“Can I have transport for one prisoner, please? Brooke Road junction with Cazenove Road.”

Oh God, how good it felt saying those words. I could barely contain my pride.

“Golf November two will deal,” the van driver said.

“Golf November two, thank you.”

Mr Petersen was very compliant, so I decided not to handcuff him, which was probably a wise thing because my hands were shaking so much from the adrenalin rush, I would have failed miserably. Instead, I got him to sit on the front doorstep, whilst I waited for the van. A few minutes later Dawn arrived.

"Well done," she said. "Any problems?"

"No, I don't think so, though he did try to run away."

"If he's tried to run away, it's probably best to handcuff him," she said.

Did I detect the slightest hint of admiration in her voice?

Dawn walked up to the prisoner, told him to stand up and applied handcuffs so naturally, she could have done it blindfolded.

"I'm sorry I didn't call you, but I couldn't get in on the radio," I explained.

"That's okay, you've done really well, Chris."

Her words were like music to my ears.

Dawn took hold of Mr Petersen's arm and led him to the road and into the rear of the van that had just pulled up.

"Get in the van with him, Chris. I'll sort his car out and join you in the charge room. Where are the keys?"

"Keys?" I replied, not quite sure what she wanted.

"His car keys, are they still in the vehicle?"

"What vehicle?"

"The vehicle he was in when you arrested him, of course."

I didn't reply.

"Chris, what have you arrested him for?"

"Disqualified driving," I whispered, my colossal mistake dawning on me.

"Was he in his car when he was arrested?"

"I don't have a car, I sold it last week. I was on my way to the station when I saw him following me. I didn't know he was a police officer. I thought he was going to rob me, so I ran. When I was getting dressed, I saw him watching my house from the alley opposite," Mr Petersen replied helpfully.

"Please get out the van, Mr Petersen and let's take these handcuffs off," Dawn said.

I sat on the bench, my head in my hands, rocking slowly backwards and forwards; my short career had hit rock bottom.

Chapter 11 – A beer with Andy

Fortunately, Mr Petersen saw the funny side of the situation and graciously accepted my earnest and often repeated apology. Ironically, he voluntarily got back into the rear of the van to be driven to work, as he was now running late. Dawn and I walked back to the nick.

"Please don't say anything, Dawn," I pleaded.

"We'll have to write this up, I'm sorry. I'll have to tell Sergeant Bellamy what's happened. It was a completely unlawful arrest and Mr Petersen could sue the job for a lot of money."

"No, I know that. I mean, here, now, don't have a go at me. There's nothing you could say that I don't already know. I feel stupid enough."

Dawn ignored my request.

"I'm not sure this is the right job for you, Chris."

"Dawn, it's only been two weeks."

"I know but I'm just being honest with you. You're very young, perhaps you need to go and get some life experience and re-join when you're like, forty."

"I can't afford to leave, Dawn; where would I live?"

"Can't you go back home?"

"No. My mother died last year, and the council have repossessed our house 'cos they say that as there is just me, I didn't qualify for a three-bedroom house; instead, they offered me a place in a hostel."

"Were your parents divorced? What about your dad?"

"He died before I was born."

"I'm sorry to hear that, but this is the Metropolitan Police; if you're looking for sympathy, you'll find it between shit and syphilis in the dictionary, but you won't find any here."

I almost lost my temper. Whatever I'd done, I didn't deserve to be spoken to like that.

"There's no need to speak to me like that; you asked me a question, all I did was answer it."

For a second Dawn looked as though she was going to apologise; she didn't, but when she spoke her tone was conciliatory, suggesting to me she realised she'd overstepped the mark.

"Well, I guess the Metropolitan Police is stuck with you then."

"Thanks for not having a go at me, *partner*," I replied.

Dawn shrugged her shoulders and at that moment, I can honestly say I hated her.

Nothing much happened after refs. We did a few tax discs and took a call to a missing seven-year-old child, who turned up at the next-door neighbour's before I'd completed the misper report. For a change, it was me who was being moody. I obstinately refused to start or continue a conversation. It felt strangely liberating, but in truth, I'm not sure Dawn even noticed.

After booking off, when I went to get changed, I expressed my mounting frustration by punching my locker door. It was a stupid thing to do. I really hurt my knuckles and hardly made a dent. I thought, *'well, that's about par for the course'*. When I'd taken the impromptu decision to damage some inanimate object, I'd believed the locker room was empty, but hearing the bang, a bloke appeared from around a corner, clad only in a towel, and asked in a cheerful voice, "You alright?"

"Just ignore me, mate. I'm an idiot," I replied, bending over double, holding my hand and grimacing in pain.

Half an hour later, I was sitting in a pub with my new friend Andy Welling, a strikingly well-built black PC, who obviously trained every day, and who was a year or two older than me.

"Bugger me, Chris, you can't resign after two weeks; you've signed up for thirty years."

"But, Andy, I just can't do anything right, and Dawn really hates me."

"Listen, you're new, you're gonna make mistakes. She knows that, or maybe her issues are not with you?"

"What?"

"Look, it might be she has a problem in her private life, but you're there, so it's you that gets it in the neck. I don't know Dawn personally, but she's got a good reputation, and she's thick as thieves with Tommy on B relief and plonks don't come much better than her. Give the girl a chance to get to know you; you're a nice enough fella."

"I've got to give her a chance! What about her giving me a chance?" I replied incredulously.

"Listen, Chris. This is a funny old job. No one gets accepted straight away. A few months ago, an ex-military guy came out of Hendon, he'd fought in the Falklands with four two Commando. Well, you'd think he would settle in easily, wouldn't you?"

"I'd have thought so; what could possibly bother a bloke like that?" I asked.

"Well, first time he sees a prisoner getting a hiding, he only goes and reports it to the Inspector."

"And that didn't go down too well?"

"I should coco. It was all squared up, but no one would work with him again. No one would even speak to him; couldn't trust him, you see. He resigned a couple of weeks later."

I was conscious not to react to what Andy had just told me, but my mind wandered. So, the police did beat prisoners up. I'd heard rumours, but never believed them.

"First you gotta earn some trust and then they'll start to accept you. Believe me, that'll be easier for you than both me and this Dawn girl. She's a woman, and they have to be twice as good as their male counterparts, and then as a black PC, I've got even more to prove."

"Why, is the Met really racist?"

"Yes and no, Chris. Everyone's fine with me now that they know me, and it's certainly not as bad as everyone thinks but it's there, just under the surface. For example, there's a genuine belief amongst most white officers that all crime is committed by black youths and that's just not how it is. Black youths snatch handbags, oh and they smoke the weed that's true, but white lads commit burglary, car theft and armed robbery and, generally, take class A. Asians go in for non-violent pursuits like counterfeiting and tax evasion, Africans commit fraud on a scale you wouldn't believe and, whilst Orthodox Jews are fundamentally honest, they're criminally bad drivers and should never be allowed behind the wheel of a car. The Scots get pissed and want to fight the world and the Irish plant bombs. Vive la difference."

Andy raised his glass in a toast.

"Are you serious? Next you'll be telling me the Italians are all mafia gangsters."

"By and large, yes, I am. And just so you know, the worst gangsters in London are not Italian but the Chinese; their extortion rackets in the West End are legendary. Of course, my template doesn't always work. You do get black blaggers and white fraudsters, and of course not all Irish people are bombers, but remember this ..."

Andy leaned forward, as if he was about to impart some great policing secret.

"What?" I asked expectantly.

"You never get an Orthodox Jew who can drive." He laughed out loud.

"Andy?" I hesitated.

"Yes, mate?"

"How do I earn trust, have I got to not bottle it in a fight or something?"

"No, it's not like that, it's not a bravery thing."

"Well, what have I got to do? I don't understand."

Andy laughed and shook his head.

"Chris, I can't tell you go and do this, this and this and everyone will trust you. It's not like that. Something will just happen, and you'll back your mates up, even if that could drop you in it too."

"Okay, I gotta more difficult question," I said, after we'd each taken a long gulp of beer.

"Shoot."

"How do I get on with Dawn?"

Andy thought for a few moments.

"That's easy. You could do her such a favour that she would be forever in your debt."

"Like what?"

"Introduce her to me."

Andy's smile was wide, deep and mischievous.

Chapter 12 – G T P

Andy was a genuinely nice guy and I really appreciated how he'd gone out of his way to help a floundering colleague. However, I wasn't convinced about it being more difficult for Andy to be accepted than myself, just because he was black. Andy was built like a Greek statue, had plenty of confidence and a great sense of humour. Quite frankly, I'd have swapped places with him any day.

When I got home, I undressed, wrapped a towel around my waist and, unusually for me, headed for the shared shower, which was down one flight of stairs. I would have used the shower more often, if it wasn't so mouldy and the drain wasn't always blocked with thick clumps of black hair. As it was, I forced myself to have at least one shower a week, whether I thought I needed it or not. I walked through an unlocked door to see the woman who lived immediately below me, with one leg up on the bath drying her steaming, naked body with a crisp white towel. She didn't bat an eyelid.

"Hi," she said casually.

"I'm sorry, the door was unlocked," I said, turning to leave.

"No problem, officer; stay there, I won't be a moment."

Officer? How did she know what I did for a living? I didn't even know her name.

I tried not to stare, I really did, but I just couldn't take my eyes off her. She was tall and slim, with small pert breasts and long thin legs; her hair was straight and dark. When she turned to check her face in the steamy mirror, which she wiped clean with one corner of the towel, my eyes dropped to admire the most perfect backside I'd ever seen. Well, it would have been had an enormous and quite ugly tattoo not adorned the lower part of her back. What I found quite amazing, and completely arousing, was her lack of self-consciousness. She didn't appear to be the least bit disconcerted that she was completely naked in front of a total stranger. Having studied a spot on her face quite intently, she tried but failed to squeeze it. She turned round and looked, without any shame, straight at my groin. The pleasure I was experiencing, having found myself in this most unusual situation, was quite visible underneath my towel. It was, after all, quite literally the first time I had been in the same room as a naked woman.

"Gosh, officer, I thought it was illegal to carry an offensive weapon," she giggled.

"Only in a public place," I replied, quite pleased with my banter.

She wrapped a larger towel around her impressive body, and, in a swift single movement, swirled a smaller hand towel around her wet hair. Then she started to collect various bottles of toiletries.

"The door lock's broken, I've told Perry, but you know what a useless landlord he is," she said.

"Oh well, tell him there's no hurry to fix it," I grinned.

The woman paused momentarily and then smiled.

"I'm Debbie, by the way."

"I'm Chris," I replied, almost forgetting my own name.

"Debbie, how do you know what I do for a living?" I asked.

"Perry's told everyone. I think he thinks it gives him a bit more stick when he's collecting the rent."

"What are you saying? That he threatens you with me if you don't pay your rent?"

"Not me, no, but the guy who lives next to me, the African, he's an illegal, so when he didn't pay last week, Perry dropped your profession into the conversation. I don't pay rent, Chris."

"How come?" I asked.

"Well, let's say I pay my rent in a different sort of way," she laughed.

"Besides, I don't live here, I live in Highams Park."

"I thought you lived in the room below me?"

"No, Chris, I only work here."

"You work here, what do you do?"

Debbie laughed.

"I'm your local neighbourhood hooker, Chris."

She turned and drew a smiley face with her finger on the steamy mirror and, for a second, I thought she was doing so to indicate to me she was only joking, but realised from the satisfied smile when she turned back to face me that she wasn't.

"And before you fret, no, it's not illegal. I don't walk the streets, so I'm not loitering or soliciting, and as I work alone, the room can't be classified as a brothel."

"So, you pay Perry by sleeping with him?" I asked; a picture of our fifty-year-old, overweight landlord came into my mind.

"I don't have sex with him, that's not what our dear old landlord is into."

"Really, do tell?" I was intrigued.

"Perry likes to bend over my knee and be spanked, and the harder the better."

"Really?" I said.

"Don't you dare say anything to him, I mean it, Chris."

"Don't worry; your secret is safe with me," I assured her.

Debbie collected up half a dozen bottles and a razor.

"All yours," she declared.

I moved to one side to let her pass and had allowed her ample room, but she deliberately brushed by me and her body pushed firmly against my erection. As she cleared the door, Debbie stopped and turned around.

"Chris?"

"Yes."

"I'm very GTP."

I had no idea what GTP meant but it sounded great.

Chapter 13 – Mini confusion

Despite Andy's pep talk, the following Monday morning I went to work without much enthusiasm.

I met my instructor in the Street Duties office; if she answered my humble *'good morning'*, I didn't hear her. Should I apologise again for the debacle with the disqualified driver? There didn't seem much point. Instead, I offered to make her a cup of tea; she still ignored me, so I made her one anyway and over the next twenty minutes it went from piping hot to lukewarm, without being sipped.

I didn't know how to handle the situation, so I stepped outside and lit a cigarette. The remnants of night duty were returning to the nick and a tired early turn was arriving after a quick change over. Quick change overs were notorious; they occurred twice in every four-week shift pattern. On each occasion the relief only got eight hours between tours of duty.

I noticed how everyone acknowledged each other; there was an unspoken something between the officers, which I could identify as camaraderie but not share. I overheard a conversation between two older constables, one from each passing shift.

"Much happening, Bill?"

"Quiet night, mate, fatacc just after four that kept a few of us busy but that was about it."

"Who was the victim?"

"They still haven't identified him, some black kid driving like an idiot. Lost it and hit the tree everyone hides behind to do the bus lane. These bloody kids, they think they're invincible."

"Tell me, I've got a seventeen-year-old who's got a Fissie."

The conversation moved from the yard, through the rear door, into the station and out of my earshot. I flicked the rest of my cigarette clean over the portacabin and checked my watch.

When I went into the office, Dawn was sitting at the desk with her head in her hands. Hearing me enter, she quickly stood up, but I noticed she turned her head away. Was she crying? Was I really that bad?

"Thanks to you I got a right bollocking on Friday. Sergeant Bellamy was furious I'd let you out of my sight."

I didn't know what to say, so I decided to look as apologetic as I could.

Without further ado, Dawn picked up her hat and handbag and headed for the door. I followed.

Parade was short and sweet but, at its conclusion, the sergeant asked Dawn to stay behind for a quick briefing on another matter. Not wanting to get in the way, I decided to make my way to the canteen and wait for her there, but as I was leaving, the sergeant impatiently called me back.

"Pritchard, where do you think you're going? This concerns you too."

Dawn's eyes looked to the heavens, her expression said it all.

"Right, you two. I'm sorry about this but can you deliver a death message? An eighteen-year-old lad was killed last night in a fatacc. His name was Jason Featherstone, and he lives on the Weir Estate. He was driving a yellow Mini; the full details are here."

The sergeant handed Dawn a piece of paper.

"According to the voters, he lives there with mum, dad and a younger brother."

"Have they reported him missing yet, Sarge?" Dawn asked.

"No. The fatacc was at four this morning. He was killed instantly but it took several hours to cut him out of the wreckage and the car's no current keeper. They found his driving licence in his back pocket when they searched the body. When you've informed the next of kin, one of them is going to have to go and ID the body in the morgue at the London. Dawn, take the Duty Officer's car and run whoever up there to do the formal identification. Then get a statement from them."

"Do we know anything else about the family, Sarge?"

"No Dawn, no previous, nothing."

"No problem, Sarge. We'll get up there straight away."

"Cheers, guys."

We booked out radios, collected car keys hanging from a hook and went to a beige-coloured Austin Allegro, which was parked in the yard. Dawn walked once round the vehicle, although exactly what she was looking for, I had no idea and didn't dare ask. Although the car was less than two years old, we got in an interior which looked many times its age and drove in silence through quiet streets. I felt quite excited; delivering a death message sounded a very dramatic and grown-up thing to do. This, I decided, was real police work.

Dawn parked on double yellow lines immediately outside the entrance to Chapel le-Street House, our destination. The tension in the car was stifling. I turned to look at Dawn for the first time since we'd left the nick but what I saw stopped any words in my mouth. She was trying desperately to conceal a giggle. When she saw me looking, laughter burst forth like a guilty child; at first it spluttered but then it grew until it was loud and unabated. I didn't know what was going on, I'd never seen Dawn smile, let alone laugh before. I thought perhaps she'd lost it and was having some kind of breakdown. Eventually, after five or six separate attempts, she gathered her composure.

“Let’s go,” she said, the old Dawn once again in charge; I wondered what the hell had got into her.

“And let me do all the talking, do you understand?”

Without waiting for an answer, she was up, out and on her way, her puppy, me, walking quickly behind her. The Featherstones lived on the first floor. Dawn knocked with a clenched fist firmly on the thickly painted blue council door and we waited. When a minute had passed, she knocked again, harder this time.

“I am coming, I’m coming,” a female voice with a heavy Jamaican accent said.

Bolts were clunked and keys jangled and a heavily set black lady in her mid-forties blinked several times before, in an instant of painful recognition, the expression on her face changed from surprise to concern.

“What is it, officer?”

“Mrs Featherstone?”

“Yes.”

“Can we come in, please?”

“Of course, of course,” she replied, stepping backwards.

“Donald, come down now, it’s the police,” she shouted up the stairs, her voice full of anxiety.

“What is it? What is it?”

“Can we go into the lounge please, Mrs Featherstone?”

“Donald,” she called again.

“Is it my mother, officers? Please tell me she’s alright?”

Dawn waited patiently; perhaps two full minutes, until Mrs Featherstone and her husband were seated opposite us on the sofa, by which time Mrs Featherstone had convinced herself her mother had died.

It was the longest two minutes of my short life. I couldn't look the lady in the face but, instead, stared shamefully at the floor. Suddenly I realised what a terrible thing we were about to do, I felt sick.

"Mr Featherstone, Mrs Featherstone. I have some bad news, very bad news. Your son, Jason ..."

Dawn paused.

"Yes, what about him, officer?"

The concern in her voice had diminished.

"We believe he died in a car accident last night."

There was silence, not the expected deathly screams and howls which I had anticipated. Then Mrs Featherstone said slowly and purposefully, "I think there has been some kind of mistake, officer."

"Are you Jason's mother?"

"Yes."

Dawn pawed quickly through her pocket book.

"Is his date of birth 1st December 1965?"

"Yes."

"Does he drive a yellow Mini?"

"Yes, he only bought it at the weekend."

"Well, we have information Jason was driving that car at about four am this morning and was involved in a fatal car accident."

Mr and Mrs Featherstone exchanged a confused look.

"Well, officer, Jason is asleep in his bed upstairs. I saw him not an hour ago when I got up to go to the toilet."

"Can I ask you to check please?"

"Go on, Donald, go and wake him up, get him down here."

Donald did as he was told without saying a word. The three of us sat silently listening to Mr Featherstone's footsteps go away and then return. As he entered the lounge, he simply nodded slowly to his wife, indicating Jason was indeed in his bedroom.

"There, I told you," Mrs Featherstone said politely.

"I'm so sorry," Dawn said. "There's obviously been a mistake, I really am quite embarrassed."

Mrs Featherstone beamed a reassuring smile that communicated nothing but kindness.

"These things happen. Now stop worrying, you two look truly awful."

Suddenly there was a spontaneous outburst of mutual relief in the room; even after my pretty abysmal first few weeks, I felt inclined to smile. I was genuinely relieved these lovely people did not have to receive such devastating news after all. As the four of us stood up, a young lad strolled casually into the room wearing only pyjama bottoms.

"Oh, Jason, my boy, these police officers thought you were dead. Come and give your mum a big hug."

He shrugged his shoulders self-consciously.

"Jason, have you lent your car to anyone?" Dawn asked.

The young man shook his head definitively.

"Perhaps someone has stolen it?" Dawn suggested.

Jason shook his head and spoke for the first time.

"No way, I disconnect the high tension lead every time I leave it."

Jason walked over to the window and moved the net curtain aside.

"I'll find out what happened and get back to you, Mrs Featherstone," Dawn said, turning towards the door.

"Call me Cynthia," she said.

A horrible thought had flashed through my mind and stopped me in my tracks. With no regard to Dawn's previous instructions to *'let me do the talking'*, I turned to Jason.

"Is your brother in?"

Jason shrugged his shoulders; clearly the teenager had said enough for such an early hour.

"How old is Jason's brother, Mrs Featherstone?" I asked.

"Cynthia, dear, Cynthia," she corrected me, giggling at her own informality.

"Max? He's only thirteen."

Thank God, I thought as my fears evaporated, but Dawn's smile had disappeared.

"Cynthia, get Max up please. Jason, can you get your driving licence?"

When Mrs Cynthia Featherstone found an empty bed and Jason said that his car, car keys and driving licence were missing, the realisation and their grief erupted with the force of a volcano.

Chapter 14 – The aftermath

Dawn and I soon put the pieces together. Thirteen-year-old Max Featherstone was, like many other lads his age, completely into cars, and couldn't resist the temptation to borrow his brother's new Mini, and his driving licence, to go for a quick spin in the middle of the night. Max had climbed out of his bedroom window and shinned down the drainpipe.

The rest of our day was fraught with the most dreadful sadness, which the recent loss of my own mother seemed to accentuate. The first hour was truly awful. Mrs Featherstone screamed and wailed, Mr Featherstone sat and cried like a baby and Jason tried to kick and punch doors, walls, windows – anything to vent his grief. I felt hopeless and so very, very sorry for them, but no words were going to help, so I sat quietly. On some level, I tried to retreat inside myself. It was the most harrowing day, but throughout I thought Dawn shone like a star. It wasn't just that she was calm and professional; there was something else about the way she interacted with people, something unquantifiable, not just with the bereaved family, but with everyone with whom she came into contact. I had never really noticed it before, but that day I could see it so clearly. The closest my thoughts could get to articulating what I saw, was to describe Dawn's manner as charming, but that wasn't it; whatever 'it' was was so much more than that. People simply wanted to do whatever she told them, it was quite amazing, mesmerising.

At the end of my tour of duty, I felt emotionally shot through, completely drained. I realised why Dawn had got the giggles just before we'd entered the Featherstones' flat. It was nerves caused by the stress of what she knew from experience was about to come. I had not the faintest idea what a dreadful thing it is to tell someone their child is dead; never again would I feel excited by such a prospect; in fact, I felt embarrassed that I could have been so insensitive.

Once home, I changed and headed straight for the Elephant's Head, where I was just in time for two swift pints. I chatted to Eddie, the affable but dim barman, but several times during the conversation my mind wandered where I wished it wouldn't go, so I finished my second pint quickly and left. I really didn't want to go to bed, even though I had to be up in six hours. I needed to talk over what had happened with someone, but there wasn't anyone, and eventually a sheer lack of alternatives forced me between the sheets for a restless but short night.

It was not until I was driving to work the following day, I remembered it had been me who had first realised that the younger brother might have been involved in the accident. I gave myself a little credit, not too much, but just enough to feel slightly less stupid than I had on the same journey the previous day. I wondered whether Dawn had noticed.

I parked my car in its usual spot and made the short, familiar walk through the backstreets of Stoke Newington. These led me into the back yard and the portacabin, which was the Street Duties office.

"Morning, Dawn," I said.

"Chris."

Well at least she'd acknowledged me I thought; the day was already looking up.

"Dawn?"

"I heard an expression the other day and I've no idea what it means?"

"Go on."

"A neighbour of mine said she was GTP, what on earth does that mean?"

Dawn almost smiled.

"And who exactly is this neighbour?" she asked.

"Her name's Debbie."

I didn't want to admit I lived above a prostitute, so I said no more.

"Is she in the job?"

"No, why?"

"Because GTP is a very *police* expression; I can't imagine people not in the job using it."

"She's definitely not in the job."

"GTP stands for good to police," Dawn explained.

I didn't understand and must have frowned because Dawn went on to explain in more detail.

"If a shop, like a jewellers, gives a discount to old bill, then other old bill will say they're GTP, good to police. Perhaps a fish and chip shop gives a free portion of chips to any old bill that wanders in, that chippie will be GTP."

"Oh, I see."

"So, exactly what trade or calling does this Debbie do? Whatever it is, she's offering it to you at a discount."

I floundered, as I couldn't tell her she was a prostitute. It would sound like I was already paying her for sex.

"I think she's a minicab driver," I replied, but I was certain the slight delay in answering was enough for Dawn to recognise the lie. Fortunately, however, it was time to make our way over to the parade room, so the conversation came to a natural end.

After parade the sergeant again pulled us to one side.

“Well done yesterday, you two. A hard but good day’s work. Mrs Featherstone contacted the Duty Officer last night to say thank you for everything you did.”

I was astounded. This woman, who’d just lost her son, had taken the time to pick up a phone and thank us for our efforts. For a few moments, I was no longer listening, so when the conversation went quiet and it was obvious the sergeant was waiting for me to answer a question, I took a guess and replied confidently.

“Yes, Sergeant.”

I had no idea about what I had just agreed to do.

“Good then, after refs report in plain clothes to DS Cotton in the CID office. He’ll give you your assignment.”

As we walked over to the canteen, Dawn said with her usual hint of frustration, “Chris, when the sergeant’s talking to you, try to do him the courtesy of listening.”

“Sorry, Dawn, but I just couldn’t believe Mrs Featherstone did that, you know, phoned in to thank us. Can you?”

“No, it was good of her, amazing really. Don’t ever forget there are a lot of nice people out there.”

That was the second proper conversation I’d had that morning with Dawn, and I felt ridiculously elated that she had ordained to speak, almost chat, with me. I wanted to continue the dialogue and to say something to compliment her on how well she’d done yesterday.

“I’m glad I was working with a woman yesterday, you know, when you’ve got to do something like delivering a death message.”

“Oh, good,” she replied.

“So do you think WPCs are good at certain jobs?”

"Oh, yes," I replied, warming to a theme that was obviously going down well with Dawn.

"Give me some examples?" she said.

"Well, like yesterday, and dealing with children and babies."

Dawn nodded. For once I seemed to have said the right thing.

Chapter 15 – Big dipper

The CID assignment was, in fact, quite interesting. Apparently, in the last few weeks there had been numerous reports of thefts from shoppers in a popular department store in the High Street. All of the victims had been elderly ladies. Dawn and I were to sit behind a one-way mirror in the store and watch for dippers, or as they are more commonly known by the general public, pickpockets. If we saw anything, we were to communicate with CID officers who were hiding in the back of an unmarked police van parked immediately outside.

By ten- hirty, the two of us were sitting on comfortable chairs in a warm storeroom watching the customers go about their business. At times it was a bit spooky, and then quite amusing, as people who were trying on clothes would stand only a few feet away admiring themselves in the mirror, completely unaware that we were immediately in front of them observing their every move. One white man in his sixties took the opportunity the mirror presented and cleaned his nose with a probing forefinger, before examining his excavation work intricately, and finally popping it in his mouth. The sight made me heave. Dawn said one word.

"Men!"

As ever, the atmosphere between us was strained, which caused me to think I must have said or done something wrong again. I lacked the confidence to try to initiate a conversation and Dawn the inclination; so, we sat in silence. Perhaps an hour passed before Dawn spoke.

"Aye, aye."

"What?"

"That woman, what's she doing?"

A white woman in her forties had a small pair of scissors in her right hand. She was using them to cut the clothes labels off several jackets, which were hanging on a circular rail. She definitely looked suspicious because her eyes were dancing everywhere.

"I don't know; is she cutting the labels out?"

She was. Having cut off about half a dozen, the woman stopped, as her task was apparently complete. She walked swiftly off towards the exit.

"How bizarre; I think she's cut off about six labels, but why?" Dawn said.

"Those jackets are about the only things which are not in the sale. Do you think that's relevant?" I asked.

"You're right, well spotted; but I don't get it?"

It was the first compliment Dawn had ever given me, but I was confident it was unintended.

"Why would you steal labels? Try to remember what she looks like, Chris; she might come again."

"Okay," I replied.

The label woman had moved out of our sight, so we settled down once again to watch and wait. Occasionally, Dawn called up the CID officers in the van outside, just to check the signal and to keep them awake. It was a while later when I next heard Dawn speak.

"Aye, aye."

To our right an old lady was searching through an assortment of clothing in a large circular basket, above which a sign read *'All Items Reduced to £1'*. She had a square, tartan shopping trolley, on top of which she had rested a matching handbag. She was a typical old lady, short, grey-haired, with a bent back and swollen ankles.

"We have a victim, now all we need ..."

Before Dawn could complete her sentence, two young white women with an assortment of bags, babies and buggies, started browsing casually through the basket. Their stiletto heels were too high, their earrings too large, and they chewed gum with open mouths. They looked cheap.

"Canning Town shoes," Dawn said.

"Pardon?" I said, not knowing what she meant.

"Watch carefully," she instructed.

"They're not pickpockets, are they? They've got young kids with them," I asked.

Dawn didn't reply but spoke quietly on the radio.

"Stand by, stand by."

One of the younger women was edging closer to the handbag, but the old woman suddenly turned and looked at some clothing on another rail, and in so doing, completely blocked our view of her shopping trolley and handbag, we couldn't see anything.

"Get out the way," Dawn said, sounding frustrated.

When the old lady did eventually move, the young women were walking away from the basket towards the lingerie section, which was off to our left. The handbag was still on the trolley and everything seemed in order to me, but Dawn spoke into the radio.

"There are two IC1 females, early twenties, both with buggies and arms covered in tattoos. They're still in the shop, but when they leave, stop them and turn them over, chaps, do you receive?"

"Yes, yes," a male voice replied.

Two minutes passed and the old lady selected two pairs of large white knickers from the sale basket. She then turned to look for the checkout.

Her right hand slipped into her handbag and stopped. She dropped the knickers and started to search frantically for her purse. It was long gone. Dawn transmitted again.

"We have a victim, guys, and the two young girls should have her purse, over."

"They're not out yet, Dawn. Oh stand by, here they come, we'll stop them, stand by."

Dawn and I left our hiding place and identified ourselves as police officers to the distraught old woman. The purse that had been stolen contained her married couple fortnightly state pension, which she had collected that morning, one hundred and nine pounds, in ten ten-pound notes and nine one-pound notes. The purse itself was a red tartan design, identical she said, to her handbag and shopping trolley, they were a set.

We had been joined by the manager, who had seen our rapid emergence, and correctly assessed the situation. Dawn asked him to take the lady to his office, so we could take a statement.

"We'll be back shortly, Sir," she said to him.

"Come on, let's see what's happening outside."

The women had been stopped and separated; three male officers surrounded each and whilst one was talking, the other two were searching their belongings. Dawn and I stood slightly apart and watched. We waited patiently, but as the minutes passed, my doubt started to rise. One of the CID officers came over,

"Can't find anything, Dawn."

"They've got it, we saw them dip it, didn't we, Chris?"

Despite not having seen any such thing, I nodded in agreement.

"I'll strip search them in the back of the van, bring them over one at a time," Dawn offered.

When the first woman was told what was going to happen, she went mad.

"She ain't fucking strip searching me, the lesbian," She howled as she was dragged, kicking and screaming, towards the van.

The woman was large and powerful and even with four male officers pulling and pushing her, she was barely moving at all.

"Do you want another female officer, Dawn?" the CID officer asked.

"I think I might."

It took a good two minutes to drag her into the van and, all the while, she shouted and swore.

A crowd of about twenty onlookers had gathered and a few voiced their concerns about police brutality.

"What's she done to deserve that?"

"Four onto one, that's about right, you bastards."

"I want your names, you ain't getting away with that."

"Are you putting her in the van so you can beat her up?"

A police vehicle pulled up and several uniformed officers got out. I recognised the WPC immediately; it was the woman who on my first day had tricked me into buying her a cup of tea. Dawn had told me her name was Tommy. Two male officers bluntly advised the crowd to move and keep their views to themselves.

"Move along. And the next person who gobs off will be nicked for obstruction."

"What you got, Matthews?" Tommy asked cheerfully.

"Couple of dippers, Tommy, they had an old lady's purse off."

"Did they now? They're gonna wish they hadn't," Tommy said.

Her voice was superficially cheerful but there was a menace, a cut in it, which everyone who heard the exchange identified.

Dawn and Tommy climbed into the back of the van and the male officers who had the female lying face down on the floor got out. As soon as the doors closed, there was the slightest of muffled screams and then perfect quiet.

"Everything all right in there?" the DC asked.

"Everything's fine, Tommy's just having a quiet word with this young lady."

Everything was fine, because, within a few minutes, Dawn emerged with a bundle of money in her right hand and a smile on her face.

"It was down her knickers. I've counted it quickly and it's the missing one hundred and nine quid. They've obviously dumped the purse. I'll check the Ladies in a minute. Tommy says, *'do you want a confession'*?"

"Did you see her take the purse, Dawn?"

"Yes, we did."

"In that case, tell Tommy, *'thanks but no'*, we've got enough."

"She'll be disappointed," Dawn said, smiling mischievously.

The DC just laughed, and Dawn banged on the van doors with a fist.

"It's all right, Tommy, we've finished with her."

The van door opened, and a quiet, completely compliant, young woman emerged. She blinked several times, her eyes adjusting to the sunlight. There were streams of mascara running down her face. She was muttering, *'I'm sorry, I'm sorry'*, over and over again. I wondered what on earth had happened to her to make her so servile.

"Your turn," Dawn said to the second woman.

“I ain’t got nothing, honestly,” she pleaded.

Dawn rolled her finger and pointed to the rear of the van; the woman looked across at her friend who was sobbing quietly.

“Get in and get it over with,” Dawn said.

Without any assistance and with her head hung low, the second woman walked over to the van and climbed in. Dawn followed. Tommy had remained in the van. As the doors closed, I heard Tommy’s voice.

“Like nicking from old ladies, do you?”

Several seconds ticked passed and then a loud chilling scream rang out.

Chapter 16 – Original notes

Dawn was of course right; I wondered if she was ever wrong. The old lady's red tartan purse was in the toilets, dropped into a cistern. The old lady herself had waited patiently in the manager's office and was delighted to be told her money had been recovered. She was less impressed when Dawn told her the cash was evidence and she couldn't have it back yet.

"But how will I buy my shopping and pay my bills, officer?" she asked politely.

"I'll see what I can do; wait there a moment," Dawn said.

"PC Pritchard, can I have a word with you outside, please?"

In the corridor, Dawn gave me her cashpoint card, told me her pin number and sent me off to withdraw one hundred and nine pounds to give to the old lady, whilst she took a statement. I was quietly impressed; what a lovely thing to do.

An hour later we were back at the station in the canteen making our arrest notes. Dawn was dictating whilst I wrote.

"Change the occasional word, or write the sentence a different way, we don't want our notes to be identical," Dawn instructed.

I did so quite effectively; where Dawn wore *'plain clothes'* I was dressed in *'civilian attire'*, when she *'observed'* I *'noticed'*, so far so good. We were soon up to the point where the young lady had moved herself next to the shopping trolley. The truth was, that was the very last thing we'd seen, but Dawn's dictation suggested otherwise.

"I saw the woman look in the direction of the old lady. When the old lady's back was towards her, the younger woman's right hand entered the handbag, which was resting on the top of the tartan shopping trolley. I saw her remove a matching red tartan purse and place it in her right jacket pocket. She and her associate then walked quickly away towards the lingerie section and ladies' toilet. I communicated with units who were outside the shop and directed them to stop and search the two women."

Dawn noticed I had stopped writing.

"Why aren't you writing this down?" she asked.

"Well, um, well I didn't see what you're saying."

"What?" Dawn said quietly.

She looked around to see if anyone was within earshot of our conversation.

"Dawn, are you suggesting I should write something I know is wrong? What happens if this goes to court? I'd have to lie under oath, wouldn't I?"

At that point DS Cotton joined us with two cups of tea.

"Everything okay here?" he asked, perhaps sensing an element of tension.

"Everything's fine," Dawn said confidently.

"Well done, you two, excellent. I'll be having a few words with old Bellamy to tell him how impressed I am. She's not having it of course. Says she keeps her money in her pants because of all the pickpockets. Says she and her old man get just over a hundred pound a week in benefits. Quite a clever defence really, what with money being unidentifiable. We should have just given her the purse."

"It wasn't feasible, Sarge; the manager knew the purse had been found in the toilets."

"Oh, I didn't realise that," DS Cotton said.

"It's not a problem; we'll give you all the evidence you need," Dawn assured him.

"Unfortunately, because she says the money is hers, we can't just photocopy the cash and return it to the old lady. She'll have to wait until the matter is settled at court," DS Cotton said.

"Oh, Dawn's ..." I went to tell DS Cotton about what Dawn had done but she kicked me so hard under the table it took all my self-control not to cry out loud.

"Dawn's what?" he asked, as I held my breath.

"Oh, Dawn said she might have to wait," I said, recovering quickly.

"Anyway, well done again. Put your IRBs with the charge sheet, we'll deal from here."

DS Cotton stood up and walked off.

"Dawn, what did he mean when he said we should have given her the purse?"

Dawn put her head in her hands and rubbed her face before she replied. She spoke quietly and slowly, leaning forward across the table and carefully choosing her words.

"Okay. Listen. If we say, when Tommy and I searched the suspect, we found the purse on her with the money in it, she would go down like a stone in water. But we can't say that because I know the manager is aware the purse was in the toilet and we can't trust him or expect him to lie. But it's okay because we saw her dip the old woman's handbag, didn't we?"

I didn't say anything but looked down; I was unable to hold Dawn's stare.

"Listen. If you do it your way, not only does the slag get away with this, but she gets to keep the money. Down her knickers because of pickpockets is complete rubbish and you know it. The old lady lost one hundred and nine quid; she had one hundred and nine quid. You know she stole the purse; we just need to oil the wheels of justice a bit. Otherwise, I'm telling you the jury at good old Slagsbrook Crown Court will acquit her. She stole that purse and I ain't prepared to let her get off."

I stood up and pushed my chair back.

"Where are you going?" Dawn demanded.

"I need a cigarette," I said and walked out of the canteen and into the back yard.

I knew by the time I'd finished my smoke I'd have made my mind up. I turned it over and could see Dawn's point, I really could, but at Training School they'd drilled into us the importance of honesty and integrity. They'd also emphasised that the punishment for perjury, lying under oath, was seven years. And if I lied today, where did it stop? Would I soon be fitting people up with bags of cannabis, flick knives and knuckle dusters? I realised this was a significant moment. I drew deeply one last time and flicked the butt clean over the portacabin. When I walked back into the canteen, I had made up my mind what sort of copper I wanted to be. This wasn't going to be easy, but I had to be true to myself and no one else.

"Well?" Dawn said.

Without saying a word, I sat down and reached across the table and picked up her notebook. I turned it around and started to copy what she'd written.

"Chris?"

"What?"

My reply was terse.

"You're doing it for the next old lady that wants to go shopping without having her purse stolen."

"I know."

My voice was no more than a whisper.

Chapter 17 – The road to hell ...

As the weeks passed, my failure to get on with Dawn was starting to wear me down. Every day I saw my instructor interact with others and she seemed a happy-go-lucky character with a keen sense of humour, well respected and liked by all. In contrast, in her relationship with me she was at best indifferent and, at worst, damn right moody. My desire to please her had grown disproportionately large but as each opportunity arose to prove myself, I managed to miss it. A good day was no longer when I did something right but instead when I didn't do anything wrong, and they were few and far between.

Dawn was never friendly towards me but curiously, I'd started to find her attractive.

I thought that when I'd backed up her evidence against the pickpocket, I might have earned some Brownie points, but I was wrong. I realised later that it was expected that one officer would always back the other up in evidence, it was a given, and therefore not worthy of any particular credit. With this realisation came the appreciation that had I declined to support Dawn, my career would to all intents and purposes have ended there and then. I suspected that officially, I would have been informed by Sergeant Bellamy that I was unlikely to pass my probation and asked to resign. As it was, I'd backed her up and still had a job.

My Street Duties course rolled on.

Part of my training involved visiting different belief groups where representatives would explain to me their religious and cultural traditions to promote understanding and tolerance. I found these boring but I was always polite and listened, feigning an interest I really didn't possess. To be honest, I wasn't convinced there was a God and I found their eccentric beliefs almost comical because they were all so convinced that their particular sect held the only keys to Heaven.

On Thursday we'd been to a synagogue in Stamford Hill and met several Orthodox Jews, one of whom was a kindly old rabbi. I did notice that every one of them wore really thick glasses and thought this might explain why they were such terrible drivers. They seemed a welcoming but introverted community, fiercely traditional and passionately religious. As our meeting was drawing to a close, a younger man came bounding into the room.

"Hello, hello. I'm Abe."

He shook our hands with gusto and the words raced from his mouth as if they were all in some sort of competition to escape.

"Oh, hi, Abe," Dawn said.

She had obviously met him before.

"I've only just been told you were here otherwise I'd have come up earlier. I am a police officer too," Abe said enthusiastically.

I had never seen anyone who looked less like a policeman. Abe was in his early thirties, very tall, very overweight, with all the Orthodox trappings: the traditional clothing, the curly hair hanging in front of his ears and of course, the thick, square glasses.

"Pleased to meet you," I said.

"I work Saturday nights and late turn Sunday. I've been doing it for three years now. Got a commendation last year for bravery for arresting a violent suspect."

"Gosh," I said.

"Are you being puppy-walked? Is that what Dawn's doing? She's good, you know. When you join your relief let me know, I'll come out with you, show you the ropes."

Dawn stood up, clearly indicating she wanted to leave, and something in her body language suggested to me she had even less time for Abe than she did for me.

"What do you do for a full-time job? I know you've told me before, but I've forgotten, Abe," Dawn asked.

I realised from the question that Abe must be a Special Constable.

"Oh, I'm a firearms dealer."

"Gosh, that sounds very glamorous," I said.

"It's not really; nowhere near as exciting as being a police officer," Abe replied.

"Have you ever thought about joining as a regular?" I asked, genuinely interested as to why he wouldn't want to if he enjoyed it so much.

"Oh no, the pay's dreadful, I mean, no offence, but how can you live on such a ridiculous salary. What is it these days, about six thousand a year?"

Dawn coughed; I took the hint and we said our goodbyes.

We headed back on a circular route towards the nick.

"Be very wary of our Abe, Christopher. He means well, he really does but ..."

"But what?"

"He tries too hard. I know the local Jewish community love him, he's like their sheriff, but just be careful. Someday, somewhere, he's going to end up in a pile of shit. And whatever you do, don't go out paired up with him unless you're casting for a remake of *Carry on Constable*."

“He’s a firearms dealer, that’s an unusual occupation,” I commented, ignoring the obvious dig.

“Yes, between you and me I reckon there are more firearms amongst the Jewish community in Stamford Hill than the black community of Brixton and old Abe there supplies them all, whether the purchaser’s got a Section 1 licence or not. But that’s just what I think and not what I know.”

“Why do they need them?”

“’Cos after the holocaust, they’re determined never to be victims again, and who can blame them?”

“That’s really fascinating,” I said.

Dawn shrugged her shoulders, her gesture of non-interest bringing our discussion to an end. I thought we almost had a conversation going there. I really wished she’d loosen up a bit with me.

When we reached the bottom of the High Street the bingo hall was turning out at the end of the afternoon session and dozens of elderly ladies were making their way home. Dawn and I stopped and lent against the railings which separated the wide pavement from the busy main road. We nodded, acknowledging each old lady that passed by.

“Pigs,” a voice shouted from behind us.

I turned around and looked across the road. At a bus stop opposite were perhaps ten youths who I guessed had come from the local sixth form college.

“Excuse me,” a voice said, and I turned back to see an old lady addressing us.

“Can I say how nice it is for you to come and make sure we all get home safely? A friend of mine was mugged last week, had all her winnings stolen; she says she'll never come again. It made me think twice too, but now you're here I know I'm safe."

"It's a pleasure," Dawn said, with a warm smile that I thought I'd really appreciate being on the receiving end of, just once.

"Pigs. Are you deaf too, you stupid swines?"

I didn't react this time but instead looked into a shop window, which reflected the scene at the bus stop opposite. I was vaguely aware that Dawn was still talking to the old woman.

"Pigs."

The voice was growing with confidence.

I identified the lad who was shouting. He was a white kid wearing a green T-shirt and brown combat trousers. Suddenly my mind flashed back to Heston Services in the middle of winter and the very first piece of policing advice I had ever been given. I walked slowly to the crossing and waited for the green man. I made sure I didn't look directly at the bus stop, as I wanted the youths to hold their ground; they did but I did notice the gobshite had gone very quiet. I stole a subtle glance. The lad in the green T-shirt was retreating to the rear of the crowd. When I reached the opposite pavement, I walked slowly, oh so slowly, towards the group. I noticed the young men were looking less confident with each step I took. I stopped some three yards short of the group and pointed a finger at the youth with the green T-shirt. I felt unusually confident and very much in control.

The youth bolted.

He ran like the clappers off down the street and away from me and I took off in hot pursuit. The lad turned left and down a side street, I followed, closing, definitely closing. The lad turned left again and in another fifty yards, left again. I knew he was doing a square and possibly trying to get back to his friends at the bus stop. A last left turn and I heard the lad shouting for help. He ran through his mates, who immediately formed a line across the pavement to stop, or at least try to impede me. I'd played a great deal of rugby and knew how to break through a tackle. I slowed my pace very slightly, dipped my right shoulder and then sprinted hard, pumping my thighs, and at the point of anticipated contact I sprang forward driving my shoulder and upper arm ahead to take the initial contact. The line parted and I charged through unhindered but straight into the side of the old lady who'd been chatting to us only a few minutes before. She was thrown completely off her feet so hard both her shoes remained exactly where they had been at the moment of impact. The collision happened in a blur but I barely checked my stride and kept running. I was determined this lad wasn't getting away and nothing was going to stop me.

I looked to the right, across the road; still standing by the railings was an open-mouthed Dawn.

Chapter 18 – Two out of three

When I got back to the nick with my prisoner, the charge room was packed. Two sergeants were working flat out and there was a queue of other prisoners all waiting to be booked in, two of whom were scantily clad young women. I sat my lad between them in the only available seating space left in the room.

The first, a bleached blonde in a tiny denim miniskirt and five-inch heels, asked the young lad.

"What you nicked for then, darling?"

"'Cos one, he," the young lad nodded at me, "ain't got a sense of humour and two, he's a really quick runner."

The women laughed.

"What did you do that he didn't find amusing?"

"I might have mentioned something about a farm animal what lives in a sty."

"Never a shrewd move, they rarely find that amusing."

"What are you here for?" the young lad asked, unable to stop looking at the young women's legs.

They both laughed.

"Tomming."

"Tomming? What's that?"

"Loitering for the purpose of prostitution is the legal term."

"Oh, I see, of course," the young man replied.

"Mind you," the second tom said, speaking for the first time, "I'd give it for free to the rozzer that nicked us."

"So would I," agreed her friend.

"What's a rozzer?" the young lad asked; a question which I appreciated because I didn't know either.

"Rozzer is what south Londoners call old bill; cozzers, coppers, Babylon, bobbies, peelers, pigs, five O and fuzz are some other well-known names."

At that moment, PC Andy Welling entered the charge room.

"Speak of the devil," the first tom said.

"Hi, Chris," he said, with genuine warmth.

"Hi, Andy."

"How are you getting on with Dawn these days? Any better?"

I shook my head.

"Sorry to hear that. What you got in here?"

"Just one for threatening behaviour."

"Oh well, well done, they all count in your record of work."

"I gather these two ladies are yours, Andy?"

"Yes, yes."

The room suddenly went quiet and when I looked up I saw the superintendent talking to one of the sergeants. From the silence I gathered the presence of such a senior officer in the charge room was a rare event.

"Is the PC with the prisoner from outside the bingo hall here?" the senior officer asked.

"That's me, Sir," I replied.

"Can I have a word, please?"

I felt nervous and guessed it must be about the old lady; I followed the senior officer into the small interview room by the front office.

"What's the prisoner arrested for?"

"Threatening behaviour, Sir."

"Was there a foot chase?"

"Yes, Sir."

"Did the prisoner assault an old lady? Knock her out of the way when you were chasing him?"

"Well, that's not quite how it happened. He ran through a crowd of his mates who tried to block me so I barged through them and the old lady was the other side."

"She's gone to hospital with a broken hip. PC Matthews has gone with her. When the prisoner's booked in, do your original notes and get up to the hospital with some flowers. The Duty Officer is at the scene taking some statements about what happened, he'll report to me. Don't go off duty without seeing me. Are you early turn?"

"Street Duties, Sir, eight to four."

"If I'm not in my office, I'll be in the library."

I nodded, although I'd no idea where the library was but I'd worry about that later. I was relieved the superintendent didn't seem too concerned.

Eventually the sergeant called my prisoner forward and asked me.

"Grounds for arrest please, Officer?"

"I was patrolling the High Street in the vicinity of the bingo hall. Many old ladies were coming out when this youth starting shouting and swearing at myself and WPC Matthews. He used the words pig, wanker and cunt. Several of the old ladies looked shocked and distressed. When I went to speak to him, he ran away but returned to the scene a few minutes later when, fearing he would continue behaving in this abusive manner, I arrested him."

It was nearly the truth, and I was pleased to have got through a process that all new officers find difficult. I was really sorry Dawn wasn't there to witness me doing something right for a change.

"You've heard what the officer's said. Have you got anything to say?"

"No, I'm sorry. I thought I was having a laugh. I didn't think about the old ladies."

The lad put out his hand to shake mine.

"I'll shake your hand when you leave the nick."

"Fair enough," he replied sheepishly.

The sixteen-year-old, who was studying for the same three A levels which I'd taken just a year ago, turned out to be quite a nice chap. He'd not been arrested previously and when he learnt he was going to have to go into a cell whilst bail checks were completed, panic set in.

"Can't you just leave the door open. I suffer from claustrophobia. I won't escape or run away I promise, mate, honest," he pleaded, as I led him down the cell passage.

"I can't but you shouldn't be here for long. Sarge's already called your mum and she'll be on the way as soon as she's picked up your sister."

I struggled to find anywhere to put him, as the cells were all full; the drunk tank at the very end had at least six prisoners in it and the single cells were all doubled up. I put him in number six and chalked his details below two other names on the blackboard next to the cell door. My satisfaction was, of course, tempered by the injury to the old lady, but I had made my first lawful arrest and allowed myself a satisfied smile as I returned the cell keys to the sergeant.

***

I hated hospitals, not just since mum died but for as long as I could remember. The smell alone would fill my stomach with butterflies, so when I arrived at Casualty, I was feeling bad in so many different ways. I was directed to a geriatric ward where I found Dawn waiting outside the door to a single room off to one side. She was sitting, reading a magazine and looking really bored.

"Hi," I said tentatively.

Dawn ignored me; she didn't even look up.

I sat next to her.

"Looks like you've got away with it," she said, still reading the magazine.

"Sorry?"

"Looks like you've got away with GBH'ing the old girl."

I didn't say anything, I knew Dawn well enough by now; if she had something to say she'd say it without my encouragement.

"The Duty Officer's been up here and spoken to Mrs Wilson and her son. Most of the witnesses say the lad knocked her over. One, a shopkeeper, says it was you. Luckily, everyone agrees, whoever did it, it was an accident. Neither she nor her son is interested in taking the matter further. Mrs Wilson is a big fan of the police; well, she would be, wouldn't she? Her belated husband was in the Met. You, Christopher, are one lucky son of a bitch."

"It was an accident, Dawn."

"What came over you? You were like a man possessed."

"I don't know. I just couldn't stand there whilst he was slagging us off."

"I was chatting to the old lady, what was he saying?"

"Pigs, wankers, cunts, that sort of thing."

"Fair enough, he needed nicking then, but you should have told me what you were doing. The first thing I knew was when you came tearing back around the corner and charged at those lads at the bus stop."

"Dawn, whatever I do, I fuck up. And now someone's got hurt. And I'm not so mind-numbingly stupid that I don't realise how much you hate me."

There was an awkward pause for several seconds, and then Dawn filled the silence.

"Hate is a strong word, Chris. Let's settle for dislike."

"Why, Dawn, just tell me, please?"

"Okay."

She took a deep breath, this was going to be more than just a few words, and mentally I braced myself, whilst Dawn continued to turn the pages of her magazine.

"You're too young to be in the job; you don't wash enough and smell of B.O. You're scruffy; your helmet's two sizes too large and looks ridiculous; you stink of cigarettes; you swear too much, every other word is fuck this or fuck that; I find you quite boring; you fancy me and that thought makes me feel physically sick; you make assumptions because of my sex that you wouldn't make if I was a man, like I'm going to have kids and leave the job and that I'd be good looking after kids. Why? Why would I be good at looking after children? I'm a single child and I've never had any kids so why would I know what to do?"

Before I could attempt to answer, Dawn's harangue continued.

"Oh, and you're so obsessed with yourself and how you're doing, you never give a thought to anyone else."

At no time during the conversation did her eyes look up from the pages of her magazine.

I stared ahead at a poster advertising a Quit Smoking Helpline. I said nothing in response to the brutal assessment. Instead, I considered her criticisms and quite frankly, couldn't really argue with any, except perhaps the last. I had realised quickly after Hendon that I was very young to be doing the job; I didn't wash every day and took no particular pride in my appearance, but I hadn't thought anyone noticed. The helmet I'd borrowed was two sizes too large. I smoked too much and probably had asked some pretty tactless questions, but I hadn't intended to insult her. As for giving a thought to her problems, I'd guessed she might be going through some crisis, but I couldn't see her wanting my help or advice.

"Go and see Mrs Wilson, Chris. Then meet me outside Casualty."

It was only then I realised I'd forgotten to buy any flowers.

***

When we were walking back to the nick, I got a message to report immediately to the Chief Inspector's office upon my return.

"That sounds ominous. I thought you said I'd be all right," I commented, gloomily.

"Well, that's the impression I got from the Duty Officer. Maybe there's been some developments?"

"Funny, I thought the Superintendent was dealing with it. He was the one who told me to go to the hospital."

"Shit travels downhill," Dawn replied.

"Have you got any advice, partner?" I asked, more in hope than anticipation.

"Yes. Wait and see what he says first, whatever you do. If you have to, say you think the lad hit Mrs Wilson first and knocked her into your path. I'll back you up."

"Thanks."

"No need to thank me, Chris, that's what we do for each other."

The Chief Inspector's office was on the first floor and the door was already open, but I knocked all the same.

"Come in," said a fifty-year-old, grey-haired man sitting at an untidy desk. From the three pips on his epaulettes, I knew he was the Chief Inspector.

"PC Pritchard, Sir; you want to see me?"

The Chief Inspector was on the phone; he covered the mouthpiece and said quietly, "Come in, Pritchard. Take a seat."

He waved to an area behind the desk where a small round table was surrounded by several low comfortable chairs.

"Yes, of course, if there's any cost implications, we'll pay. I believe its twenty-four hours. We can pick you both up and run you down there if you like. I think they call them sexually transmitted diseases these days."

I was glad the telephone conversation was obviously not about the old lady.

"Yes, okay. I'd like to apologise again. Yes, yes, goodbye, Madam."

The Chief Inspector hung up and swung around in his swivel chair to face me.

"Seriously, Pritchard. What were you thinking?"

"Sorry, Sir?"

"That's mum on the phone. She's furious."

"Is she still alive?" I asked.

I was surprised, after all, Mrs Wilson was eighty so her mother must be at least a hundred.

"Yes, of course," the Chief Inspector replied.

I was confused.

"*He's* not complaining, mind you."

"Isn't he?" I said but I didn't know who 'he' was, but still at least 'he' wasn't complaining, so that had to be good, didn't it?

"Did they teach you about the three P's at Training School?"

"Yes, Sir," I replied, even more confused.

"Well, what are they?"

"Prisoners, property and prostitutes, Sir."

"And what did they tell you about the three P's?"

"That if you drop in the ..." I hesitated to use a swear word.

"Pritchard, I've been in this job for twenty-eight years, I've heard the word shit before."

"Shit, that if you drop in the shit, Sir, it'll be because of either a prisoner or property or a prostitute."

"And you decided to bugger up two of the three P's in one go."

"Sorry, Sir?"

I was completely lost. I'd absolutely no idea what the Chief Inspector was talking about. It didn't seem to be about the old lady at all. I sat quietly for several seconds but was overwhelmed by the urge to know what I'd done.

"Sir?"

"Yes?"

"Sorry, Sir, I know I've done something wrong, and I am sorry, honestly, really sorry, but can you tell me what I've done?"

"Pritchard, you put a sixteen-year-old juvenile in a cell with two prostitutes. When an hour later his mother came to collect him, and the sergeant took her to the cell and unlocked the door, she discovered her precious baby as naked as the day he was born having sex with both of them. Let's just say, she wasn't impressed. As we speak, she's taking him down the clap clinic to get him checked out. Not your finest hour. What have you got to say, Pritchard?"

"Sorry, Sir."

"How old are you, son?" the Chief Inspector asked, his voice quieter, the frustration suddenly absent.

"Nineteen, Sir."

The Chief Inspector slowly shook his head from side to side.

"Off you go, lad," he said, almost kindly.

I got up to leave and then remembered my problems weren't yet over.

"Sir."

"Yes."

"Where's the Superintendent's office?"

"It's gone four, so he'll be in the library."

"In the library, Sir?"

"The library, the heart."

"The heart?"

"Oh, for goodness' sake, Pritchard, the Superintendent will be in the library, otherwise known as the lounge bar of the White Hart public house which is located some fifty yards east of this police station."

Chapter 19 – Lessons from a lost or stolen

That Saturday I spent the morning washing and pressing my uniform and, for the first time since Training School, ironed every police shirt I had and this time, I did the entire shirt and not just the front. I then spit and polished my boots so well you could quite literally see your face reflected in them. Fortuitously, that week my replacement helmet had arrived. Never again would anyone be able to say PC Pritchard was scruffy.

I adjusted my morning schedule always to include a strip wash at the small sink in my room and, to facilitate the process, I purchased two large bath towels to lie on the floor. Never again would anyone say PC Pritchard was smelly.

In the afternoon I had my hair cut very short and purchased from the barbers a wet shaving kit. I had only ever used an electric razor and then not every day. I spent a small fortune in Marks & Spencer's on new underwear and also bought several pairs of jeans and casual shirts.

During the evening I completely spring-cleaned my room, vacuuming, polishing, scrubbing and wiping. I threw out some of my older clothing and replaced my bedding with brand new, crisp sheets and a state-of-the-art continental quilt.

I tried to give up smoking, but the attempt only lasted a few hours.

Later that evening, I went to the Elephant's Head and felt considerably better than I'd done for some time. Listening to Dawn's criticism hadn't been easy but I was determined to take on board what she had said and change what I could.

***

When I reported for duty the following day, I looked smarter than I ever had. I met Dawn in the portacabin; she looked me up and down and nodded. She didn't say anything, she didn't have to, because I knew she'd noticed. Unusually that morning, we didn't go out immediately but went to the canteen for a quick cup of tea before setting off on patrol. We sat apart from everyone else, and I guessed correctly that Dawn wanted a quiet word with me.

"I have some bad news, I'm afraid," she said, her voice and expression serious.

I thought she was going to tell me I'd failed the Street Duties course; my heart sank.

"Mrs Wilson died yesterday."

I felt awful; I put my head in my hands to try to hide tears, which I could feel welling up; this was terrible. I wanted to protect old ladies, not kill them. Oh God! Oh Fuck!

"How come? It was only a broken bone."

"Her broken hip caused internal bleeding and she went into shock."

"Fuck, Dawn, she was really sweet."

"Listen and listen carefully. There's bound to be some sort of inquiry, and we'll have to give evidence at Coroner's Court. I've made a detailed statement and completely corroborated your version of events. The lad ran into her first and then you. It was all an accident."

"If you want to tell the truth, I'll understand," I said.

"You still don't get it, do you? That's why working with sprogs is so dangerous. I've made a statement and I'm not, I can't, change it. Not now, not tomorrow, not ever. Once it's written, that's what happened. Any other way takes you straight to prison for perverting the course of justice. Do you understand?"

I mumbled a 'yes'.

“For Heaven’s sake, Christopher, do you understand?”

I looked up, straight into her eyes.

“I understand, Dawn.”

“Let me tell you a true story. If you remember nothing else from the three months we work together, remember this. It’s about a friend of mine. We were at Training School together and she was posted somewhere south, Croydon, I think. Julie was a lovely girl, bright and bubbly and by far the smartest student in the class. Anyway, she worked hard and eventually got rewarded with a posting as operator on the area car. Now you won’t know this yet but, if you ever get into a chase with a lost or stolen, when you eventually catch the car, the occupants will star burst. If there are several of them and only two of you, you’re not going to catch them all, so try to get the driver. The passengers will say their mate just picked them up and deny knowing the car was stolen, even if the ignition column’s missing and the quarterlight is smashed. Most East End juries will acquit, so the golden rule is catching the driver. If, however, the driver escapes and the only one you can get hold of is one of the passengers, then you ‘put’ him in the driver’s seat. Do you understand what I mean by that?”

“Yeah, you say the passenger was the driver.”

“That’s right; everyone knows this is what you do.”

“Anyway, Julie is the operator on the area car and they get behind a lost or stolen Triumph Dolomite Sprint. It’s a short chase; the guy loses it on a bend and wraps it around a tree. Now you, me, Marc Bolan, we wrap a car round a tree, we die. Not this guy, he jumps out and gives it legs. The passenger’s not so lucky, he’s okay but his door is damaged in the accident and before he can get out, the area car driver nicks him. The area car driver writes up his notes whilst Julie's booking the prisoner in. When she walks into the canteen the area car driver hands her his notes and she copies down the evidence, making the odd change here and there so both sets of notes, though essentially the same, are not identical. Both notes say, categorically, that the person they arrested was driving the stolen car.

"They go to court, the defendant's charged with taking and driving away, he pleads not guilty saying he was only the passenger and had no idea the motor was nicked. They give their evidence; he's convicted and gets a bender.

"Years pass and everyone moves on, except the area car driver's kid gets leukaemia and mum and dad suddenly find God. The son gets cured and one morning the area car driver, completing some pact he's previously made with the Almighty, goes to see his Chief Superintendent and confesses all the wrongs he's ever done including, of course, fitting up the passenger as the driver of the lost or stolen Triumph Dolomite Sprint. The area car driver gets a year's imprisonment and Julie two years, the full works, not suspended. Do you see what I'm saying, Chris? When you lie, you lie forever, or people go to prison. This is no game; this is a really serious business."

"No wonder you can't really trust me, yet."

"Maybe now you'll start to understand."

I nodded. From what Dawn was saying and remembering how we'd had to gild the lily to make sure the dipper was charged, it seemed that a police officer regularly had to lie in order to secure a conviction. If you didn't, if you decided to be an entirely honest cop, then you would be both ineffective and more importantly, ostracised by your colleagues. If, on the other hand, you chose to oil the wheels of justice, then you risked being convicted yourself of some pretty serious criminal offences. And the more I thought about it, the more I understood Dawn's line that when you lie, you lie forever, because the second you change your account of events, it makes what you said originally a falsehood, and an evidential falsehood is called perjury by the criminal justice system.

"Now, let's get out of here," Dawn said, apparently satisfied her words had sunk home.

As we collected our stuff and walked across the yard, Dawn turned to me. I was, as ever, a few paces behind her.

"Oh, what you doing on Thursday?"

"Late turn, with you of course, why?" I replied.

"No, you're not. You're going to Mrs Wilson's funeral."

Chapter 20 – Advice given

After nearly a month of Dawn's careful tutelage, I gradually got to know the basics. Like most probationers, first I got the hang of process, the official term for reporting motorists for traffic offences. By the Friday of each week, Dawn made sure my bright yellow 'record of work' book contained the details of numerous bus lanes, red lights, untaxed cars, failing to accord precedence on zebra crossings and driving without insurances.

Whilst Dawn was never friendly, as the weeks became a month, she did at least become slightly less curt; but in my company, she rarely smiled. I noticed too, she never enquired about my private life or domestic circumstances. If I mentioned a subject other than work, even if it was as bland as a television programme, which had been on the night before, Dawn would change the subject back to policing. Working with PC Matthews was bloody hard going but I was learning fast.

One early turn about midday, when Dawn and I were leaving the nick, we got a call to a domestic dispute in a flat on a council estate a short walk away.

"Most domestics are rubbish. If you nick the husband, you'll end up fighting his wife too, even though she's the one that bloody called you," Dawn commented, sceptically.

The flat we were called to, number sixty-eight, was on the top floor and as the lift smelt so strongly of urine, we mutually decided to walk up the six flights of stairs without a word of discussion passing between us. When we got to the right door, instead of knocking, Dawn put her finger to her mouth to indicate I should be quiet, knelt and pushed the letterbox open slowly and looked inside. She then turned her head and listened intently; somewhere inside a television was on. She stood up and retraced our steps along the landing and I followed, a little surprised we weren't going to call at the address. Instead, Dawn knocked at the neighbour's door. A little old lady answered.

"Hello, officer," the occupant said, clearly surprised by her unexpected callers.

"Yes, sorry to disturb you, madam, it's nothing to worry about," Dawn said reassuringly.

"What could I have to worry about, officer? All the bad news in my life has long since been delivered. Now, can I help you?" the old woman said, smiling kindly.

"Can you tell us anything about the people next door at number sixty-eight?"

"Edith and the twins? Edith's a lovely lady but those sons of hers are a handful."

"In what way?" Dawn asked.

"Oh, she has dreadful trouble with them."

"How old are they?"

"Oh, twenty-five, thirty, I'm not very good with ages."

"And does their dad live there, too?"

"No, Ralph died many years ago. He was a lovely man, but he liked his rum too much."

"Have you heard any noise coming from next door this morning?"

"Yes, but there's always shouting. Edith screams and shouts but they take no notice."

"Thank you very much, sorry to disturb you."

"Oh, would you like to come in for a tea, I don't get much company these days."

There was barely hidden desperation in the old lady's plea; in that second, I felt her loneliness.

"I'm sorry; we've got to call next door, perhaps next time," Dawn said, firmly ending the conversation.

This time Dawn knocked on the door of sixty-eight, and a few moments later a black lady in her mid-fifties answered.

"Did you call police?" Dawn asked.

"Yes, yes, come in, come in," she said.

We stepped into a tidy but sparsely furnished council flat and followed the lady into the living room. Sitting on the settee were two very similar-looking men in their twenties who were wearing only boxer shorts and had their arms folded across their chests in exactly the same manner. They were watching a children's cartoon on the television and barely moved when the three of us walked in. They were well-built men with square powerful shoulders but something in their gaze suggested they were not all there.

"I want them out now, officers," the woman demanded, and she stamped her foot; her sons ignored her.

"Christopher, take this lady into the kitchen and find out what's going on. I'll speak to these two," Dawn instructed.

The kitchen was small and sparse but the smell of spices hanging in the air suggested this lady really knew how to cook.

"Can I ask your name, madam?"

"Edith, Edith Gloria Vincent, officer."

"And what's the problem, Mrs Vincent?"

"I want my boys out now."

"Do they live with you?"

"Yes, but they've gotta go now."

"Why, what have they done?"

"Such a disgusting thing, officer. Today, I was doing the washing in the bath and they come up behind me and did it. I'm not having it."

"They did what, Mrs Vincent?"

"They took me. And where no woman should be took. I'm not having it."

I had absolutely no idea what she was talking about; I knew I'd have to ask very specific questions.

"When you say 'they', Mrs Vincent, to whom are you referring?"

"The twins, officer," she replied, as if I was stupid.

"And are they your children, Mrs Vincent?"

"Yes."

"And are they the two men sitting in the lounge?"

"Yes."

"And when did this 'thing' happen, Mrs Vincent?"

"It happens most every day, officer, but today it was different."

"And where does 'it' happen?" I asked, feeling I was making slow but definite progress.

"It happens sometimes in the kitchen, sometimes in the bedroom and this morning in the bathroom when I was doing me washing."

"And this morning in the bathroom, what exactly did the twins do?"

Mrs Vincent looked to the heavens in frustration and let out a long sigh.

"Please, Mrs Vincent, tell me exactly what the twins did to you this morning."

"They held me down and had their way."

"Had their way doing what?" I asked, determined her next answer would reveal all.

"Officer, if you cannot understand me then I need to speak to the lady officer, you are perhaps too young to understand."

This was the very last thing I wanted; that would make me look really stupid. I was determined to get to the bottom of the matter. I thought hard, there only seemed to be one explanation.

"Mrs Vincent, are you telling me that this morning your sons had sexual intercourse with you in the bathroom?"

"No," she replied decisively.

I gave up. I would have to get Dawn after all, so I went to leave.

"This morning they took me in my bottom," she declared.

"What?" I replied, somewhat unprofessionally; then gathering myself, I spoke slowly and clearly.

"This morning your sons buggered you in the bathroom whilst you were doing the washing?"

"Yes, officer, that's what I've been trying to tell you," an exasperated Mrs Vincent replied.

"And this has happened before? You mentioned the bedroom and the kitchen."

"Before they do not take me in the bottom; today it has gone too far."

Suddenly I realised Dawn was alone with the twins and felt an urgency to make sure she was all right.

"Wait there, Mrs Vincent, I need to speak to my colleague."

I darted back to the lounge where a distinctly uncomfortable Dawn was in conversation with the twins who were on their feet and now standing between her and the door. As I entered, I caught the tail end of a sentence.

"It's women like you, it's your fault," one of them said; the other was nodding.

"Sit down," I said firmly, almost aggressively, and when they did, I was impressed with my own authority.

Dawn walked across the room, there was a definite look of gratitude in her eyes; would it have killed the miserable cow to thank me?

"Wait there, I need to speak to my colleague," Dawn said to the twins.

We stepped outside the front door.

"I think they raped her this morning," an incredulous Dawn said.

"I know, up her arse over the bath whilst she was doing the washing."

"Per anus, you say per anus not up her arse," Dawn corrected me.

"Sorry."

"Does she want them arrested?"

"I didn't ask. It took me ages to realise what she was alleging."

"I don't blame you for that," Dawn said.

"It's not every day you get a call like this," she added.

"When I realised what was going on and that you were alone with them, I just came to check you were all right. When I think about it, I think she just wants them ejected," I said.

"This is their house, it's not that simple and they have rights; where are they going to go? If she wants them arrested, we can get them out, but she'll have to come to the nick, be examined and make a statement. Then if they are charged, we can ask for a bail condition requiring them to keep away from their mum and this house. Social services will have to find them somewhere to live," Dawn explained.

"Go back and speak to her and see if she'll make a statement. If she won't, explain that we're a bit stuffed, I'll finish my chat with Tweedledum and Tweedledee but this time they're not coming between me and the door."

As I walked back to the kitchen, I noticed the boys had resumed watching cartoons.

"Mrs Vincent. We can take your boys away, but you'll have to make a statement about what happened this morning."

"I'm not making no statement, officer; I'm not getting my own children arrested. If they get a criminal record, they'll never find a job. But I can't take it in my bottom, that's too much. Just speak to them about that. Tell them if they put it in my bottom again, they'll have to find somewhere else to live. I am not having it in my bottom, never again. I was bleeding, officer."

When we left the flat, I contacted the Reserve to give the result of the call.

"Golf November, four six six?"

"Go ahead."

"The call to sixty-eight Keir Hardie House, domestic dispute, advice given, over."

"All received, out."

Advice given? Advice given? I had told two twenty-five-year-old men that next time they wanted to have sex with their mother they've got to use her vagina. I thought this must be the strangest piece of advice ever given by the Metropolitan Police.

Chapter 21 – Funeral

I wore the same black tie my trembling hands had knotted on the morning of my mum's funeral. During the short service I stood well back from the well-attended graveside. I was weighed down by guilt and reminded of a gangster film I'd once seen where the killers attended their victim's funeral and kissed the grieving widow acting as if they were completely innocent of the crime. It was my intention to melt into the background and then leave quickly and quietly as soon as it was over, but my plan failed for as soon the service finished, Mrs Wilson's son, who I'd met briefly at the hospital, made a beeline for me.

"Oh, officer, how very kind of you to come," he said, shaking my hand enthusiastically.

"It's the least I could do," I replied, feeling as awkward and embarrassed as I'd ever felt in my life. This was even worse than when I'd arrested the disqual driver who hadn't actually been driving.

"My mum died last year so I know what you're going through, Mr Wilson," I added, glad to be able to say something which was both honest and heartfelt.

"Mum was eighty-three, she had a good innings. She didn't suffer for months with a long painful illness like Dad who had the big C. She was at bingo on Friday and only forty-eight hours later had passed on. Now that can't be a bad way to go, can it?"

"No," I replied meekly.

What else could I say?

"Oh, and thank you for the flowers, they are lovely."

I mustered a smile and thought perhaps if I didn't say anything more, Mr Wilson would move along and speak to someone else, hopefully a long-lost uncle or distant cousin.

"You must come to the hotel. We've laid on drinks and some food. Some of Dad's old colleagues are there, George and Henry; I'm sure they'd appreciate the chance to talk job with you."

"No, no really, I've already intruded enough, and I've come by bus ..." but before I could finish my feeble excuse, Mr Wilson interrupted.

"Nonsense, you can ride with us, there's room in the car 'cos Aunt May's going straight home from here."

I felt compelled to go. On the solemn thirty-minute drive from Abney Park Cemetery to the impressive oak-beamed hotel adjacent to an old Elizabethan hunting lodge in Chingford, I tried to reconcile my guilt. I knew I'd never meant to hurt Mrs Wilson and that if the lad at the bus stop hadn't been such an idiot, the chain of events which led to her death would never have been set into motion. I was also aware that if my neighbour Gerald hadn't primed me to do so, I wouldn't have reacted as I did. By the time we'd arrived at the wake, I'd browbeaten my conscience into coming to terms, at some superficial level at least, with what had happened.

Almost immediately Mr Wilson introduced me to two elderly gentlemen who were his late father's colleagues, the most talkative of whom was a chap called George who'd joined the Met in 1920 and retired in 1953, ten years before I'd been born. George had more stories than Agatha Christie; he'd been an Inspector during the Second World War and one of Churchill's personal protection officers. For three pints I listened genuinely fascinated as George regaled me with tales of the Blitz, doodlebugs, unexploded bombs and a very drunken wartime Prime Minister. The second man, Henry, who I guessed had heard these tales countless times before, smiled and nodded appropriately but kept his own memories to himself.

When the stories had temporarily dried, Henry spoke for the first time since our introduction.

"Your hands are tied these days, young man. Too many do-gooders doing no damn good at all. In my day every prisoner you arrested got a decent hiding just to remind them who was in charge. I feel sorry for you; lay one finger on them and you'll lose your job, but trust me, that's what's needed. Today the criminals have the upper hand."

"It's not that bad, we've not lost the streets yet," I said, trying to sound reassuring.

"I'm not so sure, young man. You see, most people, say ninety-nine out of a hundred, are good honest folk who don't need the police to stop them committing crime. But that one per cent, and don't forget that's five hundred thousand people in an island of fifty million. You're there 'cos if you weren't you'd have anarchy. The day the criminal minority no longer fear the police, we're in real trouble. Every liberal who undermines what you do takes society another step towards the abyss. Let's hope someone realises before it's too late."

"Oh, Henry, don't be so depressing," George rebuked his friend.

Henry shook his head despondently.

"Are you on the square, young man?" George asked.

I wasn't sure I knew exactly what I was being asked but assumed being 'on the square' was akin to being on the level, above board so to speak. I took a calculated guess that I was being asked whether I was honest and truthful. Then I panicked, why were they asking me this? Were they going to ask me about how Mrs Wilson died? Did they suspect something? What had they heard? I knew they were waiting for an answer.

"Yes. I'm on the square," I replied cautiously.

At that precise moment Mr Wilson tapped a fork against a wine glass and the room almost instantly fell silent. I exhaled a long slow breath in relief. I decided as soon as the speech, or eulogy, was over I'd make as if going to the toilet and then slip away.

Mr Wilson opened by thanking everyone for attending and went on to talk about his mother's early life and how she had met his father. My mind started to wonder and just when I was paying no attention at all, I noticed every eye in the room had fallen upon me.

"... that my mother should die helping, albeit unwittingly, to arrest a hardened criminal seems to me rather fitting. I have been assured that without her assistance the suspect would have escaped; instead, he is where he belongs, behind bars."

Several heads were nodding in agreement and approval, a ripple of humble applause circulated around the room and I felt obliged to join in but I looked down unable to meet anyone's gaze, for I knew the 'hardened criminal' was in fact a pleasant young man who, following a genuine apology, hadn't been charged with anything.

A few seconds later everyone was raising their glasses and toasting the late, great Mrs Lydia Wilson. The speech was over; my time to beat a quick retreat was at hand. I looked for somewhere to leave my pint glass which, as it remained half full, would support my pretext to be going to the toilet and then coming back.

"Can we have a discreet word with you, young man?" George asked.

Shit. George and Henry had tracked my slow drift across the room and weren't going to let me escape that easily.

"Of course, what is it?"

"Not here, can we step outside?" Henry asked seriously.

This was it. This was definitely where they're going to confront me about Mrs Wilson. I followed them into the car park; lighting a cigarette as we stepped outside, I offered them one, but both declined. George looked about, apparently checking we couldn't be overheard. I felt my hands start to shake.

"What lodge?" George asked.

"I'm sorry?" I replied, taken aback by the strange question.

"What's your lodge's name?"

"What lodge?" I replied, mystified.

For a second, I thought George had suddenly gone senile or had a sudden stroke or something but when I glanced sideways at Henry, I couldn't read anything in his facial expression to suggest the question was unusual. Suddenly the penny dropped: the lodge, of course; they were asking me about the old hunting lodge next to the hotel. I had read the sign as we'd pulled up into the car park.

"I think it was Queen Elizabeth's."

"A royal lodge? How impressive," George said.

"Yes, must be five hundred years old," I added, helpfully.

"I hope you don't mind us asking but ..." George hesitated.

"Go on," I said, the tension inside me evaporating as this had nothing to do with Mrs Wilson's death.

"Well, could we visit?"

"Of course."

"Well, if I give you my telephone number perhaps you could arrange it?" Henry asked.

"Okay," I replied, somewhat perplexed as to why they needed me to take them; the sign I'd seen stated the hunting lodge was open to the public.

"Excellent, excellent. Let's go back inside, I think the buffets just started and I'm starving," George suggested.

I agreed to join them again once I'd finished my cigarette. In truth, I wanted a few minutes to myself. The voice behind me made me jump.

"Christopher, have you got a spare one of those, I'm meant to be giving up," Mr Wilson asked.

"Yes of course," I replied and dug the packet out of my jacket pocket.

"Mr Wilson?"

"Yes?"

"George and Henry have asked me to take them to the lodge."

I nodded towards the impressive old Elizabethan building.

"Oh, you don't have to, really. Just tell them you're busy. My dad was on the square. In fact, I think that's where they all met. I've never bothered, myself."

"Oh," I said, starting to think I was missing something.

"I really don't mind taking them, they're really good company and it's great to hear their stories."

"Well, it's up to you but don't think you have to."

I finished my cigarette and flicked the end an impressively long distance across and out of the car park.

"I really need to be going, Mr Wilson. I'm sorry about your mum, it was a nice funeral."

"Of course, Chris, but before you go there's just one thing I need to know?"

"Yes?"

"The bloke that ran into mum. Exactly what had he done?"

Chapter 22 – High places

As we set out on patrol the following day Dawn was eager to learn how Mrs Wilson's funeral had gone. I took her through my graveside guilt, my failed attempts to escape the wake and then finally being cornered by Mr Wilson.

"So, what did you say?" Dawn asked.

"I lied, Dawn, I had to. I could hardly tell Mr Wilson the person he'd described in his eulogy as a hardened criminal was a not unpleasant sixteen-year-old who'd just called me a few names."

"So, what did you say?"

"I said I thought I recognised the man as someone wanted for murder and that the CID were dealing and had yet to inform me whether he'd been charged."

"You probably did the right thing; there are occasions when the truth just isn't what's required."

"So I'm beginning to learn."

And as I completed the sentence our eyes met and just for a second, and for the first time in all the weeks we'd been working together, something passed between us. It was the strangest thing; was it a mutual understanding or a common thought? I wasn't sure what it was, but I was certain it was something.

***

Several hours later we saw a brand new Land Rover with darkened windows parked on the zig-zags on the approach to a pedestrian crossing in Church Street. I stayed with the vehicle whilst Dawn called on several nearby shops to locate the driver.

Dawn returned with a white woman in her forties who was smartly dressed in an expensive dark blue trouser suit and her styled shoulder-length brown hair looked as if she'd just come from the hairdressers. She had an air about her which suggested the parking matter was so trivial she was doing us an enormous favour simply speaking to us about it.

"Oh, officers, come on; I've only been here for a few minutes. I'll move it and we'll let the matter rest there."

Usually, Dawn would stand back and let me deal with these traffic matters but on this occasion, she seemed to take a particular offence to the woman's attitude.

"Madam, you parked on the approach to a zebra crossing without any consideration that people might wish to use the crossing safely. You will be reported for the offence."

"Oh officer, don't be so damn silly. You're starting to irritate me. Now go and catch some real criminals and leave respectable, law-abiding people like myself alone."

"You will be reported for this offence, you do not have to say anything but anything you do say may be given in evidence."

"Oh you silly woman, go away," the woman remonstrated as she went to get into the vehicle.

Dawn put her hand on the driver's door, preventing the woman opening it.

"Take your hand off my car now," she said, with considerable authority.

"I haven't finished with you yet, please hand me the keys."

Dawn was holding her ground.

I thought the woman was going to explode.

"How dare you?"

"Keys," Dawn demanded, putting her hand out.

The woman threw them on the pavement and headed off towards a telephone box which was only a few yards away.

"I'm phoning my husband," she declared.

I looked at Dawn who picked up the keys and mouthed something to me but I couldn't make out what she was saying.

"What?" I asked.

"That's the woman in the department store, the one with the scissors."

I did recognise her, although I have to confess, I wouldn't have done so had Dawn not pointed her out.

"When she's finished on the phone, we'll search the car. If she kicks off, nick her, Chris, she's getting right on my nerves."

I could hear the woman shouting down the phone and then she pushed the door open and called to Dawn.

"My husband wants to speak to you."

"Does he?" Dawn asked, walking towards the telephone box.

"Yes, here." She offered the handpiece to Dawn who took it as if she was going to put it to her ear, and then hung up.

"Your husband might want to speak to me, but I do not wish to speak to him. Now please join me at your car."

The woman huffed and puffed with an exaggeration which bordered on the comical.

"You'll be sorry you didn't speak to my husband but that's your problem now, I tried to help."

Dawn ignored her.

"Have you got anything in the vehicle that you shouldn't have?"

"Of course not, will you kindly stop upsetting me. My husband will have your job; you're making a huge mistake, young lady. I hope you like being unemployed."

"Please don't threaten me," Dawn said, almost politely.

"I am going to search your vehicle because I believe you may have stolen property."

"And do tell me, young lady, on what grounds is that speculation based?"

The question caught me by surprise, it was just not the way members of the public usually spoke, but fortunately Dawn was unflustered.

"A woman fitting your description was recently seen acting suspiciously in a department store; it is believed she may have been shoplifting. I am going to search your vehicle for any evidence of that offence."

"Oh, poppycock."

Dawn handed me the keys.

"Open the boot."

She guided the woman to the rear of the vehicle and after a little fiddling, I turned the catch and the boot swung sideways open. Inside were piles of neatly folded clothing. It looked brand new. There were trousers, shirts, jackets, jeans, pullovers, cardigans, T-shirts, polo shirts and every other type of clothing I could imagine. The back seat was covered too.

"Why have you got all this clothing?" Dawn asked.

"I like to shop," was the woman's curt reply.

The clothes seemed so neatly organised and perfectly set that I was loath to disturb them. Dawn flicked through a few labels and asked, "Are these all for you then?"

The woman looked to the sky as if it was the most stupid of questions.

"Well? Are they?"

"What do you think, officer?" was the woman's enigmatic reply.

"I'll tell you what I think, they're not for you because they are all different sizes."

"Oh, I'm surprised you're not a detective," the woman said sarcastically.

Again, there was something in this comment that wasn't quite right; I started to feel uneasy. We searched the rest of the vehicle. On the front passenger seat was a brown leather briefcase; inside were over two hundred pre-printed price tags and a small gun-like device with a needle and thin plastic cord wound around a small drum. Throughout the search the woman stood with her arms folded and her nose raised as if to avoid a pungent odour. Her attitude was detached and arrogant and, if she was worried about what we'd found, she never showed the slightest concern.

In a large diary in the case was a comprehensive list of department stores, locations, directions, telephone numbers and sale dates.

Most significantly of all, in the glove compartment, attached to a bull clip, were dozens of receipts which flicking quickly through, I noticed seemed to account for most of the clothing in the vehicle. This proved she'd not stolen the clothes and presumably explained why she wasn't worried by our interest. I was perplexed about what exactly we were dealing with. It didn't seem to make any sense so whilst Dawn continued searching, I questioned the woman to see if I could shed any light on the matter.

"Why have you got all these clothes?"

"Why not? It's not an offence to buy clothes is it, Constable?"

The use of my rank to address me I also found slightly disconcerting.

"Are you in the clothes business?"

"Yes and no."

"What do you mean?"

"I'm agreeing with your question and disagreeing."

"Do all these clothes belong to you?"

"I purchased them. I have the receipts. They are mine."

"What are you going to do with them?"

"Some I will wear, some I will keep, some I may give to friends and relatives, others, if they don't fit or look right, I shall return."

I was getting nowhere. Dawn called me over; in the woman's handbag she'd found an envelope containing hundreds of pounds worth of store vouchers but there was also a pocket-sized Metropolitan Police diary.

"Is this yours, madam?" Dawn asked, holding up the diary.

"Yes," she replied.

"Are you a police officer?"

"No."

"Where did you get it from?"

"That is no concern of yours."

Next, Dawn found the woman's driving licence and read the name aloud.

"Mrs Florence Farrington-Smythe."

Dawn put the driving licence back and stopped her search.

"Mrs Farrington-Smythe?"

"Yes."

"This officer will take your details but other than that, we are finished here. Please do not park on the approach to a zebra crossing again; you will receive a verbal warning for that offence."

I was taken aback; although I couldn't work out what was going on, I knew something wasn't right and was amazed that Dawn had decided to bring our stop and search to a premature end. I took the woman's address and date of birth and recorded the registration mark of her Land Rover and the location and time of the incident.

"We're sorry to have troubled you, Madam," Dawn said, all sweetness and light.

I realised, of course, Dawn's attitude had changed the minute she'd found the woman's driving licence and learnt her name. I waited until she'd driven off before saying anything.

"So, who's Florence Farrington-Smythe then?" I asked.

"It's such an unusual name; I am guessing she's the wife of Denis Farrington-Smythe."

"And who, pray tell, is Denis Farrington-Smythe?"

"He's our D A C."

"DAC?"

"Deputy Assistant Commissioner, or to put it another way, he's your boss's boss's boss's boss's boss's boss's boss; or something like that."

"Oh."

"And as we weren't getting anywhere, I didn't see the point of pushing it. We couldn't nick her 'cos she'd got receipts for everything."

"But she was up to no good, wasn't she?" I asked.

"I don't know. I mean, her old man must be on like, fifty grand a year so she's not going to be doing anything illegal surely?" Dawn said.

"Stinks to me," I said.

"Gotta know when to fold 'em," Dawn said pragmatically, and probably for the first time, I didn't agree with her.

***

We were strolling back to the nick when our next 'customer' appeared. This time Dawn had no doubt in her mind when the young lad dropped onto the pavement and as soon as he saw us ran quickly in the opposite direction. Dawn was after him before I realised what was going on and a minute later had her nose broken in the struggle to arrest him.

An hour later I was sitting in the canteen sipping a cup of tea and staring at a blank arrest notebook. I had no idea what to write and the person whose job it was to help me was in hospital. I'd tried to find Sergeant Bellamy, but he wasn't in his office and when I asked around was told he'd gone to a meeting and wouldn't be back.

I was going to have to write something, and it was really important that I got it right because I'd have to give my evidence from these notes when the case came to court.

The truth was I couldn't definitely say the person we'd seen climb over the fence was the same person I'd arrested, nor could I say he assaulted Dawn as it was more of an accidental coming together than a deliberate head-butt. Should I write in the notes that I punched him? What should I write about the black bin liner containing the stolen property? That a PC had given it to me and told me to say it was on the prisoner when I arrested him? I didn't think so. What about the horrendous injury to the prisoner's eye?

Several times I picked up my pen only to put it down again. I was slowly but surely getting myself into a state when in walked the one person who could save me, PC Andrew Welling.

"Hi, Nostrils, I hear Dawn's been injured, how is she?"

"Oh God, am I pleased to see you? Yeah, she's broken her nose I think, she's down the London. I'll go and see her in a bit but I've got to write up my arrest notes and I'm really struggling. Please, please help me?"

"Of course, Nostrils, no sweat, let me a get a cup of tea and we'll have it done in no time."

I talked Andy through the episode and set out all my quandaries; he listened without saying a word for a good five minutes and when I'd finished, he asked several really detailed questions about the black bin liner and its contents, the prisoner's clothing, his injuries and even his previous convictions.

"Nostrils, it sounds to me like you've definitely got the right man."

"Do you think?"

"One hundred per cent."

"Okay, so where do we go from here?" I asked.

Andy nodded towards my notebook, closed his eyes deep in concentration and although he'd been nowhere near the incident, dictated my notes as if he'd been right there beside me.

On Friday 24th June 1983 at about 1600 hours I was on duty in Wordsworth Road N16 with WPC Dawn Matthews. We were walking south on the east footway. About twenty yards in front of us I saw a man climb over a fence and jump down onto the pavement. He was a black male about 18 years old and he looked straight at us. It was a bright sunny afternoon, and I got a clear and unobstructed view of his face. He had short black hair and was clean shaven; he was wearing blue jeans and a beige T-shirt and white training shoes with blue stripes. As soon as he saw us he ran in the opposite direction. As he'd come from the rear garden of a residential house and because of his actions in running away, I immediately formed the suspicion he'd committed an arrestable offence, probably burglary. I gave chase. The man turned left into Belgrade Road towards the High Road and as he turned the corner, I noticed he was carrying something black in his right hand, it looked like some type of a bag and as he ran, I could hear the contents of the bag jingling. He turned right into the High Road and I temporarily lost sight of him. A few moments later when I came around the corner, I couldn't see him anywhere but ran on down the High Road past a crowded bus stop and on for about fifty yards. He was nowhere to be seen. I stopped and turned round; I saw the crowd at the bus stop near Belgrade Road had formed a circle and were facing inwards, apparently watching something which was happening in the middle. I ran back and as I got near heard a commotion from the crowd. I pushed my way through and saw WPC Matthews and the man I had been chasing were fighting on the floor. I noticed the black bag, it was in fact a bin liner, was next to them. WPC Matthews is only 5'4" and slim and the man was much bigger and stronger than her. She had her arms around the man's chest but he pulled back, turned to face her and brought his forehead forcefully against WPC Matthews' nose. I heard a crack and saw her grimace as if in pain. Blood started to pour from her nose. WPC Matthews, however, refused to let go and then the man again moved his head slowly, deliberately backwards and I feared he was going to head-butt WPC Matthews again, so to prevent this I punched the man as hard as I could with the fist of my right hand, I struck his face, I think I hit him in the jaw. The man fell unconscious on top of WPC Matthews striking his face on her knee as he fell and catching his eye socket which immediately started to swell. He gained consciousness a few moments later and I arrested him on suspicion of burglary and assault on police and seized the black bin liner that was by his side. I cautioned him, he replied 'I want my solicitor, I ain't saying nothing.'

"Thanks, Andy," I replied.

My hand was really aching from writing so quickly and I opened and closed it to ease the cramp.

"You're welcome, Nostrils, now get up the hospital and give Dawn one from me."

Chapter 23 – Apologies

As soon as I could, I made my way to the hospital to find Dawn. I bought a bunch of flowers from a stand in the car park. They looked fine in the fading light of dusk but when I examined then more carefully in the dazzling brightness of the hospital entrance, discovered they belonged in the bin. Then the smell hit me, that distinctive hospital aroma, and I felt nervous; for a few seconds I faltered.

"Are you okay, young man, are you in pain?" a kind voice said, as its owner gently squeezed my arm.

A middle-aged black nurse was looking at me with genuine concern; it was Cynthia Featherstone.

"Oh my God, Mrs Featherstone, how are you?"

Cynthia smiled.

"I came back to work today, Christopher."

I was amazed she'd remembered my name, but I didn't know what to say.

"I … err … I didn't know you were a nurse."

Cynthia smiled again. There was genuine kindness in that smile.

"Come this way, Christopher. Dawn's in here," she said gently. "I've been looking after her for you."

She ushered me along a corridor and into a small side room where Dawn was lying on her back with her eyes closed and a huge ice pack resting on the bridge of her nose and forehead. If she heard me enter, she gave no indication. Her uniform was on a nearby chair, and she wore an undignified light green hospital gown. Her hair was down; I'd never seen it down before.

"Hi Dawn," I said tentatively.

She turned her head towards me.

"Barry?"

"No, it's Chris."

She said nothing.

"I bought you some flowers."

She said nothing.

"I'll put them on the side."

In the process I knocked over a glass of water and the plastic cup bounced on the tiled floor.

"Dawn, how is it?"

"Broken and reset. I have to keep this ice pack on for another hour and I can't open my eyes. After that I can go home."

There was an unpleasant tone in her voice; I knew I'd made a mistake in coming.

"Can I give you a lift home?"

"Don't you think you've done enough? Where the hell were you?

"I ran past. I didn't see him at the bus stop. I came back as soon as I saw what was going on."

"You're bloody useless."

"I'm sorry if I let you down."

"Oh, just fuck off, Chris."

Dawn's words hurt. I stood there for a few long seconds but having realised there was nothing I could say which would recover this situation, I turned and left. As I walked through the hospital reception, Cynthia Featherstone gave me a look which asked why I'd left so soon. I smiled lamely and kept walking; the truth was I didn't want her to see I was crying.

By the time I'd reached my car, I decided my short inglorious career was all but over. I headed for my only friend, the Elephant's Head, and started to understand how my mum had turned to drink after my dad died. Eddie the cheerful barman welcomed me.

I sat quietly at the bar deep in thought. I was in a dilemma; I knew I should resign. If Dawn blamed me for what happened, then everyone else at the nick would too. My life would be unbearable, and I'd have to leave, but where would I go and what would I do? I had no money, in fact I'd less than that: I owed two hundred and seventy pounds to Mr Barclaycard. When mum died I'd inherited nothing except her tab at the local corner shop. The owner, a sweet Asian gentleman called Vee-jay, had been good to mum. He'd refused to sell her alcohol but when she'd spent all her money elsewhere on vodka, Vee-jay would let her buy food and cigarettes on a tab which she rarely repaid. After she died, I'd settled this by getting a Barclaycard and using one of the new cashpoints.

An hour later I was still considering my options when I became vaguely aware that someone had sat on the stool immediately to my left. The way my luck was going, it was bound to be the pub bore with the big red nose, so I turned slightly away to avoid providing any opportunity for him to spark up a conversation.

"I'm really sorry, Chris, please forgive me," Dawn said quietly.

I swung round in total surprise.

Dawn had two black eyes, I'd seen worse, but they weren't pretty.

"Oh God, Dawn, are you okay? I'm so sorry I didn't get there sooner."

She placed her hand on my knee and squeezed. It was the first time we'd ever touched. It was the simplest, kindest gesture I'd ever experienced.

"You did great. Really you did. Forget what I said earlier, I was being a bitch and blaming you because someone else did something, or rather he didn't."

"Can I buy you a drink?" I asked.

"No, you cannot, this one's on me."

She ordered and Eddie served, I would have been grateful if Eddie had not asked Dawn, "Did he do that to you?"

She shook her head politely. I gave Eddie a look which told him to fuck off and leave us alone and he read it well.

"Dawn, how the fuck did you recognise him at the bus stop?"

"I didn't."

"I don't understand?"

"If you walk down a road in uniform, what does everyone do?"

"They stare at you," I replied; it was the first lesson Dawn had taught me.

"Quite right; you ran past that bus stop and everyone at the bus stop, everyone in the street was watching you. A policeman running down the road, loud excited voices on his radio, now you don't see that every day. Everyone was watching you, everyone that is except one person, who was facing the other away. When I saw him, I was suspicious. When I went to speak to him and he was panting heavily, I was certain. I knew I had to get hands on, otherwise he'd bolt again."

"Fucking hell, Dawn, you're brilliant."

"No, I'm not; stick with me and you'll learn."

"Are CID dealing with him?" she enquired.

"Yes. He's got loads of previous, including three for burglary and one for assault on police."

"Well, well done to you. Your second arrest, Chris, and for burglary too."

She raised her glass in a toast.

"You pack quite a punch, young man."

"I broke his jaw. It's the first time I've ever punched anyone, Dawn. I just wanted to help you. But I think I've broken my thumb."

I wiggled the injured digit.

"If you can move it like that, it's not broken," she suggested.

We chatted, we actually chatted for a good ten minutes. Dawn was worried about what her mum would say, before remembering mine had died and apologising for being insensitive. All too quickly though, she had finished her drink and shifted off her stool.

"Oh, have another," I pleaded, so glad of the company.

"No, really, I've got to get home, have a shower and stuff."

"Sure, perhaps ..."

"Perhaps what?" Dawn asked.

"Perhaps we can do this again?"

"Why, are you attracted to women with two black eyes?" she asked jokingly.

"Dawn?"

"Yes?"

"I've never fancied you more."

I'd said it as a joke, reminiscent of when she'd said it to me after I'd fallen in the dog shit that first day when we were doing the bus lane, but the truth was, I'd never fancied anyone more.

Chapter 24 – Alternatively

The following week Dawn was off sick recovering and was temporarily replaced by Dean, a twenty-stone giant of a Mancunian with an overgrown beard who was considerably friendlier than Dawn but much less inclined to work. We spent the first hour having a 'quick frame of snooker' in the basement which Dean won easily and he pocketed the fifty pence bet we'd had, as he put it 'to make the game a bit more interesting'.

When we eventually went out on patrol, the contrast to working with Dawn was immediately apparent. With her there was always a reason to be doing what we were doing or going where we were going; with Dean we were just wandering and chatting. He seemed a nice bloke, and I learnt more about his domestic circumstances in the first five minutes of our conversation than I had about Dawn in a whole month. Dean had been playing his first season of professional rugby league when his career was ended by a serious knee injury. He lived with his very attractive wife, an opinion which was supported by a photograph Dean plucked from the back of his warrant card, and between them they had more debt than a small third world country.

About an hour out from the nick a young black youth on the same side of the road but walking in the opposite direction, approached us. The lad dropped his head down, avoiding eye contact.

"Good afternoon," Dean said politely when the lad was a few steps away.

The youth sucked his teeth.

"Rassclot," he replied, through barely moving lips.

I had no idea what that meant but it seemed only polite to say it back.

"Rassclot," I replied, with a friendly smile.

Dean's reaction was, however, very different; he stepped to his right and into the path of the young man who had no choice but to stop. His cheerful northern accent was replaced by a low, aggressive whisper.

"Listen, cunt. I was polite to you. Now I'm going to try again and if you don't wish me a similarly happy post-meridian, me and my friend here will have to witness you kicking in that front door and arrest you for attempted burglary."

Dean pointed to the yellow door of a nearby terraced house.

"Let's try again, shall we? Good afternoon."

The youth nodded slowly, apparently considering his options.

"Good afternoon," he muttered.

"That's better; wasn't difficult, was it?"

Dean stepped aside allowing the youth to pass.

"Have a nice day, Sir," he called.

"Got to keep them in check," Dean said, out of the corner of his mouth.

"Anyway, mate, you'll have to come to dinner. The missus would love to meet you; just don't let her have too much to drink otherwise she gets extremely flirty."

I thought I wouldn't mind if she did if she was half as good-looking in real life as she was in the photograph.

A call came out about an abandoned lost or stolen car in Lordship Lane.

"Shall I take that as we're in Lordship Lane?" I suggested.

"Are we?" Dean asked.

The question surprised me as Dawn had always taught me to know the name of the street you're in, so that if you have to call for assistance, you can let the Reserve know where you are.

"Yes, we can't be far away."

"Go on then, Nostrils, but you're doing the writing."

"Golf November, four six six will deal."

"Four six six, thank you."

As it transpired, we were literally around the corner from the informant, a middle-aged Asian man. He explained the blue Ford Cortina outside his house had been parked there for days, he'd never seen it before and when he'd looked closer had realised it was unlocked. The nick had already done a PNC on the vehicle, which had showed it had been stolen from King's Cross the previous week.

"We'll deal with this now, Sir, thank you," Dean said, rather rudely I thought.

We started a quick, cursory search. I assumed there would be nothing of value but when we lifted up the back seat there was a five-pound note and a silver-coloured lady's wristwatch. Dean quickly swooped them up, slipped the money in his pocket and examined the watch.

"Fucking hell, it's a Cartier, they're worth a fortune. I wonder how long the owner's been looking for this?"

"Shall I make a list of the property in my pocket book?" I asked, aware this was the correct procedure.

"No, don't worry. I'll stick it straight in the one three two when I get back to the station. There's too much damn paperwork in this job."

Dean slipped the watch into his pocket alongside the five-pound note.

Not ten minutes later the Reserve called me up.

"Four six six, are you still in the vicinity of Lordship Lane?"

"Yes, yes. Go ahead, Golf November."

"I knew we should have kept quiet; they're going to lumber us with a pile of shit now," Dean berated.

The voice on the radio continued.

"Can you deal with an abandoned call for police at seven two, seventy-two Orchid Court?"

"Yes, yes."

Seventy-two Orchid Court was on the top floor of an unattractive twelve-storey council tower block but at least the lift was working. An elderly white man answered the door and Dean asked whether he'd called police.

"Yes, yes, officer. There's been a burglary, come in, come in."

Dean entered first but as he did so he turned to me.

"You're reporting this."

We followed the old man into his lounge. The place was 'old people' dirty.

"How did the burglar get in?" Dean enquired.

"I don't know but it's not the first time."

"What's been stolen?"

"A couple of socks, my egg pan and the top to my Parker pen."

Dean and I exchanged a glance.

"When it happened before, what did he take?" Dean asked.

"A letter from the Gas Board."

"Well, we'll report it at the police station, we'll tell our colleagues to keep a careful eye on your flat and we'll put an all stations out to see if we can recover the stolen property."

I was pleased Dean was being patient with the old man, who was clearly going senile.

"We'll have a quick look round. See if there are any clues."

"Oh, thank you, thank you so much."

Of course, the old man hadn't been burgled but I had a funny feeling he was about to be.

Chapter 25 – Day two with Dean

As I drove into work the following afternoon, I turned the previous day's events over in my mind. Could I be certain Dean had stolen the watch and the five-pound note? Or for that matter that he had appropriated any other articles from the old man's house? I hadn't actually witnessed him doing so. I decided to check the station records to see if Dean had handed in the cash and the watch, as the property should be recorded somewhere in the Station Office. Dean had said he was going to enter details of the property in the one three two; I knew this was a binder where details of recovered stolen vehicles were recorded, so it was here that I checked first.

It was not a great surprise when I could find no trace of either the money or the Cartier on any documentation. I considered speaking to Dean about it at some stage during the day but picking the right moment would be difficult and I wasn't at all sure how Dean would respond. As I turned things over, I realised I had another very obvious problem. If Dean admitted taking them, what would I do then? I couldn't arrest him, and I knew reporting him to the sergeant would end my own career as certainly as handing in my resignation, because no one would ever trust me again. Perhaps I'd have been happier if I'd not known? Actually, the more I thought about it, the more annoyed I was with myself for checking. After all, legally, ignorance was bliss, or more precisely, an acquittal.

I met Dean in the canteen and although our tour of duty officially started at two, we didn't finish our second game of snooker until gone three. Once again, I lost and this time I handed over a pound to my erstwhile tutor. If my policing skills weren't going to improve this week, at least my snooker ability would.

Just about the time the schools were turning out, we commenced our patrol.

"So, Dawn Matthews is your Street Duties instructor, Nostrils?"

"Yes, she's very good," I replied loyally.

"Really? I've always found her a miserable cow. For years we all thought she was a dyke and then it transpires she'd been shagging a DS on the Flying Squad, a geezer called Barry who I've known since Training School. He played the happily married man and she was very discreet. Anyway, apparently in the last couple of weeks, after like five years, she's dumped him 'cos it's actually dawned on her that he ain't going to leave his wife and kids. She thought it would force the issue and that he'd turn up at her place with his tail between his legs and a suitcase in his hand, but he hasn't and she's like devastated."

"Oh," was all I could say.

"Nostrils, when she puts on the old slap and lets her hair down, WPC Dawn Matthews is quite a stunner."

I nodded; I really didn't want to say anything in case my comments somehow found their way back to Dawn.

"She's certainly had it rough. Nearly died a few years ago, you know. She had cancer and the doctors only gave her like a one in ten chance of surviving. Can't say getting through the ordeal made her very happy though. And since this Barry thing, seems to me, she's been like a bear with a sore head, which is ironic really, 'cos one month out and about with you and that's exactly what she got, a very sore head."

Dean chuckled.

"I did my best to help her, I really did."

"I know, Nostrils," Dean interrupted. "I'm only kidding you; you did well, everyone says."

I felt immensely relieved and very grateful to Dean for letting me know.

"And well, after our day out yesterday, well I can vouch for you too. You're alright, Nostrils."

Dean slapped me firmly across the back. Suddenly I felt uncomfortable; did 'being alright' mean what I thought it did? Was I 'alright' because I'd acquiesced to theft from motor vehicle and burglary?

Dean continued, "But seriously, Nostrils, would you consider giving old misery guts something to cheer her up?" He winked, ridiculously.

"I don't know, I haven't really thought about Dawn like that."

"Fucking hell, mate, you ain't queer, are you? We don't really like queers in the police you know, can't trust 'em. Just when you need your colleague to be helping you out in a pub fight, the last thing you need to discover is he's a fucking poofter."

"Why? Can't they fight?"

"Oh, for fuck's sake, Nostrils, you're starting to worry me. Listen, we're on aid on Friday, ten to six, so come round for dinner in the evening and meet the missus. If you don't fancy her, you *must* be fucking queer."

"Thanks, I'd like that," I said, grateful of any opportunity to enhance my dull, monotonous private life.

"I'd say bring your partner, but you'd probably turn up with another bloke."

He laughed again.

"I am normal, Dean, don't worry about that. Listen, I could see if Dawn wants to come. She'll probably say no."

"Don't bother, mate, I'm not a big fan of hers, Nostrils; besides, my missus ain't particularly fond of plonks."

"Okay, it was just a thought."

"Is there anything you don't eat?

"Cheese, I can't eat cheese."

"I'll tell Jess. She's a fantastic cook and great fun. I promise you we'll have a good evening. You can stay over if you like; we've got a spare room."

"Thanks."

"Oh, hang on."

Dean looked at a group of black youths that were exiting the Arndale shopping centre.

"What's the matter?"

"Nothing's the matter but you see that kid there, in the blue top, smoking."

"Yeah."

"That's David Hector."

"Who's he?"

"He stabbed a PC last year. Got off with the assault saying it was self-defence and only went down for off wep. He got fuck all and became a bit of a local hero. So, we decided to deal with him, let's say, in a different way."

Dean called out in a friendly, cheerful, carefree voice. "Hi, Dave, how are you doing?"

I was confused; why was Dean being so friendly?

David Hector was clearly annoyed by Dean's salutation. The young man made every gesture he could to distance himself from Dean's dialogue.

"Every time a PC sees David, he says 'hi' and acts like he's his best friend. One, it drives him mad; two, it undermines his status as the best thing since sliced bread; and three, with any luck they'll think he's a grass and impose the sentence the court had failed to."

Dean's explanation was interesting, but I couldn't imagine Dawn doing it.

"What we doing today, Dean?"

"We're keeping Stokey safe, Nostrils. Anyone fucks with us, they're ..." Dean fought for the right word.

"What?" I asked.

"History," Dean replied, apparently content from the satisfied expression on his face, that he'd found the right one.

Chapter 26 – Shoplifting and extortion

Working with Dean was something of a paradox. The company was great, the man chatted incessantly, and I learnt about everyone else at the nick, who was doing what to who and why; but the work itself was boring: we just strolled, we didn't patrol. Dean seemed to put more effort into avoiding work than it would have taken just to do it. On one occasion, we'd witnessed quite a serious RTA about a hundred yards in front of us involving a lorry and a small three-wheeled disabled car. What did Dean do? He took the first left and headed off as quickly as possible, muttering that RTAs were for Traffic. As it transpired, the driver of the car was trapped and had to be cut out by the fire brigade, but by the time that happened Dean and I were back in the canteen having refs. If a shout came up and we were nearby, it was almost impossible to persuade Dean to let me take it, so I was particularly surprised when he put up to take a bomb threat at the Arndale shopping centre.

"Why are we taking that?" I asked.

"Because there's no writing, we just help evacuate the shops a,nd you know what empty shops mean?"

"No?" I replied.

"Rich pickings," Dean laughed.

Evacuating a shopping centre wasn't as easy as it sounded. Many shopkeepers didn't want to close and technically you couldn't force them. Threats were becoming increasingly common as the IRA brought their reign of terror across the Irish Sea to mainland Britain.

I kept a careful eye on my partner as I didn't trust him at all; I had a feeling he'd seize any opportunity to steal. This time, if he had taken anything, I didn't witness it. We'd just completed getting everyone out of the main department store when we received the 'all clear' and even though it was still quite early in the shift, Dean insisted we return to the nick for a quick cup of tea. As we walked into the back yard and I turned left into the canteen, Dean made an excuse to go to the locker room.

"I'll catch up with you in a minute; don't forget, no sugar and leave the tea bag in," he called, as he descended the stairs to the basement.

I was suspicious: why did Dean have to go to the locker room? I decided to follow him but at a discreet distance. Using the reflection in a conveniently positioned glass door, I saw Dean open his locker and remove his helmet. Sitting on top of his head was a boxed bottle of Chanel perfume. I slipped quietly back up the stairs. I was impressed with my ability to spot a thief but depressed that my ability was wasted, and my efforts wouldn't be reflected in my record of work.

***

Later that day things went from bad to worse when we were returning for refs and Dean asked me, "What you doing for grub?"

"I'll get something in the canteen," I replied, not really having given the subject any thought.

"Do you fancy a kebab and a coke?"

"Sure."

"We'll go to the kebab place just up the road from the nick. It only opened last week and it's about time the Metropolitan Police gave them some business."

As we walked in, I went to the end of a queue of half a dozen customers, but Dean completely ignored them and placed his order as if the shop had been empty.

"Two large doners and two cokes please."

"Yes officer," the owner replied.

I felt really uncomfortable, I'd have much rather queued, so I busied myself working out how much the order would cost and getting the exact money ready; I hoped this would allow us to leave quickly without impacting too much on other customers. Dean saw me looking through my change.

"What are you doing?"

"Getting the money ready, I'll get yours."

"You fucking won't, mate, we ain't paying."

I said nothing but kept the money in a clenched hand just in case.

Having ascertained our requirements regarding sauce, the owner wrapped each kebab in paper and dropped them into a small plastic bag, placing two cans from the fridge on top.

"Two pound forty please, officer," the owner asked politely.

"I beg your pardon?" replied Dean in a voice which suggested he had been mortally offended.

"Two pound forty, I've not charged you for the cokes," the owner replied rather sheepishly.

Slowly, deliberately, Dean withdrew his truncheon and admired it. Panic started to rise inside me; surely, he wasn't going to threaten the owner over two pound forty's worth of kebabs? Dean walked over to the large plate glass shop window.

"I see you still haven't got a shutter blind, Sir."

"They're very expensive, officer."

"But worth it; after all, how much would one of these windows cost to replace if it got, let's say ..."

He tapped the window suggestively with his truncheon.

"... smashed by vandals during the night?"

It was a question which required no answer.

"Please, officers, have the kebabs on me."

"I'll tell you what," Dean replied, now all smiles, as he reached across the counter to collect his free supper. "In recognition of your generosity, we'll do our best to regularly patrol this stretch of the High Street and make sure nothing happens to that window."

Now I had only studied the basic sections of the Theft Act 1968 but was fairly certain what I'd witnessed would amount to blackmail.

Chapter 27 – Unnecessary obstruction

My last day with Dean was gloriously sunny and for the first time it was short sleeve order. This created a problem which required careful planning to overcome. My police jacket had six pockets, and each contained an important piece of kit: I had a general notebook, several arrest books and two accident report books, three process books, a producer pad, a Road Fund Licence pad, handcuffs and whistle, a warrant card, pens and a ruler, a small torch. In short sleeve order, I had to relocate this equipment to my belt and two trouser pockets which already contained personal effects. Fortunately, from the shop at Training School I'd purchased an assortment of belt attachments designed for just this purpose: I had a pen pouch, a handcuff pouch, a torch clip and even a bespoke holder for my various notebooks. As I left the portacabin, the enormous Sergeant Bellamy was entering, his huge belly hanging over and obscuring his own belt.

"Nostrils, how do you manage to carry all that stuff on your belt? It can't do your back any good, you know."

I just smiled, resisting the temptation to point out the obvious irony.

"Oh yes, while I remember, Dawn's back on Monday; try and take better care of her this time, Nostrils, she's really quite popular you know, and you'll be most unpopular if anything like that happens again."

Sergeant Bellamy disappeared inside. No pressure then, I thought.

"Don't look so serious, Nostrils, he's only kidding," Dean said, as he waited outside the portacabin.

We set off on patrol.

"I've told Jess you're coming for dinner tomorrow; she's looking forward to meeting you," Dean said enthusiastically.

“Gosh, tell her not to be too excited, it’s only me,” I replied modestly.

In all my concerns over Dean’s honesty, I’d forgotten I’d agreed to go round, but as I was about as lonely as anyone could be, a night out in company was not to be sniffed at, even if it was with dodgy Dean.

“Dean, you know you said we were aid tomorrow?”

“Yes.”

“What is aids?”

“Not aids, that’s a queer’s disease, you wanker; aid is where we’re sent off the division somewhere to police a specific event, like a football match or a demonstration.”

“That sounds exciting?”

“Trust me, it’s not. It’s very, very boring. Most of the time you sit around all day in a carrier, which is why policeman are good card players.”

“What?”

“There’s always a game of cards going on and often it’s for quite serious money. Do you play?”

“Yes, but not for money.”

“Fuck me, Nostrils, you are so ...”

He didn’t finish the sentence, but I could guess what he wanted to say.

“We’re up at the Polish Embassy, there’s some demonstration or something.”

As we turned the next corner, we came across an unexpected queue of traffic.

“What the fuck’s going on here?” Dean asked rhetorically.

A quick assessment identified the problem. A removal lorry was parked immediately opposite a bus stop and so, every time a bus came along, all movement along the road in both directions came to a halt for however long it took the passengers to alight and then board. If the van moved perhaps twenty yards along the road, the matter would be resolved. We split up to locate the driver. The first door I called upon was answered by a short white man in his mid-forties wearing stained denim jeans, a white T-shirt and black steel-capped boots.

"Is this your van, Sir?" I enquired politely.

The man looked past me.

"What that one there?"

"Yes, is it yours?"

"It's on a single yellow and it's obviously loading, so what's the problem?" he replied.

"I know it's a single yellow but as you're parked opposite a bus stop the traffic is getting blocked every time a bus stops."

The man took several steps out onto the pavement and examined the situation. Then he looked me up and down.

"Ain't my problem, mate, tell the buses not to stop there; the van's parked legally and I certainly ain't moving it."

"Can't you just move it twenty-five yards down the road, please? I'd really appreciate it."

I was trying to be charming.

"No can do," the man replied.

I was completely taken aback; I hadn't been rude to the driver and my request to relocate the vehicle had been eminently reasonable. After all, it wasn't as if I was sticking him on. I turned the problem quickly over in my mind. Was the man, in fact, right? No, he wasn't; there was an offence of unnecessary obstruction which had nothing to do with yellow lines and was committed if you blocked the road. I would rather have had Dean by my side, but I was fairly confident I knew what I was doing.

"Sir, I must insist you move your vehicle, it is causing an unnecessary obstruction. I'm only asking you to move a few yards so it's not opposite the bus stop. I'm not being unreasonable. Really, just a short distance will do."

"My vehicle is certainly not causing an obstruction and you are one twenty-four-carat arsehole. I'll tell you what, do yourself a big favour, fuck off and leave me alone. I ain't moving it."

And with that, he turned around and headed back to the house. I was gobsmacked; they never taught you at Training School how to deal with such irrational behaviour. I had to act, and act now, because within seconds this man would be back in the house behind a closed door. I took several quick strides, overtaking him in the process, and blocked the route to his front door.

"What are you going to do, you little runt? Get out of my way or I'll send you home to mummy with a few less teeth."

I took a deep breath, braced myself for the fight I knew was about to come and, very formally announced, "I am arresting you for unnecessary obstruction ..."

Before I got another word out, from nowhere, Dean appeared behind the man and over-spoke me.

"We won't be arresting this gentleman today, PC Pritchard, now stand aside and let him enter."

I was confused and angry but did as I was told. The door slammed.

"What the fuck, Dean?"

Dean said nothing but looked back towards the road. I followed his gaze; the removal van was signalling and pulling slowly away and into the traffic. The man hadn't been anything to do with it. What an idiot I was. When I recounted the conversation in my head, he'd never said it was his lorry. If I'd nicked him, that would have been my second unlawful arrest. For the first time that week, I was really glad to be working with Dean. Dawn would have made such a fuss; in contrast, I knew Dean really didn't give a damn.

Chapter 28 – An evening in with the Campbells

Dean was right, aid was very boring. Sitting for nearly eight hours in the back of a police carrier van with twelve others on a scorching hot day was nobody's idea of fun. Dean had introduced me as Nostrils to the others when we'd paraded, and they'd exchanged a few words about the shotgun incident, but thereafter, no one took any notice of me. I sat at the back, carefully watching how the others interacted, how they spoke to one another, who was the most influential and who the least. The group took the piss out of each other constantly; mostly it was very funny but some of their humour went above my head as the references were apparently to matters or events of which I'd no knowledge.

Three activities dominated the day: cards, always for money; leering at passing women – some of the comments were truly graphic and completely inappropriate; and farting. Several of the officers managed to partake in all three activities simultaneously. In the social pecking order, Dean was somewhere in the middle. He was loud and brash and acted the hard man, but I noticed he was careful about whom he made the butt of his jokes. I didn't attempt to join in; even if I'd wanted to, I wouldn't have known where to start.

Apparently, four of the officers were ex-military: two had been in Northern Ireland together, one had been a Military Police dog handler, and the fourth on an aircraft carrier. What struck me more than anything that long day, was the fact that every part of the United Kingdom seemed to be represented. There was a Scot, perhaps two Irish guys, several northerners, two Welshmen, a Geordie and a fella from the Black Country. The only area completely unrepresented was London. From his accent, even the sergeant was from a long way west, perhaps Cornwall. Was this representative of the Met? Where on earth were the Londoners?

At the end of the day, when we were in the locker room getting changed, Brian, the chap who'd been driving the carrier and whose locker was only three away from mine, unexpectedly started up a conversation.

"I hear you're having dinner at Dean's tonight?"

"Yes, he says his wife's a great cook."

"She certainly has quite a reputation," he replied.

"Great," I said, "I haven't eaten all day. I'm starving."

***

The drive to Dean's, who lived in police married quarters in Wanstead, took me a little over half an hour. En route I stopped to buy a bottle of wine and a box of chocolates. I knew nothing about either, so I chose by price, which meant I spent as much as I could afford. Dean answered the door with a warm smile and a welcome which suggested we'd known one another for years rather than days.

"Come in, come in. Darling, Nostrils is here."

"Christopher, please," I replied, handing over the wine and chocolates.

"Get him a drink, I'll be through in a mo, just a few more things to do," a delightful female voice called from the kitchen.

The flat felt like a home and the contrast to my own domestic circumstances was striking. I took Dean's offer to make myself comfortable and kicked off my shoes, curled my legs under me and sank into the most comfortable sofa I'd ever sat in. From the kitchen the sounds and smells of cooking wafted in equal measure into the lounge. Music was playing at just the right volume so as to be present without interrupting and at the far end of the room, a dining table was set for three. Dean disappeared into, and then emerged from the kitchen through two saloon doors which were straight out of a cowboy film. He was carrying two glasses of wine; handed one to me and raised a toast.

"To a pleasant evening."

"I'll drink to that," I replied.

Dean had just sat in a chair to the right of the sofa, when the kitchen doors swung open and in blew Mrs Campbell; my bottom jaw nearly hit the floor.

"Oh, hello, darling, I'm delighted you were able to join us."

Recovering my composure, I jumped to my feet and took the outstretched hand which was offered.

"Oh, thank you for having me, Mrs Campbell."

"Don't you dare call me that; you make me sound so old. I'm Jessica, Jessie or Jess, whichever you prefer."

Jessie was in her thirties, noticeably older than Dean, and absolutely drop dead gorgeous. Tall, with long curly brown hair, a stunning face, large voluptuous breasts and a tiny waist; at the instant I saw her, I fell completely in lust. She was wearing a tight white T-shirt, a dark navy blue pencil skirt with a slit in one side, and high heeled cocktail shoes. When she sat, the skirt rose. She crossed her legs at which point, and with a gargantuan effort, I forced myself to look away and towards Dean, who seemed to be watching me carefully whilst wearing a confident smile.

"I told you she was lovely, didn't I?"

I felt awkward; I wasn't sure what an appropriate reply would be.

"Don't embarrass the young man," Jessie said.

"Now tell me, Chris, where is your girlfriend tonight, or will she be joining us later?"

"I'm afraid it's just me, Jessie," I replied, grateful the conversation had moved on.

"Just you? Tonight? Or in life generally?"

"Both, I'm afraid. I don't have a girlfriend. I've only been at Stoke Newington a month and live alone in a flat in Hackney."

I knew 'flat' was a small lie but it made me feel slightly less embarrassed about my miserable existence.

"Are you working tomorrow? Dean's off."

"No, I've got the weekend off; I don't start proper shifts until I join my relief in about two months."

"Then you must stay the night. It'll mean you can have a decent drink and get up in the morning and go in your own time. I've made up the bed in the spare room."

"Okay, that'll be good, thank you."

I welcomed the opportunity to be away from my 'flat'.

During dinner, and when I was certain both of my hosts weren't looking, I stole glances at Jessie's wonderful breasts, perfectly round and firm in the tightest top I'd ever seen. At one stage I even deliberately dropped my fork so I could admire those shapely legs beneath the dining room table.

Jessie was a complete and utter bundle of bouncing fun throughout the evening and several times I found myself feeling more than a little jealous of Dean. The wine kept flowing and by one o'clock, the evening, a very pleasant one at that, was drawing to a natural close.

"Oh, Christopher, let me show you to your room and I need your advice on something before you turn in."

Jessie took hold of my right hand and pulled me up off of the sofa; I was, in fact, grateful for the assistance otherwise I might have just stayed there all night. She led me into the hall and pushed open a door to a small unlit room, but she made no attempt to enter.

"The bathroom's there and," she pointed to a second door, "that's your bedroom and you're right next door to us so no snoring, otherwise I'll be in to sort you out."

If only, I thought. Jessica opened the third door and led me into the master bedroom still holding my hand.

"Sit on the end of the bed and give me your honest opinion, Chris."

This was clearly their bedroom and I felt uneasy being in there. Jessie turned and opened the doors to a large pine wardrobe and appeared to be searching through hanging clothes. I seized the opportunity to study her shapely calves, but she turned around and I was caught bang to rights. Jess smiled broadly and I shrugged my shoulders, admitting the capture.

"Sorry," I said apologetically.

Jessie gently stroked the side of my cheek with the red painted nail of her right forefinger, her gesture suggesting she was not the least offended. Then she selected and held up two outfits, in her left hand was a maid's uniform and in her right, a black basque.

"Which one do you think I should wear for Dean? I'm always so horny when I've had red wine."

An older, more experienced me would have insisted on seeing them on before offering an opinion but the nineteen-year-old virgin sitting nervously on the edge of the bed didn't know what to say.

"I, er, I er, um, well ..."

"So, either then," she smiled.

"Now off to bed, you; I've got to get changed."

I went to the bathroom and had a quick shower before wrapping a towel about myself, carrying my clothes under one arm and going back to my room. The flat was now in darkness and through the wall I could hear Dean and Jessie talking, although couldn't quite make out what they were saying.

I dried, folded the towel over a radiator, turned off the light and climbed into a single bed. I was tired, had drunk a little too much and knew I would soon be asleep. Just as I was drifting off, the unmistakable sound of Dean and Jessie having sex began. I was soon fully awake and very, very horny. I'd never had sex but I'd fooled around with a girlfriend in the Upper Sixth before losing her to a bloke with a job and a car. I'd also read and re-read my impressive collection of pornographic magazines that lived under my bed, so I knew enough to be able to imagine exactly what was going on only a few feet away through the wall. Neither of them was making any attempt to conceal what they were doing, knowing as they did that I was right next door. Jessie was doing most of the talking and as she grew louder, I started to make out some of what she was saying.

"I'm going to fuck his brains out."

"I'm going to go in there and ride his cock and then I'm going to let him cum in my mouth."

"You're not going to stop me."

"You brought him here for me and now I'm going to have him."

"I bet he's got a bigger, harder cock than you."

"He's nineteen, he's gonna be able to fuck me all night."

I had started to masturbate but when I heard what she was saying I stopped and lay very still, listening intently for any hint that they had uncoupled, and she was now on her way to my room. God, I hoped so. I knew it was all weird, but I really didn't care, my cock was burning with desire.

From the elongated grunt a few minutes later, I figured Dean had finished. The room next door fell suddenly quiet. I waited hopefully, and then I waited some more and then I fell asleep.

It was the smell that woke me up, and I'd never before been woken up by a smell, a delicate sweet aroma. I opened my eyes, the curtains had been pulled and moonlight illuminated the room. In the half-light I saw Jessica, in black basque, black stockings and stilettos standing by the bed.

"Move over," she said.

"God, you're lovely, everything about you, you even smell fantastic."

"You're so sweet," she said, pulling back the covers and exposing my immediately erect cock.

"It's Chanel, you know, very expensive, Dean bought it for me the other day."

Jessica sat on the edge of the bed, took my cock in her hand and started to play with me slowly.

"Who's a big boy then?"

I was so aroused I could barely speak.

"You know that's going into my mouth, don't you?" Jessica said.

I was panting heavily; my cock was rock hard. I put my hands under my buttocks. I wanted to see this moment, to witness this stunningly attractive woman sucking my cock. I looked down, something glistened in the moonlight and caught my eye, I looked closer. On Jessie's left wrist was the Cartier watch from under the back seat of the lost or stolen.

Chapter 29 – The ice melts

I was greatly relieved when Dawn came back to work the following week. Although I would have been somewhat at a loss as to how to interact with Dean after the events of Friday night, the main reason was that working with PC Dean Campbell seemed a sure way of ending up in prison. I hadn't seen or spoken to Dawn since our brief drink on the night she'd been assaulted and when we met again I was pleased to see only the slightest hint of two black eyes remained.

I sat opposite her in the canteen at just after six o'clock; Dawn was sipping from a mug of tea. She smiled, she actually smiled at me; my heart melted.

"Hello, Chris."

"Good to have you back, Dawn."

"Who did you have last week?"

"Dean, Dean Campbell. I think he's on A relief when he's not on Street Duties."

"I know Dean. How did you get on, he's a bit of a handful?"

"Well, I am anticipating being arrested for four indictable offences any second now."

I looked into Dawn's eyes to read her reaction.

"Only four?" she asked; clearly, she knew Dean well.

"As long as he didn't take you home to his wife, then consider you've had a lucky escape."

I shifted uneasily in my chair.

"Can I get you another tea?"

"Oh, Chris, you didn't?"

"Oh, Dawn, I did."

She shook her head from side to side.

"You men, you're a nightmare. Your brain is in your bloody pants."

"So, I'm not the first then?"

Dawn nearly choked on the remainder of her drink.

"No, Chris, you are not ...' she paused, "... the first."

"I'm not the second either, am I?"

"No, but let's stop this conversation now or we'll never get out the canteen. Instead, you can tell me what Dean told you about me."

The sudden change of topic and the nature of the question caught me somewhat off guard.

"Nothing really," I replied sheepishly.

"Chris, I've just started to warm to you. Don't spoil it."

"Sorry, fair enough. He told me you were having an affair with a married man. Really that's about it."

"I was but it's over. Barry was a DS here but he went to Training School with Dean. I guessed he'd tell you. My fella, my ex-fella, is on the Flying Squad now."

"Look, I'm sure there's no earthly reason why you'd want to but if you ever want to talk about it to a nineteen-year-old kid with absolutely no life experience and who's never been in a serious relationship except with his right hand, you know I'm always here."

"Thanks, I'll take a rain check but I appreciate the sentiment."

As we left the nick, we walked through the front office. At Dawn's prompting, I asked the Reserve if there were any outstanding calls we could take; there weren't. It was great to be working with Dawn again; it was a complete contrast to Dean. Where Dean and I had ambled and chatted, Dawn and I patrolled and watched. When she walked down a street, her eyes were everywhere. She rarely made idle chitchat because she was working. At one point, she stopped an old Vauxhall Chevette for no reason I could see, but after a few words with the driver she waved the car on.

"What was that about?" I asked curiously.

"There's a disqual driver in The Grove who drives a brown Chevette, but that was not the one."

"I'd have given the driver a producer, if you'd wanted," I replied, mindful of previous advice she'd given me that 'when you stop a car, always give the driver a producer'.

"No need, Chris, sometimes you just know they're fine."

We walked on and as we rounded the next bend, heard a man shouting, screaming almost. No one was in sight, so it seemed likely the disturbance was taking place inside a house. Instinctively our pace quickened until we were outside number fourteen, a very ordinary terraced house. The noise was coming from an open upstairs bedroom window, and the voice belonged to a man with a very heavy Nigerian accent.

"What's he saying?"

Dawn shook her head.

"Knock at the door but check through the letterbox first. If he does come to the door retreat back, give yourself space."

I could see an uncarpeted hall and stairs, up which appeared to be a trail of blood; not too much, as if someone had cut themselves on a kitchen knife. I knocked and rang the electric doorbell; a few moments later a face appeared at the upstairs window.

"What?" a small black African man in his mid-twenties said.

He was very dark skinned, had tribal scars on his cheeks and was not wearing a top.

"Is everything okay, Sir? We heard shouting."

"What?" the man said again.

"Can you come down and open the door?" Dawn asked, but her tone of voice suggested it was a demand more than a request.

"What?"

"I think there's blood on the stairs inside, have a look," I said.

Dawn looked through the letterbox.

"Yes, I think you're right."

The man had disappeared and the shouting recommenced.

"Let's speak to the neighbours," Dawn suggested.

We didn't gather much but what we did learn was important. The man lived there alone, which probably meant we didn't have to worry there might be someone else in the flat who was either injured or in danger. He didn't appear again for several minutes, until a suitcase came tumbling out of the window, then some clothes rained down and finally a wooden bedside table came crashing onto the pavement. Dawn and I relocated to a safe distance and Dawn called for some assistance.

"Golf November, one eight two receiving?"

"Go ahead, Dawn.

"Can you ask the Section Sergeant to come to Wattling Avenue? We have a male inside number fourteen who seems mentally ill and has decided to empty the contents of his house onto the street through an upstairs window."

"One eight two, eighty-two, I'm on my way," a male voice said.

"Thanks, Sarge. There's no immediate hurry, the situation is quite contained."

More furniture was being thrown: a mattress, a bin and then several pairs of shoes were hurled nearly to the other side of the street. Neighbours had come out to watch the unfolding drama and several moved their cars as a precaution. An old lady who lived several doors up offered to make us some tea, which we gratefully accepted. At about the same time the tea arrived, the Section Sergeant pulled up in his panda car. I didn't recognise him, but he obviously knew Dawn.

"Hi, darling, how you doing?"

"Good thanks, Sarge, how are you?"

"Fine, sorry to hear about you and Barry, I'd have put money on you two ending up together."

"Me too," Dawn replied, with a sad smile.

"So, what's going on here?"

"The occupant is an African male who lives alone. We heard him shouting, we knocked at the door, but he refuses to open it. As you can see, he keeps throwing stuff out of the window and there's some blood on the stairs inside but not too much."

A toilet seat came crashing down right on cue. A considerable pile had started to grow beneath the window.

"Golf November receiving, eighty-two over?"

"Go ahead, Skip."

"Can you contact three-one? We need the DSU down here. Get me a running time please?"

"Stand by, I'll go on the main channel."

The old lady returned with a cup of tea for the sergeant.

"Thank you, my love," he said, with a broad smile.

"That's quite all right, officer. If I can help at all, just ask."

"Well," he said, hesitating.

"Go on, Sergeant, do you want a biscuit?" the old lady asked.

"No thank you, but I was going to ask if we come through your house, can we get into the back gardens and across to the rear of his premises?"

"Yes, but you'll have to climb over two high fences," she replied.

"I won't but he will," the sergeant replied, pointing at me.

"Off you go, lad; see what you can see from the back."

The old lady took me through her house, and I climbed over one six-foot wooden fence, and a slightly shorter brick wall, and dropped with the agility of youth into an overgrown back garden, littered with rubbish and discarded household furniture. The back door was slightly open. I could see no movement inside. In fact, the house had been quiet for some minutes now.

"Eighty-two and one eight two, I'm in the back garden. The back door is open but there's no sign of the occupant."

"Received; it's gone very quiet in there."

"Eighty-two, Golf November?"

"Go ahead."

"Three-one running time two zero, twenty minutes over."

"Received."

"Four six six, eighty-two?"

"Go ahead, Sergeant," I answered.

"Stay at the rear, when three-one gets here we'll come in through the front door, over."

"Yes, yes, received."

I stood, waited and got a little bored. I smoked a cigarette and as I was flicking the filter end across several back gardens, heard the carrier's siren coming from a good mile away. When it arrived, I imagined the boys kitting up in riot gear. There was still no sight or sound from within the house.

"Four six six, eighty-two, they're about to go in, stand by."

"Received, Sarge."

I calculated my quickest escape route should the man come out the rear door armed with a knife or some other weapon. As I was doing so, I heard banging, and assumed they were forcing the front door. I wondered briefly why they didn't just come round the back like I had but then realised they'd probably struggle to climb over the walls wearing riot gear. A minute later I heard dozens of footsteps charging about the house and then it went quiet. I opened the back door and went into the dirtiest kitchen I'd ever seen and met two officers in full riot gear; they were panting heavily and the inside of the clear plastic visors of their helmets had steamed up.

"Where is he?" the first shouted.

"Upstairs, I think," I replied.

"Four six six, has he come out the rear?"

"No, Sergeant."

"He's not in the house, he's not anywhere."

The two officers in the kitchen took their helmets off and they and several others congregated with me in the back garden; most lit cigarettes and their sergeant questioned me about the missing man.

"When did you last see him?"

"Which room was he in?"

"What was he shouting?"

"Could he have escaped through the back garden before you got here?"

We all agreed that was the only plausible explanation when a falling roof tile missed the sergeant's head by no more than four inches and smashed into pieces on the patio. Before we had time to look up, there was an almighty cry and we all instinctively moved away from the house.

The Nigerian man was hanging over the side of the roof from a creaking horizontal drainpipe; his feet were a good twelve feet above the hard patio floor. He hung by both arms and made no attempt to climb back up. As I walked down the garden and further away from the house, I could see a gaping hole in the tiled roof through which the man had climbed.

We stared at each other hesitantly; personally, my prevarication wasn't because I didn't want to help the man, but I was acutely aware that if I got under him, and he fell on me, I'd suffer a significant injury. I guessed we were all thinking the same. The man was wearing only a pair of white and blue striped pyjama bottoms and these were slowly and irretrievably slipping down until after only a few moments they fell off and catching his feet, hung down towards the ground as if leading the way for the inevitable fall.

"Call on all the neighbours, get a ladder now," the sergeant barked and his crew starburst leaving only us there.

I knew we didn't have enough time to find, erect and climb a ladder and was about to suggest getting a blanket to catch him in, when there was a crack from the drainpipe as it broke away; the right-hand side gave way first and the break moved across the flashing slowly as each screw untwisted in turn and so the man fell to the ground in a series of jerks and landed with no more force than he would have experienced jumping from a few feet.

The man immediately pulled his trousers up and secured them with the cord. He was sweating profusely and the look on his face was a curious mixture of fear, presumably of the sergeant and me, and relief at having survived what should have been a back-breaking fall. He looked shy, almost childlike.

"You okay, son?" the sergeant asked, in a not unfriendly way and without making any movement towards him.

He nodded.

"Shall we get you a doctor?"

The sergeant's voice was kind, gentle and reassuring.

He nodded again.

The sergeant smiled; the man smiled back.

"You had a mighty lucky escape there, son."

"Will you do me a favour?"

The man frowned but nodded; he hadn't said a word, but the sergeant's quiet calmness seemed to have won him over. I assumed the sergeant was going to ask him to get in the police carrier so he could be taken to hospital, so I could have fallen over when the sergeant asked, "Will you get on my shoulders?"

A look of confusion flashed across the man's face.

"I want to play a little trick on my colleagues. I promise, I won't hurt you."

The man nodded slowly.

The man was small and light which made the task quite easy and following the sergeant's clear and concise instructions, having stood momentarily on a low-lying brick wall, he was up and onto the sergeant's shoulders like a child on his father's back in a swimming pool. The man started to laugh, and we did too.

I had an idea what was going to happen, but I kept quiet and waited to see the deception unfold. Within perhaps half a minute, three of the carrier's PCs came back through the kitchen with the news that a ladder was being brought from a neighbour's house, but the sight of the man sitting on the sergeant's shoulders stopped them in their tracks.

"Bloody hell, Sarge; what's happened?"

"He couldn't hold on any longer so I stood directly under him so that he could drop on to my shoulders. He dropped and I caught him, but I think I've injured my back; can you help him down?"

I had guessed Sarge was going to make a joke by pretending to have caught the man, but the others were taking him seriously. They helped him down and called an ambulance both for the man and Sarge, who was feigning a back injury. They were soon joined by the rest of the crew who were congratulating the sergeant for his bravery. The longer this farce lasted, the more uncomfortable I felt. I wondered how long Sarge was going to let this run but when the ambulance arrived and took only the sergeant away, I had my answer.

Chapter 30 – Aiding and abetting

Throughout the incident, Dawn and I had been on opposite sides of the house and so the first time we were together was on the walk back to the nick.

"So, what exactly happened?" she asked.

"Well, the bloke climbed onto the roof from his loft by removing some tiles but having got out he must have slipped or tripped or something because he came sliding down the roof and nearly landed on top of us. He was hanging from the gutter."

"You mean the guttering?"

"Yes, the guttering."

"So what's this about the sergeant catching him when he fell? I don't get it."

"Neither do I," I replied.

"What was he standing on? I thought they were trying to find a ladder."

I didn't reply immediately. I was in something of a dilemma. Should I stick to the sergeant's incredible account, which was that he'd literally caught the man on his shoulders as he fell, or should I tell her the truth? Dawn's earlier advice about 'once you lie, you lie forever' kept running through my mind.

"I don't really know what to say, Dawn," I said, quite honestly.

Dawn's frown suggested she hadn't entirely fallen for the account she'd heard.

"Can I tell you exactly what happened? And before you say yes, I warn you that you might wish I hadn't told you."

"I appreciate the warning, I really do, but just tell me the truth."

I noticed a definite change in Dawn's attitude towards me today; I hoped it was permanent.

I then spent several minutes relaying to Dawn exactly what had happened and how I was certain it was intended to be a big joke but when no one laughed, the sergeant seized the opportunity to play the injured hero.

"Maybe he's looking for the old ninety days?"

"What do you mean?"

"If the sergeant's got twenty-six and a half years in and gets an injury on duty, he can get retired on a full pension which is immediately index linked. With inflation at eight per cent that could be worth a fortune. Perhaps that's it."

"Should I say anything to anyone?"

"No, just keep your mouth shut and keep out of it. After all, the man's not been arrested or anything so you won't be required to give evidence. When you make your notes about the whole thing just be vague about how he got down. I'll dictate if you want."

Dawn didn't seem too concerned and of course she was right, I wouldn't be going to court or anything like that, so no one was really going to be affected. It wasn't until several months later I realised the true extent of the sergeant's dishonesty. Not only did he receive an award from the Royal Humane Society for saving the man's life. He also got a Commissioner's Commendation for bravery and most prized of all, an index-linked ill health pension.

***

As we were booking off later that day, Sergeant Bellamy emerged from his small office.

"PC Pritchard?"

"Yes, Sergeant."

"Report to the nick at 3.30 tomorrow morning for a briefing in the canteen."

"Me too, Sarge?"

"No, Dawn, we're going to let Nostrils out on his own. Well, not quite on his own, he'll be with eighteen heavily armed Flying Squad officers, so even he should be safe."

He laughed but all Dawn could manage was a weak smile. I speculated that her Barry would be amongst them and this was why Sarge had excused her.

"The Flying Squad are gonna nick a blagger and do a ticket on his drum. I thought you were an ideal choice to assist them, what with your expertise in the area of armed robbery."

"Drum, Sergeant?"

"His house."

"Ticket, Sergeant?"

"A search warrant, lad," Sergeant Bellamy replied, shaking his head.

I couldn't resist, although I actually knew this one.

"Blagger, Sergeant?"

"An armed robber. Christ, what do they teach you at Training School these days? Don't be late, breakfast rules apply."

That got me back. I had no idea what 'breakfast rules' meant but didn't have the courage to ask again; Dawn must have read my thoughts.

"I'll tell you later," she said.

***

I had an early night but didn't sleep a wink. I'd set two alarms but required neither. At three o'clock on a dark, damp summer morning, I drove my brown Ford Fiesta through deserted streets. I turned left onto the one-way system and lit a cigarette, inhaled deeply and unwound the window several inches to allow the smoke to escape. I'd already learnt to treat red lights as give-way signs, safe in the knowledge that if I was stopped by police, I was wearing half blues, that is to say, wearing my uniform but with a civilian jacket on over it, so I wouldn't even have to pull out my warrant card.

I arrived early and parked the car in the back streets behind the police station. After a quick visit to my basement locker to collect my uniform jacket and helmet, I made my way to the canteen. I'd noticed police canteens were the strangest of places. Whatever the time of day, whatever the day of the week, whether the canteen staff are in or had gone home, these rooms were the hub, the heart and the soul of the nick. All the lights and every radiator were always on and every ashtray full. By three in the morning most tables were covered in discarded paperwork and used crockery. I was first to arrive, took a chair by the back wall and picked up yesterday's Sun newspaper, whose headlines heralded the arrival of Prince William. If I read the newspaper, I hoped to feel less awkward, less out of place, when the others started to arrive, and over the next twenty minutes, the Flying Squad arrived in some style. They drove their cars straight into the back yard – a Ford Granada, several Rovers and finally an impressive BMW – and swaggered into the canteen with plenty of attitude and a smell of stale alcohol; each carried a holstered handgun. They were all male, white and in their forties and they were all, to a lesser or greater extent, overweight. I reflected that only a year ago I'd been at school; in contrast, this early morning I was a real man doing a real job amongst real men, hardened armed Flying Squad officers.

Two dog handlers joined us, their dog leads fastened and worn diagonally across their bodies almost ceremonially. I interpreted it as a signal to others they were no ordinary uniform officers; they were a specialist, elite breed. Their charges remained in their vans barking at anyone who dared pass by. We were finally joined by two uniformed officers who I vaguely recognised. I assumed they must have been from night duty relief. One introduced himself to the guy apparently in charge of the Flying Squad as the van driver.

The Flying Squad Detective Inspector briefed us.

"We go in at four thirty. The house is a middle terrace in Amhurst Lane, number one one two. We can get access to the rear garden, so we'll go through the front and back door simultaneously on my call. Harry and Geoff, you got the keys?"

Two men nodded.

Keys, I wondered how they'd got the keys?

"I won't give the go until I've heard from the uniform chaps that the street is secured. You?"

He pointed at me:

"Yes, Sir."

"When I transmit five, you secure the junction with the High Street. Don't let anything, pedestrian, cyclist, car, turn into Amhurst Lane until you get the 'all clear'. Understand?"

"Yes, Sir."

"When you get the 'all clear' you can clear off. Van?"

The van driver nodded.

"You take the other end of the street and secure it on my order but when you get the 'all clear', come to the address because we'll need you to transport the prisoner."

Seems easy enough I thought, trying hard not to be too disappointed. Okay, it wasn't the most glamorous of roles, I wouldn't be kicking the door in, or charging upstairs, or fighting the prisoner to the ground, I'd be stopping traffic. Oh well, we all have to start somewhere.

The briefing continued.

"We can't put the dogs in first because we think there are children in the house. It's a three-bedroom terraced, and our source tells us Charlie sleeps in the rear bedroom on the first floor. Once we've secured him, he'll be nicked for the robbery on the Securicor Van in Peckham Rye last month and we'll execute the ticket. His wife's meant to be a handful, over twenty stone as well, so be warned. If anyone finds the shotgun, make sure it's loaded."

I must have misheard; surely the DI meant 'unloaded'?

The address was only a short distance from the nick so as no one offered me a lift, I walked along the deserted High Road to take up position at the junction with Amhurst Lane. From the numbering of the houses, I calculated the house the Flying Squad was going to enter was about two hundred yards away from my position. I stood in the shadows and awaited the 'Five' transmission which would be my signal to move to the centre of the road and stop any traffic which might seek to enter. I glanced at my watch, ten minutes to go. As I stood there the sweetest aroma of freshly baking bread drifted my way from a baker's, situated about five shop premises along the High Road from the junction. Oh, how good it smelt. I decided when I got the 'all clear', I'd pay a friendly visit and see if I could mump anything for breakfast.

I lit a cigarette; technically of course, I shouldn't have, not when in uniform in a public place but no one would see me at this time of the morning.

Five minutes to go. I wandered about ten yards into Amhurst Lane and noticed a small, unmade access road running behind the shops to either side. I saw, perhaps twenty yards along and behind the baker's, a white van facing towards Amhurst Lane. The engine was running, and a man was loading boxes of bread and other freshly baked produce into the rear. The van was a potential problem. If I stood at the road junction as instructed, the van would emerge behind me and could then turn right away from the High Street and towards the house. I decided to speak to the driver.

I walked quickly, hoping my watch wasn't slow.

"Listen, mate," I called, as I approached.

"Yes, mate," The short stocky white man replied.

"Are you the driver?"

"Yes, mate?"

"How long you gonna be?"

"If you give me a hand, two minutes."

I walked to the rear of the baker's van and helped load half a dozen brown cardboard boxes whilst I explained to the driver that, when he got to the end of the road, he had to turn left and onto the High Street.

"I was going to anyway, mate. My first delivery's in Islington," the driver replied helpfully.

As I walked back to Amhurst Lane, the van followed behind me at walking pace. I walked into the road and waved the vehicle out and away from the target house. The problem had been resolved.

My radio, which had been silent since I'd left the nick, crackled to life.

"All units. Three hundred and forty-two, three four two, Stoke Newington High Road, Stoke Newington, premises of Newington Electricals, suspect on premises now. Units to deal please?"

That call was nearby. Could I leave my position to go to the burglary? I really needed to know just how close I was and walked quickly into the High Road to see exactly where three hundred and forty-two would be in relation to my current location.

The shop on the corner of the junction was a newsagent, where was the bloody number? My eyes flicked quickly about searching up and down. There it was: three, three, two. I was practically on top of the crime, and it was happening now. My adrenalin started to pump. Surely, I could go to investigate? I reached for my radio and waited for a gap in the radio traffic to transmit and tell the Flying Squad DI what I was about to do. Several units had taken the call, but none had declared they were especially close. A second prisoner for burglary so soon in my career would be outstanding. This had the potential to secure my reputation for years. My fingers twitched over the transmit button.

"All units stand by. We have further information. The informant is in the bakery next door. The suspect, a white male, is loading stolen goods into a white van parked at the rear."

I froze. White male, white van, the rear? That was the bloke I'd helped!

I should, of course, transmit what I knew, which way the driver had driven off, how long ago, his detailed description; but I had helped him load the van, my fingerprints were literally all over the stolen goods. Oh my God, I would never live this down. I had unwittingly committed burglary, handled stolen goods, assisted an offender and aided and abetted a crime. My hand slowly dropped away from my radio. I stepped quietly back into the shadows where I'd decided to hide for about the next ten years.

Chapter 31 – Waiting for the call

After the Flying Squad DI had given the 'all clear', I found I'd gone off the idea of going to mump breakfast at the baker's. Instead, I accepted a series of routine calls to postpone my return to the station and the inevitable storm which awaited me. Every time my personal radio crackled, the precursor to any transmission, I feared it would be an order to report at once to the Station Sergeant or perhaps even the Duty Officer. I was glad Dawn wasn't about to witness the end of my remarkably short inglorious police career. And just when we'd started to get along too.

Eventually, when I could put it off no more, I slunk back to the station, ordered a light breakfast although I really wasn't hungry, and took the same seat in the corner at the back which I'd vacated only a few hours before when I had a career.

I picked at my food but left most of it. After I'd finished, I saw Dawn walk through the back yard towards the portacabin; she would have usually popped in to get a takeaway tea but this morning she kept walking and I guessed she was avoiding the canteen in case Barry was still at the nick. There were a few of the Flying Squad still about but as I didn't know what Barry looked like, I couldn't tell whether he was there or not. Now I came to think about it though, I couldn't imagine she'd have been going out with any of the blokes I'd seen earlier that morning, they were all fat and middle-aged.

I glanced at my watch; it was just before nine. Time was ticking by and still no one had spoken to me; was it possible that no one knew about my catastrophic fuck up? I decided to tempt fate and go outside and have a smoke. I played a little game with myself; I told myself that if no one had mentioned my mistake by the time I'd finished my cigarette, then I'd got away with it.

With a cigarette in my mouth, my hands unsuccessfully searched the numerous pockets of my tunic and trousers to locate matches. An outstretched arm holding an expensive gold lighter came to my rescue; its owner I immediately recognised as the Flying Squad Detective Inspector.

"Thank you, Sir," I replied, with suitable deference.

"That's alright, son," the DI said, as he lit my cigarette and then his own.

We both breathed in deeply and exhaled almost in unison. I really didn't know what to say to this man, anything I said would be either stupid or mundane, so I decided to say nothing. A full minute passed, both of us seemed content with the silence, and just when I was about to drop and stamp, the DI commented, almost as an aside, "You did well today, lad, very well indeed."

Did well? Was he taking the micky? All I'd done was block the road off. I frowned, unsure how to respond and keen not to offend.

"Sir, I ..."

"You kept your mouth shut, lad. You fucked up but you're young, you'll learn. I saw you reach for your transmit button, but you made the right decision and said nothing. And don't worry; I'll keep schtum too."

The DI held out his hand.

***

"Hi, Chris, were you on time?" Dawn asked, as I entered the portacabin.

"Yes."

"Good job; would have cost you a fortune if you'd been late."

"Why?"

"I heard Sarge tell you breakfast rules apply."

"I did," confirmed an unseen Sergeant Bellamy, from his small office.

"What does that mean?" I asked.

"It means, if anyone is late, even by one second, they have to buy breakfast for everyone else at the briefing. How many people were there at the briefing this morning?" she asked.

"Twelve Flying Squad blokes, a couple of dog handlers, some guys off night duty and an ambulance crew."

Sergeant Bellamy emerged from his office.

"Well at a pound a go, maybe one fifty, that would have cost you twenty quid if you were lucky and thirty if they all went to town and ordered everything," he said.

I wasn't convinced the debt could be legally enforced but I phrased my next question cautiously.

"It doesn't seem very fair, Sarge."

"Listen, Nostrils, was anyone late this morning?"

"No."

"That's why it's done; it guarantees everyone gets in on time even if it is three thirty in the morning."

Dawn was nodding, she obviously agreed.

"Did it go all right?" she asked.

"Yeah, they nicked the bloke; all I had to do was block one end of Amhurst Lane."

"I'm sure even you couldn't mess that up, Nostrils," Sergeant Bellamy said, who then spoke to Dawn, changing the subject.

They clearly hadn't heard anything about the bloke in the white van.

"Dawn, I'm leaving early today."

"Going to one of your meetings, Sarge?" she asked, with a smile.

"I am, as a matter of fact. Of course, Barry was on the square, wasn't he?"

Dawn grimaced. In my opinion, my partner would have been happier if people didn't keep mentioning her former boyfriend.

"Yes, but he only joined so he had an excuse to see me. I think he can't have gone more than three times but if you were to ask his wife, she'd tell you he went at least once a week for nearly five years. In fact, he was so devoted to the lodge his duties would take him away several weekends a year and for a whole week every May to Florida."

Dawn and Sergeant Bellamy laughed but something in their conversation was nagging at me. I felt like I was experiencing déjà vu; on the square, the lodge, what did it all mean? I decided to wait until Sergeant Bellamy had gone into his little office before asking Dawn.

"What did Sergeant Bellamy mean? When he said Barry was on the square?"

"Both Barry and Sarge and half the Met's male police officers are on the square, Chris."

"What does on the square mean?" I asked.

"On the square means they are freemasons."

"Freemasons?"

"It a secret society thing, all very mysterious. But apparently they do a lot of work for charity so that makes it okay."

"Don't you agree with it then?" I asked, detecting derision in Dawn's voice.

"I don't really care, Chris. If grown men want to get dressed up in an apron and white gloves once a month and undertake quasi-religious ceremonies, then more fool them."

"Is that what they do? That sounds ridiculous?"

"Don't mock it, Chris, it is your destiny." She said the last four words in a deep voice mocking Darth Vader from Star Wars.

"Never," I said resolutely, and then I remembered.

"Dawn, you know I was at Mrs Wilson's funeral the other week?"

"Yes."

"Well, I got asked by some of the old guys, well two retired police officers, whether I was on the square. I thought they were asking me whether I could be trusted, you know, whether I was decent and upstanding."

"So, you said yes?" Dawn replied, almost laughing.

"I did."

"Oh, you idiot. They were asking you whether you're a freemason."

"These old men at the funeral asked me to take them to the lodge."

Dawn was laughing out loud now.

"And how are you going to do that?"

"I was going to take them to Queen Elizabeth's Hunting Lodge; you know, the one in Chingford?"

Dawn didn't say anything; she couldn't stop laughing long enough to speak. She had caught a serious case of the giggles.

Chapter 32 – A gratuity and a rape declined

The following week saw Dawn's approval rating of me increase slightly, when we took a call to a burglary at a clothing factory warehouse right on the edge of the ground. We were met by the victim, Toby Saunders, a white man in his mid-fifties and from his sycophantic manner, a particularly unpleasant character whose business was the manufacture of gentlemen's fashions.

He took us around to the rear, where the fire exit doors had been apparently forced with a jimmy, and then showed us rows of empty rails from which he claimed a large quantity of suits had been stolen. I started to take details for the crime report but could tell from Dawn's line of questioning she was sceptical. She asked him for invoices, queried why he'd not set the alarm, told him he'd have to provide elimination prints, even asked him directly whether we were investigating a burglary or an insurance fraud but Mr Saunders couldn't be shaken from his account and Dawn eventually admitted defeat. Throughout his interrogation, Mr Saunders remained calm, unruffled and excruciatingly polite; the crocodile smile never wavered from his face.

When Dawn's questions dried up and Mr Saunders wandered out of our earshot, I quietly asked Dawn what was blindingly obvious to the three of us.

"Don't you believe our Mr Saunders, then?"

She shrugged her shoulders and pulled a face to suggest she wasn't sure.

When Mr Saunders reappeared, he was carrying a dark grey two-piece suit over his right arm.

"There you go, officer," he said.

"You're a size thirty-two waist? That'll fit perfectly. Don't worry, I'll just show it as stolen with all the others and claim it on the insurance."

Upon hearing the offer, Dawn turned her back on us and walked off towards the fire exit, I knew she was disassociating herself from the conversation.

"No. No thank you," I said, firmly and loudly enough for Dawn to hear.

"Don't be silly, officer. No harm to anyone. Perhaps you'd like to come back and collect it on your way home?"

"We cannot accept gratuities, Mr Saunders. Thank you but no thanks. Dawn, have we finished here?"

We left the ever-happy Mr Saunders, who waved us farewell as if we were leaving his dinner party, and continued on our patrol.

"Golf November, one eight two?"

"Go ahead, Dawn."

"Riverside Way will be a crime sheet; we'll give you the number later."

"All received."

"And PC four six six?" Dawn said, as if she was still speaking into her radio.

"Go ahead," I replied, copying her theme.

"Well done," she said.

She didn't have to say what I'd done right, I knew.

***

The following day, and the day after that, Dawn and I were directed to cover Assistant Station Officer for the last two hours of our shift. As Dawn explained, the job of the ASO was to deal with callers at the front counter of the police station, and she said there were a thousand reasons why people came to the police station: to report a crime; to report an accident; because they'd lost a dog or found one; to comply with the conditions of their bail; to seek directions; to complain about a noisy neighbour; to leave a birthday/valentine/anniversary card for an officer; to request validation of a passport photograph; to produce their driving documents; to declare themselves homeless; and so on and so forth.

Dawn took me through the different procedures with each new caller. After about an hour or so a rough-looking white woman in her early thirties asked to speak to us in private and I ushered her into a small interview room adjacent to the front office.

Dawn nodded towards me to indicate she expected me to take the lead.

"How can we help you, madam?"

"I'd like to report a crime."

"Tell us what has happened."

"I've been raped."

The statement came as something of a shock, not least because she simply didn't look to me like she'd been raped. I looked across at my mentor but got no help.

"Do you require any urgent medical assistance?"

Apparently, I'd selected the appropriate question because out of the corner of my right eye I could see Dawn nodding very slightly.

"No, no, no."

"Do you know who did this to you?"

"Yes of course, my boyfriend Del, Del Wright."

"And where is he now?"

"Probably with his whore."

"And when did this happen?"

"Last Wednesday, or was it Thursday? No, no, definitely Wednesday because Coronation Street was on."

"And where did the offence take place?"

"In bed of course."

"At home? At your home address?"

"Yes, yes. 127 Bellingham House, Rochester Road."

"Do you and your boyfriend Del Wright live together?"

"Yes, but I haven't seen him for a couple of days."

I scribbled three letters on a blank statement form which was already on the desk and turned it so Dawn could read them 'C I D'. She shook her head with the tiniest of movements. Apparently, calling in the cavalry wasn't an option. I realised Dawn was testing me to see how much I'd learnt in my first few months. I recalled what I'd been taught at Hendon, the five key investigative questions; of these I'd asked where and when, leaving what, why and how to come.

"Mrs?"

"Samantha Davies, with an E."

"Are you happy if I call you Samantha?"

"Of course, young man."

The woman was, contrary to her appearance, very well spoken.

"Samantha, what exactly has occurred?"

"Last Wednesday Del came home about eleven. Of course, now I know he'd been with my best friend but I didn't know then. I was asleep, I mean really fast asleep. Anyway, he wanted sex, he always wants sex but I was annoyed. I'd not heard from him all day and when he started mucking around I told him no, several times. He ignored me, pulled down my pants and had his way. But no is no, isn't that right, officer?"

"Yes," I said, with the only reply which can be given to that question under those circumstances.

For the first time Dawn spoke.

"Did he wear a Durex?"

"No, no need, I'm on the pill."

"Did he ejaculate inside you?"

I was surprised by Dawn's bluntness; I would never have thought to ask such direct and personal questions.

"Did he have an orgasm? Yes of course, so did I but just the once, that's how annoyed I was with him."

Dawn once again nodded towards me, effectively handing control of the interview back. The next key question was why but that seemed stupid as the reason was obvious; then I realised that was the wrong 'why' question.

"Why are you reporting this now, I mean it happened five days ago?"

"Because, officer, I've just discovered the dirty rat is sleeping with my best friend."

"Do you want him arrested; will you make a statement and press charges?"

Again, out of the corner of my eye I could just make out Dawn indicating I was on the right track.

"Yes, definitely."

"We'll need to come to your house."

"Good Lord, why?"

"We'll need to seize your bedding and clothes for forensic evidence."

"What will that prove?"

"That he had sex with you; your statement will say you didn't consent."

"Yes, but that was Wednesday night?"

"Yes."

"We had consenting sex twice on Friday, at least three times on Saturday and, of course, Sunday morning."

Dawn coughed; I moved my chair a few inches back and she took over.

"We'll need you to sign a statement, I'll refer it to CID, you'll probably hear in a few days," she said in a matter-of-fact kind of way.

"Very well, officers."

Dawn selected the blank front page of a statement from amongst an untidy pile of paperwork lying on the desk. She clicked open a black biro and wrote:

'On Monday 13th June 1983 I attended Stoke Newington police station and made an allegation of rape against Mr Del Wright who resides with me at the address overleaf.'

"Please read and if you agree, sign and date this statement, there and there." Dawn pointed at two of the three appropriate places and I noticed that she hadn't asked the woman to sign immediately after the last written word, which was the usual practice.

"We'll be in touch, Samantha."

As the woman left, she thanked us.

Dawn wrote immediately after the word 'overleaf':

'I wish to withdraw this allegation and do not want police to take any further action.'

Of course, I realised Dawn's carefully inserted addition meant that no one would be investigating anything.

"The Metropolitan Police has got better things to do than deal with this shit. Now witness her signature withdrawing the allegation by signing here and here," Dawn instructed firmly.

I did as I was told.

***

When we emerged from the interview room, there were several people waiting to be served. I spent the next hour at the front counter recording a complicated fail to stop traffic accident reported by a Yugoslavian lorry driver whose negligible command of the English language meant the interview was conducted largely in mime, much to the amusement of Dawn and the member of the public she was serving. When at last I got rid of the Eastern European, a white woman in her late thirties, wearing far too much make-up and perfume, strode up to the counter with purpose and in what appeared to be a most unnatural act, banged a clenched fist on the counter. The gesture almost made me laugh out loud, but I swallowed hard and with some effort held my guffaw in.

"Can I help you, madam?" I asked.

"I want to see WPC Dawn Matthews immediately."

It would have been the most natural of things to have turned to my left and introduce my partner but somewhere at the back of my mind, an alarm bell sounded.

"Can I enquire what this is about madam?" I asked politely and without any indication that WPC Dawn Matthews was standing immediately next to me.

"Yes, that slut is having an affair with my husband."

Chapter 33 – Clear directions

I sat whom I assumed to be Barry's wife in the small interview room which Samantha Davies 'with an e' had earlier vacated. She was visibly shaking, and the occasional tear ran down her cheek creating dark tracks of her mascara.

"Can you bear with me for two minutes, madam, so I can see what WPC Matthews is working today?"

The woman nodded.

As soon as I stepped outside the room, I heard a desperate tapping on the glass which partitioned the waiting area from the front counter: it was Mr Toby Saunders. I waved him through assuming he had urgent and vital information about his burglary, but from the looks on the faces of the other people who were waiting patiently, they thought he had jumped the queue.

"Officer, officer, I'm so glad it's you."

He seemed really agitated. I wondered if he'd come to admit the whole thing had been a scam.

"Calm down, Mr Saunders, and tell me what's happened."

Very conscious that I had Barry's wife in the interview room, I wanted to rattle quickly through what Mr Saunders had to say.

"I've got this."

He pulled a small piece of paper from his pocket and then several documents from another, all of which he handed to me. I was looking at a producer, issued several hours ago by a constable on an adjoining division.

"So, this isn't about the burglary?"

"No, not at all. I just got a producer and wanted my friend, PC ..." He looked at my shoulder, "four six six to deal with it."

"I'll get the book."

I retrieved the HORT/2 pad from the shelf behind me and started to examine Mr Saunders's documents. The driving licence was in order, his MOT was fine, but his insurance was fifteen days out of date. I started filling in the paperwork.

"Have you brought the wrong insurance certificate, Mr Saunders? This one's out of date."

"I know, I know. I just forgot, you know how it is, officer. I'm a busy man. I'm sure you can do me a favour in return for the one I did for you?"

I stopped writing and looked up. Mr Saunders was all smiles.

"Sorry, what favour did you do for me?"

"The suit, the suit, the one, or perhaps two, you're picking up later."

"Mr Saunders, I made it very clear we can't take gratuities."

"Well, how about we call it something else?"

"What?"

"A present, call it a thank you present for being so efficient yesterday. If you don't want a suit, perhaps you would prefer the money?"

Mr Saunders reached into his trouser pocket and pulled out a large wad of banknotes from which he unrolled several twenty-pound notes and placed them with deliberate fussiness on the counter between us. I shook my head.

"You don't understand, Mr Saunders ..."

"If it's not enough I'll double it, there."

He pulled more and laid them down.

"Two hundred pounds officer, don't be stupid, do yourself a favour."

It didn't cross my mind, not even for the briefest moment, to take the money; in fact, Mr Saunders was starting to aggravate me.

"No Mr Saunders, no. If you do not have insurance, I will report you for that offence. You do not have to say anything but anything you do say may be given in evidence."

"Now officer, if you're not careful I could say you were asking me for a bribe."

In an instant and for the first time, Mr Saunders' smile had disappeared; his voice was suddenly full of threat and menace.

"I know several very senior officers very well. We meet quite regularly if you get my drift. I am a very credible man. Now what do you think, officer? Do we have a deal?"

I'd kept my head down and continued to complete the paperwork. I hadn't got time for this, I had to sort out Dawn's problem and what was more, Mr Saunders was insulting me, threatening me and irritating me all at the same time. When I'd finished my report, I pushed his driving documents back across the desk and looked up.

"Mr Saunders?"

"Yes?" he replied hopefully.

"Go fuck yourself."

***

I left Mr Saunders at the front counter; the look of shock on his face was a picture. I walked back into the interview room. In the five minutes I'd been gone, Barry's wife had composed herself, stopped crying, wiped the mascara from her face, reapplied her make-up and completely unnecessarily put on more perfume, which caught in my throat and made me cough as soon as I'd sat down.

"I'm so sorry to keep you waiting. I had an urgent matter at the front counter. I've checked with Duties, WPC Matthews is annual leave this week."

She'd obviously planned for the news that WPC Matthews was unavailable because her next statement was delivered calmly and firmly.

"I thought she might be."

She smiled sarcastically but I didn't react.

"In that case PC four six six, I'd like to see the Chief Superintendent."

"Yes of course, can I take your name?"

"Mrs, Mrs Emma Jones. My husband is Barry Jones, he used to work here," she replied.

I excused myself again.

Dawn was nowhere to be seen. I looked round the Station Office but everyone was going about their usual business, so I assumed no one else was aware of what was going on. I waited for about a minute, a vague plan was forming at the back of his mind, and then I re-entered the interview room.

"I'm afraid all the senior officers are at a conference today but his secretary has asked me to take your telephone number so she can contact you and make an appointment for later this week."

She looked me straight in the eye and I guessed she was trying to gauge my honesty.

"Very well, but I'm telling you now, PC four six six, that if I don't hear from the Chief Superintendent's secretary by the end of tomorrow with a date and time for my appointment, I'll be back and asking for you."

"You will hear, I assure you."

"And the appointment must be during the day, I pick the kids up at three."

Barry's wife started searching earnestly through her enormous handbag; her perfume still dominated the tiny room and I coughed again to clear my throat. Eventually, she found what she was looking for and laid on the desk facing me a photograph of three young children on an indeterminate beach.

"What lovely kids," I said.

"That bitch, Dawn Matthews, is trying to ruin their lives by taking their father away and I'm not going to sit back and let that happen."

"Can I ask, Mrs Jones; are you certain your husband's been seeing someone else?"

"Absolutely."

Her reply was so definitive it slammed shut that avenue of our conversation.

"Can I get you a tea?" I asked, simply because I could think of nothing else to say and Mrs Jones was making no attempt to leave.

"Yes please. I need to gather myself before I leave."

I thought she'd already managed to do that but was grateful for any excuse to escape the stifling perfume-stuffed atmosphere in that small room. I used the kettle by the telex machine; it had just boiled, and I returned with two polystyrene cups of piping hot tea and some sugar in a third. Dawn was still nowhere to be seen.

"So do you know this slut?"she asked, before I'd even sat down.

"Mrs Jones, I've only just started working here a few weeks ago, I hardly know anyone."

She sipped her tea and flinched.

"I'm sorry, I should have warned you, it's really hot."

"Why can't she find an unmarried man? Why has she got to want somebody else's?"

I hoped the question was rhetorical, it wasn't.

"Well?"

"I don't know what to say, sorry."

We both took simultaneous sips. God, it was hot. Seconds ticked slowly by.

"Is it your husband's first affair?" I asked, desperate to fill the uncomfortable silence.

Mrs Jones pushed her chair back, stood up, leaning forward and tipped her cup of tea slowly over my head. It burnt for a few seconds but most of it went on my shirt. I blinked.

"You bastard," she said, as she slammed the door behind her.

What had I said?

***

Instead of going home at the end of our early turn, Dawn and I sat in the Street Duties portacabin discussing how we were going to deal with Barry's wife.

"Stop; whatever you're going to suggest, don't. Don't get involved, Chris. This isn't your problem, it's mine," Dawn said, as she stared into the bottom of her cup of coffee.

"Tell me what will happen if she speaks to the Chief Superintendent?"

"I'll get transferred, very quickly, and probably to the other side of London."

"Okay. Just hear me out for a moment. She didn't recognise you, so she certainly won't recognise the Chief Super."

"So?"

"Well, we could arrange for her to meet someone she thinks is the Chief Super but isn't."

"Go on."

"Well, that's it really. The pretend Chief Super will say all the right things, tell her you're going to be transferred to, let's say, Heathrow. She'll be happy. You can stay at Stokey, so you'll be happy; everybody's happy."

Dawn said nothing so I went on.

"Unfortunately, she wants the appointment during school time."

"Well forget it then, maybe of an evening but ..."

"Hang on; I may have only been here a few weeks but even I know the Chief Super's in the pub at lunchtime from twelve to two every day. I presume his secretary takes a lunch break too. If we can get Barry's wife here about twelve, we can get her into that office when it's clear. All we need now is to find someone to play the part of the boss; any ideas?"

Dawn thought.

"Yes. There's a guy on my old relief who's spent the last three years trying to get in my knickers. He's a nice fella, and he owes me one 'cos I witnessed one of his dodgy arrests some time ago. The prisoner alleged he'd been fitted up; I backed this guy up in the box, got him out of a hole."

"Isn't that what you're meant to do? That's what you keep telling me."

"Not really, not when you're off duty and thirty miles away at the time of the arrest."

"Oh."

"He'll help. I know he will. We'll need to get a couple of crowns and stars so he can replace his shoulder numbers and be temporarily promoted."

"It'll be a piece of cake," I said, thinking exactly the opposite.

"What could possibly go wrong?" Dawn asked.

Chapter 34 – The best laid plans

The person who owed Dawn a favour was William Rees, the PC with the locker next to mine who I'd met on my first day. We three conspirators met the following day in the canteen and planned the deception with military precision. It seemed luck was smiling on us as enquiries had already established the Chief Superintendent was off on Thursday playing golf. Dawn, pretending to be the Chief Superintendent's secretary, put in the call to Emma Jones and made an appointment for that day at noon. William said he'd replace the shoulder numbers on one of his tunics with the requisite insignia and temporarily promote himself by five ranks.

When Thursday came, things got even better when Dawn said she'd been upstairs with some vague idea of chatting to the Chief Superintendent's secretary who she knew quite well and perhaps arranging to go out to lunch with her, only to discover the secretary was also off.

Well before noon I loitered about the front office and when Mrs Jones arrived, I ushered her quickly into the interview room. I noticed she looked much better today, less flustered and quite attractive for a woman who was considerably older than me.

"I haven't got long, young man. I hope the Chief Superintendent will not keep me waiting."

"I'll make a quick call to his secretary, I'm sure he'll see you shortly, ma'am," I replied.

"Do that and please don't come back with any excuses," she said.

I called the Chief Superintendent's office, Dawn answered.

"She's here, shall I bring her up?" I asked.

"Yes, William is in the office, I'll tell him. I'll make myself scarce; I don't want her to see me again."

I stuck my head around the interview room door.

"Please follow me, Mrs Jones."

I led her slowly up the two flights of stairs, giving Dawn time to disappear, into what was known colloquially as the attic where William, or rather Chief Superintendent Rees, met us on the landing.

"Mrs Jones, good afternoon. I am very pleased to meet you."

William took her hand, shook it and buried his eyes into hers with a promise that whatever she wanted, she could have. When I'd first met William, I'd been impressed with his quiet charm; now he was really turning it on.

"Please come this way."

William walked into the secretary's small outer office and then through a second door into what I assumed was the Chief Superintendent's office. I waited a few moments and then turned to walk back down the stairs.

"Constable, please get us some drinks," William called, as I turned back.

"Tea, Mrs Jones?"

"Please."

"Two teas please, Constable."

I hoped Mrs Jones was going to drink this one.

When I got to the first floor, Dawn was waiting for me.

"How's it going?" she asked nervously.

"So far so good but William's only bloody ordered two teas, cheeky sod."

"Yeah, but that's what would happen, isn't it?"

"I suppose."

"Shall I get them from the front office?"

"No, we're not working there today; you'll have to use the canteen."

I looked at my watch, ten past twelve.

"The canteen will be packed."

I was right, the queue was ridiculously long. It was a good ten minutes before I carried the drinks back up the two flights of stairs so I hoped Mrs Jones would be long gone. Standing in the secretary's office, I listened for a few moments at the Chief Superintendent's door but couldn't hear any conversation or other sound within. Thank goodness I thought; we've only bloody pulled this off. I put the teas down on the secretary's desk and went towards the office intending to make sure the room was neat and tidy so the real Chief Superintendent wouldn't know anyone else had been using it. I moved quickly as I'd no right to be there.

I opened the door and strode several paces inside. To my surprise the room wasn't empty at all. Emma Jones and William Rees were very much there. She was bending forward over a big oak desk, her skirt up around her waist, her white knickers down and around her ankles, and William was shagging her from behind. I stopped dead in my tracks; Emma had her back to me and was unaware I had entered, but William looked to his left, gave me a thumbs up sign and a cheeky grin, and continued as if I wasn't there.

***

I only got the full story later that day. Apparently, William had said all the right things to Emma Jones, how sorry he was, how immoral Dawn's actions were, how she would be transferred to West London by the end of the week as a punishment, and then he said *the* line.

"I can't understand why your husband would even consider sleeping with another woman when he's got such an attractive wife at home."

"That's a very nice thing to say, Chief Superintendent, but you don't really mean it."

"I most certainly do, Mrs Jones. If you were unattached, I'd ask you out here and now."

"Well, if I was unattached, I'd be happy to say yes."

William smiled; their eyes met for just a second too long. When William stood up and stepped around the desk, he intended leading Mrs Jones out of the office but Mrs Jones had other ideas. She moved close to him, breaking into his personal space, and dropped to her knees.

Chapter 35 – One six three, where are you?

The following day, the last of my eighth week at Stokey, was coming to an uneventful close. It was just before two and I was waiting for Dawn in the Street Duties office to book off. I was plucking up the courage to ask her to join me for a drink that evening at the Elephant's Head when the door burst open, and she came in with a face like thunder.

"Everything okay?" I asked, actually meaning 'What the fuck has happened?'

She ignored me and knocked abruptly on the sergeant's office. My insecurity, which only ever lurked just below the surface, assumed I'd done something wrong. My mind raced; I thought she must have heard about the burglar I'd assisted.

"What is it?" shouted Sergeant Bellamy, obviously annoyed at being disturbed.

"There's a PC from early turn missing, Dave Perryman, one six three," Dawn replied.

There was a huff, several puffs, the portacabin rocked gently and Sergeant Bellamy emerged.

"What do you mean, missing?" he asked.

"Apparently, he's not been answering his radio since refs and now he's failed to appear to be dismissed. They say he's as sound as a pound normally. All hell's breaking loose."

"Nostrils," the sergeant barked, "go and get three radios; Dawn, go to the room above the stables, there's two Home Beats in there studying. Tell them to get their arses down here now."

The radios were booked in and out from a cabinet in the Station Office and at busy times, shift changes for example, an orderly queue formed. As early turn were being kept on, they'd not handed their radios in and late turn were already booking theirs out, so by the time I reached the front of the queue, there were none left. I'd have to return empty handed.

The Station Office was organised chaos with a dozen things happening at once, but every twenty or so seconds the Reserve, a female officer with an immaculate radio voice, depressed the red transmit button and said with serene calmness,

"One six three, one six three, Golf November, are you receiving over?"

And each time she did, the noise in the room dropped for just a few seconds as subconsciously everyone listened in the hope the missing officer would respond. During the five minutes I'd been queuing for the radio, I must have heard the same message perhaps fifteen times; each time it was spoken in the same rhythmic monotone delivery. As I turned to leave, the message started again but this time the last three words had changed and were bursting with raw emotion.

*"One six three, one six three, **where are you**?"*

For the first time I looked at the Reserve; tears were pouring down her cheeks. I must have been frowning or otherwise looking confused, because a passing officer whispered in my ear to answer my unspoken question.

"One six three is her kid brother."

I returned to the portacabin where the sergeant, Dawn and two Home Beats were waiting.

"No radios left, Sergeant," I said.

"For goodness's sake, Nostrils, Dawn was right, you are completely useless. Dawn, go and find a couple."

The words annoyed me, but only momentarily; there were more important things to worry about. As Dawn left, a plain clothes officer stuck his head into the office and announced, “Briefing in the canteen in ten, please bring any radios you've got 'cos I can't find any anywhere.”

Fuck you, Sarge, I thought.

***

The canteen was packed, every seat was taken, and many officers were standing. The Chief Superintendent, whom I recognised as the short man who'd attacked my prisoner in the charge room, was standing before us deep in conversation with several other senior officers. Dawn was one of the last to arrive. She carried a radio in each hand.

The room settled as the Chief Super spoke.

“PC Perryman was early turn today but he hasn't been heard from for several hours.”

He paused and looked slowly around the room.

“He paraded at six o'clock and left the station ten minutes later.”

Several in the room exchanged glances suggesting no one ever left the station at that time. The parade might only take ten minutes but then there was always a brew in the canteen. Anytime between six thirty-five and seven would have been a more accurate departure time.

“He was posted to six beat, about a forty minutes' walk east of the nick. It contains Franklin Park, the canal and the delightful Bromsgrove Estate. There's mile upon mile of terraced housing and a few expensive drums near the border with J Division. I am told there's a council rubbish tip, some waste land and a hectare or two of allotments. PC Perryman's been on six beat all month so he might have formed some routine to his patrol. We know he took ...”

The Chief Superintendent looked down at some writing which had been scribbled in a note pad.

"... a call at seven thirty-two to a theft from motor vehicle in Radley Road and at eight twelve he did a car check and a name check for a process. He returned to the nick for refs at ten and so he would have left at ten forty-five."

Again, there were several raised eyebrows to suggest such accurate time keeping was unlikely.

"The Reserve called him at ..." he took another glance down, "twelve fifteen with a domestic but he failed to respond. We know the reception that side of the ground can be intermittent, so she thought nothing more about it. It's now two forty and he's still unaccounted for so I'm about to officially declare him missing. Before I push the button and we go nuclear, I need to be certain he's not shagging or similarly indisposed. If *any* of you know where he might be, even if that means telling me he's with a girlfriend who lives on the ground, or he's seeing somebody else's wife, or anything else which might explain why he's missing, now is the time to speak up, gentlemen."

There was a brief silence before a PC put his hand up.

"Go on."

"He's not got a girlfriend or anything like that, Sir. Dave's genuinely happily married, I'd put my pension on it. If he's not returned, he's in serious trouble."

At least half of those assembled nodded firmly in agreement. The Chief Super had his answer and left the room with the instruction to all of us assembled to wait there.

***

I was mesmerised watching events unfolding. By three thirty it seemed that every police officer in London had either arrived at Stokey or was descending upon it; there was even a rumour the Commissioner was on his way. An incident room had been set up in the canteen and actions were being issued to officers in pairs. In the back yard, groups of DSU officers were being individually briefed to search specific public areas. India nine nine, the police helicopter, was hovering a few hundred feet above, awaiting instructions. Police dogs were everywhere. Early turn were directed to swamp beat six and speak to as many members of the public as possible. As the station still had to deal with the usual business, late turn were assigned to all calls unrelated to the missing officer. A BBC news crew was setting up a camera by the rear entrance to the yard.

As Dawn and I were waiting in the actions queue, she said, "I hope they don't send me to tell his wife."

"Why, you haven't been sleeping with him too, have you?"

It was a cheeky response, but I just couldn't resist.

"Do you think that's funny?" Dawn feigned annoyance.

"Why would they choose you?"

"Because looking around, I'm one of only a few female officers on today, and they'll want to send a woman. But I warn you, if I go, you're coming too."

"Of course, partner," I replied obediently.

"Oh, I'm sorry about what Sarge said earlier, you're not *completely* useless," she said.

"Thanks."

"Just useless," she added, with a grin.

When we reached the front of the queue Dawn spoke for both of us.

"WPC Matthews and PC Pritchard, Street Duties."

The CID officer wrote down our names next to a long list of actions and handed us a piece of yellow carbonated paper without saying a word. Dawn read it quickly as we made our way into the yard.

"According to this, two days ago PC Perryman did a name check on a male he'd stopped. They want us to call on the male and see if he has any information."

"I don't get it. That's ridiculous, how will the bloke he stopped two days ago be able to help?" I said, really disappointed.

Dawn didn't answer immediately; she seemed to be thinking the matter over carefully.

"Don't you agree?" I pressed; I wanted her to ask for a more relevant enquiry.

"We'll see," she replied. "But at least I didn't get the wife."

***

The male we had to question, Mr David Forrester, was a white thirty-two-year-old with several previous convictions. He lived about twenty minutes away in a first-floor council flat; that afternoon the urgency in our step got us there in fifteen. A black man with dreadlocks answered the door; he immediately had attitude, but Dawn was the epitome of patience and manners.

"What you want?"

"Sorry to trouble you, Sir, but is Mr Forrester in?"

"He don't live here no more."

"He gave this address to police on Wednesday."

"I don't know nothing about that but he don't live here no more. He gave this as his parole address, but he only stayed here two nights."

“Can we come in and check?”

“You got a warrant?”

“No.”

“I know the law, you gonna need a warrant if you wanna come in. What’s he done, anyway?”

“Probably nothing. Will you contact police if he comes back?”

“No.”

So that was the end of that but as soon as the front door was closed on us, Dawn took a few paces and then broke into a run. She sprinted along the short landing and down the stairs. I was at a loss as to what was happening but followed anyway. As we got to the ground floor, instead of leaving by the front way we had entered, Dawn tried to open a fire exit that led to the rear of the flats. The door was locked but it had a long thin vertical opaque window, and she pushed her eyes up against it.

“Damn,” she said out loud.

“What?” I asked.

“Look.”

I cupped my hands as if forming make-believe binoculars, and peered through the glass. I could just make out a white male running away from the flats, across open land towards what looked like a cemetery. The male seemed to be limping, but pursuit would be fruitless, his lead was too great, and by the time we found our way around the outside of the flats, he would be long gone.

“Whilst we were at the front door Mr Forrester was dropping from a window and making good his escape,” Dawn said.

“What’ll we do now?”

Dawn spoke slowly.

“We have a missing PC. We know he stopped Forrester two days ago and today, we have reason to suspect Forrester had committed a crime, a serious crime, otherwise why would he drop ten feet from a first-floor window to escape us? I believe the missing PC and Forrester’s actions may be linked.”

“Go on?” I said, following her logic.

“So, we’re going to search the upstairs flat?”

“Without a warrant?” I asked nervously.

“We don’t need one if we have even the slightest suspicion the missing PC might be in there.”

“But we don’t really, do we?” I said.

“I do,” Dawn replied unequivocally.

“Dawn, we could really land in the shit here,” I said.

“Listen. There’s a PC missing, he could be in there. I not leaving here until I know one way or another. With or without you I’m going in and I’m going in now.”

“Okay, okay,” I said.

A minute later we were once again knocking at the flat.

“What?” the surly occupant said.

“You know what,” Dawn replied tersely, “warrant or no warrant, we’re coming in. You try to stop us and Nostrils here will knock you out.”

The occupant looked me up and down and smiled. I felt stupid, at five foot ten and eleven stone, a heavyweight boxer I wasn’t. The occupant, a six-foot-two muscular Rasta man, wasn’t going to be intimidated by me. In fact, I estimated I’d last about ten seconds.

“He’s a lot tougher than he looks, or at least I hope he is,” Dawn said, with a hint of humour. “Please let us come in.”

Dawn dropped her voice to no more than a whisper, but it worked, and the man stepped aside to indicate we could enter. Sometimes Dawn knew just how to speak to people; it was a real skill.

"Thank you," she said.

"Where's Mr Forrester's room?"

He nodded towards a door at the back of the flat. We entered a small bedroom; one curtain was open and the window through which he must have climbed out, swung on its hinges, the TV was on. Dawn touched the unmade bed.

"Still warm," she commented.

She knelt on the bed to open the other curtain and let more light in. The room was no more than ten feet by eight. I pushed a button and the TV turned off. Dawn started to look around, opening drawers and looking in the cupboard.

"Look under the bed," she instructed.

I didn't know what I was looking for but wasn't going to ask. I pulled out a damp towel which was curled into a tight ball. As I picked it up, it seemed unnaturally heavy, when suddenly, the towel unwound itself and a meat cleaver thudded onto the floor. I went to pick it up.

"Don't touch it," Dawn said, just in time.

I opened the towel out. It was covered in blood and as I stared at the cleaver, I realised it too was bloodstained. I looked at my hands, blood was everywhere. There was something else; something was on the carpet next to the cleaver. It was small but vaguely familiar.

"What the fuck is that?" I asked.

Dawn knelt down and studied it carefully.

"I think it's an ear!"

Chapter 36 – Red wine in a harem

For Dawn and me, Friday early turn didn't end until four on Saturday morning; we had worked a twenty-two-hour shift. The flat had been declared a crime scene and we'd rolled from one job to another until we were eventually dismissed just as it was getting light. The good news was that the missing PC, minus an ear, had been found alive but unconscious on the allotments at the rear of some expensive houses.

As we walked across the station yard, now devoid of the turmoil that had been there some twelve hours earlier, "I was going to ask you to join me for a drink this evening," I said.

Of course, I actually meant the previous evening.

"We can still get a drink if you want one?" she replied.

"Where in London can you get a drink at four in the morning?" I asked incredulously.

"The early house, of course."

"The early house?"

"Yes, early houses are pubs near markets; they have different licensing hours because everyone works nights. If we shoot over to Smithfield we'll be able to have a few pints, but I'll tell you what."

"What?"

"Let's go home; I'm shattered."

"Me too," I said, but the truth was I'd have done just about anything to avoid returning to my bedsit.

We entered our respective locker rooms through adjacent doors. I felt the impending doom of a boring weekend weighing me down but when I opened my locker saw someone had slipped a white envelope through the angled vent. It had 'Chris' written in very feminine handwriting, so I ripped it open and read a short, neatly written note.

Dear Chris,

It would be great to see you darling. Perhaps you would like to sample my delights again? Perhaps you would like to come over on Sunday? Say six?

Jessica xxx

I knew I shouldn't but knew I would. I slipped the note into my trouser pocket, changed into half blues and left. By coincidence, I emerged from my locker room at exactly the same time as Dawn. We exchanged a pleasant smile and then I followed her up the stairs. I really fancied her now. I certainly hadn't had any such thoughts when I'd started on Street Duties but the more we worked together, the more attractive I found her. It was academic though; she definitely didn't fancy me. She had been seeing a DS for seven years who was probably in his mid-thirties; I was a nineteen-year-old boy who still occasionally suffered from spots. My chances with Dawn were non-existent but I gave myself some credit for realising that fact.

"You got anything planned for the weekend?" she asked me, as we reached the top of the stairs.

"Nothing," I lied, and checked the note was firmly planted in my pocket. "What about you?"

"No, washing, ironing, cleaning. I might go and see my cousin on Sunday, but it always makes me depressed."

"Why?"

"She has the perfect life. She lives in Twickenham, hubby's a stockbroker on a hundred kay a year and she drives a new Porsche. She's got two lovely kids and the cow is two years younger than me."

"Dawn?"

"Yeah."

I paused, uncertainly and then said, somewhat unconvincingly, "Nothing."

"What?"

"Do you want to see a film later? If you're not busy. I know, like, you know, but the truth is I'm pretty bored of a weekend."

"Yeah, okay, but I choose. Pick me up at seven."

She retrieved a pen from her handbag.

"Got any paper?"

I was so shocked I handed over the note from Jessica Campbell, but fortunately, without looking at the paper, Dawn folded it several times and quickly scribbled an address on a blank side.

As I drove home, I thought over this most unexpected turn of events. Where on earth did I find the front to ask her out? Perhaps it was because I was so tired? But then again, I knew, and she knew, and she knew that I knew, it wasn't that sort of date. I remembered how only a few weeks ago she'd been pretty brutal to me, but instead of being offended, I'd decided to take it on board, to smarten up, to clean up and generally try to shape up. I also had another visit to Dean and Jessica's to look forward to. I knew it wasn't normal to be shagging some bloke's missus whilst he was in the next room, but I did get to have sex with one of the sexiest women I'd ever laid eyes upon and, quite frankly, that negated any other moral or ethical consideration.

As I climbed the stairs to my sad little bedsit, I quite literally bumped into Debbie, who was emerging from the bathroom wrapped as usual in a towel.

"You're late, Chris," she said cheerily.

"Flat out all day, Debbie."

"Me too," she replied, with a wry smile. "I've just got rid of my last client. Do you fancy a glass of wine?"

"Yeah, go on then. Let me get out of my uniform and pull on some jeans."

I looked at my watch; it was a quarter to five. Ten minutes later, I was sitting in the most extraordinary room, sipping a glass of red wine with my prostitute neighbour who'd changed into a tracksuit and training shoes. The room was decorated like a harem: there were no chairs, beds or tables but cold plastic mattresses all over the floor and perhaps thirty cushions of various shapes and sizes; coloured net curtains hung at irregular intervals and the lighting was low and seductive. The room smelled sweet and when I saw a spilt bottle of baby oil, I knew why. I stood the bottle back up and clipped the top into place.

We chatted for the best part of an hour. I was amazed to discover my neighbour was only a year older than me. She said she was working to support her young child and that they lived in Chigwell with her mother.

"Mum thinks I'm a casino croupier in the West End which explains the late nights and irregular hours. I am only going to do it for another year 'cos I earn a fortune, Chris, up to three hundred a day. All cash in hand, do you know what I mean? I don't know what to do with the money, honestly, its everywhere."

She lifted up a mattress and underneath I saw in the half-light what appeared to be piles of banknotes.

"I drive a Mercedes with a personalised plate and buy my daughter the best clothes money can buy. She's only three but she has her hair and nails done professionally every week. Do you know what I mean, Chris? It's crazy, it's like mental; my mate from school, she works at Barclays Bank in Tottenham and she like knows what the players earn, and I'm like, Glen Hoddle earns what? Is that all? Do you know what I mean?"

I was really tired, and the wine was going to my head; gradually, the whole experience was becoming surreal.

"How long you been a copper then?" she asked.

"Only a few months."

"Where you based, Hackney?"

"Stoke Newington."

Debbie thought hard.

"Nope, don't know anyone there."

"Do you know lots of policemen then?" I asked, a little surprised she knew any at all.

"One or two, one or two," she replied coyly.

"Have you got a proper boyfriend?" I asked.

"Why? You offering? After all, it is always useful for someone in my business to have a boyfriend who's a policeman. You know, to protect me and stuff. Do you know what I mean?"

"I'm new, Debbie, and I don't know all the rules but I'm pretty sure that's not allowed."

"Really?" she asked, sounding a little too surprised.

Chapter 37 – Another visit to Wanstead

I didn't wake up until two o'clock the following afternoon and when I did, felt really rough. I wasn't used to red wine and I'd had three large glasses. I popped out to buy a paper and some toothpaste when Eddie, seeing me walking by the open door of the pub, came out and handed me an envelope.

"That woman, the one who had the black eyes, dropped this off for you. She didn't know where you lived but knew you came in here."

"Thanks, mate."

"Do you want a pint before we close?"

"No, no, I'm fine, mate, thanks."

I immediately identified Dawn's handwriting and inside was a short note:

Chris,

Sorry but I can't make tonight, see you Monday, don't forget we're nights.

I was disappointed but grateful she'd gone out of her way to tell me. What's more was that although she'd obviously now changed her mind, at least for a few hours she'd agreed to go out with me.

By mid-afternoon I was bored, so I wandered into a betting office only to leave thirty minutes later still bored but twenty quid lighter. I ended the day in the Elephant's Head, sitting at the bar watching the usual customers doing the usual things. At ten o'clock or thereabouts, several officers from Hackney police station came in wearing half blues. I watched them carefully for the next hour.

They had an air of unpleasant arrogance about them emanating, I assessed, from their perceived invulnerability, which they demonstrated by having the tops of their truncheons sticking out of their right trouser pockets. As they were technically off duty, they shouldn't have been carrying them.

The old Canadian landlord, Red, seemed happy enough to have them in his pub but the other customers, those with whom I was becoming very familiar, were distinctly indifferent. For once though, closing time came and went without being called and at eleven thirty the landlord locked the pub up with everyone inside. Clearly, if those responsible for enforcing the licensing laws were drinking in your pub, you were exempt from them.

On Sunday I set off in good time for my drive across the East End of London to Wanstead. En route, I witnessed quite a serious car accident: a white Austin Metro had inexplicably left the road and driven straight into a tree at what must have been at least forty miles an hour. On any other occasion I would have pulled over to assist but not today, because my cock was driving and wasn't stopping for anyone.

I arrived at six thirty and climbed the stairs to the first-floor flat; naturally, I carried the requisite bottle of red wine in one hand and box of Milk Tray in the other. I knocked, and my cock and I waited.

Jessica opened the door and stood back. She was wearing a red basque, black stockings, suspenders and black stilettos. She looked absolutely gorgeous.

"Wow!" was all I could utter.

"Well thank you, kind Sir, do come in."

I headed for the lounge but was stopped when the lovely Jessica asked forcefully, “Where do you think you’re going? I want you in the bedroom; you can put the wine and chocolates on the dresser, put your clothes on the chair and get onto the bed.”

This time there was no smell of cooking coming from the kitchen, nor was there any sign of Dean.

“Is, um, Dean about?” I asked tentatively.

“No, he’s late turn but I’ll enjoy telling him what we got up to when he gets home.” She smiled.

As I entered the room, I saw two pairs of police handcuffs in the middle of the bed.

“Handcuffs?”

“I want to tie you up, make sure you don’t get away. Then I’ll fuck your brains out.”

And that was exactly what Jessica Campbell did. She secured my hands and feet at each corner of the bed, she used the cuffs for my wrists, and ropes, which were already in place, for my ankles. Then she rode my cock. When she had reached orgasm she dismounted, got a glass of wine, relaxed for ten minutes and then started over again. At first, I couldn’t believe my luck but by nine o’clock I was genuinely feeling abused. What’s more, she knew completely what she was doing and never let me climax, so I was getting really frustrated. When I asked to be released Jessica just laughed and started over. Nearly four hours, countless fucks and just one miserly orgasm right at the end later, she did let me go. I was exhausted and very, very sore.

When I set off home, I made the definite decision not to return, but by the time I got in I couldn’t wait to be summoned again.

I showered and just after ten slipped over to the Elephant's Head for a swift pint; the pub was, for the second night running, full of old bill in half blues. They acted like they owned the place; at one point one bloke even came behind the bar to help himself but Red the landlord really didn't seem to mind. I was watching them carefully but discreetly from my stool at the end of the bar when the landlord placed a pint in front of me which I hadn't ordered.

"Have this one on me, son, you've bought me enough."

"Thanks, Red, cheers."

"Boisterous lot, aren't they?" he commented, following my gaze.

I had never been in the pub in half blues, as I deliberately wanted to keep my occupation to myself.

"Are you okay with them drinking here?" I asked.

"Yes and no. They drive some other customers away, but they don't half drink and they pay their way. Mind you, they all drive home. And I know I'm not going to get any grief from the licensing sergeant, which is always good to know. This lot are okay but the CID, now they're another story, always blagging, for this charity or that. I ain't stupid, there ain't no charity, but what can you do?"

"I don't understand."

"They collect 'donations' of bottles of spirits. They say they're for a charity raffle."

"Oh, and if you decline?" I asked.

He shrugged his shoulders.

"Don't really want to find out."

I felt a pang of guilt, by not owning up about what I did for a living; I knew in a way I was deceiving him. Just then a couple entered, and Red wandered off to serve them. She was an attractive, thirty-something blonde; the bloke with her was much older, perhaps by fifteen years. As I watched them, I realised something was different, I no longer felt like an outsider looking in. I wasn't quite sure why but was sure it had something to do with Mrs Jessica Campbell.

Before leaving I used the toilet, or more specifically, the wall urinal. I was in full flow and several pints of lager were making their way to the Thames when the bloke who was with the blonde came in and stood downstream. The chap coughed, there was a clatter and his dentures, top and bottom set, dropped into the urinal where they were immediately surrounded and enveloped by my urine.

"Jesus!" spluttered the man, before he bent and in one quick swoop, retrieved them.

He took them to the sink, rinsed them under the cold water and popped them back in his mouth. I tried not to, I really did, but I must have looked disgusted because the man felt compelled to justify his actions.

"I've got to put them back in, we've been going out for months and she hasn't got a clue that not one of the teeth in my mouth is my own."

Chapter 38 – Nights begins with an alarm

I was really looking forward to my first week of nights. Ever since I'd been working with Dawn, she'd impressed upon me that nights was 'proper policing'. In preparation, I'd bought an expensive torch to replace the cheap one which the Met provided, and a set of thermal underwear because she'd told me just how cold it was at five in the morning even in mid-summer. As soon as I entered the nick, I was struck by the different atmosphere: the administration departments were deserted, in the canteen the counter shutters were down, no cleaners or garage hands went about their business and even the ever-present queue of people waiting to be served at the front counter had disappeared.

At the end of parade and after reading out several messages from the parade book, which included an entry about a missing prostitute from an adjacent division, the sergeant gave us an update on PC Dave Perryman.

"He's out of intensive care and in a stable condition. He's had surgery on his head wound and seventy stiches but except for the fact that getting a pair of glasses to fit is going to be a nightmare, he is. thank God, going to be okay. Apparently, he'd turned Forrester over two days previously and when he once again caught him hanging around behind those expensive drums on Elm Avenue, Dave arrested him for loitering. He wasn't expecting the guy to produce a machete and plant it in his helmet. If he hadn't been wearing the old tit, he'd be dead. Forrester's still wanted. Are there any questions?"

There were none and the sergeant, a small well-built Scotsman with a beard, who I thought would have looked more at home in a kilt than his uniform, dismissed us. After Dawn and I had booked out our radios we were almost immediately sent to an alarm at a Cohen Jewellers in the

High Street. We checked the premises over, there didn't seem to be any sign of a break-in, so we got the Reserve to call the keyholder, unsurprisingly a gentleman called Joseph Cohen, to come out and reset the alarm.

"Do we need to wait for him?" I asked, keen to get on with the night's work.

"No, let's get going. It seems secure to me," Dawn replied.

We set off to patrol our beat.

"Your lesson this week is stop and search. Hopefully, the next person we turn over won't be related to a senior officer," Dawn said, referring of course to Mrs Florence Farrington-Smythe.

"We use the powers in the Metropolitan Police Act 1839. Turning someone over is one of the most difficult skills to learn but it is the most useful. Half those on parade this evening will never have acquired it. You see it can get very confrontational very quickly. It's when you're most likely to get into a fight. There are a few tricks I can teach you and you'll develop some of your own and then, who knows, in three years or so, you'll be imparting them to your own sprog."

I knew sprog was a derisory term for a probationer constable.

"Sorry about letting you down on Saturday."

"That's all right, thanks for letting me know. I was surprised when you agreed to come."

"Did you go anyway?"

"No, I had a quiet weekend, ended up in the Elephant's Head as usual."

We walked on in silence for perhaps a hundred yards.

"I saw Barry on Saturday."

I was really surprised because even these days Dawn rarely talked about her personal life; I tried to make my reply sound casual.

"Did you? How did that go?"

"He's emigrating to Australia and wanted me to hear it from him first."

"Oh, Dawn, I'm so sorry. How do you feel?" I asked gently.

"Pretty stupid, I thought he was going to tell me he'd decided to leave his wife after all. He never ever saw me at a weekend, so when he called and asked to see me on a Saturday evening, I assumed he'd already left her."

"Sorry."

"I got all dressed up, I looked the business, if I say so myself."

I didn't know what to say.

"I was really excited, shaking with nerves. We met in our favourite pub, sat at our favourite table, everything was just perfect and then he tells me, he, she, and their three kids are going to the other side of the world."

We walked on for another hundred yards in silence.

"Dawn? I'd leave my wife for you."

"You gotta find one first, though now you've smartened up at least you stand a chance."

"Seriously, are you gonna be all right, partner?"

"Got to be, haven't I? And no more dating married men, they never bloody leave their wives."

"Did you feel tempted to tell Barry about his missus and William?"

"No, I'm not a bitch."

"One eight two receiving?"

"Go ahead."

"Are you a van driver?"

"Yes, yes."

"Can you drive Golf November two from four please? The driver and operator are at a.m. court tomorrow."

"Yes, yes."

"Thank you, Golf November out."

"You're in luck, Chris; we won't be walking all night after all. It's unusual actually, they don't normally post plonks to the van?"

"Plonks?"

I'd heard the word a few times now but was none the wiser as to what it might mean.

"WPCs. It's what the old boys call WPCs."

"Why plonks?"

"There are two theories about the origin of the word. The first is that it comes from initials stamped on the service records of American troops stationed in England during the war and stood for Person of Little or No Knowledge. The second is this: the first WPCs wore wooden clogs; whereas male officers' hob-nailed boots made a 'plod' when they struck the cobblestones of the old London streets, these clogs made a 'plonk'. And so, PCs were known as plod and WPCs as plonk."

"So, is it an insult, to call a WPC a plonk?"

"Some WPCs get upset about it. I'm not that bothered. It depends on who says it and what context it's said in."

"A bit like sprog for a probationer then?" I said.

"Exactly," Dawn replied.

Within an hour we were on our way back to the bloody jewellers. The owner had reset the alarm, but it had gone off again and was obviously faulty. We checked the front and back of the premises, once again everything was fine. We asked the Reserve to call the keyholder.

"This time we'll wait for him, try and convince him to turn it off. Otherwise, we'll be back and forwards all night," she added.

The keyholder only lived a few miles away and was there in ten minutes. A pleasant, if slightly frustrated, Jewish gentleman offered profuse apologies.

"I don't understand it, officers. It's never caused any problem before."

"Do you want to try leaving it off? You can get the alarm company out in the morning," Dawn suggested.

"But I have a fortune in stock, officer. I've just taken a consignment of two hundred gold sovereigns; if they get stolen and the alarm is off and no one is on the premises, the insurance won't cover me."

"Look," Dawn said, "we're patrolling the High Street all night; we'll keep an eye on the place. What more could you want?"

"I'm not happy, officer."

"Listen, trust us, it'll be all right."

Mr Cohen deactivated the alarm and entrusted two hundred gold sovereigns to our charge.

Chapter 39 – Voices

It was an unusually busy night and calls came out at regular intervals; rather frustratingly they all went to the mobile units and we were left patrolling the High Street and High Road. Stoke Newington has both a High Street and a High Road, which meet roughly in the vicinity of the nick. Eventually a call came our way.

"One eight two receiving, over?"

"Go ahead."

"Before you take the van out can you take a quick call to three eight, thirty-eight Blenheim House? A disturbance. The informant's the male occupier, possibly suffering harmless delusions. I don't think it'll tie you up for long."

"Received."

Blenheim House was a tower block; there were two lifts, each serviced every other floor but only one worked. The lift opened into a square central landing off which there were four flats, one in each corner. The whole place was an architect's dream but a resident's nightmare: what looked good on paper was in reality bland, cold and characterless.

The occupier of thirty-eight was awaiting our arrival; he was a thin nervous-looking white man in his mid-fifties, with tobacco-stained teeth and brown dirty fingers which he offered by way of a limp handshake.

"Oh, officers, I'm so sorry to trouble you, do come in."

His voice was soft and effeminate, his mannerisms and movements equally so.

He led us into a smoke-filled lounge with several overflowing ashtrays and a dozen empty cans of beer atop a dated coffee table.

"Please take a seat."

"We're fine, we'll stand, thank you. Now what's the problem?" Dawn replied quite briskly, and I sensed she had taken an instant dislike to this man.

"I keep hearing a voice."

"Go on."

"I keep hearing a child crying for help."

Dawn nodded towards me to indicate I should continue asking the questions.

"How often do you hear these voices?"

"Not voices, voice. Just the one voice. It started last night, at about three o'clock, every ten minutes, and again tonight."

I noticed Dawn had started to examine several magazines which were on a coffee table.

"Do you mind if we look around?"

"No, no, carry on," he said passively.

I had no idea what we were looking for; Dawn knew what she was doing; she seemed to think, to operate, at a different level to me. We were searching drawers, looking in cupboards, under beds, in the fridge but for what?

"Do you work, Mr … ?"

"Mr Field, James Field. Yes, at the Town Hall. I'm a clerk, I deal with planning applications."

"And how long have you worked there?"

"Thirty-two years."

Dawn interrupted me.

"So, whose voice do you think you are hearing?"

"I don't know, I really don't. But will you just sit with me for ten minutes? I'm sure you'll hear it too. If not, then I know I'm going mad. Please, please."

"Very well."

And so, we did just that. In complete silence we waited, and waited, and waited.

"Enough," Dawn declared after about three minutes, but it felt much longer.

"PC Pritchard, please record Mr Field's full details and verify them with documentation. I'll see you outside."

***

As we walked back to the nick, Dawn was silent. The silence reminded me of those first few weeks when she hardly spoke at all. I was starting to worry that I'd done something wrong. Eventually she spoke.

"What do you make of Mr Field then, Chris?"

From her tone I knew she wasn't annoyed, that she'd just been turning things over in her mind. I reminded myself that I needed to relax a bit.

"Strange bloke, bit sad, bit lonely."

I realised I could be describing myself.

"Paedophile," Dawn said definitively.

"A pedo what?"

"A paedophile. A man who likes kids, you know, sexually."

"What on earth makes you think that?"

"Don't know, just a hunch."

I'd got to the stage with Dawn where I was prepared to accept without reservation almost anything she said.

"Dawn?"

"Yes, Chris?"

"When we were searching his house, what were we looking for?"

"Anything that can help us work out what's going on. Nothing specific."

"But he was just mad, wasn't he? Normal people don't hear voices."

"A voice, Chris, singular. You see, he's had a full-time job for over thirty years, and a reasonable one at that, one where he's going to be dealing with people every day. So, he can't be mad. If he's hearing a voice, there might be a psychosomatic reason."

"A?"

"Psychosomatic, it's where the mind influences the body."

"Go on."

"No, I'll keep my thoughts to myself at the moment. If I'm wrong, I'll look really stupid. We'll go back to the nick and check the Collator's. By the time we've done that and had something to eat it'll be time to take the van out."

"Did you notice anything about the bedside drawers?" continued Dawn.

"No, of course not, they were locked," I replied.

"Exactly; they were locked. Why would someone who lives alone lock a bedside drawer?"

"Maybe he keeps his valuables there?"

"Did anything about him or the flat suggest to you he had anything valuable?"

"No, it was nearly as horrible as where I live."

"There's something wrong, Chris, but we'll get to the bottom of it. Did you do a PNC check?"

"Yes, no trace."

We were nearing the nick now and it started to rain, we quickened our pace. In the Collator's Office Dawn flipped through the 'Fa – Gi' drawer, from which she triumphantly produced a card.

"I knew it," she said, reading the information on the back. She handed it to me.

On the front was an old black and white photograph of Mr Field, taken a long time ago; on the rear was one typed entry dated 3rd July 1972:

Suspect arrested by PC 371H for loitering with intent to commit an indictable offence when he was observed in Nightingale Park watching children in the play area. Insufficient evidence. Released NFA.

"That was over ten years ago, Dawn, and he wasn't even charged."

"I know, but my instincts were spot on."

"What are we going to do?"

"I don't know. I'll have a word with CID. I wonder if the voice he thinks he's hearing is an old victim."

"Next you'll be telling me he buried him under the floorboards," I joked.

Dawn looked at me without smiling and a chill went down my spine as I realised that was exactly what she was thinking.

Chapter 40 – A drunk is bailed

I was more than happy to be taking the van out because compared with walking the streets of East London in the pouring rain in the middle of the night, being driven through them in a dry warm police van was luxury.

We'd only been out for about ten minutes when we were called back to the nick and told to report to the charge room where a sergeant whom I didn't recognise was sitting at the desk completing some paperwork; on the bench opposite sat a smelly old drunk, fast asleep.

"You asked for the van, Sarge?" said Dawn.

"Who are you?" the sergeant asked, clearly expecting someone else.

"We're Street Duties, on attachment for this week. The night duty van driver is court tomorrow, so we've been asked to cover."

"You're obviously the instructor?"

"Yes, Sarge, Dawn Matthews."

"Oh, you're Tommy's mate, I've heard of you but what about him? Is he all right?"

The sergeant nodded towards me. After enough of a pause to suggest she'd given both the question and her answer some thought, Dawn replied, "He's sweet."

They held one another's stare for a few telling seconds. I was quietly delighted that Dawn had described me as 'sweet' and was well aware of the context in which it was said; she was telling the sergeant I could be trusted, it was really quite a significant moment. The sergeant looked me up and down and just as I was beginning to feel awkward, he broke the tension with one word.

"Good."

He turned back to Dawn.

"I'm just bailing this prisoner. He's got his property in his pockets and here is his 57c."

He handed Dawn a long, slim piece of paper with red lettering on it.

"Pop it in his jacket pocket, please."

Dawn took it and gave it to me; I walked around the desk, folded it and handed to the man; he didn't respond.

"There you go, mate," I said encouragingly. There was no response.

"Just put it in his top pocket, there's a good lad," the sergeant said, so I did.

The man was in a very deep sleep and stank of alcohol. I couldn't work out why he was being bailed; surely, he should be sleeping it off in the tank. And what did him being bailed have to do with the van? And why was it so important that I could be trusted? None of it made any sense but I'd learnt to keep such thoughts to myself; time, I knew, would reveal all.

"Where shall we take him to?" Dawn asked, without any suggestion in her voice that this wasn't quite right.

"Anywhere off this ground, preferably Y or J."

"No problem, Sarge, consider it done."

The man was so deeply unconscious the sergeant and I had literally to carry him to the van, where he was unceremoniously laid down on the cold metal floor.

"Shall I get in the back with him, Dawn, in case he wakes up?" I suggested helpfully.

"No, I think he'll be okay, jump in the front."

"Are we taking him home?" I asked as I climbed into the passenger seat and slid the door forward and closed.

"He's of no fixed abode, Chris; we're just taking him ..." she paused, apparently seeking the most appropriate words, "far away from the nick."

I was confused; why were we 'taking him far away from the nick'? I turned around but Dawn hadn't put the light on in the rear and I could only just make out the man's outline in the dark; he was still fast asleep.

We drove in silence, off the ground and down the Lea Bridge Road towards Walthamstow. At a roundabout not too far across the border with J we turned left off the main road and several turns later down ever-diminishing roads, were soon driving along a dirt track near a canal or a river; it was difficult to tell in the darkness.

"This'll do," Dawn said, pulling the van to a halt where the track opened out.

"This'll do for what?"

"Dropping off our passenger, of course. Come on, give me a hand, we can slide him out."

She stopped the engine, slid back the door and jumped out; I followed. The rain was falling heavily now and the ground was a mixture of mud and gravel. Although only a minute or two ago we'd been driving through residential streets, now we were in the middle of nowhere.

"Where are we?" I asked.

"The marshes," Dawn replied.

She opened both the back doors of the van and took hold of the drunk's ankles.

"Well, are you going to help?" she asked.

"Help with what?" I asked.

"Help me get him out."

One long yank and the man slipped across the metal floor and out onto the ground where he landed without ceremony or dignity. She slammed the rear doors shut and started to walk back to the driver's door. I stayed where I was.

"We can't just leave him here," I shouted, trying to raise my voice above the wind and rain.

Dawn called something back, but I couldn't make out a word, so I followed her to the front of the van.

"Dawn, we can't leave him here, he'll die."

"Christopher, he'll be fine. He's not our problem any more. Get in the van."

"What do you mean he's not our problem, whose problem is he?"

"Whichever Coroner covers the Lea Valley."

"I don't understand?"

"Chris," she said.

Her gloved hands were on the steering wheel and her head turned towards me.

"Yes?"

"He's dead."

She turned the ignition; the engine started, and we drove off into the miserable night.

Chapter 41 – Superman, Part 1

Sleeping after nights was a nightmare. Just as I was climbing into bed, the rest of Hackney was waking up. To make matters worse, the neighbours had chosen that week to have their windows replaced with double glazing. By three, I was getting into a state of panic as I had to be back at work at ten, was yet to get a minute's sleep and was actually feeling wide awake. I decided the situation needed urgent action, dressed and went into the Elephant's Head where I downed three pints of strong lager in less than thirty minutes. It did the trick; by four thirty I was fast asleep. In fact, I was still fast asleep at seven, at eight and at nine. When I eventually awoke it was nine fifteen and I was going to be late, late for night duty.

That night I made it to the parade room with just two minutes to spare by contravening every traffic law and regulation ever written, red lights, stop signs; speed limits meant nothing to me. I walked in a few paces ahead of the sergeant and inspector and took my place next to Dawn.

"You're late," she whispered, as the parade got under way.

"Tell you about it later," I replied.

When the sergeant once again posted Dawn and me to the High Street beat, he looked up and added, "I hope you do a better job tonight. Cohen's Jewellers was burgled last night, and they even blew his safe. That's something which doesn't happen much these days."

Dawn and I didn't join the rest of the shift for tea after parade but set off straight away. For a while neither of us said a word about the burglary but I didn't think it was a coincidence that we'd set off in the opposite direction to the jewellers. Finally, Dawn broke the silence.

“I made a stupid mistake last night. I should have recognised the oldest trick in the book. Burglar Bill keeps setting off the alarm until the police, the owner and Uncle Tom Cobley and all are convinced it’s a fault and deactivate it. Then he screws the place.”

I wanted to reassure Dawn that it wasn’t her fault but guessed my words would be hollow and meaningless. Anyway, who was I to pass judgement?

“I’ll have a look in the burglary book later, when there’s no one in the CID office, see what was taken and more importantly whether there’s any mention of my fantastic advice. Of course, when I said that we’d keep an eye on the place I’d forgotten we’d been asked to take the bloody van out.”

Again, I said nothing. If the truth were known I was less concerned about the burglary and more worried about other events of the previous evening.

“Dawn, are we often told to dispose of dead bodies?”

I wasn’t sure but out of the corner of my eye, I thought I saw Dawn check her stride.

“I’m just asking, I need to understand. Don’t get worried, I haven’t, I wouldn’t say anything to anyone.”

“Before we have this chat, take your battery out of your radio,” she instructed.

I did as I was told and she also removed hers.

“Show me your battery.”

“Why are we doing this?” I said, as I held my battery up cupped in the palm of my hand.

"Because sometimes you get an open carrier on the radio and you transmit even though you're not depressing the transmit button and I don't want anyone to overhear the conversation we are about to have."

"Okay."

"The prisoner last night died in the police cell. No one had hurt him; he was just an old alcoholic. If the sergeant had, how shall I put it, formally dealt with the incident, you know called a doctor and all that, it would be what's called a death in custody. That's a very serious matter, even if no one's done anything wrong. The cell would be treated as a crime scene; A10 would be called out; anyone who had anything at all to do with the prisoner would be suspended from duty. It's such a load of shit; it's easier to deal with it like we did."

"A10?"

"Complaints, you know, they're the police that investigate the police."

"Does that happen every time someone dies in the cells? What if someone dies after they've had a kicking?"

"No, 'cos in a case like that I wouldn't get involved. In this job what you gotta decide is what you will do, and what you won't do. Draw your own line and stick to it. It's nothing like they teach you at Training School. It's nothing like Dixon of Dock Green. It's nothing like the Sweeney. This is a fantastic job but it's also really dangerous, and I don't mean in a physical way, although there's always that. Look, to make the job work you gotta be prepared to do things that are not completely kosher. If you did everything by the book, it just wouldn't work. And when you do these things, you gotta be smart about it, and back one another up. Bottom line is, no one's filming what we're doing so as long as we're smart and stick together it's ...

"A piece of cake."

I added hopefully but I'd misjudged the moment and Dawn reproached me swiftly. In all the months I worked with her it was the only time she ever raised her voice to me.

"This ain't a bloody joke, Chris."

"Sorry; I know, I understand," I assured her, suitably contrite.

"You'll make it, Chris. At first, I thought you were a total idiot, but I was wrong, you'll be okay, you might even be quite good. Have you got any questions? Because we're not having this conversation ever again."

"So, what if someone fits someone up with like a bag of cannabis, what then, do you back them up?"

I was, of course, thinking back to my first day at Stokey and my little chat with William.

"I've never fitted anyone up in my life and never would, so no. Remember what I said, you draw your own line in the sand and stick to it."

"But what about the pickpocket, wasn't she fitted up? You know when we said we'd seen her hand go into the old lady's bag?"

"That's not the same, Chris. She did the dipping and we just made sure she went down for it. When I talk about someone being fitted up, I mean they didn't do the crime in the first place. There's all the difference in the world between the two and between them is where I draw my line."

I understood, I really did.

"I get it."

"Do you?"

"Yes."

"Good; now put your battery back in and never mention last night again. As far as you and I are concerned, we never did anything. Understand?"

I clicked the battery home and nodded.

***

It was another miserable night. Few people were about, and Dawn and I tried hard but failed to find anyone to stop and search. By four in the morning, we'd both had enough, and Dawn had just suggested tea and bagels – there was a bagel shop in Dalston which opened really early – when the radio sprang to life.

"One eight two receiving, Golf November over?"

"Go ahead."

"Did you take a call to Blenheim House yesterday?"

"Yes, yes. Male suffering from harmless delusions."

"Well, he's suffering from them again; keeps hearing voices; can you attend?"

"Yes, yes."

"Tonight, Chris, we're getting to the bottom of this. He's got something he wants to tell us and we're going to be all ears," Dawn said.

Once again Mr Field was waiting for us when we got out of the lift; he looked tired and agitated. As we went into the lounge, I noticed a smell of cooking.

"Strange time to be making dinner, Mr Field," Dawn said.

"I'm not," he replied, looking confused.

"Well, what's that smell then?" she asked.

"I can't smell anything," Mr Field replied innocently.

"I can; it smells like meat, perhaps pork?" I said.

"What's the problem tonight, Mr Field?" Dawn asked.

"It's the voice again; I'm sure it's a child calling for help. When I get into bed and the house is perfectly quiet, I can hear the faintest voice shouting help, help."

"Put the kettle on, Mr Field, my colleague and I will have a cup of tea if that's all right?"

"Yes, of course."

He set off for the kitchen and as soon as he was out of sight, Dawn started looking about the room. She examined some utility bills that were on the coffee table, glanced quickly under the sofa and looked at some old photographs which were on the mantelpiece. She was still holding one when Mr Field reappeared with a tray and three very different mugs.

"I'm sorry about the cups; I haven't got two that match. I'm not used to having company."

"Who is this young boy?" Dawn asked.

"That's me. I was six and on holiday in Wales."

Mr Field put the three cups on the coffee table and sat in an armchair.

"Did you go to work today, Mr Field?" I asked, remembering Dawn's observations from the previous day.

"I did but honestly I shouldn't have bothered. I was half asleep and made loads of mistakes. My manager was getting really annoyed. In the end she let me go early."

"Mr Field, when did you last see a doctor?" Dawn asked.

"I knew it, I knew you'd think I was mad."

He slumped forward and put his head in his hands.

And then it happened.

"Help, help, help."

Dawn and I looked at one another aghast; Mr Field looked up, the expression on his face desperately asking whether we'd heard it too. Though I was tempted to pretend I hadn't, I couldn't be that cruel.

"Help."

The voice was very faint, very weak and it was high pitched, definitely a female or a child, and croaky.

"Where's it coming from?" Dawn said, standing up.

"I've no idea," I replied.

"Is it louder in here or the bedroom, Mr Field?"

He thought momentarily before replying.

"It's about the same in both rooms."

"Who lives next door?" Dawn asked.

"By the lift it's Mrs Fellows but I saw her this evening, she lives alone. On the other side of me are an Indian family but they're fine, I've seen them too."

"Help."

"I think it's coming from above. Who lives above you, Mr Field?" Dawn asked.

"No one, it's been empty for a year, most of the flats above are empty 'cos they evicted a load of squatters last month. I think only one flat is occupied, the one by the lift above Mrs Fellows."

"Who lives there?"

"Some bloke who's on his own I think. He's about my age. I don't know his name, but we walked up the stairs together the last time both the lifts were broken, but I'll swear that's not his voice."

We stood in silence for several minutes waiting for the next 'help' but the voice had gone quiet.

"Let's have a look upstairs, Chris, Mr Field, you can come too."

We used the stairs. The landing was exactly the same as the one below: four flats were off the central square, one in each corner; two had metal bars padlocked across them; apparently, these were where the squatters had been evicted. Dawn nodded towards the letterbox of the flat by the lift and I bent down and pushed the metal plate open. I was immediately hit by the strangest smell; something was definitely cooking, the lights inside were on and the place had definitely been lived in recently.

"What's that smell?" Dawn asked.

"I don't know, but I think someone's cooking. It's what we could smell downstairs," I replied.

"I couldn't smell it in my flat, but I can now," Mr Field said.

"Is someone there?" a feeble female voice asked from within.

"Are you okay?" I shouted.

"Help me, I can't move. Call the police," the voice pleaded desperately.

"Find out whether anyone else is in the flat," Dawn said.

"Is there anyone else in the flat?"

"Yes, no. I'm not sure. Please call the police."

"We are the police."

"Chris, put the door in," Dawn ordered.

Whenever I'd watched TV programmes, kicking a door in had seemed the easiest of activities: stand back, square up, bend knee, kick and pop, the door would fly open. I was about to discover, however, the reality was very, very different. I kicked and kicked, and when that failed, I shoulder charged several times until I was fairly certain I'd broken something in my upper arm.

"'Cos of the burglary problem, the council changed all the front doors last year, these are reinforced," Mr Field said, his information a little too late to be useful, I thought.

"I don't think I can open it, Dawn," I declared eventually.

"We'll have to get the fire brigade," I suggested.

"Perhaps, but first let me just try one thing."

Dawn walked over to the door, knelt down and opened the letterbox. I assumed she was going to explain the delay to the unseen occupier and ask if there was any way we could get in, but instead she reached in with her right hand and withdrew a string upon the end of which was a key. She allowed herself a little triumphant grin before slipping it into the lock and opening the door.

"Draw your truncheon, Chris."

The instruction surprised me, and I must unwittingly have expressed doubt about her instruction because Dawn said quite forcefully, even though I hadn't actually said anything, "One, because I told you and two, because we don't know what we're walking into here and whatever is happening it ain't a tea party."

I regretted even silently questioning Dawn, and for the first time in my police career withdrew my truncheon.

"After you, Chris; Mr Field, wait here please," Dawn said.

The smell in the flat was intense, strangely familiar but quite unpleasant.

"Where are you?" I called several times, but the voice had stopped.

We checked the kitchen, empty, and interestingly nothing was cooking in the oven. We checked the lounge, which was untidy.

"A bloke lives here alone," Dawn said, almost to herself.

Then the bathroom, yuk; toilet, yuk yuk; and finally, the last room, which must by elimination be the bedroom. The door was closed. I turned the handle and standing back pushed the door open with the end of my truncheon, I was fearful what secret the room might be hiding. I was right to be.

Chapter 42 – Superman, Part 2

In years to come, when I told the Superman story those listening would laugh but in reality, there was nothing amusing in the tragedy which had occurred.

The occupier, Michael Cooper, was a fifty-four-year-old bachelor who'd decided, before life passed him by completely, he would fulfil a burning sexual fantasy. He wanted to be a superhero, to save a maiden in distress and for her then to show her gratitude by having sex with her saviour.

Mr Cooper found his maiden advertising her services in a newsagent's window and as far as Candy was concerned, she'd been asked to do a lot worse. He hired his costume from a Fancy Dress shop, telling the shop assistant it was for a party.

He'd planned everything down to the finest detail and purchased rope from a hardware store and even taken out and studied a library book on knots. When the evening came and Candy arrived, she was, save for about fifteen additional years, everything he'd dreamed she would be. They'd discussed his fantasy over the telephone when he had made the appointment, so Candy knew what to expect and charged him a little extra because she could. Candy undressed completely and was blindfolded and tied firmly to the bed. It was a surprisingly cold summer evening, so she asked her client to put some heating on. He left the room and returned a few moments later with an electric bar heater, which he plugged in and turned on. He wasn't in costume at this stage and retired to change in the living room.

When ten minutes later, as prearranged, Candy cried desperately for help, Superman came bounding into the bedroom to save her. He jumped up onto a carefully placed chair from which he leapt across the room towards the bed. Only his head struck the ceiling with considerable force and he went immediately unconscious, which in itself wouldn't have been too great a problem had his head not caught the side of the bed as he fell to the floor. Mr Cooper's neck snapped like a twig underfoot and the superhero was dead before he came to rest at the side of the bed and some eighteen inches from the heater. Candy heard two quick bangs and felt the bed vibrate with the second, but she was unable to see what had happened because of the blindfold. She wasn't sure what was going on and whether or not this was all somehow part of the fantasy. For a minute or two she said nothing. Then she called tentatively, "Mike, are you all right?"

She was soon trying to extricate herself from the bed, but the ropes around her wrist tightened the more she pulled. Within twenty minutes panic had set in but it was to no avail, she was completely and utterly stuck. She assumed Mike had been knocked out and would eventually come to but when several hours had gone by, she started to fear the worst and thought he must have had a heart attack or something. Every so often, she called for help but after a while, started to lose her voice. Then her hands started to hurt like hell, it was almost as if they were burning. They were being held slightly suspended and the ropes were painfully tight; she feared blood was being cut off.

After what felt like a week, in reality it was only a day, she became aware of a strange smell in the room, like someone was roasting meat. Then she remembered the heater and guessed quite correctly her deceased client was slowly cooking. She soiled herself several times and fell in and out of consciousness. She still called out occasionally, but she was losing the will to live and had started to want to die to put an end to this hell. At one stage, during a dream which was so very real, all her family and friends came one by one to say goodbye.

When Dawn and I entered the room, our senses were momentarily overwhelmed. A naked white woman was tied to a bed, her hands viciously swollen and a deep purple colour. She was lying in her own excrement; she was perfectly still and, if we'd not heard her voice only a few minutes earlier, both of us would have assumed she was dead. On the floor by the bed, was a man wearing a Superman outfit; one of his legs was near an electric heater, the heat from which had burnt through the costume and turned his calf a deep brown. The man's head was at a very unnatural angle and no medical expert was needed to diagnose a broken neck.

I went quickly to the kitchen and returned with a sharp knife, but when I went to cut the woman's hands free, Dawn shouted, "Don't!"

"Why?"

"Don't, we need to get an ambulance. You've got to leave them like that; it's something to do with septicaemia."

"What's that?"

"Blood poisoning. The bad blood from her hands will go to her heart and brain, it's very dangerous. You must leave her, Chris."

"Disconnect the fire and put it somewhere safe. Check the male's pulse, just to make sure he's dead."

"Golf November active, over?"

"One eight two, go ahead."

"Two four, twenty-four, Blenheim House. I require an ambulance for a female, early forties, with severe ligature injuries. Then I need the

Divisional Surgeon, the Duty Officer, a photog and CID in that order please, as I also have a sudden death."

"Received."

"One eight two, Golf November one?"

"Go ahead, Sir."

"What on earth have you got there?"

Dawn paused for a moment, gathering her thoughts.

"I suspect we've found the missing prostitute that was mentioned on parade yesterday. Oh, and we've also got a dead Superman, he's been slow cooking for several days, who died during a valiant attempt to rescue her."

"One eight two, have you been drinking?"

"Not yet, Sir, but I'm going to need a few later to get this scene out of my head," she replied.

Chapter 43 – Radioactivity

When I got home that morning it was nearly ten o'clock. I exchanged pleasantries with Debbie as we passed on the stairs.

"When I've not got to get some sleep, I'll tell you a tale about the dangers of your profession," I said, through a tired smile.

"Why, what's happened?"

"Really, I need to get to bed, I'll tell you later."

"You working this weekend?" Debbie asked.

"My last night duty is Saturday."

"Do you fancy a day out? Shall we go down to Brighton on Sunday?"

"Yeah, okay," I replied.

"I'll pick you up about twelve, I'll do a picnic," Debbie said.

"Yeah, that'll be nice."

As I climbed into bed, I briefly wondered whether the job would have a problem with me going out for the day with a prostitute. The solution seemed fairly obvious: don't tell them.

***

The fourth of the seven nights was quiet and unremarkable until about four when Dawn and I were called into the nick with the curious and specific instruction for me to see the Station Officer, Sergeant Rose, alone.

"Have I done something wrong?" I asked Dawn.

"No, you haven't, Chris, don't worry about it, it's probably nothing."

Sergeant Rose took me into a small interview room adjoining the front office. He looked serious, really serious, and I thought I must have made some catastrophic mistake, so I was mightily relieved to hear him tell me, "Listen son, there's been a serious radiation leak at a nuclear plant in

Oxford. They've contacted all the police stations in the Met and they're asking us to collect samples of water from the Thames. I'm giving you this responsibility. The first sample, called sample GN/1, should be taken from the water next to the bank, but the second, GN/2, from the middle of the river. You'll need to exhibit each sample so take some bags with you and use the urine jars from the drink drive kits in the Divisional Surgeon's room as they're sterile. Dave will take you there in the van but no one else is to know, and that includes PC Matthews, as the last thing we need is news of this leaking into the press."

"Yes, Sarge."

The pun went completely over my head at the time as I was too busy trying to work out how the Devil I was going to collect a sample of water from the middle of the Thames?

The question as to how was on the tip of my tongue when the sergeant turned on his heel and walked out and back into the front office where the presence of others meant the subject could be discussed no more.

Dawn had disappeared, which relieved me as she would have been certain to ask me what was going on. Having collected the necessary equipment, two plastic tubs with screw-on lids, and still somewhat perplexed, I wandered into the back yard where Dave the van driver, a cheerful Brummie in his mid-twenties and who I'd learnt from an earlier conversation was already a father of four, was waiting with the engine ticking over. I climbed into the front passenger seat.

"Hi, Dave, you okay?"

"Yes, Nostrils, I'm fine. Can't believe this has happened again."

"Have there been other leaks?"

"Apparently, it happens several times a year; I can definitely remember doing this last year."

"You're joking?" I replied, amazed that news about a radioactive leak had never got out before.

We drove quickly through empty streets on a blue light, the absence of cars making the bell unnecessary, and into an area of London with which I was unfamiliar; well, that is to say, any area of London which wasn't the London Borough of Hackney. After about twenty minutes I asked Dave where we were.

"Near the Rotherhithe Tunnel, mate," he replied, as we drove into a park adjoining the Thames.

Dave stopped the van at the top of an old disused slipway which led down to the river, or what would have been the river had the tide not been out. The van's headlights illuminated twenty-five yards of mud.

"You'll find gloves in the back."

"Gloves?"

"Listen, Nostrils, you're taking samples of radioactive water; even the Met wouldn't expect you to do that without some protection."

I opened the rear door and returned seconds later wearing a ridiculously long pair of thick, bright, luminous yellow rubber gloves which reached up the entire length of my arms. I picked up one of the small glass sample bottles and set off to save London from a nuclear disaster. With every step my boots sank slightly deeper into the mud. When I guessed I was about halfway, my left foot disappeared completely before, in a moment of panic, I pulled it quickly out. Mud almost up to my knee. And it stank too. As I neared the water, I found slightly firmer footing on gravel and quickly scooped up the sample and carefully replaced the lid; I didn't want to lose the sample if I dropped it so I pushed the jar deep into my trouser pocket. I decided to return by the same route: although I knew the going was hard, that path was illuminated by the van's headlights and at least I could be confident the mud could take my weight. Or so I thought. At one stage both my feet sunk rapidly, and my descent only stopped when the mud had come up to my shins; I was genuinely scared I would get stuck. When I eventually stumbled up the slipway, I was covered in mud which filled both my boots to squelching point and caked my trousers and lower jacket. I was in an utter mess but I had my sample. I wondered whether Dave would be impressed, but all he said when I slid the passenger door back was a curt "You're not getting in my van like that. Get in the back."

"But I've got to get a second sample from the middle of the river."

"They've never wanted a second sample before, are you sure?" he asked.

"Yeah, that's what Sergeant Rose said."

"And how are you going to do that?" Dave asked curiously.

"I've no fucking idea. Is there a bridge near here?" I asked, with some vague concept of dangling the second urine jar by a string over the side of the bridge.

"Listen, Nostrils, if I were you, I'd go and get another sample and just tell them it's from the middle; after all, the river is so low there can't be much difference between the side and the middle."

I thought Dave had a point. I liked the idea of completing the task but didn't relish a second foray into the stinking disgusting Thames mud. Why, oh why, hadn't I thought of this before I'd set off the first time? I should have got two samples whilst I was out there. And so, once again illuminated by the van's headlights, I set off to collect the second sample. When I returned to the van for a second time, I'd lost one boot and all my dignity to the river.

When we got back to the nick Dave told me to remain in the rear of the van to wait testing and clearance.

"What testing? What clearance?" I asked.

"It's nothing to worry about, Nostrils, just wait here."

All I wanted to do was peel out of my uniform, have a warm shower and go home. Now I had to wait in the rear of the van for testing, whatever that meant.

Some thirty minutes later the rear doors opened and someone, I assumed it was Sergeant Rose, although I couldn't be sure, pointed a small spherical object attached to a wire at me. I heard a series of fast clicks and then several expletives from the sergeant; it was Sergeant Rose, I recognised his dulcet tones.

"Listen, son, the Geiger counter reading's not good; you'll have to go to the London for a thorough check-up. They've got an isolation ward there."

"What do you mean the readings not good, Sarge?" I said, trying not to sound worried but actually quite petrified.

"Nothing to worry about, son, it's just, well, there's a safe level and you're a little high."

"What's the safe level?"

"Anything under twenty's fine."

"What am I?"

"Three hundred and forty-two."

Sergeant Rose slammed the door shut. I felt gripped by panic and started breathing heavily and rubbing my hands backwards and forwards across my head before I realised I was rubbing mud into my hair.

A good thirty minutes later, and it felt a lot longer, Dave climbed into the front of the van and turned around; I was sitting at the front end of the bench.

"Where the fuck have you been, Dave, I've got to go up the London. It sounds fucking serious."

"Sorry, mate, I was having a game of snooker, took us ages 'cos neither Mike nor I could pot a thing."

Great, I thought, so glad it was important.

"Mate, sit at the back by the door will you, I don't want you anywhere near me, Sarge told me that your reading was lethally high."

"Lethally?" I said nervously.

I moved back.

"Dave, when you've done this before, were anyone else's readings high?" I asked, hoping to find some assurance in his answer.

"Oh yeah, and they checked out okay. Honestly, Nostrils, don't worry, you'll be fine. Sarge says he'll phone ahead and tell them you're coming."

"Great," I replied, meaning anything but that.

"So, tell me about the others."

"What others? I can't really hear you, mate," Dave said.

Having a conversation between either end of the van wasn't particularly easy but I desperately needed to know.

"The other ones who took the samples, what were their readings?"

"I've only done this once, Nostrils, and the last time must have been a year ago, I can't really remember."

"Well try," I implored him.

"Well, it was Knocker, he's been IDT'd to Fulham. He did it last time."

"And?"

"Oh, he's fine, just got married, some of the relief went to his wedding a few months ago. I didn't get an invite."

"And what was his reading, Dave? Please try and remember."

"Oh, I remember 'cos it made us laugh."

"Yes?"

"Sixty-nine, his reading was sixty-nine. Well bugger me, Nostrils, who'd have thought I would have remembered that?"

That didn't make me feel any better, as I was at least six times higher than this Knocker chap.

As we drove through now slightly busier streets, it was nearly five o'clock; several of night duty called up to wish me well, I'm sure it was a nice gesture, but it made me even more worried.

"Four six six receiving over?"

"Go ahead," I replied.

"Good luck, mate, we're all thinking about you."

"Thanks," I replied, sounding positively heroic.

We pulled up in an area outside Casualty usually exclusively reserved for ambulances.

"Wait here," Dave said and then he jumped out and disappeared into the hospital.

Several minutes later, through the front window I saw Dave walking back towards the van; next to him was a very attractive nurse whose serious expression only heightened my anxiety. She was carrying something in her right hand and a clipboard in her left. She went momentarily out of sight and then the rear doors opened; she was now wearing a face mask and surgical gloves.

"I understand you may have been exposed to radiation," she said through her mask in a very businesslike manner.

"Yes," I replied.

"I need you to provide two samples for testing, the first urine, in here please."

She handed me a glass cup.

"The second, semen, in here please."

She handed me a test tube.

"Semen?" I asked, not sure whether I'd heard her correctly.

"Yes. Radiation kills sperm, that's why exposure can make men infertile. We'll be able to assess your exposure by undertaking a simple sperm count; it's the easiest and quickest way."

I'd heard something similar previously, so the test seemed a logical one.

"When the results are in, we'll know whether to take you straight to the isolation ward or if we can admit you through the usual process."

The van doors closed abruptly.

"Do you want me to turn the light on?" Dave said helpfully.

"Yes please, and then can you fuck off for twenty minutes? This is not my idea of fun."

"No problem, mate."

With the light in the rear of the van on, I looked at myself. I was in a right state, covered head to toe in wet, smelly and very probably radioactive mud. To cap it all, I now had to piss in a jar, not a great problem but difficult when not in a toilet, and then masturbate into a little tube whilst sitting in the rear of a police van. I really wasn't in the right mood.

I stood up for the first task but for the second I had to lower my trousers and pants. Having tried unsuccessfully to produce the sample of sperm whilst sitting upright on the bench, I decided to lay flat on the cold metal floor. Just as I got going, both rear doors opened, and several bright flashes blinded me. I blinked. When my eyesight cleared, I saw the entire night duty relief standing there watching a mud-drenched, uniform constable with his trousers and pants around his knees, one boot missing, playing with his penis in the rear of a police van. There were howls of laughter, cheers and clapping. Several nurses were also there, including the attractive blonde who had donned the face mask and given me my instructions.

I made no attempt to cover myself up, what was the point? I just lay back and resigned myself to the embarrassment. In all honesty, I was just relieved it was a wind up.

Chapter 44 – A pub visit and a fire extinguisher

As we set out on patrol the following evening, Dawn explained to me that new probationers were always subject to a wind up of some kind and that I should view the experience as a kind of initiation ceremony.

"You took it in good spirits though, Chris, that's important."

"I'll be honest, Dawn, after a moment of embarrassment; I was just pleased it was all a joke."

"When you were collecting your samples from the Thames, the entire night duty were lined up along the bank of the Thames watching you."

"Did that include you?" I asked, because I was fairly certain she wasn't in the crowd at the hospital.

"Yes, but I didn't go to the hospital. I thought you might appreciate my absence as we're working so closely together."

"Thanks."

"If you're a new WPC they hold you down, bend you over the desk in the Station Office, pull your skirt up and ink your bottom with the station stamp."

"You're kidding me?"

"I'm not."

"Did that happen to you?"

"Oh yes."

"I'm not sure having your arse stamped is more embarrassing than wanking in front of an entire relief."

Dawn considered for a moment.

"Now I think about it, you might be right. They came unstuck when they tried to station stamp Tommy; she put two of them in hospital."

"You're kidding?"

"I'm not. She broke one guy's wrist and kneed the other so hard in his groin he fainted from the pain."

"What is it about her, Dawn? How come she is so tough?" I asked.

"Tommy? She was the European judo champion in the late seventies. She's a top instructor now."

So that, I thought, was her secret.

"She's as prone as anyone to a knife in the back or a bullet, but if she lays her hands on someone, no matter how big and hard they think they are, they're going down. There's a good lesson there, Chris: never judge a book by its cover."

I nodded thoughtfully.

"You know Dean?"

"The old van driver on A relief?" I asked.

"No, Dean as in Dean and Jessica," Dawn explained.

"What about him?"

"He's like six foot six and twenty stone, right?"

"Yeah."

"Rumour has it that last year he bottled it when a guy off his relief was getting a hiding, you know, walked the other way pretending he hadn't seen what was going on."

Somehow that didn't surprise me.

"That would never happen with a WPC 'cos they'd want to prove themselves. A WPC will always get stuck in when the chips are down."

I didn't doubt Dawn, but my mind wandered back to my first day on patrol with her and I realised how much my attitude had already changed.

The pair of us were once again asked to cover the van from two o'clock. Dawn was determined to use the first four hours, when we were on foot, to find someone to stop and search, but it was a quiet Thursday night and just after midnight light rain started to fall. The radio, too, was quiet, with very few calls coming out and those that did went to the mobile units. All we'd done in nearly three hours was report a stolen Ford Capri.

Several times during that evening our High Street patrol had taken us by the front of the Three Horseshoes public house and at just after eleven, we'd noticed the lights had been switched off and the doors locked. At about quarter to one, we found ourselves in an alleyway at the rear of this pub and the landlord was putting out a crate of empty bottles.

"Good evening, officers," he said in a soft Irish twang.

"Good evening," we replied in unison.

"Would you like a swift half or perhaps a wee Irish coffee to help you through the night?" he asked, through a wide friendly smile.

As usual, I said nothing and waited for Dawn to politely decline, so I was surprised when she agreed.

"An Irish coffee would be just the thing, thank you, landlord."

The landlord tilted his head towards the back door which he then entered and held open, waiting for us. We followed and walked through a small, untidy kitchen and emerged into the bar. All the lights were off, the juke box and fruit machine had been unplugged and the doors were bolted but the Three Horseshoes public house was heaving with two rooms full of customers. As we entered, silence immediately descended and every eye fell upon us. From the looks on their faces, the customers believed the pub was being raided and they'd all been caught drinking after hours. I felt even more embarrassed than I had the previous night outside the hospital. I knew we were completely compromised. We couldn't do anything about the after-hours drinking as we'd agreed to accept free alcohol from the landlord, which incidentally, Dawn told me later, was a specific criminal offence under the Licensing Act.

"So that's one Irish coffee and a pint of bitter for you, young man," the landlord announced, in a loud enough voice to dispel the customers' fears.

In that instant, the tension in the room evaporated and everyone resumed their interrupted conversations as if we weren't there.

I still felt really awkward, and it didn't help me that even Dawn, who was always so cool, so collected, so in control, looked uneasy. Fortunately, she knew how to manipulate the position we'd found ourselves in.

"Whilst we're here, is there anything you can tell us which might be useful fighting crime?"

The landlord thought for a few moments then glanced to either side conspiratorially and leaned across the bar.

"An Irish fella was in here earlier with a large wad on the hip, his name's Danny something," he said quietly.

"Can you tell me anything else about him, that's pretty vague?" Dawn asked.

"He's always up on the Heatherside estate although I don't think he lives there. Oh, and he drives a beat-up old green Mini one two five; oh yeah, from what he was saying, he was in Wandsworth last Christmas."

"Thanks," Dawn said.

"But if anyone asks, I never told you a thing, officer."

Dawn winked.

Two hours after closing time, the landlord continued to serve other customers whilst we, two police officers in full uniform, stood at the bar drinking. It really wasn't right. We drank up quickly and left.

As we walked off Dawn said, "That was embarrassing. Never saw that coming. I thought the place was bloody empty."

"Me too," I replied.

"Useful information about the Irish geezer though. We'll have a punt up to Heatherside when we get the van later, see if we can find the green Mini and identify the driver. More importantly, Chris, we've covered ourselves; we've got a decent piece of criminal intelligence which will justify our visit to a licensed premises should anyone say anything."

Once again, I was impressed with my mentor; she was shrewd, so very smart.

"Dawn, Wandsworth is in south London, right? One of my class went there from Training School."

"Yes, why do you ask?"

"Why would this bloke with the green Mini go to Wandsworth for Christmas? Perhaps he has relatives who live there?"

***

After refs, Dawn showed me how to submit the information we'd had received in the Three Horseshoes to the Collator and told me to familiarise myself me with a list of London prisons, explaining that when the landlord said this Danny had 'been in Wandsworth', he'd meant he'd been serving a term of imprisonment in Wandsworth prison, not visiting relatives in a south London borough. Dawn then wandered off to do some paperwork and I waited for her in the front office chatting to the Reserve, an affable chap called Fitz who was several years my senior and an ex-submariner. I appreciated the fact he'd gone out of his way all week to make me feel welcome. The radio, which had been silent for ages, suddenly sprang to life.

"Chasing vehicle failing to stop for police Haslett Road east towards Shepperton Lane. Alpha Charlie Romeo three two four Tango."

I identified the index immediately; it was the Ford Capri which Dawn and I had earlier reported stolen. Fitz moved quickly over to the PNC terminal at the rear of the front office. As he did so he called over to me, "Tell him I'll do a PNC."

"No need, Fitz, it's a lost or stolen Ford Capri 2.8. I've only just reported it."

"I can't keep up, any units assist, Shepperton Lane, Shepperton Lane," the voice said urgently.

"He won't stand a chance, he's only in a Metro," Fitz commented.

"Tell him its lost or stolen, Nostrils," Fitz shouted at me.

"From four six six, that vehicle is a recent lost or stolen, I repeat lost or stolen," I said.

I heard sirens from the back yard and knew several of the relief were on their way to assist. I could have run and tried to jump into the rear of one of the vehicles but I was conscious Dawn wouldn't approve if I went off without her. Since my unlawful arrest of the disqualified driver, she didn't like to let me out of her sight. So instead, I elected to remain in the Station Office and listen to the unfolding drama on the radio.

"It's a loss, I repeat a loss, Victoria Avenue," the driver of the Metro declared.

"That was short and sweet," Fitz remarked.

Minutes ticked by as other police cars joined the search. Just as I was about to go to find Dawn the radio snapped to life again.

"Golf November, two eight four, the white Capri's north at speed in the High Street towards Golf November."

Fitz sprang to his feet, picked up the large red fire extinguisher which was holding the Station Office door open, jumped over the front counter and ran down the front steps. I followed. Several innocent vehicles passed and then the white Capri came into sight, travelling at speed. Fitz stepped marginally into the road and lifted the extinguisher with two hands above his head preparing to launch it at the speeding car. I'd been at a loss to work out why he'd picked it up in the first place, but now I knew.

I could see this all going terribly wrong but I'd neither the strength of character nor wherewithal to prevent it; I was just a spectator.

When the Capri was only yards away, Fitz launched his intercept extinguisher. The red cylinder flew several feet over the Capri's black roof and landed with a crunch on the bonnet of a parked and unattended red Jaguar XJ6; it bounced once and slammed into the middle of the windscreen which instantly shattered. It went up and across the roof and down the boot, where it gathered momentum before falling to the pavement and gently rolling across to come to rest in a newsagent's shop doorway. Then, with a violent hiss the fire extinguisher discharged its foam contents. By the time the cylinder was empty, the stolen Capri was a mile away.

"Shit," Fitz said.

I stood aghast.

Seconds ticked by, somewhere a dog barked and to cap it all the burglar alarm in the newsagent went off.

And then an armada of police cars raced past us in desperate pursuit of the stolen car. I watched as perhaps ten, maybe fifteen police vehicles of all shapes and sizes sped by; several Rovers led the way followed by, in no particular order, three police vans, at least two Austin Metros, perhaps three Allegros, a dog van and two traffic motorcyclists. I was vaguely aware of a female voice on my radio, the operator on channel one, asking,

"Can a unit confirm there are only three police vehicles chasing, all other vehicles are to withdraw."

"Only three, that's correct," a dishonest voice said.

"Shit," Fitz repeated.

Now it was safe to do so, I walked across the road to inspect the damage. The Jaguar, brand spanking new and on an A plate, was a complete mess. The bonnet, roof and boot were all dented and scratched, and the front windscreen was smashed in.

"Shit," Fitz said.

I gathered myself. The Capri had once again been lost, which afforded me a brief opportunity to call up for a vehicle check.

"Golf November, four six six, is there anyone in the front office who can do a quick vehicle check please?"

"Four six six go ahead," Dawn said; she'd obviously made her way there.

"Alpha two three two Yankee Hotel Hotel."

"Four six six, you should have a red Jaguar XJ6, no reports."

"Can I have the owner's details please?"

"Yes, yes. Peter Terence Adams, 19 Staples Road, Loughton, Essex."

"Thanks, all received, out."

Then unexpectedly, the Duty Officer called me.

"Four six six receiving, Golf November one?"

"Go ahead, Sir."

"Are you free to speak?"

"Yes, yes; go ahead."

"If you've stopped the vehicle you've just done the PNC check on, you ought to be aware that Peter Adams is our new Superintendent."

"Shit," Fitz said.

Chapter 45 – Christopher in the charge room

Our last night duty looked like being the quietest of the week. Although it was a Saturday night, it was tipping down and the people of Stoke Newington had apparently decided not to venture out. We were walking along a side road which ran parallel to the High Street when Dawn first mentioned the events of the previous night.

"The repair's going to cost two grand."

I didn't have to ask what repair.

"The Superintendent doesn't believe a word of it. He's ordered an audit of all the fire extinguishers in the nick."

That didn't worry me too much. Soon after the event someone had been dispatched to surreptitiously acquire a replacement from another police station.

"That's what happened, Dawn," I said stoically.

"You're telling me the driver of the Ford Capri threw a fire extinguisher out of his window at you and Fitz as he was driving past the nick?" she asked incredulously.

"That's what happened, Dawn."

"Good job the driver was never traced, isn't it?"

I said nothing but I'd been very relieved to learn the Capri had earlier been found abandoned, ironically undamaged, in Chelmsford and that the thief was long gone.

"I know it wasn't you, it was Fitz, he's got a reputation as a bit of a nutcase."

I said nothing.

"Come on, Chris, tell us what really happened. I know Fitz tried to stop the stolen Capri by chucking the fire extinguisher from the front office at it. And do you know how I know?"

I shrugged my shoulders.

"Because when I heard your voice on the radio confirming it was a lost or stolen, I made my way to the front office, which was deserted. But when I entered, I had to open the door, and in the five years I've been at this nick, I've never had to open the door between the main corridor and the front office. And do you know why I've never had to open that door? Because it's always propped open by a fire extinguisher. In fact, I didn't even realise there was a door there."

"I've made my statement, I supported Fitz and that's all there is to say, Dawn."

"I must confess, because you're so young in service you have a little bit more believability than an old stick would. Anyway, just so you know ..." She paused, waiting for me to ask.

"What?"

"You did the right thing, earned yourself just a smidgen of credibility."

"With Fitz?"

"With Fitz and the rest of night duty."

"And me," she added after a further pause.

***

At about three in the morning Dawn and I were drying out in the CID office, which was otherwise deserted. It had poured all night and we were just about as wet as it was possible to get.

"Any Golf November unit available to assist in the charge room with the search of a violent prisoner?"

Dawn nodded towards the radio sitting on my lapel.

"Four six six and one eight two; two minutes."

"Thank you, Nostrils."

It was Fitz's voice.

We made our way quickly to the charge room but well before we got there, we could hear the commotion.

"I'll fucking kill you, take these cuffs off, they're FUCKING breaking my arms, cunts, cunts, CUNTS!"

Inside, the small stout Scottish Station Sergeant was standing over a topless white man, probably in his mid-twenties, who was shouting and cursing. He was on his side in a corner of the room facing the wall, partially under the bench the prisoners sat on when they were waiting to be processed. The sergeant's right boot was applying considerable pressure to the man's back to make sure he stayed there until sufficient reinforcements arrived. Several free-standing chairs were on their sides suggesting there had been a considerable struggle.

"We got the handcuffs on but it was a bit of a battle. He'd just bitten Fitz, who's cleaning himself up," the sergeant said, in his strong Glaswegian accent.

"What's he in for, Sarge?" Dawn asked, having to shout above the man's continuing protests.

"Violent behaviour in a police station. He's not making a lot of sense but it would appear he's just discovered his missus is having an affair with a police officer, but from the look in his eyes he's high as a kite on a blustery day."

"CUNTS."

The man was screaming; when he wasn't screaming, he was panting frantically.

"He must be hyperventilating," Dawn said.

"Good, with any luck he'll pass out and we can get him in the cell," the sergeant replied.

Fitz returned; his right hand was wrapped in a tea towel.

"Fucking bastard's bitten right through the skin."

"CUNTS, fucking CUNTS, fuck my wife you bastards, I'll fucking kill you CUNTS!"

The man was still struggling but he was very effectively wedged in.

"I think he's off his head, his eyes are really bloodshot, and his pupils are really dilated," Fitz said.

"CUNTS, fucking CUNTS, I'll fucking bite anyone that comes anywhere near me."

"I don'ae think four's going to be enough," the sergeant said, affecting a stronger than usual Scottish accent.

"Oh, it will be, just tell me where you want him and leave the transportation issue to me," Fitz said, with more than a hint of revenge in his voice.

"In that case, Fitz, cell one if you please."

"Allow me," Fitz said.

He unwound the tea towel and dropped it to the floor; with two hands he took hold of the prisoner's brown hair at the back of his head.

"I'll teach you to fucking bite me; take your foot off his back, Sarge."

As soon as the sergeant stepped back, Fitz yanked the prisoner violently by the hair and his head jerked upwards and backwards. Then Fitz tugged again and walked quickly backwards. The prisoner was dragged out from under the bench, across the charge room floor, along the corridor and into cell one. Every inch of the way he screamed as if his arm was being hacked off with a machete. Whilst being pulled along by one's hair wouldn't be comfortable, I thought the man was seriously overreacting. In fact, I admired Fitz's restraint as he could have very easily have given the prisoner a damn good kicking. The sergeant, Dawn and I followed.

The bed was along the left wall of the cell, at the far end of which was the toilet. Fitz had taken the prisoner to the far-right-hand corner.

"Keep hold of his head whilst we strip search him," the sergeant instructed Fitz.

"You," the sergeant said to me, "lie across him, pin his legs down to stop him from thrashing about too much."

I did as I was told whilst Dawn and the sergeant stripped him of his jeans, socks, pants and shoes until he was completely naked. As each article of clothing was removed it was searched and then literally thrown out of the cell into the corridor. In the pocket of his jeans was a clear plastic bag which contained several white pills. The man continued to struggle and shout but gradually he tired and his strength ebbed.

"Get ready to take his cuffs off," the sergeant mouthed.

I was vaguely aware there was a special procedure for doing this but as I'd never practised it, I hoped to get clear instructions.

"Young lad, you can be the last on him; when I've got the cuffs off, get out before he has time to get up."

The prisoner was put on his side facing away from the door. I put all my weight between his shoulder blades whilst the sergeant, with a key supplied by Dawn, leaned over and unlocked each cuff. Fitz held the man's wrists tightly so that even with the cuffs off, he couldn't move. Then it happened very quickly: Dawn was out first, then the sergeant was off and away, then Fitz; then, as soon as possible, I got to my feet, stepped away from the man in one deft movement and backed quickly towards the door, but when I saw the man was making no attempt to get up, I slowed down, not wanting it to appear that I was running away.

The prisoner rolled onto his side and for the first time I got a proper look at his face and knew instantly why the sergeant thought he had taken drugs. His eyes were so bloodshot the white was red and his pupils were huge.

From behind me someone threw a white all-in-one disposable suit into the cell; it landed on the bed. The prisoner spoke between pants.

"Your mother sucks big black cocks."

From nowhere, an image of mum lying on her hospital bed flashed across my mind, her body and arms punctured by needles from which tubes led to bags which surrounded her. Her head was turned to one side and despite all the pain, she was smiling at me like only a mother can. Her skin had turned yellow, and she was really thin, but her deep blue eyes emanated love.

"What did you say?" I whispered.

The man smiled. He knew he'd hit a nerve.

"You heard. Your whoring bitch mother sucks big black cocks and swallows their cum."

Something somewhere took control of my body. I was aware that I was no longer walking away from the prisoner; but rather moving towards him. A hint of fear showed in the man's face before he quickly curled into the foetal position and wrapped his arms around his head. Not effectively enough, I thought, as I could still see a small area of his head visible above his ear. I clenched my right hand into a fist and drove it down hard. The contact was excellent and made a satisfying sound which I appreciated with a detached objectivity. I punched a second time, harder, but the blow was less accurate and glanced off the man's arm. The third was a solid, gratifying strike and the man's head cracked with a thud against the cold cell floor. I was vaguely aware that the prisoner's body had gone limp and his arms had dropped from around his head. The fourth punch was going to be much easier but as I drew my arm back, other arms pulled me backwards, away from the prisoner and out of the cell.

Three voices spoke at once.

"Alright, mate, calm down," the sergeant said.

"Chris, Chris, Chris," Dawn said.

"Nice one," Fitz said.

"Go and sit on the bench," the sergeant ordered. "Dawn, get him a glass of water."

"Yes, Sarge," she replied.

"Fitz, call the Divisional Surgeon to examine two officers and a prisoner."

"Yes, Sarge," he replied.

I was shaking, really shaking, but mentally felt a serene detachment from what had just happened. Dawn put a polystyrene cup of water on the bench next to me.

"Thanks."

As my breathing slowed and the adrenalin rush subsided, a sense of almost overwhelming grief crept into my consciousness and I closed my eyes to better see my mum's face. Oh, how I wanted to see her and be with her again.

"You can come back now 'cos God, I really miss you."

"Sorry?" Dawn said.

She must have thought I was talking to her.

"Dawn, can I have a word?" the sergeant asked.

"Yes, Sarge."

I vaguely wondered how much trouble I was in. Would I lose my job? Would I be arrested? So what? My mum would never know, so did it really matter? How dare that bastard speak about my mum like that? I could feel anger again and was aware my breathing was increasing and then I thought, if I'm going to get nicked for assault, I might as well make it worthwhile.

I looked up; Dawn and the sergeant were in the fingerprint room, obviously discussing what had just happened. The cell keys were on the desk, Fitz was back in the Station Office calling the doctor.

Right, you bastard. I stood up, gathered the keys and deliberately wrapped my fingers around them to dampen any jangling. As I walked by the fingerprint room, I ducked under the small square window and then turned right and down the cell passage. At the cell door I flicked the catch, dropped the metal wicket down and looked inside. The prisoner was lying on the floor exactly where he'd been when I'd been dragged off; he hadn't moved an inch. The light in the cell was dim so I waited for my eyes to adjust and then watched carefully to see whether the prisoner was breathing. He was. I looked through the fifteen or so keys to select the right one for this lock and as I did, heard Dawn and the sergeant emerge from the fingerprint room. I peered at the prisoner again; my desire to inflict more violence was waning. I stopped searching for the key, closed the wicket and walked back to the charge room. As I entered the Charge Room the sergeant looked at my right hand.

"Oh, there they are," he said.

"Sorry?"

"The cell keys. I was looking for them."

I handed them over and the sergeant clipped them to his belt.

Dawn came in from the Station Office.

"Oh, there you are. Where did you go? I was looking for you."

I ignored the question.

"Chris, are you all right?" Dawn asked.

I didn't know what to say.

"Sarge wants a quick word with you."

"Sarge?" I said, slowly becoming more aware of what was going on.

"Nostrils, come here."

The sergeant walked off into the fingerprint room.

This is it, I thought; this is where I get told my fate.

As I entered the small room, the sergeant closed the door behind him.

"Look what you've done to your shoe," he said, looking down.

Automatically, I followed his gaze.

Thud.

"What the fuck?" I said, completely gobsmacked: the sergeant's head-butt had landed squarely in the middle of my face.

***

At half past six Dawn and I were sitting at a small table in the corner of the saloon bar in a packed early house. The bar was full of Smithfield market workers at the end of their day.

"When I heard what the prisoner said, I thought it might hit a nerve."

"Just a little," I replied.

"I must say you pack a decent punch; how's your hand?"

"Never mind my bloody hand, look at my nose."

Dawn tried but failed to conceal a giggle.

"Don't bloody laugh, it's crooked," I said, feeling my nose for the hundredth time.

"We make a fine pair; mine's been wonky since that burglar head-butted me."

"Rubbish, yours is perfectly straight. The middle of my nose, you know that bit whatever it's called, is now in blocking my left air passage, look."

I leant my head back to show Dawn what I meant; the four men on the adjacent table gave us a strange look.

"We'll have to re-name you Blocked Nostrils," Dawn laughed.

I laughed too.

"What did Sarge want to talk to you about, you know, when he said he wanted a word?"

"He told me what he was going to do and asked me how you'd react. I said you'd be fine."

"So you knew he was going to do this?"

I studied my nose in my reflection in the window.

"Look, it's like this." Dawn lowered her voice. "You can lawfully assault a prisoner, but it has to be self-defence. Self-defence is a lot easier to justify if you've got some tangible injuries."

"Tangible?" I asked, although I did actually know what the word meant.

"Visible. It literally means something that can be touched."

"I know."

"Now if this chap makes a complaint saying he was beaten up, the Divisional Surgeon will be asked to make a statement. He'll confirm that you and Fitz had injuries. Get it?"

"Yes, but couldn't I have had something a little less permanent?"

"Like what?" asked Dawn, a barely concealed smirk still lurching.

"Oh, I don't know, just something that doesn't make me look like I've just gone ten rounds with Joe Bugner and lost."

"You don't look like you went ten rounds with Joe Bugner and lost," Dawn said encouragingly.

"Don't I?"

"No, you look like you went one round with Joe Bugner and lost."

I felt my nose for the hundred and first time and then remembered I'd arranged to go out with Debbie at twelve.

"I need to get home; I've got to be up in a few hours."

"And another thing: don't punch the head, the injuries show really easily and tend to look much worse than they are. Always punch the body," Dawn said, quite seriously.

I found it surprising that Dawn was giving me this lesson because I couldn't ever imagine her losing her temper and thumping someone.

"Dawn, have you ever done anything like that?"

"No never. It's a bloke thing; female officers don't tend to react like that."

"Am I missing something? I mean, I thought I might be in trouble, but no one seems particularly bothered."

"Chris, the prisoner was an idiot; the doctor confirmed he'd taken hallucinogenic drugs. For what he said, he got what he deserved. But don't get in the habit of assaulting prisoners, because if you do it's a fairly short road out of the job and into prison. Also, you earn a reputation for being punchy and people are reluctant to work with you."

"I won't," I said, and I meant it.

"No, I know you won't, you're not that type. Actually, Chris, you've done well this week. You took the wind up in good spirits, helped old Fitz out of his spot of bother and you've not mucked up at all. A few of the guys have said they hope you go on their relief when you finish Street Duties. Well done."

I stopped examining my nose.

"Thanks," I said, quietly holding back a rush of emotion. I composed myself with a deep breath and I asked one final question.

"Dawn, why am I called Nostrils?"

Chapter 46 – Brighton and a tom

Debbie had arranged to knock for me at twelve, but she didn't turn up until nearly two. When I opened the door, I couldn't contain my impatience.

"I thought you weren't coming."

"Sorry, darling, don't be like that. I had a really late client last night; he didn't go 'til four."

Her hair was wet, and I assumed she'd just washed it. She wore an expensive-looking black leather jacket, the tightest pair of blue Gucci jeans, which extenuated her slim figure and tight behind, and a pair of black cowboy boots which matched her jacket.

"Do you still wanna go? It's pouring with rain," I asked, genuinely hoping she would back out.

"Of course, it'll be fun. What happened to your nose?"

I mumbled something about a fight with a prisoner and Debbie took my right hand and studied the knuckles closely; the first two were red and swollen.

"If you ask me, the other bloke looks a lot worse than you this morning."

The fact that my injury had been inflicted by the sergeant gave the conversation an ironic twist. I picked up my own jacket, a cheap plastic model from a market stall in Walthamstow, and we headed down the stairs to the small car park at the rear. I had hoped Debbie was going to drive, but there was no sign of a Mercedes sports car.

"Where's the Mercedes, then?" I asked, more in hope than anticipation that the vehicle was parked nearby.

“Oh, I don’t keep it here, it would get vandalised. It’s at my mum’s in Leytonstone.”

I couldn’t quite put my finger on the reason why, but at that moment her credibility started to crack.

“So you don’t use it to travel to work then?”

“Oh no, I always use cabs. That way if I give the driver a blow job, I don’t have to pay the fare.”

I had no idea whether she was being serious.

When we reached my Fiesta, I politely opened her door, and she swung her enormous handbag into the footwell of the passenger seat and climbed in.

“I thought you were bringing food? Doing a picnic were your exact words. Unless it’s in that huge bag of yours?”

“I couldn’t be bothered. We’ll get something on the pier; they do really good fish and chips.”

We drove into town, over the Lambeth Bridge and down the A23. When I stopped at a petrol station somewhere south of Brixton, Debbie took the opportunity to make several calls from a phone box on the opposite pavement. In the end, I grew impatient with waiting and tapped on the window to encourage her to return to the car; she ignored me and came in her own time.

“I was just chatting to an old friend of mine who lives in Brighton, I said I’d pop in and say hello. I’ll only be ten minutes. You don’t mind waiting outside, do you? He don’t like the old bill and he’d kill me if I brought one to his door.”

I shook my head and shrugged my shoulders; I suspected this was not going to be the relaxed day at the seaside I’d hoped. We chatted intermittently on the journey but as I was determined to avoid asking Debbie anything about her job, it was difficult at times to pick a topic or interest which we shared. I told her about Superman and the girl tied to the bed for three days, but she didn't seem especially interested; it seemed to me her mind was elsewhere. In the silences I noticed her almost constant sniffing, it was not attractive. For the last half an hour of the journey Debbie fell asleep; I was quite happy and put the radio on, but quietly so as not to wake her.

When we got to Brighton the first thing Debbie wanted to do was visit her friend, but she'd forgotten exactly where he lived and had to phone him again to confirm the directions.

When we found the address, Debbie told me to park around the corner and wait. I was starting to feel more like a taxi driver than a mate, but Debbie was only gone for a few minutes and when she reappeared, she seemed more relaxed and eager to get on with the rest of our day out.

All afternoon a constant onshore wind blew an unremitting light drizzle. Despite our best efforts to keep dry, we got damper with each passing hour. We drank in several pubs, went window shopping in The Lanes, ate fish and chips on the pier and ended our trip sitting in a seafront hotel watching waves crash on the pebble beach.

I thought Debbie was a bit of a contradiction: she was attractive without being the least bit sexy, young in years but old in life, expensively clothed on the outside but cheap inside. What's more, she really liked a drink and consumed pints of Stella at almost set hourly intervals. Although she never seemed to get drunk, it did mean she was constantly looking for a toilet; and boy, could she smoke. For every cigarette I had, she smoked three.

We'd only just set off to return to London and were still on the outskirts of Brighton when Debbie asked me to find a phone box and then, after making yet more calls, asked, "Can you drop me off at a mate's? I don't need to go back to Hackney until tomorrow evening."

Debbie's 'mate' lived near Tottenham, so it wasn't much of an inconvenience.

It was late and the road was quiet, so I put my foot down, determined to get this disappointing day over. I decided I wouldn't be doing it again. I was ploughing down the outside lane of the dual carriageway as it descended from the South Downs when I saw a police car on the inside lane. It was too late; I passed by doing at least ninety miles an hour. In my mirror I saw the blue lights come on. I slowed down and pulled over in a lay-by before it had actually caught up with me. I was quite confident I'd be able to talk my way out of any formal procedure. I did notice, however, that Debbie looked suddenly very nervous and thought perhaps she had some outstanding fines or something.

"And why have I stopped you, Sir?" asked the policeman, a Sussex officer.

"Because I was speeding, officer."

"And what speed were you doing?"

"Just under ninety, I think."

"Have you been drinking?"

"I had a couple of pints in the afternoon, officer; that was three hours ago now."

I was pretty sure I wasn't over the limit.

"I require you to take a breath test."

"No problem."

The officer returned to the police vehicle to collect the breath test kit. I recognised the device instantly, having practised its use several times at Training School.

"Have you done this before?" the officer asked.

"Sort of?" I replied suggestively.

The officer frowned.

"What do you mean?"

And there it was, just the question I'd was fishing for.

"Well ..."

I paused to consider how best to phrase my answer.

"Are you in the job?" the officer asked.

"Yes."

"Met?"

"Yes, officer."

"Warrant card?"

I reached into my back pocket and handed it over unopened.

The officer examined it.

"Fuck off, Mr Pritchard, but slow down," the officer advised in a not unfriendly manner.

"Thanks, mate," I said, taking back my warrant card.

When I jumped back in the driver's seat and fastened my seat belt. I looked across at Debbie; she looked really flushed. I didn't ask why.

When we hit the outskirts of south London, Debbie decided she needed to use the toilet and asked me to pull into the next pub we passed. When she got out, I noticed her large handbag in the footwell of the front passenger seat and realised it was the first time she'd been parted from it all day. Without knowing exactly what I was looking for, I turned the internal light on and slipped my left hand into the bag. I felt around and removed a rectangle block, roughly the size and shape of a large paperback and quite heavy. I glanced up to make sure Debbie was still in the pub, placed the item on my lap and examined it. I carefully unwrapped several pieces of paper to expose a rectangular block of white powder in clear plastic cling film.

"Fuck," I said out loud.

I wasn't quite sure which one, but I realised I was holding a considerable amount of an illegal drug, probably cocaine but possibly amphetamine. I quickly replaced the paper and put it back in Debbie's bag.

"Fuck," I said again.

I considered leaving Debbie in the pub, driving off there and then and dumping the drugs in the Thames but as I dithered, the passenger door opened and Debbie jumped back in. I manoeuvred my Fiesta out of the parking space, and out of the corner of my eye I noticed Debbie checking the drugs were still in her bag.

I decided to get her to Tottenham as quickly as possible, drop her off and have nothing to do with her ever again. Then it hit me that I'd been stopped by Sussex Police with a large quantity of drugs in my car. I'd been close to going to jail; I felt nauseous.

Debbie must have sensed something in my demeanour because a few minutes later, she asked, "Are you all right, Chris? You seem uptight all of a sudden."

"Yes, I'm just tired. It's 'cos I've been on nights."

"Listen, I told you I was good to police. Perhaps tomorrow evening you can pop down and I'll give you a massage."

Whilst I'd no intention of taking her up on her offer, I was reminded of what Dawn had said about the GTP or good to police expression.

"You said you know other policemen?" I asked.

"A few," she replied coyly.

"I'm not asking their names."

"I wouldn't tell you if you were."

"I'm not, it's just, are they customers or friends?"

For a moment I thought Debbie was ignoring me, but when I glanced sideways I saw she was contemplating her reply.

"He," she said firmly, indicating that we were in fact talking about only one person, "is neither. He's more like a business associate; do you know what I mean?"

I didn't understand but guessed I would get no further if I asked how on earth a police officer could be a business associate of a prostitute, so I let it go.

As we neared Tottenham and before the opportunity was lost forever, I considered confronting Debbie and telling her that I knew what was in her bag. Then I realised if I did, I should really nick her, which would then lead to me having to explain exactly what I was doing with a woman I knew was a prostitute on a day out in Brighton. I decided I'd only got one choice, to play dumb.

I dropped Debbie off on some indeterminable council estate near White Hart Lane, said goodbye and left it at that. I knew Debbie had used me and felt both stupid and disappointed, but, at least, I'd learnt one lesson: why cops and prostitutes should keep themselves to themselves.

Chapter 47 – A dying trade

The following week was the start of my tenth week on Street Duties. I felt my relationship with Dawn was improving with each passing day. I couldn't help it but I'd started to have feelings for her and it wasn't just a physical attraction; there was just something about her, and whatever it was, it did something to me.

All week we were working twelve to eight, which I considered a very sociable shift providing both a decent lie-in beforehand and several hours in the pub afterwards.

I'd not had any contact from the Campbells and my mind frequently wandered back to the voluptuous Jessica. Now I was off nights and back in the real world, I hoped to bump into Dean and perhaps receive another invitation.

When Dawn and I met in the Street Duties portacabin on the Monday, she was friendly and relaxed.

"Hi, partner, good day yesterday?"

She had never called me partner before, it felt good.

"Hi, Dawn, quiet day really," I said.

I could hardly tell her that I'd had a day out at the seaside with a prostitute and oh, by the way, we collected a kilo of class A whilst we were down there.

"What did you do, go and see your cousin in Twickers?" I asked, happy to be changing the subject.

"No, just caught up with some sleep and housework. You did well last week, Chris. I wasn't too embarrassed at all and the way you backed up old Fitz, very impressive."

"I didn't back him up, that was exactly what happened."

Dawn smiled broadly.

"Well done, you've passed the first test of the week and as a prize you get to buy me a cup of tea."

Over tea Dawn discussed what we were going to try to achieve that week and it centred upon the information we'd received from the landlord of the Three Horseshoes.

"Let's find this Danny chap and see exactly what he's been up to. We'll spend some time around Heatherside and see if we can locate the green Mini."

We made our way via the Arndale Centre, where there'd been yet another bomb hoax. En route, and as usual, Dawn was like a hungry lioness looking for her next meal. Even after working with her for two months, I still loved to watch her. I tried to mimic her style but was a poor imitation; Dawn seemed to have a sixth sense which told her not only when something wasn't right but more importantly, when something was.

We'd been on the Heatherside estate for no more than twenty minutes and were doing a street-by-street search for the green Mini, when I saw it driving straight towards us and stepped out to stop it before Dawn had realised what was going on.

The driver was a heavily tattooed white male in his mid-thirties who spoke with an Irish accent. I asked him to join me on the pavement.

"What's the matter, officer?" he enquired confidently.

"Is this your vehicle, Sir?" I asked.

"Yes and no. I bought it yesterday but I ain't paid for it yet."

"You bought it yesterday?"

I knew this contradicted what the landlord had said.

"Yes, from this geezer in the Oak, Peter something."

"Have you got your driving licence?"

"No."

"Have you got anything with your name on?"

"No, I don't think so."

I pulled out my pocket book.

"Name and date of birth please?"

"Danny McDougal."

"How do you spell McDougal?"

"I've no idea, officer; I don't read and write so good."

"Date of birth?"

"Two, two, fifty-three."

"How old are you, Danny?" Dawn interjected.

"Thirty-two," he replied.

"Try again, Danny?"

"Thirty-one, I don't know; I don't count so good either."

Whilst Danny and I were talking, Dawn had been walking round the vehicle examining the tax disc and the tyres and regularly glancing inside; she joined us on the pavement.

"Danny, is there anything in the car that shouldn't be there?" she asked.

It was the second time I'd heard Dawn ask this question as a prerequisite to a search, the first time was with the DAC's wife, and I realised what a great question it was; if the recipient replied 'no' then the next line was an obvious 'well, you won't mind if we have a look then, will you?' whereas, if the person said 'yes', he or she was admitting having in their possession something they shouldn't.

"I don't know. As I told this officer, miss, I only got the car yesterday. I don't really know what the last owner might have left in there."

"Danny, I'm going to search the vehicle as I'm not happy with some of the answers you've given, and I believe it might contain stolen or other illegal items."

"Go ahead, officer, I'll help you. I'm quite interested to see if there's anything myself."

With that, Danny walked to the back of the car and helpfully opened the boot, then the passenger door and he even leaned across and opened the small glove compartment.

"Stay with him," Dawn said to me.

"Oh, she's the boss is she, son?" Danny said jovially. "My wife is the same, always telling me what to do."

Dawn started her search in the boot. A few seconds later she held up two wires, one black, the other red, and a plastic battery compartment which had been removed from a radio or electric toy.

"What's this electrical equipment for?"

"No idea, it must have belonged to the previous owner, officer."

I realised this was going to be Danny's reply to every question.

Dawn then began to search inside the car.

"Turn him over," she called.

I got Danny to empty the contents of his four jean pockets on to the bonnet of the Mini. He pulled out a packet of cigarettes, a lighter, several disgusting handkerchiefs and then a huge bundle of banknotes. I checked his pockets, which were empty, and took possession of the banknotes.

"Dawn," I called.

"What?" she replied.

I held the bundle of banknotes in front of the windscreen so she could see them.

"How much is there?" she asked from inside the car.

"About two G's."

"Where did you get that money?" she called.

"I had a win on the gees-gees, officer, it was only a pound Yankee, but the first horse, Buzzards Bay, came in at fifty to one. The other three were all about fours so it was a nice little earner."

I didn't have a clue what he was talking about but apparently Dawn did, because she asked, "Which bookies?"

"William Hill, I think, but I cannot be sure, officer."

"What's in this washbag hidden under the driver's seat?" Dawn said as she got out of the vehicle holding a small black bag with a zip on the top.

"No idea, officer, never seen it before, must belong to Peter."

Dawn undid the zip at the top and holding the bag in her left hand, opened it up with her thumb and forefinger, and peered inside.

"Never seen this before?" Dawn asked, without saying exactly what she was looking at.

"Never."

"Golf November receiving, one eight two?"

"Go ahead, Dawn."

"Trafford Drive, Heatherside Estate. Can we have transport for a prisoner, and we'll need to bring his car in too."

"Yes, yes. Golf November two, can you assist?"

"Running time from the nick," the van driver said.

Dawn nodded towards him and I took a two-handed hold on Danny's right arm.

"Chris, arrest him for handling stolen goods, but I suspect from the electrical equipment in the boot we actually have in our custody one of a dying trade?"

"A bomber?" I asked incredulously; surely we hadn't arrested someone from the IRA?

Dawn laughed.

"No, not a bomber, you idiot, a safe blower," my partner replied.

Sometimes I really wished I knew when to keep my mouth shut.

Chapter 48 – Strip search

Back at the nick I gave the grounds for arrest to the sergeant and throughout, Danny kept protesting he'd only just purchased the vehicle and knew nothing about the bag stuffed with gold sovereigns or the safe-blowing equipment in the boot.

When I'd finished, Dawn nodded approvingly and mouthed 'well done' to me; it was a nice touch and very much appreciated. She then went to do a name check on him and to inform the CID, who would be dealing with our prisoner, and she handed the washbag to me. It was really heavy; I unzipped the top and just couldn't resist the temptation to look in: the bag was full of gold coins.

"No trace on the name check, Sarge," Dawn said, sticking her head around the charge room door.

The sergeant looked at Danny over his reading glasses; he spoke slowly, quietly, but with striking authority.

"Listen, Danny, or whatever your name is, don't muck me about. I want your real name."

"That's it, Sarge, Danny McDougal, on my mother's life."

"If I discover you're lying, you'll regret it," the sergeant said.

I was quite taken aback by the sergeant's aggressive attitude.

Danny just shrugged his shoulders.

"Very well. PC Pritchard, please empty the contents of the bag out on the desk."

I tipped the washbag forward and coins spilt onto the desk.

"Christ, they must be worth a fortune. Are you honestly telling me, Danny, or whatever your name is, that the man who sold you the car yesterday forgot that he'd left thousands of pounds worth of gold sovereigns in it?" the sergeant asked.

"I know nothing about the stuff, on my children's lives. May the Lord strike them dead if I'm not telling the truth."

I put the sovereigns into ten piles of ten.

"Stick them back in the washbag for now, PC Pritchard. Before we list his property, let's search him properly to see whether he's got anything else on him. PC Pritchard, get a couple of male officers from the canteen; tell them I need some help to search a prisoner," the sergeant said.

"That's all right, Sergeant, I searched him on the street."

"Can I have a word?" the sergeant said abruptly.

He stood up and walked into the nearby fingerprint room; I followed.

"Close the door, son."

"PC Pritchard, when I say get two officers from the canteen, I'm not opening a debate on the subject, I'm giving you a direct fucking order."

The sentence had started at barely a whisper, but the volume and intensity rose with each passing word until it ended with a crescendo of anger.

"Yes, Sergeant, on my way now."

I hesitated just to make sure I was doing the correct thing. The sergeant nodded once and off I shot to the canteen to see if anyone was about.

I returned a minute later with the two officers whom I knew only by their first names as Adrian and Nigel; they were the ones who'd given me a lift from headquarters on my first day when I was shot at. As we walked across the yard, Nigel asked, "Which skipper is it, Nostrils?"

"Twenty-two I think, I don't know his name."

"Oh, Dave Franklin, our kids go to the same school. The prisoner better not play up 'cos you cross him at your peril."

I know, I thought.

When we walked in the charge room Sergeant Franklin's instructions were crisp and clear.

"PC Pritchard, take your prisoner to the tank."

"You," the sergeant pointed to Nigel, "come with me. You," to Adrian, "guard the door, no civvy comes in here, do you get me?"

"Yes, Sarge," Adrian replied.

I knew that 'civvy' referred to the civilian staff who worked in the administration department. I had started to get a really bad feeling about this. I remembered Dawn's advice, to decide your own line in the sand, but then thought about Andy's counsel when he told me being trusted was about backing your colleagues up, when to do so might drop you in it too. What's more, wasn't I being hypocritical after what I'd done on nights? The fact that no one seemed especially bothered about what I'd done suggested to me that perhaps such things were a common event. I took Danny to the tank, a large cell which could accommodate up to four prisoners at once, which was usually used for drunks. For perhaps thirty seconds there were just the two of us in the cell.

"Listen, Danny; don't fuck the skipper about 'cos he's a real handful and he's looking for a fight."

I hoped by offering this advice, Danny might capitulate and bloodshed would be spared.

"Really?" he asked, with a hint of nervousness in his voice.

"I ain't joking, I'm new here but I know what goes on. That's why the female officer has made herself scarce; she doesn't want anything to do with what's gonna happen. That's why he's ordered a PC not to let anyone in. You'd better cooperate."

I knew I sounded convincing because Danny looked really worried all of a sudden. I kept the pressure up.

"Danny, for fuck's sake. We know you did the jewellers last week; we had a tip off, and we've been looking for you all week."

Danny didn't reply because at that moment we were joined by Sergeant Franklin and Nigel.

"Right, Danny, let's start by asking you again, what's your name? Don't give me that Danny McDougal bollocks 'cos there ain't no way you're no trace on the PNC."

Danny looked at me.

"It's all right, tell him," I said.

"It's Danny, Danny Daly, D A L Y."

"Thank you, Danny. Now strip."

Danny undressed, first his T-shirt, then his jeans and finally his shoes, socks and pants. As each article came off Sergeant Franklin threw it to me to search. It was immediately apparent that Danny rarely washed or changed his clothes; in fact, everything about him stank. When his jeans were thrown over, knowing I'd already searched them on the street, I was amazed when in the front right-hand pocket, I found two gold sovereigns.

"Sarge," I called triumphantly, holding up the coins.

"There you go; I said he needed to be searched properly," the sergeant replied.

Danny looked surprised and then resigned. I was pleased because evidentially, the discovery irrefutably linked Danny to the stolen jewellery, but I was at the same time disappointed because I'd missed such a vital clue and didn't relish the prospect of telling Dawn.

When Danny had undressed completely, Sergeant Franklin got him to bend over and pull his arse cheeks apart. I looked away as it reminded too much of what had happened to me during the selection process. Then, in an apparent act of sheer defiance, Danny Daly farted long and hard. Even Sergeant Franklin laughed.

Strangely, when we all returned to the charge room and I listed the property from the washbag, there were only ninety-eight sovereigns; I could have sworn there had been ten piles of ten.

Chapter 49 – Intelligence circle

"So, Danny McDougal isn't Danny McDougal?" asked Dawn, as we sat in the canteen writing up our arrest notes.

"No, he's Danny Daly; loads of previous, all for dishonesty. He's spent most of his life in prison. He claims to live on a travellers' site, just on Hackney's ground, but the bail enquiry has come back negative."

"He won't want us to know where he lives for two reasons. Firstly, if he gets bail, he'll fail to appear and we won't know where to find him; and secondly, because the rest of the sovereigns, well what he hasn't sold yet, will be there."

"Yes, of course," I replied.

"I can't tell you how pleased I am to have recovered at least half of Mr Cohen's stolen jewellery. I can honestly say, I've lost sleep about advising him to turn his alarm off. What a stupid thing to do."

We hadn't talked about it since the day after the burglary, when Dawn had mentioned something about checking the crime book.

"Don't be too hard on yourself, partner."

"No, Chris. That was a big mistake and I'm just surprised nothing more has come of it. If I was Mr Cohen, I'd have hit the roof and would definitely have made a complaint."

"Did you realise this Danny chap might be connected to the jewellers?" I asked.

"If I'm absolutely honest, not in a million years," Dawn replied.

"When I saw you holding up the wires and battery thing, and what with him being Irish, I thought we'd got ourselves a member of the old provisional."

"Do you know, Chris, now you put it like that, I can see why. Perhaps I should take back calling you an idiot, but I'll tell you what, I'll bank it, and next time when you make a complete arse of yourself, I'll say nothing."

We continued writing our notes for several minutes. As usual, Dawn dictated as she wrote and I copied.

"I must admit," I said, looking around to check we couldn't be overheard, "I thought Sergeant Franklin was going to, you know, when he told me to take Danny into the cell to search him?"

"Thought he was going to what, Chris?" Dawn asked.

"You know, beat him up."

"Only if he was being a right arsehole, like that guy the other night with you; but Danny was all right, wasn't he?"

"Was he?"

"He wasn't fighting or shouting and swearing. Yeah, so he wouldn't recognise the truth if it sat on his head, but you don't get a hiding for lying. If someone gets beaten up, Chris, and as we know, it does happen, then they deserve it."

Dawn started to write, so I felt guilty, but I had to disturb her again before we got too far into our notes.

"Dawn?"

"What?" she said impatiently.

"You know I looked through Danny's pockets when you were searching the car?"

"Yes," Dawn said.

"Well, I missed two sovereigns that were in his jean pocket.

"It's not the end of the world, Chris; these things happen."

"Sergeant Franklin suggested I leave out of my notes the bit where I searched him on the street. Otherwise, he says, I'm going to look pretty stupid if it goes to court."

"Well, then I suggest you do as Sergeant Franklin says. But remember?"

"Remember what?"

"Once you write it down, that's what happened, and forever."

"Understood, partner."

After we'd finished writing up our original notes, we were told to go to see DS Cotton, so we made our way to the CID office.

"Listen, you two, we'll interview your prisoner, but he's bound to *'no comment'* as he's got that hooky brief Saunders from Clark & Co. If we take him to court tomorrow, he'll probably get bail and we'll never know where he lives, so this is what I'm going to do. I'm going to charge him and bail him tonight. When he's released, I'll get the Crime Squad behind him and hopefully, he'll take them to his home. Then we'll get a ticket and turn his drum over first thing tomorrow morning. It's a bit of a risk but I think it's worth it to recover the rest of Mr Cohen's uninsured losses."

"I agree, do you need us to do anything, Skip?" Dawn asked.

"Yes. The prisoner's apparently taken a bit of a shine to young Christopher here. Apparently, you had a quiet word with him earlier in the cell.

"Did you?" Dawn said, unable to contain her surprise.

"Did I?" I said almost simultaneously, before I realised what he was talking about.

"Go and have a chat with him, son; let him ask you about getting bail. You say you'll do what you can and then when he does get released,

Danny might be a little bit more relaxed. Basically, Nostrils, my plan will be more likely to work if he thinks you fixed it for him."

"Okay."

We went back over to the canteen to discuss how I was going to do this and decided the best approach was the simplest; I would take Danny a cigarette.

Sergeant Franklin unlocked the cell and, ignoring the overwhelming stink of body odour, I entered.

"How are you doing, Danny?"

Danny, who had been on the bed, sat up and swung his legs round. I sat next to him and offered him a smoke.

"Thanks. And thanks for tipping me off about the sergeant. I behaved myself, didn't I?"

"Well, apart from farting at him, yes."

We both laughed.

"Listen, officer, I need bail, my son's really ill and I gotta get home and see him."

I was amazed how quickly the subject had come up; I hadn't even lit my own cigarette.

"I can't help you mate; bail is a decision for the sergeant."

"I'll make it worth your while," Danny said.

"I don't think they'll listen to me, I am only a probationer, bail's nothing to do with me; honestly, Danny, I'm not fucking you about."

"Listen, officer, I've more coins. If you get me bail, I'll make a nice present of one to you."

I hadn't expected this turn of events and acted as if I was considering the option. Then, after an elongated draw on my cigarette, I replied, "No,

Danny, I don't want your sovereigns. I want to progress my career. I want to get in the CID. Give me some information, like who you've sold any to. You do that and I can't promise you bail, but I do promise I'll see what I can do."

I stood up and walked out, deliberately not giving him an opportunity to make a decision there and then.

On Dawn's advice, I gave Danny two hours to consider his options. When I went back, I took him another cigarette but this time, I spoke to him through the wicket.

"All right, mate? CID been down yet?" I asked.

I wanted Danny to mention bail first, not me.

"No, officer, the CID won't come down 'til my solicitor gets here, and he's tucked up at Bethnal Green and says he won't be free for a couple of hours."

"Why don't you use the duty brief?"

Danny ignored my question.

"How's bail looking, officer? I've really got to get out of here."

"You tell me?" I said, putting the ball back in his court.

"I'm not a tout, officer."

I said nothing.

"It's complicated. You see, I gave a dozen sovereigns to this bloke, but he's got them on bail."

I didn't know exactly what Danny meant but I pretended to understand.

"How badly do you need bail, Danny?"

There was silence whilst we smoked the remainder of our cigarettes. I stubbed mine out and went to close the wicket.

"I'll see you tomorrow, Danny. I'm off in half an hour."

"Okay, you win," he said reluctantly.

"Go on."

"I gave twelve sovereigns to Billy Brown."

"Who's he? I'm going to need more than that, Danny."

"Billy Brown, you know him; he's the landlord of the Three Horseshoes."

Chapter 50 – Dawn opens up

The rest of the week rolled quickly by and, on Friday evening, Dawn and I were sat in the Elephant's Head.

"So, the Crime Squad did the warrant on Danny Daly's drum but only found six sovereigns. That's a bit disappointing. It would've been great if we'd got all, or most, of Mr Cohen's losses back," I said.

"Yes, *evidentially* they only found six," Dawn replied, her voice full of scepticism.

"What are you suggesting?"

"It doesn't matter," Dawn said, but she'd said enough.

Clearly my partner thought the Crime Squad might have pocketed a few for themselves.

"I don't understand; if the landlord had bought twelve of the stolen sovereigns, why would he drop old Danny in it, by telling us he'd suddenly come into money?"

"Because the landlord had the coins on bail, which means he'll pay for them when he's sold them. If, in the meantime, Danny gets nicked and sent down, well then, he'll never have to pay for them, will he?"

"Oh, I get it now. What a bastard though."

"There's no honour amongst thieves, Chris. They all have this big thing about not being a grass but, as soon as they're nicked for something serious, they turn on their mates, even sometimes their own family. Barry reckoned some of the biggest villains in London are in fact our top informants."

"Really?"

"Really."

"Is tout the same thing as grass?" I asked, remembering what Danny had said about not wanting to be a 'tout'.

"Yeah, tout is an Irish term," Dawn explained.

"Oh, some bloke was asking after you today, apparently," Dawn said.

"What, someone at the front counter?"

"No, a detective on the Regie; some DS called Gerry; big bloke, well over six five."

"What's the Regie?"

"The Regional Crime Squad, it's like detective heaven."

"What does he want with me?"

"No idea. Perhaps you've hit a flag."

"Yeah, that'll be it, almost certainly," I said, despite the fact I'd no idea what she was taking about.

"Dawn, can you speak English; what's a flag?"

"If the Regie or the Squad are looking at someone, like a first-division criminal, you know C eleven."

I didn't really know what C eleven meant but I got the gist.

"They'll put a marker on his criminal record so that, if anyone does a PNC check on him or his vehicle, then they'll be notified. Then they'll come and see why you did that check. It's nothing to worry about. This Gerry bloke spoke to Tommy, she knows him vaguely, says he's a wrong 'un and to mind your step, but really don't concern yourself over it. If he gives you any shit, tell him to see me."

"Okay, thanks. Where am I going to be in a couple of weeks, when you abandon me?" I asked.

"You'll be fine. Oh, you're going on C relief by the way. Sorry, Sarge mentioned it earlier, but I clean forgot."

"Do you know anyone on that relief?"

"A few; there's a couple of really strong characters and one, called Paul, who's an area car driver. He's just left his wife and kids for some young WPC called Sarah. Actually, she is quite stunning, everyone fancies her and that includes most of the women, too."

"Is she tall and blonde? Used to be a model, apparently."

"Yes, that's her. I might have known you'd have spotted her."

"What are you going to do, Dawn; are there any more sprogs needing your tender guidance?"

"No, I'm going onto Beat Crimes. I want to go into the CID and that's the first step."

"So, I will be your last then?"

"Definitely. I couldn't have another you, Chris, you were really hard work, but I love you now." She smiled sweetly.

"So that's what they mean by tough love, is it?"

"You were pretty hopeless, but your arrival did coincide with Barry and me splitting up, which didn't help matters."

"How are you about that?"

"Broken hearted, completely and utterly devastated. Chris, this is mad, I dream about Barry every night. It's doing my head in."

"I'm sorry."

"I never want to feel that way again about anybody."

"I know it's not the same, but when my mum died ..."

"Do you know what? It probably is the same. It's like Barry died. He's just disappeared out of my life and left a hole I just can't fill. And now he's going to the other side of the world."

"Can I help? I know I probably can't but, well, oh I'm not asking you out or anything."

"As it's turned out, you've been a bit of a Barry antidote. You know, you're everything he's not. He was confident, charismatic, good-looking, funny, bright, articulate ..."

"Dawn Matthews?" I interrupted.

"Yes?"

"I'm going to give the same advice I gave a certain Mr Saunders a few weeks ago."

"And what exactly was that, PC Pritchard?"

"You can go and fuck yourself."

We laughed too loudly for the Elephant's Head. People stared.

"Eddie, two more pints please," I called.

"What you doing tomorrow?" Dawn asked.

"Well, I don't know; the options are too numerous to mention."

"Seriously, Chris, you busy?"

"Seriously, Dawn, no."

"In that case you can pick me up at eight. Once a month three friends of mine and their partners meet up for an Indian. As Barry could never do weekends, I am allowed to bring honorary boyfriends. Over the years I've taken along several of my working partners. It'll be a laugh, I promise. We've got a rather cruel trick to play on Roger – he's my best mate, Sue's, husband – but he deserves it, as he's a complete shit."

"I'd love to come, thanks," I replied, really pleasantly surprised to have been asked.

"But Chris, don't take it the wrong way will you?"

I knew exactly what she meant. I looked her in the eyes and replied, with complete sincerity, “I promise you, I won’t.”

I knew my place.

Chapter 51 – The big pools fraud

I spent Saturday shopping for clothes, had my hair cut again and cleaned my old Fiesta inside and out. I knew Dawn wasn't interested in me physically, but I still wanted to look as good as I could that evening; firstly, so I didn't embarrass her in front of her friends, and secondly, just in case she got hopelessly drunk and seduced me. I figured the chances of that happening were slim, but it did no real harm to allow myself to think there was always a possibility.

Before I set off, I looked up Dawn's address in the A to Z. She lived in a place I'd never heard of called Buckhurst Hill. I gave myself plenty of time to get there and was really early. I parked up several streets away and listened to Capital Radio for half an hour. I turned the music up loud when one of my favourites, Bonnie Tyler's *Total Eclipse of the Heart*, came on and, for the first time, I actually listened to the lyrics, instead of just singing along. They seemed to me to be about a woman having an affair with a married man and I thought of Dawn and Barry. Somehow, I knew that song would always make me think of Dawn.

Dawn's mum owned a very impressive, detached house in Buckhurst Hill, immediately opposite Epping Forest. I parked up and walked nervously to the door that opened, as if by magic, as I approached. The warm smiling face of Dawn's mum welcomed me like a long-lost friend.

"Christopher, my dear, do come in. Dawn's still getting ready."

"Thank you, Mrs Matthews."

"Would you like a drink?"

Jenny Matthews was in her mid-forties, her blonde hair was straight and immaculate, her features precise and her voice soft and kind. We chatted easily and, several times during our conversation, I thought to myself how lucky Dawn was to live in a perfect home with such a lovely mum. I was jealous but not in a selfish way. Two cups of tea later, Dawn was ready. When she swept into the lounge, I couldn't believe my eyes. The woman I'd worked with for months, who wore no make-up, always tied her hair up and plodded around in the most unflattering plain flat black shoes, was in fact gorgeous. I almost didn't recognise her.

"Gosh, you look absolutely stunning, Dawn," I said.

"That's kind of you; thank you, Chris," Dawn replied.

"Thank you for the tea," I said to Dawn's mum.

"It's a pleasure, have a great evening."

"We will, thanks Mum," Dawn replied as we left.

On the journey from her house to the Indian, Dawn explained to me the practical joke they were intending to play on Sue's husband, Roger.

"Roger does the pools religiously, he even won a few thousand pounds a couple years ago, and he does the same numbers every week. He plays golf on a Saturday afternoon, and misses the classified results, so he always asks the waiter, Taz, to check Ceefax on the TV in the kitchen and tell him the score draws. Well tonight, the waiter has been primed to return with Roger's eight numbers. It's all been carefully plotted and, if Sue's suspicions are correct, might trick her husband into showing his true colours."

"That's a bit cruel, isn't it?" I asked.

"You haven't met Roger yet, the guy's an arse. He deserves worse. Poor Sue spends half her life making excuses for his bad behaviour, and the other half, spending his money."

In truth, I felt a little out of place all evening. Dawn's friends were pleasant enough, but they were considerably older than me. They chatted about kids, potential schools, au pairs, mortgage rates and a dozen other subjects of which I knew nothing.

The women had all been at school together and were completely at ease with one another, but the men, less so. Dawn had been right, Roger was a dick: if you'd done it, he'd done it twice; if you owned it, he owned a bigger one. He did something in the City and, apparently, earned lots of money. He was brash, loud and arrogant and about half as clever and a third as witty as he thought he was. All evening he picked on me. I did my best to take it well, when all I really wanted to do was to remove his teeth with my fist.

"Did you hear about the wanker Dawn's working with at the moment? Only tripped over and fell in some dog shit, went all in his hair," Roger said, as his shish kebab was being served.

"That was me, Roger," I replied with a smile. "But don't worry, I washed my hair especially for tonight."

Everyone laughed except Roger, who went on spitefully, "Oh, so does that mean you're the young lad that's never going to be a policeman as long as you've got a hole in your arse." He laughed, no one else did.

There was a moment's awkward silence before Sue chastised him for being *'so unkind'* and the conversation moved on. Dawn winked at me reassuringly.

When it appeared Roger had forgotten all about the pools, a carefully rehearsed line from Dawn reminded him.

"A friend of mine at work won a thousand pounds on the Met lottery last week; I wish I could have some of her luck."

Within seconds Roger had dispatched the waiter, Taz, to the kitchen. In less than a minute, he had returned with a small piece of torn newspaper that he handed to Roger. Everyone did their utmost to act normally but conversations faltered, and then stopped, as they awaited his reaction. He arose abruptly and to everyone's surprise, went to the bathroom.

"Are you sure you got the right numbers, Sue?"

"Of course."

She looked over to Taz, whose thumbs-up signal suggested his part of the plan had been executed.

"Maybe he forgot to do the pools this week and he's in the toilet sobbing his heart out."

"No, no, that can't be right. He does them by standing order."

Several minutes passed and then a particularly nervous looking Roger returned from the toilet; he was carrying his coat.

"Listen," he said to everyone, "I've got to go, sorry."

"What? Don't be stupid," Sue said.

"No, shut up a second, you don't understand. I've been seeing your sister for over a year now. We're really in love. You can keep the house and the car ..."

He placed a set of Mercedes keys on the table in front of Sue.

"I'm sorry, but I never want to see you again."

With that he turned on his heels and walked away. Every eye fell on Sue, who seemed remarkably well composed under the circumstances; she beckoned the waiter over.

"Taz, you can bring them now."

Taz disappeared for a few seconds and returned with another waiter. They were both carrying ice buckets and in each was a bottle of Moët et Chandon. A broad smile spread across Sue's face.

Chapter 52 – Dawn's mum

When the two bottles of champagne were empty and everyone was getting ready to leave, I saw Dawn use the payphone by the toilets several times. She was a little drunk and I was worried she might be trying to contact Barry, but I didn't say anything.

"Chris, I need to ask you a favour," Dawn said quietly, as she returned to the table.

"Ask whatever, Dawn, you know I'll do anything for you."

I was trying to flirt and desperately hoped she was going to ask me to spend the night with her.

"I really need to go home with Sue tonight. She's my best mate and, although she's all big and brave, I think she'd probably appreciate the company. The fact Roger was over the side was not a surprise, but that it was with her sister has come as a bit of a shock. She thought they were really close."

So, I was going home alone; my heart sank but I didn't show it.

"Of course, I'll get off then; don't worry about me, I'm fine."

"No, that's not the favour. I need to tell Mum I'm not coming home. I know it's ridiculous at my age, but I always let her know. I've tried phoning but I can't get through. She won't be on the phone at this time of night, which means it's off the hook, which happens quite a lot. On your way home, can you just call in and let her know I'm staying at Sue's?"

"Sure, but will she still be up?

"It's half ten. Yeah, definitely."

"No problem, partner. I'll see you next week."

I drove over to Dawn's house and was pleased to see the lights still on in the lounge. I rang the doorbell and stood well back, a habit which, after only a few months' policing, was well embedded into my routine.

"Who is it?" Dawn's mum called, through the closed door.

"It's only Chris, Mrs Matthews. I've got a message from Dawn, she's been trying to get through, but your phone is off the hook."

The door opened and Dawn's mum, now wearing a long comfortable dressing gown, insisted I come inside, despite my protests that I was just delivering a message. Five minutes later, a cup of tea in hand, shoes kicked off and feet curled up under me, I felt very much at home, chatting away, as if I'd known Dawn's mum all my life.

"I really don't think Dawn should have done that to you. I mean, it's really rude. You're her date and she should have come home with you."

"Oh, I'm not her date. I'm really just a work colleague. Dawn has been puppy-walking me. I'm just out of Training School."

"I know. I know lots about you, Chris. Dawn has told me you've got no parents, or brothers or sisters. You live in a bedsit in Hackney, and you saved her when that bastard broke her nose."

I was surprised. I was aware that after our difficult start, we'd been getting on much better recently, but never in my wildest dreams had I imagined Dawn went home and talked about me.

"Dawn's brilliant at her job, Mrs Matthews. She's taught me such a lot."

"So I've been told. If only her private life was as successful."

I didn't like where this conversation was going and wanted to steer the subject back towards work.

"Dawn tells me she wants to get in the CID."

My attempt to change the topic failed.

"She was seeing some married man for years, but I think that's over now, thank goodness."

"I don't know anything about that. Dawn doesn't talk about her private life much, she's quite discreet."

"Barry, his name was Barry. She didn't tell me for years, but you kids forget we're not as daft as you think we are. I could read the signs. He used to park up down the road, drove a Volvo estate with kids' seats in the back. I never actually met him."

I finished my tea quickly. I wanted to extricate myself before the conversation got difficult.

"I'd better be making tracks," I said.

"Sorry if I've embarrassed you. I worry about her so much, I worry about her at work, and I worry about her private life. I just wish she'd find a nice single man, settle down, leave the police and have a family."

"Dawn will be fine, Mrs Matthews. I promise, I'll look after her."

"You'd better," Dawn's mum said, her face momentarily serious, and then she relaxed and a smile emerged.

For the briefest moment, I felt I'd actually committed to something.

As I got up, I saw a picture on the fireplace that caught my eye. A young bald woman was lying in a hospital bed, with a broad cheerful grin on her face.

"Who's that?" I asked, genuinely curious.

"That's Dawn a couple of years ago. She had leukaemia; we nearly lost her. They told us, at one stage, she would almost certainly die. They were the hardest, darkest days of my life. They said she'd have to fight with everything she had if she was going to pull through. She was so ill, Chris; so ill."

Her eyes started to fill with tears. I looked down. She coughed several times, composed herself and went on.

"I keep that photograph and, whenever I'm worried about her at work, I look at it to remind me how much better things are now."

"She's never mentioned it to me, although now I come to think about it, I think someone did say something about it," I said, vaguely remembering a conversation I'd had with Dean Campbell.

"That married bloke used to visit her in the hospital after I'd left. I suppose it showed he really cared about her, at least. She is so precious to me, Chris."

"I know."

"Mrs Matthews, does Dawn's dad live here too? She's never mentioned him."

"David? No, David left us when Dawn was ten. He went off with his secretary, a stunningly attractive girl called Victoria. Actually, David's been good; he paid more maintenance than he had to and signed the house over, so I can't really complain. He loved Victoria and he was right to do what he did. Of course, I didn't think so at the time, but you move on, don't you? Dawn was the apple of his eye; when he was here, they were inseparable. It must have been so hard for him to walk out on her; that's what makes me realise how much he wanted to be with Victoria. But since the day he moved out, Dawn's had nothing to do with him. He used to drive to the hospital and park under her window, so he could be near her when she was ill because she would have never let him near her. She never mentions his name and if I do, she'll change the subject. I know her reaction broke David's heart and, at first, I didn't care, but these days it really upsets me. After all, you only have one dad, don't you?"

"If you're lucky," I replied, with a smile.

"Oh God, that was tactless. Please forgive me."

"Of course."

"You're a nice man, Chris, no wonder Dawn is so fond of you."

"I beg your pardon?" I replied.

Chapter 53 – Eviction night

Sunday was boring, so, in the late afternoon, I went to see the latest Star Wars film at a cinema in Walthamstow. At seven, I was waiting for the Elephant's Head to open; at one minute past, I was the first in and took my usual place at the bar.

"Bloke was in here looking for you this lunch time," the landlord said, as he poured a pint of Fosters.

"Really?" I said.

"Yeah, mid-thirties, tall, big build."

"What did he say, Red?" I asked.

"He spoke to Eddie, but Eddie played dumb. Reckoned the guy was old bill. You're not wanted, are you?"

I had never told them in the Elephant's Head what I did, so the assumption was a logical one.

"Not that I know of, Red."

"Eddie said he was a right nasty piece of work. Even threatened him! Said that if he discovered he was lying, he'd punch his head in."

"Sounds a charming fellow."

I sipped my pint and wondered who the hell was going to my local to try to find me. I didn't have long to wait: two sips later an enormous hand rested on my right shoulder.

"Chris Pritchard? I want a word in your shell like."

I looked up to see a dark-haired white man, about thirty-eight years old, with broad shoulders and tough looking features. The hand squeezed and led me to a seat by a table in the far corner of the bar. I looked back over my shoulder; the concerned look on Red's face was strangely reassuring.

“I hear you’ve been seeing my girl.”

“Who, Dawn? She told me you and her were over, Barry.”

“Who the fuck is Dawn?” he replied and with each word spittle shot from his mouth.

I could smell alcohol on the man’s breath, not beer but deep-rooted spirits.

“Are you Barry?”

“No, you wanker, I ain’t. My name’s Gerry, Gerry Stone.”

“Oh, so you’re the DS from the Regional Crime Squad that was looking for me at work last week.”

I relaxed, knowing that whatever the matter was, it must be work related and how much danger could I be in from a fellow officer?

“How can I help you, mate?” I said cheerfully.

“Are you taking the piss?” Gerry said, with venom.

“Listen, Gerry, I’m confused; the only girl I’ve seen in months is Dawn Matthews and I’m not even going out with her, we’re just mates. Are you sure you’ve got the right Chris Pritchard? There are two of us in the job, I know ’cos I occasionally get the others guy’s correspondence by mistake; I think he works at Staines.”

“Shut your fucking mouth and listen, you lying cunt.”

“You’ve been seeing Debbie. You even did a Brighton run with her. She’s fucking mine; you speak to her again, you even fucking look at her again and you’re fucking dead. I’ll dump your body in the Thames and it’ll pop up at Teddington Lock like the other people that have crossed me.”

I was absolutely speechless. Debbie? Debbie? I’d already decided I never wanted anything to do with that drug dealer ever again.

"She's told me all about you, you fucking little prick. Did you have a nice day out, just the two of you?"

"What, she's just a neighbour and we went to Brighton for the day. I never laid a hand on her."

"She was doing a bit of business for me and it had nothing to fucking do with some fucking kid lid. I am going to tell you your future, right. You're going to be moving out real soon. I don't want you living above her. If I ever hear your name or see your face again, you'll end up a bloated rotting corpse."

"Okay, I get it. I'll find somewhere else to live. Just give me a week or two."

Gerry looked at his watch.

"It's seven thirty now; I want you out by ten. At ten, I put your door in and if you're there or there's a trace of your stuff, I'll kill you. Oh, and if you think you're going to go to A10, just remember I've got a kilo of coke wrapped in cling film that's got your dabs all over it, I've already checked. Now fuck off, you've got some packing to do."

I didn't wait to be told twice, I shot out the pub and ran home. When I got in and sat on my bed, my heart was pumping and my hands were shaking. I looked around the room; I didn't have too much to pack and could probably get it all into the Fiesta. Then I remembered I was six weeks in advance with my rent; was I ever going to see that money again? Perry the landlord didn't appear the most charitable individual I'd ever met. When I'd left Training School, I could have moved into the Section House, but had worked out I could make more money by living cheap and claiming rent allowance. The obvious thing to do would be to present myself at the Section House and ask for a room, but then I'd have to explain why I was suddenly homeless, and someone might start making enquiries. I started to pack. Half an hour later, I was loading up the car and just after eight thirty made a final check that everything was gone.

I left the door open so Gerry could get in without kicking it in; I knew if there was any damage, my chances of seeing any of my deposit would be even smaller.

As I walked down the stairs for the last time, I nearly collided with Debbie, who was coming out of the bathroom. We didn't say a word, but I saw she had been badly beaten; she was holding a flannel to a very swollen lip. I looked down and kept walking.

I drove through the East End streets just glad to be putting distance between myself and my Hackney bedsit. It was nine and everywhere around me lights were coming on. I pulled into the car park of the Reindeer pub. I was somewhere near Epping Forest. On the opposite pavement was a telephone box. I took a two pence piece from my pocket and called the only friend I had in the world.

Chapter 54 – House rules

It was good of Dawn to help me out and words couldn't express how much I appreciated it, but after I thanked her for about the twentieth time, I could tell my gratitude was beginning to annoy her, so I decided to say no more.

"It's a good job Mum took to you," Dawn said.

"I won't be here long, honest. As soon as I can find somewhere I'll be out of here. I'm embarrassed to have to ask but I really have no choice."

"Okay, now Mum's gone to bed you can tell me what's happened, and I want the truth, the whole truth and nothing but. I must know everything, Chris; if I ever discover you've lied to me tonight, I'll never forgive you."

It actually wasn't a long tale; it started with GTP, took a visit to a popular south coast seaside resort and ended in the Elephant's Head.

"What's A10?", I asked when I'd got to the part of the story where Gerry had threatened to involve something or someone called by that name.

"I've told you before about A10, also known as the rubber heelers. It's a squad set up by Robert Mark to investigate bent coppers. If they get hold of the cocaine with your fingerprints on the cling film, you'll be lucky not to go inside for a decent stretch."

"But I didn't do anything wrong, Dawn."

"Chris, when you find ten grand worth of class A on someone, you nick them. No ifs, no buts, 'cos you're either old bill or you're not."

"Okay but ..."

"No, Chris, no buts. The moment you decided to befriend a tom you made the mistake from which everything else flowed."

"I know," I said quietly.

"Were you after sex?"

"No, Dawn, really I wasn't. I was after ..." I paused, too embarrassed to complete the sentence.

"What?"

"Just company. No one likes to admit it, Dawn, but you said you wanted the truth. I'm lonely. I've got no family and no mates, not in London anyway. Weekends drag by very slowly. A day out with Debbie was something to look forward to."

"Did you go last weekend?"

"Yes, last Sunday," I replied.

"I'll bet Debbie is Gerry's informant; he's probably shagging her, and they'll have the old recycling scam going on."

"Recycling scam?" I asked.

"Debbie buys cocaine in Brighton and brings it to London where she re-sells it. There might be a small difference in price between Brighton and London which she'll exploit to make a little profit, maybe a hundred quid, then in her capacity as Gerry's informant she tells him who she's sold the gear to. Gerry then does a ticket on the geezer, arrests him and seizes the cocaine. He books in about a tenth, and thieves the rest along with any cash the bloke's holding. Debbie will get ninety per cent of the original cocaine back to re-sell. If he's really bold, Gerry will even put in for a reward for Debbie, which they'll split. Gerry will get a pat on the back for another good job. Everybody wins."

"Except the bloke she sold it to," I said.

"No, Chris, if Gerry's clever, even he'll think he's won too."

"I don't get it?"

"Well, instead of going to court as a major drug dealer, he'll look a very minor player. Instead of getting ten to twelve, he may even get a bender. He's going to lose any money he's got anyway, so he won't be bothered about Gerry nicking the cash. See, if Gerry does it right, the geezer will think he's done him a big favour and might even turn himself. Really shrewd bent coppers even give the drug dealer's wife a few quid back, maybe a grand, which goes down well and almost always guarantees cooperation."

"When you say Gerry might even turn the drug dealer, turn him into what?"

"No, turn means he persuades the guy to become his informant, a grass, a tout, remember?"

"And does this recycling scam go on a lot?"

"I honestly don't know how widespread it is, but Barry used to suspect it was quite common."

"How much danger am I really in from this Gerry?"

"If you steer clear of Debbie, you'll probably be fine. I can't imagine he sees some nineteen-year-old sprog as much of a threat."

"Thanks again for putting me up, partner."

"It's all right, Chris, but I'm going to lay down a few rules."

"No problem."

"Firstly, don't tell anyone you're living here otherwise everyone will assume we're shagging. If I hear from anyone that you're staying with me, you'll be gone that evening."

"Understood."

"Next, you don't smoke or drink in this house, and you don't bring anyone back either."

"Like who?" I laughed.

"Fair point. I was going to say don't upset Mum, but you won't because I know you well enough by now. And this is only a temporary solution, you must find somewhere else."

"Of course."

"And lastly, I don't want any trouble brought to this house, so if this problem with Gerry hasn't gone away, then I need to know. In fact, what I'm saying, Chris, is simple: whilst you live here you don't ever lie to me. Deal?"

"Deal," I replied.

"No, look me in the eye and promise me that whilst you live under this roof, you'll never lie to me."

"I promise," I replied, with sincerity.

"And another last thing."

"Finally, finally," I said.

"Don't let me find you going through my knicker drawer."

"I won't."

"You won't let me find you or you won't do it?"

"Both."

I placed my right hand across my heart and smiled.

Chapter 55 – Mother's pride

I was acutely aware that living and working with Dawn would place a real strain on our growing friendship, so I did everything possible not to get on her nerves. We travelled to and from the nick in separate cars, at work I never asked her personal questions or alluded to the fact we were living under the same roof, and when I got home, I ate with Dawn and her mum, washed or wiped up and went straight to my room and stayed there, despite finding it mind-numbingly boring. I bought a Sony Walkman and spent hours listening to cassettes and I also started jogging every day, but I really missed the Elephant's Head.

In order to find alternative accommodation, I advertised in several newsagents' windows and got the local weekly paper as soon as it was out on Thursday afternoon. There was plenty of accommodation but little I could afford, and what made it really difficult was that I had no money to put down as a deposit until I got paid in a couple of weeks, and even then, I'd struggle as I still had six weeks of rent tied up in Hackney.

On our penultimate week together we were late turn, which meant we were frantically busy reporting crimes when everyone got home from work and discovered they'd been burgled or had their car broken into or stolen.

On Thursday we set out at just after two p.m. and took yet another bomb threat at the Arndale shopping centre. Once again, we got halfway through the evacuation when we were told to re-open the centre as the call had been traced to some schoolchildren.

"One eight two, one eight two receiving, Golf November?"

"Go ahead."

"Dawn, can you deal with a sudden death, three four, thirty-four, Acacia Avenue?"

"Yes, yes."

"The informant is the LAS who are on scene and are requesting police attendance."

We'd dealt with the Superman sudden death on nights and we chatted about that case as we made our way to Acacia Avenue.

"I want you to take the lead on this one, Chris. I'll stand back and only step in if I think you've made a mistake. After all, in a couple of weeks you'll have to do it on your own."

"That's great, thanks," I replied.

My confidence had been growing recently and I appreciated the ever-increasing trust Dawn was placing in me.

We met the ambulance crew outside, a black female and an Asian male; the female spoke first.

"Thanks for coming so quickly, guys. I'm just not happy with this one. The deceased is an eighteen-year-old lad. He apparently died in his sleep last night and his mother found him in bed at about lunchtime when she came back from doing her weekly shop. There are no signs of violence on the body, no ligature marks, and no signs of a struggle in the premises. Mum is the most unlikely murder suspect you will ever meet and only the two of them live in the house. There's no evidence of alcohol or drug abuse or suicide by overdose or otherwise."

"If he's not been murdered or committed suicide, it must be natural causes, mustn't it? Why are you unhappy?" I asked.

"Because eighteen-year-old lads just don't die in their sleep."

"What has mum said?" I asked.

"She got up this morning but didn't go into her son's bedroom as he didn't have to get up. He'd just completed a college course and was having a few weeks off before looking for a job. She went out about ten, as she does every Friday to do the weekly food shop, and when she came home, was surprised he was still in bed. She went to wake him up with a cup of tea and found him dead in his bed. Here's the thing though, he doesn't look dead, he looks asleep."

"What are their names?"

"Mum is Liz Gaydon, and the deceased is Grant."

"Is there anyone else inside?"

"No."

"Can you take us to see the body please?"

As we went upstairs, I saw, sitting in the lounge, sobbing quietly, the mother who had just lost her son. I knew I'd have to speak to her shortly and remembered the dreadful day I'd had to spend with Cynthia and her husband after their son had killed himself in a car accident.

The boy's bedroom was the second of only two and was remarkably tidy and spotlessly clean. An array of sporting trophies on the windowsill suggested the room's occupant had been a successful swimmer. Grant was lying on his back, eyes closed and a slight smile on his lips; he looked at peace.

"We found him literally tucked up in bed. We immediately attempted resuss but he's been dead for several hours as rigor had started to set in, so we just went through the motions and didn't try for too long."

"Have you examined the body?"

"Yes, but nothing; would you like to see?"

"Yes please."

They pulled back the sheets. Grant was wearing pyjama bottoms but nothing above the waist. They rolled him onto his front. There were no marks anywhere on his body, although it looked as if he had soiled himself.

"That's quite common," the ambulance woman said. "Sometimes, upon death the bladder and bowels open."

"Thank you," I said and looked across at Dawn, who shrugged her shoulders, suggesting she could bring nothing to the conversation.

"I'll have a chat with mum in a minute but first I'll contact the nick and ask them to inform the usual."

We walked back downstairs and out the front door. Mrs Gaydon was in the kitchen emptying the washing machine; although her back was to me, I could see her shoulders rise and fall and I knew with certainty that tears were falling from her unseen face.

"Golf November, four six six?"

"Go ahead, four six six."

"We're at the sudden death in Acacia Avenue. Can we have the Divisional Surgeon to pronounce life extinct and can you inform the Coroner's Officer, and ask the Duty Officer and CID to attend?"

"Yes, yes. Any suspicious circumstances?"

"No, no, out."

Dawn and I then spoke to mum. As expected, she was distraught and it was difficult for her to speak for sobbing, but one thing she wasn't was responsible for her son's death, I would bet my life on that. Mum's account was simple, she came home from shopping and when her son wasn't up by one, she went into his room to get him up and make sure he wasn't sick. She found him asleep but when she was unable to wake him, realised something terrible had happened and called nine nine nine and asked for the ambulance.

The Divisional Surgeon came and went in about three minutes, and two and a half of that was taken writing out his expenses claim. When he was asked, the doctor made no guess at the cause of death, merely saying to me.

"The p m will establish that, sonny."

CID turned up, quickly dismissed the idea of foul play and left. The Duty Officer never arrived, being called to a more serious incident several miles away. Finally, at just before six, the undertakers removed Grant in a black body bag and Dawn and I walked slowly back to the nick on a warm but breezy summer evening, contemplating life's fickle nature. In the canteen, I wrote up my notes and sipped tea whilst Dawn chatted to several officers from an adjacent nick, whom she clearly knew well.

"Are you done yet, Chris? I want to go home," Dawn called over hopefully.

"Dawn?" I replied questioningly.

She excused herself and joined me, sitting down on the chair opposite.

"If I say something stupid, will you forgive me?"

"What you talking about?"

"Something has been bothering me, but I couldn't put my finger on it. I've just realised what it was, but it seems pretty trivial."

"Chris, just tell me and I'll give you my honest opinion. If it was worth saying, then I'll buy you a pint after work. If it's complete rubbish, I'll have a large G and T, thank you."

"Why, when her son has just died, was Mrs Gaydon doing the washing?"

"Go on?"

"Well, when we were there, when we came down after examining the body, she was emptying the washing machine. It was one of those new, all-in-one ones. That doesn't make any sense, does it? Why would she need to do the washing unless she was trying to remove something she didn't want us to see?"

"Do you know what she was washing? Was it bedding or clothes or what?" Dawn asked.

"I don't know, but if we go back, I'll bet she's got it on the line drying."

Ten minutes later we were walking back to Acacia Avenue when Dawn suggested, "Let's try and get a view of her rear garden from a house behind, I think that's Maple Close. I really don't want to disturb Mrs Gaydon unless we have to."

"Agreed," I replied.

The Asian lady occupier at 13 Maple Close was very helpful and showed us into an upstairs rear bedroom. Hanging on Mrs Gaydon's washing line was bedding for a single bed, and it wasn't the bedding that had been on when we'd examined Grant. After we'd said thank you and left, we discussed what that meant and its implications, but couldn't make any sense of it.

"She's not stabbed him to death; there were no signs of injury. Whatever's happened, she felt she needed to wash the sheets. Maybe he just soiled himself really badly and she didn't want him to be found like that?" I suggested.

“Maybe, but we’ll go back and tell the CID. I know you spotted this but let me do the talking. Don’t be offended but they’re not the most approachable bunch and they’ll take more notice of me than you. You okay with that?”

“Yes, of course, they’re probably more likely to respond to the older woman.”

Dawn smiled.

“You cheeky sod.”

“And Chris?”

“Yes, Dawn?”

“I owe you a pint.”

Chapter 56 – DI congratulations

The following day in the locker room, as I was getting changed into my uniform, I bumped into Dean Campbell.

"Hello, Nostrils," Dean said enthusiastically.

"Hello, Dean, I haven't seen you in ages, where have you been?"

"I've been on aid all the bloody time; you'll do your fair share when you go on relief. Do you know what relief you're going on?"

"C."

"Oh, that blonde ex-model's on that relief, she's bloody lovely."

I laughed.

"That's all everyone says when I tell them."

"You going to Chigwell tomorrow?"

"No, what for?"

"There's a big do up at the Sports Club, have you ever been there?"

"No, never."

"Well, are you busy tomorrow?"

"No."

"You still living in Hackney?"

"Yes," I lied.

"Well, come round about seven and we'll give you a lift up there. I'm sure you'd like to see Jess again."

"Don't you want to check with her beforehand?"

"No, don't be stupid, mate. Stay at our place; you never know what might happen."

"Well. I must say I'm tempted."

"That's settled then, see you at seven."

As I walked to the Street Duties portacabin, I was in a bit of a dilemma. I'd told Dawn I would always be honest with her, but I really didn't want to share the fact I was seeing the Campbells again. I decided if Dawn asked me directly where I was going on Saturday, I'd tell her, but I wasn't going to volunteer the information.

"The DI wants to see us about yesterday," Dawn said, before I'd even closed the door.

Five minutes later we were sitting in his office as the strange events of the previous day were being explained.

"Because of what you told them, Dawn, they ordered a special," the DI said.

I had no idea what a 'special' was but later learnt it was a protracted post mortem examination which was normally only ordered when there were suspicious circumstances.

"When the pathologist opened the lad up, he had a hole through his body from his anus to his throat. It appeared someone had driven a sharpened circular weapon with a single thrust, up his anal passage with such force it had gone twenty-one inches into his body, through several of his vital organs, including his heart, before finally coming to rest at the nape of his neck. He would have died instantly and probably painlessly. When we discovered this and bearing in mind what you'd told us, we assumed the scene of the attack was his bed. I went round to the address and spoke to mum and like you, quickly concluded she wasn't involved, but then, why did she clear up? She must have known who'd done it and been protecting him."

The DI leaned to his right and opened a bottom desk drawer. I expected him to produce a vital clue but instead, a bottle of Johnny Walker appeared. A second dip and reach produced three glasses.

"Drink?"

"No thanks, Guv," Dawn said.

I shook my head too.

The DI poured an enormous glass and put the two unneeded tumblers back in his drawer.

"I asked her to come down to the nick. I didn't arrest her but I wanted the place empty so the boys could do a thorough search. I told them to behave themselves too."

"Thank you," Dawn said, apparently understanding what that meant; I hadn't a clue.

"They found it in the loft. A wooden broom handle, sharpened to a point and covered in blood for a length of twenty-one inches."

"What?" Dawn said disbelievingly.

"Poor old cow. When Mrs Gaydon came home from shopping she found her son impaled on the handle. He'd fixed it to the banister at the top of the stairs and hung from the open loft hatch."

"What a way to commit suicide," I said, aghast.

"No, no," the DI said.

Dawn was shaking her head as if I'd said something pretty stupid. I was very confused.

"I'm sorry, I don't understand."

"I suspect Grant Gaydon got sexually aroused by raising himself up and down on the sharpened broom handle. He was a very strong lad, a county swimmer, and he thought he could take his own weight. Or maybe he got off on the risk? Whatever it was, on Friday it all went terribly wrong, and he slipped, or fell, onto the handle. When mum came home, she found her son impaled and very dead. I cannot imagine how she felt."

The DI took a large gulp of neat Scotch.

"Anyway, she didn't want anyone to discover how her son had died so she somehow got him down, removed the handle and cleaned him up. She put him to bed but he bled quite heavily, so she had to change the sheets, turn the mattress over and clean him up again. Well done, Dawn, for noticing the washing machine was on; thanks to you we got to the truth a lot quicker than we might otherwise."

"Not me, Guv, Chris here spotted it. I merely told the CID."

"Well, well done, lad. Have you ever considered a career in the CID?"

"No, Sir, I just want to get through my Street Duties and then my probation."

"Quite right too, I like your attitude."

As I walked out of the DI's office, for the first time since I'd joined all those months ago, I felt proud. I'd helped solve something; okay so it wasn't a crime, but it was a mystery.

"Thanks for giving me the credit, Dawn."

"You deserved it. Remember the driver who pretended to be deaf but had his car radio on?"

"Oh yeah."

"Now think how far you've come?"

"It's down to you, Dawn, all down to you," I said, and I meant every word.

"I know," she replied, with a grin.

***

On the way home that evening we stopped for a few drinks in a pub a stone's throw from home. I'd been turning something over in my mind since an earlier conversation with Dawn's mum and I wasn't going to be happy until I'd broached the subject with Dawn.

"You know how much you've taught me and all that?" I said, as we settled into a corner table.

"Yes," she said tentatively, perhaps sensing this conversation was leading somewhere.

"Well, would you be really offended if I offered some advice about something I think I know quite a lot about?"

Dawn frowned.

"Go on," she said.

"Dawn, I never knew my dad."

Dawn didn't give me a chance to complete my sentence.

"Leave it, Chris; you've obviously been talking to Mum. It's nothing to do with you."

I said nothing; instead, I took a long thirsty gulp of lager.

"The bastard walked out on us, why should I ever have anything to do with him again?"

"Because it would make your mum happy."

Apparently, Dawn hadn't anticipated that line of argument because her facial expression changed from anger to confusion. I took another sip of my beer.

"Is she that bothered?" Dawn asked.

I nodded.

"Enough to mention it to me."

"I never realised."

“Several months ago, in the London you gave me some pretty direct feedback. I listened; knowing you were right, I did my very best to change. Now I’m going to return the favour. Get in contact with your dad, Dawn, and make your mum and him very happy. Life’s too short to hate your own father.”

“We’ll see,” she replied, but I knew she meant yes.

Chapter 57 – Sports Club games

When I knocked on the Campbells' door, I was ridiculously excited to see what Jessica was wearing and when she opened it, I wasn't disappointed. She had a low-cut black dress, which was off one shoulder and came down to just above the knee and black court shoes with five-inch heels.

"Hello, darling, come in, come in."

She kissed me politely on both cheeks but her right hand cupped and then squeezed my right buttock.

My reaction was instant and quite obvious; her hand moved round and pushed firmly against my erection.

"Steady, tiger, you'll have to wait," she whispered into my ear, and at that moment Dean emerged from the bedroom.

"Put him down, Jessica Campbell, you're insatiable. Would you believe it, Nostrils? We had sex not ten minutes ago and now she's all over you like a rash."

"She's just saying hello, Dean, it's all very polite."

Dean was wearing a suit and tie and I suddenly felt underdressed in open neck shirt and trousers.

"Should I have worn a suit? I asked.

"You should have really, but don't worry, you'll do."

"Can I borrow a tie?"

"No, you can't, you cheeky sod! I don't share clothes."

En route to the police club I learnt that the 'do' we were going to was to celebrate Barry leaving the job to emigrate to Australia.

"I'm not sure Dawn's going to be too happy that I'm socialising with her ex-boyfriend."

"Why, you're not shagging her, are you?"

"No, Dean, but you know."

"Don't tell her, problem solved."

It was only then that I remembered I'd met Barry's wife before and what she'd done with William Rees in the Chief Superintendent's office.

The Metropolitan Police Sports Club in Chigwell was very impressive. A substantial house set in about forty acres of rolling Essex countryside, most of which had been converted to football and rugby pitches; there was a large play area for children, tennis and squash courts, and even a bowling green.

We parked next to a very impressive Mercedes 500SL which sported the personalised number plate 'DE 85'.

"That's nice, isn't it?" I commented to no one in particular as we got out.

"That car's always up here," Dean said, and he exchanged a smile with Jessica.

"What?" I said, picking up on something in their body language.

"Well," Jessica said, moving close and taking my hand, "a few weeks ago, Dean had me over the bonnet. But the guy who runs this place, an inspector, was checking the car park and nearly caught us."

"You two are outrageous," I said.

"Play your cards right, young man, and I might be outrageous again later."

As Dean, Jessica and I entered the main building we walked almost straight into Barry's wife, so I took swift evasive action and turned quickly right into some very conveniently placed toilets. A man, who was washing his hands in a sink, looked up at my sudden and unusually forceful entrance and said in a friendly manner, "Steady on, you must be desperate."

"I'm just trying to avoid bumping into someone," I replied honestly.

"Well, hello anyway," he replied pleasantly.

"Hi."

"I've not seen you up here before, where do you work?"

"Oh, I'm at Stoke Newington, I'm on Street Duties."

"Oh, I used to work there. Street Duties eh, has the almighty Sergeant Bellamy exploded yet?"

I smiled.

"Any day now I think."

"Well, when he does, he'll have the dubious and unique privilege, albeit very briefly, of serving the Commissioner on several districts at once."

I liked this man; he was friendly, charismatic and amusing and he smiled throughout our conversation as if talking to me at the precise moment was all he wanted to do.

"Are you enjoying the job?"

"Yes, but I'm a bit embarrassed here 'cos I'm coming to some guy's leaving do and I've never even met him. When we get outside, can you point Barry out to me, please?"

"I'm Barry. You're at my leaving do." He laughed. "Who'd you come with?"

"Dean and Jessica Campbell."

Barry laughed out loud.

"Dean still playing the cuckold, is he?"

I had no idea what the word cuckold meant, but I guessed Barry knew the games Dean and Jessica liked to play. For just a moment I felt awkward, but Barry must have sensed this because he immediately changed the subject.

"Let me take you and introduce you to the wife; what's your name?"

"Chris, Chris Pritchard, but everybody calls me Nostrils."

"Nostrils? Oh, you're the guy at Stokey that was shot at on his first day?"

"Yes, that was me."

"My team picked that job up. We've still no idea who the gunman was."

I really didn't want to meet Barry's wife again but Barry led me out of the toilet and into the hallway, where Emma was still chatting to the Campbells.

"I wondered where you'd gone? I turned round to introduce you and you'd disappeared," Dean said to me.

"Emma, this is Nostrils."

I nodded politely.

"Hi, Nostrils, what's your proper name? I hate all these job nicknames."

"Christopher, Emma, pleased to meet you."

"Haven't we met before?" Emma asked, apparently recognising me but fortunately unable to place exactly when and where.

"I don't think so, I'm very new."

I was grateful when at that moment, three children appeared from behind and demanded Emma's attention.

The Campbells and Barry kept chatting and whilst they did, I studied Barry, conscious of the fact that Dawn was still completely in love with this man. He was a good ten years older than her, and despite being quite charming, was nonetheless overweight, bald and not at all good-looking. I'd expected so much more and wondered what Dawn saw in him.

In a group, children and all, we walked into a packed bar; to the right was a hall where music was coming from and on the left was a bar.

"It's a free bar until the money runs out so just order up," Barry said.

"In that case, what can I get you?" Dean asked, and everyone laughed.

Dean took the order and told Jessica to find a table in the hall.

"Give me a hand carrying the drinks, Nostrils."

I followed Dean through the crowd at the bar but stopped when I saw, sitting at a table in an alcove, which overlooked a bowling green, two very familiar faces. Apparently not part of Barry's social function but just there for a drink, were my former neighbour Debbie and her charming boyfriend Gerry; they were holding hands. I quickly extricated myself from the crowd and for the second time in five minutes beat a hasty retreat to the toilet. This time I locked myself in a cubicle just in case. I sat there for several minutes and considered my choices; I had two, I could feign illness and make my way back to Wanstead and pick my car up or I could front it out. I chose the second option as it came with a significant likelihood of sex.

Instead of returning to the bar to tempt fate, I turned right and into the disco. The DJ had set up on a small stage at the far end and above him several banners wished 'Bon Voyage' and 'Good Luck'. Although the tables around the outside were busy, only a few children were dancing; the atmosphere was similar to a wedding reception which had yet to get going. I saw Dean and Jessica had settled on a table just inside the door and I went to join them.

"Where the fuck did you go? Why do you keep disappearing? Have you got the shits?"

"No, I haven't," I said, keen to let Jessica know I was fit and well.

"Not drinking either?" Dean asked, obviously surprised not to see a glass in my hand.

"In a minute."

"Don't leave it too late otherwise you'll have to start paying, I'm on my second already."

The evening was good fun, the Campbells knew most of the people there and I recognised a few from Stokey; by and large though, I was quite content to sit quietly and observe.

Towards the end of the evening, the Joneses gathered on stage for speeches and presentations.

They looked the perfect family and I wondered how many people in the room knew it was by and large a charade. For years Barry had been seeing Dawn, and only a month ago Emma had been happy to have sex with a police officer she'd only just met.

Barry's speech was very funny and had everyone in stitches. Having wondered what Dawn had seen in him only a few hours before, I now understood. He was so self-assured without any suggestion of arrogance and he was really quick-witted, which he demonstrated whenever there was some friendly heckling. He was clearly very bright, his enunciation and articulation were way beyond that possessed by most of the officers I'd met. Yes, I decided, there was something about Barry Jones, and for a few minutes, I appreciated what Dawn was missing.

I'd deliberately drunk very little to avoid having to walk through the bar to the toilet. Several hours had passed since I'd seen Debbie and Gerry and the evening was drawing to a close. I hoped they would have left by now. Of course, I'd realised the Mercedes sports car with the registration mark DE 85 belonged to Debbie. When I did eventually venture out of the hall, I immediately checked to see if they were still there, but they had vacated their seats, so I loosened up, used the toilet and stepped outside for some fresh air and a cigarette. When the smoke hit the back of my throat, I relaxed, but then I felt a familiar hand on my shoulder.

"I thought I gave you some advice?" Gerry Stone said.

I'd prepared for this moment and now delivered the line I'd been rehearsing all evening.

"I'm sorry, I think you've got me mixed up with someone else, I've never met you before."

I figured it was a gamble, but by playing it this way I was sending an unambiguous message that I thought Gerry might understand. I was right. I didn't even need to turn around.

"Okay, fair enough. If we've never met, we've never met. I can live with that, Pritchard. In fact, for a worthless piece of shit, I kind of like your style."

Gerry walked off. I'd not even looked him in the face. God, I thought, that went well; perhaps it was going to be my lucky night after all?

It was midnight when the DJ played *The Last Waltz* and then turned up the lights to signal the evening was over. We said goodnight to the Joneses and made our way to the car park; I walked a few paces behind to admire Jessica's fantastic legs.

Jessica spoke to Dean, threw him the car keys and took my hand.

"Let's play chauffeurs. Chris and I will get in the rear and you can drive. I'll tell you where to go."

I knew Dean had drunk at least ten pints of lager, but neither of them seemed concerned, so I wasn't either.

Dean opened the nearside rear door of the Audi 80 and Jessica got in.

"Thank you, my man. Now don't forget to open your master's door too."

Dean duly obeyed.

"Thanks, mate," I said, a little awkwardly.

"Home please, driver," Jessica ordered.

Jessica's dress had ridden indecently high as she sat, but she made no attempt to pull it down. She leant into me and my arm went naturally around her.

"Driver?"

"Yes, ma'am."

Dean was playing his part well.

"Keep your eyes on the road, do you hear me?"

"Yes, ma'am," Dean replied, as he adjusted the rear-view mirror down to watch his wife's head nestle in to my groin.

Chapter 58 – An unexpected invitation

The following day I found somewhere to live. It was a room in a shared house near Wanstead underground station. It was pretty dire, but I was desperate not to outstay my welcome. Over the last week, encouraged by Dawn, I'd ventured out of my room more often and on several nights, we'd sat up into the early hours chatting. Consequently, I'd learnt more about my partner, how she'd battled and beaten cancer, how she'd stuck with her mother through a traumatic divorce, how much she missed Barry and a hundred other fascinating insights into her life. Her company filled a massive void in my life, which would open up like a chasm the day I moved out. I knew I would miss her terribly. There was only one upside to the move: I was getting out before I really fell for her.

It was during one of these conversations that Dawn told how she'd met Barry. She was an indexer, which she explained meant she'd been trained to record information on a complicated card system: a process which was utilised for major enquiries, especially murders.

There'd been a murder at a petrol station in Upper Clapton Road, and a squad was formed to investigate. Barry and Dawn were drafted in; he was the Enquiry Team Detective Sergeant, and she was one of the indexers. Before then, they'd barely said a word, but the longer the murder investigation went on, the better they got to know one another. They became friends and then good friends and whilst nothing had happened between them, there were times when they were alone together in the office after everyone else had gone home when Dawn wished it would. The fact Barry was married was the only thing that kept her from making the first move.

Then one day at an office meeting, the DCI announced his decision to charge one of the suspects with the murder. He was a nineteen-year-old Portuguese lad and there was considerable circumstantial evidence against him. Barry was convinced of his innocence and argued long and hard to persuade the DCI that he was making a grave mistake.

"But if I get him before a jury, he'll go down," the DCI declared.

"I agree, Guv, but that's even more reason not to charge him. He's innocent, and I'd bet my reputation on that. In fact, I'd swear upon it at court."

It was an impressive display, and his final statement settled the matter: no DCI would dare charge someone in the knowledge that his DS would be a witness for the defence; but it was potentially a career-ending play by Barry and he knew it. Everyone else at the meeting knew it too and the room went silent, people looked to the floor, no one dared move. Eventually, the DCI got to his feet, took a slow walk across the room to where Barry was seated, and he held out his hand in a conciliatory gesture.

"Good for you, son, you've convinced me. Now go and get whoever is responsible."

The release of tension in the room was palpable; it had been a long day, and everyone got up and prepared to leave. Everyone except Dawn Matthews, who remained rooted to her chair, because in that moment, the young indexer had made up her mind: she wanted Detective Sergeant Barry Jones and she wanted him more than she'd ever wanted anything in her life.

***

I made my announcement at dinner that Friday evening.

"I'd like to say thank you for having me, guys. You'll be pleased to learn I've found somewhere to live. I'll be moving out in three weeks."

"Oh," Dawn's mum said awkwardly. "We need to talk to you about that."

I assumed they needed me out more quickly.

"If it's too long I can find a cheap hotel for a week. When do you need the room?"

Dawn and her mum exchanged a strange look.

"Listen, Chris; mum and me have been talking. We're quite happy to make your stay here more permanent. You're no trouble and mum could do with the extra money."

I was really shocked. I'd never anticipated this turn of events and I was both delighted but also a bit confused.

"Gosh, um."

For the first time, Dawn's mum spoke.

"Look, Chris, if you want to go, that's fine. But if you want to stay, you're very welcome. You can put a TV in your room if you want. You've been the perfect house guest and we'll relax madam's rules so you can have friends back, say on a Friday or Saturday, and you can have a few beers if you want."

"Your daughter is very strict," I whispered, but my eyes smiled at Dawn.

Suddenly I remembered something.

"I've just put down six weeks deposit and I haven't got my deposit back from the place in Hackney yet; if I don't get one or the other back, I'm absolutely broke."

"I tell you what, we'll sort something out. What do you say?" Dawn's mum asked.

"I'd love to stay."

Dawn's mum stood up and collected the three plates.

"Well, good, that's settled then."

As Dawn's mum walked out of earshot, I leaned across the table and lowered my voice.

"Dawn? You know you're going to relax some of the rules?" I said, smiling naughtily.

"No, Chris, my knicker drawer is still out of bounds."

I joined Dawn's mum in the kitchen and as was my custom, started to dry the dishes and then put them away.

"Thanks, Christopher," she said.

"No, thank you for asking me to stay."

"No, not that."

Dawn's mum looked over her shoulder, apparently checking Dawn wasn't within earshot.

"Dawn called her dad yesterday; they're meeting up next week. I don't know what you said to her but whatever it was, it worked."

"Oh, that's great news."

At that point Dawn walked into the kitchen carrying the last few dirty dishes and put an abrupt end to our clandestine conversation.

Much later that evening, after Dawn's mum had gone to bed, I enquired as to how Sue was getting on with the divorce.

"Funnily enough, when Roger discovered he hadn't won the pools he wanted to give their marriage a second try."

"And what did she say?"

"She told him exactly where he and her sister could go. Oh, I know what I've been meaning to ask you. Have you seen Mrs Campbell lately? She only lives down the road. Oh, what am I saying, silly me, you already know that," she said, in a mocking self-reprimand.

"All right, all right. I've seen her a few times," I replied, being deliberately vague.

"She's quite a lot older than Dean, isn't she?"

"Yeah, eight years or so. I think she's in her mid-thirties. She's very attractive, Dawn; have you ever seen her?"

"Once, up at the sports club; she didn't do it for me. She wears too much make-up and too few clothes; mutton dressed as lamb, Chris; but I do share something with Mrs Campbell."

"Do you?" I asked, curious to discover what their similarity might be.

"I occasionally fancy younger men."

"Really?" I could feel my heart pounding. Was this the moment for which I'd been waiting?

"Yes. Do you know Andy Welling? I think he's gorgeous."

I felt sick.

Chapter 59 – Chasing a familiar face

Monday's early turn was nearly over; Dawn and I were late coming in because we'd taken a bail enquiry on the edge of the ground at half one.

"We'll get an hour's overtime if we take a slow meander in," Dawn said.

We walked towards a short parade of shops which no doubt contained the usual newsagents, launderette, hairdressers and chemist. I was imagining climbing into bed for a mid-afternoon early turn nap and then going out for a few beers and a curry, and had been casually glancing along the building line when from the right and out of an as-yet-unidentified doorway, walked a white male in his forties. He looked to his left, our eyes met and in that nanosecond we both knew.

The man shot across the road, causing several cars to brake, and the driver of an old-style Rover, with slower reactions, crashed into the rear of a white van.

"Golf November, chasing suspect High Street east, male IC1 forty years."

He ran down the road opposite and for a few moments I lost sight of him behind a double-decker bus that had crossed between us. Then I saw him again in the distance; if anything, the gap between us was growing. I'd chased and caught much younger men, this guy was quick for an older bloke.

"Four six six, are you receiving over?" the Reserve was calling.

"Yes, yes," I panted.

"Can you give an update?"

"Suspect left into, stand by."

I turned left into another road and clocked the name.

"Stapleford Avenue," I shouted.

This was a long straight road of terraced housing with a line of cars parked along either side. The suspect had crossed over to the far side and I mirrored his movement.

"IC1 male, white, forty years old, blue jacket, black jeans, black shoes."

I couldn't talk any more; although I was fit, such a sudden explosion of energy quickly saps your strength, but I was closing now, perhaps only fifty yards behind at the next junction, which the suspect ran straight over without hesitating. A yellow BT van flashed by only seconds later and could have only missed running him over by a few yards.

"Four six six, can you maintain the commentary please, you have units running to you, but they are a long way from you, I repeat they are a long way from you."

I was vaguely aware it was just before two o'clock, the time when the shift changed over. Everyone would be back at the nick and we were on the very edge of our ground. Help was going to be a very long way away.

"Right, he's turned right into, hang on."

"Roding Lane."

"Four six six, what's the suspect done?"

"Robbery, he's wanted for armed robbery on the Abbey National Building Society and attempted murder," I replied, almost breathless, "on me."

I was only twenty yards behind at this junction, but when I took the next bend there was no sight of him.

"Suspect lost. Last seen Stapleford Avenue junction with Roding Lane."

I was surprised that I could hear a siren now, only a few streets away. The suspect couldn't have made the end of the road, so he'd either gone into an address or he'd gone to ground. I figured if he was using those shops and on foot, he probably lived nearby, in which case he might just have made it back to his house.

For a moment, I didn't have the energy to care. I stood leaning forward with my hands on my knees, breathing heavily. When I'd gathered my breath, I looked under several nearby cars before an open gate by the last of the terraced houses caught my eye.

Without waiting for the unmarked car with flashing blue lights under the grille, which was coming towards me from the other end of Roding Lane, I started to walk towards the gate. I didn't really think the suspect would be there but there wasn't any other place to look.

The gate opened into an alley, which went the length of the house and then turned left where the building ended. As I rounded this corner, a fist hurtled towards the right side of my face; instinctively, I ducked and swayed back but the blow fell with some force on the side of my head, and I stepped back, feeling dazed.

When I looked up, in front of me was the man I'd been chasing. He was short and powerfully built and was doing a very good impression of a boxer. His fists were raised on either side of his face, his body had risen up on his toes and he was rocking irregularly backwards and forwards, left and right. My right hand felt inside my trouser pocket and pulled out my truncheon, but by the time I'd completed the move I'd been hit twice more about the head. He had moved quickly towards me, punched and then retreated. The punches hurt and caused me to drop my truncheon.

A quick glance past the suspect and I saw an overgrown garden and very high brick walls. I was blocking his only avenue of escape.

"Step aside, copper, or I'll put you in hospital."

I remembered Gerald, my elderly neighbour who had given me a lift to Training School all those months ago. His words ran through my mind as clearly as if he was whispering them into my ear.

"When you wear that uniform you never, ever, ever, take a step back."

I decided retreating wasn't an option.

"You fight until one of you goes unconscious," Gerald's voice said.

I was pretty sure I knew which one of us that would be.

"Chris, where are you?"

Dawn's voice was calling on my PR but I was so focused on the suspect that it never crossed my mind to answer her.

"I'm at your last location, Chris. Where are you? Abe, what are you doing?"

Abe? Who was Abe?

I could hear Dawn's footsteps coming down the alley at the side of the house but I didn't want to take my eyes off the suspect for fear he would strike again. I knew that with Dawn by my side we'd be able to win this fight. I knew with equal certainty that without her, I was in real trouble.

Suddenly the suspect put his hands up. That's impressive, I thought; well done, Dawn.

I glanced to my right; Dawn was nowhere to be seen. Instead, Abe the Special, dressed in Orthodox Jewish clothing, was pointing a sub-machine gun at the suspect.

"Lie on the floor, face down, hands behind your back," Abe ordered.

The suspect instantly did as he was told, and with shaking hands, I handcuffed him.

"What the hell are you doing, Abe?" Dawn said as she joined us.

"Put the bloody gun down," she ordered.

"It's all right, no sweat, it's not even loaded," Abe replied.

To prove his point, he tilted the weapon in the air and pulled the trigger. A dozen rounds fired off and Dawn and I hit the deck beside the prisoner.

Chapter 60 – Receiving

I'd got hold of the landlord of my bedsit in Hackney. He'd agreed to meet me that evening in the Elephant's Head and return half of my deposit, which I thought wasn't too bad a deal as I'd left without giving him any notice.

I arrived early; I hadn't been to the pub for a couple of weeks and had missed the place. The landlord, Red, greeted me with touching enthusiasm.

"Chris, my old friend, where the devil have you been?"

"I've moved, Red, I'm living over Buckhurst Hill now."

"Moved up in the world, have we? Didn't know whether to report you missing? I was only saying to the twins the other day that I hadn't seen you since that geezer gave you a tug."

"Oh, Gerry?" He's all right, has he been in again?" I said casually.

"No, but I see him occasionally in the newsagents next door so he must live nearby. What was his beef, anyway?"

"It was a bit of a misunderstanding. He's going out with a girl who lived below where I used to live and he thought I was trying to chat her up."

"Is that why you've moved?"

"It is, Red; I thought discretion was the better part of valour, and besides."

"Besides what?"

"He'd have beaten seven bells of shit out of me if I hadn't."

The landlord laughed.

"I'm owed some rent and I'm meeting my old landlord to get some of my deposit back."

"You lived above the chemist, didn't you?"

"Yeah, why?"

"'Cos Perry owns those, and if you're getting your deposit back that'll be a first."

From out the back an unseen Eddie called Red. Through an open door, I saw a black lady emptying several large bags onto the top of a large chest freezer. Red was obviously taking a delivery to which I wouldn't normally have paid any attention if I had not recognised the woman. I didn't know her name because absolutely everyone I worked with called her 'darling': she was one of the canteen ladies from Stokey.

"Chris," a voice said, and I turned round.

"Hello, Perry, do you want a pint?"

"No thanks, I don't drink and haven't got long. I'm parked on zig-zags."

"Sorry I had to leave in such a hurry."

"Yeah, I heard the rumours."

"I must confess, Perry, I appreciate you giving me some of my rent back, I really do."

"If I'm being honest, Chris, I wouldn't normally be so generous, but let's say I was persuaded."

"By Gerry?"

"Who?"

Obviously not Gerry then, I thought.

"Who persuaded you, Perry?"

"Why, Debbie, of course."

"Oh."

"I think she must have had a soft spot for you 'cos she was very insistent."

"Really," I replied.

"Anyway, water under the bridge now, mate."

Perry reached into his inside jacket pocket, took out a roll of banknotes and separated two with a deftness born of repetition and handed them to me. I had to look twice at what I was being handed.

"Fuck me, Perry. I've never seen a fifty-pound note before."

"Neither have I, mate, but the Irish geezer that took your place gave me four. They're not counter, I've checked. Even if they were, I'd hardly pass them on to you, knowing what you do for a living."

"Shush," I said, looking around. "They don't know what I do in here."

"Oh, no problem, sorry. Anyway, must shoot."

We said our goodbye and shook hands. A few minutes later, Red appeared again and surveyed the bar. There were only the twins and me in the place; the landlord wasn't going to get rich on our trade.

"Christ, business is slow."

"Just because I've moved?"

"No, it's been pretty dire recently. That's why I've decided to implement a new business strategy."

"What's that, then?" I asked.

"From tomorrow at lunchtime, I'm going to start doing food."

"Really? Where are you getting it?" I asked, although I already knew.

Red lowered his voice.

"There's a woman that runs the canteen at Stoke Newington police station. She's going to sell me their surplus deliveries."

"Surplus deliveries?"

"Come on, Chris, you're a man of the world."

"You mean she's nicking from the nick?"

"Got it in one."

Chapter 61 – Operation hoax

"Nostrils, how do you fancy leaving Street Duties with a bang?" Sergeant Bellamy asked the following day; it was the Tuesday of my last week being puppy-walked.

"What have you got in mind, Sergeant?" I asked.

"The GPO has traced the Arndale Centre bomb hoax calls and have identified they've all come from the same T K. The Collator has analysed the data and identified they're made between three and five in the afternoon and it's always on a weekday. It all fits in with the suspicion that they're being made by kids on their way home from school. It may sound pretty trivial, but they are a pain in the arse, thirty-three calls in six bloody weeks; the shops in the centre are up in arms, they reckon they've lost thousands of pounds in business. We've got to get it sorted and it's all down to you. Well, you and Dawn. Where is she, anyway?"

"No idea, Sarge, it's unusual as she's normally on time."

"I want you to get an off-street O P on the T K and cover it this week from, say, two to six."

"I hope Dawn arrives soon, Sarge. I need someone to translate what you're saying."

"I've heard you're shagging her, Nostrils. The rumour mill informs me you provided a shoulder to cry on when that DS from the Sweeny dumped her."

"For the record, she dumped him, Sarge."

"So you are shagging her then?"

"I wish, but alas, the rumour is untrue, Sarge."

"If I shagged her just once I'd die happy, Nostrils."

"I have to agree with you, Sergeant, she is lovely. But I know my place; she'd never be interested in me."

"You're probably a bit young for her but at least time is on your side. You've got it all in front of you. For some of us, the Dawns of this world are a dim and distant memory. But for the record, I think she is absolutely gorgeous too."

With that ultimate compliment, Dawn walked in.

"I bet you two are talking about the WPC on C relief; for goodness' sake, guys."

Sergeant Bellamy and I exchanged a look.

"Actually, Dawn, we weren't talking about her, we were talking about someone even more attractive."

For a second, I wondered whether he was going to tell her.

"Well, please introduce me to her, 'cos with the luck I've had with men so far, I'm thinking of becoming a lesbian."

My mind started to wander.

"Christopher!" Dawn barked sharply.

"I'm just thinking about what you've just said; perhaps you could expand?"

"Re-focus, you little pervert."

"I'm never allowed any fun, Sarge."

Apparently, Sergeant Bellamy's mind was wandering too, because he just ignored me.

"I've got some news which concerns you both."

"Sorry I'm late, Sarge, but the DI collared me as I was coming through the back yard. He wanted to explain why they've had to NFA your armed robber, Chris."

“What? They didn't charge him?” I asked incredulously.

“No, and they're not going to,” Dawn said definitively.

“I don't understand. Why? It was definitely him, absolutely no doubt about it.”

“Well, they found nothing at his home address, he no commented the interview, there's no forensics and his alibi checks out.”

“Apart from that, he was bang to rights,” Sergeant Bellamy added sarcastically.

“But it was definitely him; and why did he run away? I could pick him out on an ID parade,” I suggested hopefully.

“Yeah, but you’d pick out the man you chased and arrested yesterday, not the bloke that shot at you three months ago,” Sergeant Bellamy said.

“Here’s the insurmountable problem, Chris,” Dawn said.

“When you made your statement all those months ago, you said you weren't sure you'd be able to recognise him and that's undermined your identification evidence. But the main issue is that when you were shown albums, remember when you went through those books of photographs, you didn't pick him out and his photograph was there.”

“So, he’s got away with it?”

“I’m afraid so.”

“If his photograph was in the album, doesn’t that mean he's got previous?”

“Yeah, lots, and one for armed robbery back in the early seventies,” she explained.

“No one doubts you, Chris. He was the bloke that shot at you.”

It didn’t make sense to me, but I had to accept what I was being told by these two experienced officers, and then I had a thought.

"Is the NFA anything to do with Abe and his Uzi machine gun?"

"No, it's nothing to do with that; it's your ID evidence, it's just not sustainable."

Dawn and Sergeant Bellamy exchanged a look which suggested they had some sympathy for how I was feeling.

"He'd walk at trial, Chris. The DI is convinced of that," Dawn said.

"You must be frustrated, Nostrils, but sometimes it's the way it goes; don't let it eat you up," Sergeant Bellamy said.

"He's right, Chris. You win some, you lose some," Dawn added pragmatically.

Sergeant Bellamy turned to Dawn.

"Anyway, Dawn, as I was saying to Nostrils, I want you two to set up an off-street O P this week and catch those kids that keep making the hoax bomb calls. The GPO have identified the T K and Chief Inspector Ops has told me to get my finest men on it. Unfortunately, they're all busy so it's down to you two." The sergeant laughed at his own joke.

"The Collator's got a briefing for you; see him before you go out."

"How's the studying, Sarge?" Dawn said.

"Okay thanks, I got eighty-four per cent at classes last week and my average is over eighty but it's traffic this week and I find it really boring. Did the DI say what happened to Abe?"

"Yes, he's been suspended, and they've taken his warrant card off him. It also looks like he's going to lose his firearms dealer's licence. Stupid idiot. The DI said the rounds landed about half a mile away because the following morning he found a criminal damage in the book where some woman's discovered the roof of her Mini Metro peppered with gunshot holes. Fortunately, she wasn't in it at the time. The lab should match the bullets to Abe's sub-machine gun. Anyway, when they had a look at his car, that blue Ford XR2 he drives, they discovered he's only had two-tones fitted under the front grille and bought himself a magnetic Starsky-and-Hutch-style blue light. He kept his car radio permanently tuned to channel one so he could take any calls that he wanted. Can you believe that?" Dawn said.

"So, it was his car I saw coming along Roding Lane? Not a real one?" I asked.

"Yeah, he pulled up before I'd rounded the corner. I didn't know where you were, so I called you on the radio, but you didn't answer. Then I saw Abe open his boot and, a few moments later, emerge with a bloody machine gun. I shouted at him, but he ignored me and came round the side of the house. What annoyed me most at the time was that although he'd seen where you'd gone, he never told me."

"It's been a long time coming; that guy had trouble written all over him from the moment he started working here. The last Chief Super was warned many times but 'cos he didn't want to upset the Jewish community he ignored the advice. Anyway, enough idle chit chat, I must get on with the studying, traffic regs await," said Sergeant Bellamy, and he disappeared back into his small office.

Dawn collected the bomb hoax briefing sheet from the Collator and we studied it in the canteen over a cup of tea. All the thirty-three nine nine nine calls had been timed and dated, and all but one had come from the phone box immediately outside the southern entrance to the shopping centre; the other had been made from the phone box at the western entrance. Significantly, all the calls had been made on a school day between three thirty and four fifty in the afternoon.

"First thing we need is an off-street O P on the main T K. When we see anyone we suspect, we'll leave the O P and keep them close until the call comes through and then we'll have them off. We'll need to be in plain clothes and you'll need to be wearing trainers. As soon as we get near them, if these kids realise what's happening before we get hands on, they're certain to be on their toes and it'll be your job to catch them. I know you're quick but don't worry, I won't be far behind. If we get the O P today, we'll start tomorrow at three. Any questions, Chris?"

"Just one, well two, I suppose."

"Yes?"

"What's an off-street O P and what's a T K?"

Chapter 62 – Andy comes out too

I'd bumped into my old friend in the locker room at the end of another busy day at Stokey. Andy was the only person I knew who took a shower before, during and after work. When I'd met the towel-clad Adonis, against the true wishes of my heart, I'd decided to try to do some matchmaking. I liked Dawn, in fact I suspected I was already in love with her, so it wasn't the easiest decision I'd ever made, but I knew it was the right one.

"So, what's this you need to talk to me about so desperately that you have to drag me into a pub at four o'clock on a Tuesday afternoon?" said Andy as we settled onto adjacent bar stools.

"It's about Dawn."

"You're not still struggling to get on with her, are you? I'm sure I saw you two in the canteen the other day and you were deep in conversation, so I assumed you were getting on better now. Oh, and that's right, and I heard from a reliable source you're seeing her."

"Andy, I'm not, never have been and never will. But you're right; we are getting on better now."

"Hang on, my source told me he'd seen you leaving her house early one morning. She lives with her mum in Buckhurst Hill, and he was driving by early one Saturday and saw you sneaking out. Captured bang to rights, Nostrils. Admit it."

"Andy, shut up and listen. I am not shagging her. Once a week I stay overnight because I have dinner with her and her mum. There is nothing going on, I'd tell you if there was."

"OK, so what do you want to see me about then?"

"Andy, Dawn fancies you and I know you fancy her. Why don't you ask her out? She's had a rough time lately and I think it would really cheer her up."

Andy looked genuinely surprised.

"Christ, I never saw that coming. So, you're really not shagging her are you, Nostrils?"

"No, really I'm not. Andy, I'd love to: she's really attractive and she's got a heart of gold. If I'm being honest, I've got something of a crush on her, so getting you to ask her out isn't the easiest thing I've ever done, but it is perhaps the noblest."

"Bloody hell, Nostrils. A crush on her. Last time we spoke, you couldn't stand her. Make your mind up. Honestly, men."

"I know, I know; I'm a complicated character; blah blah blah; but what do you say, are you going to ask her out?"

Andy shifted uneasily on his stool and ordered two more pints.

"It's not that simple, mate."

"Oh, you're married?"

"No."

"You're living with someone?"

"No."

"You're seeing someone?"

"No, not at the moment."

"Why can't you ask her out then?"

"I don't think I'm what she's really looking for."

"You're joking, aren't you? You're young, articulate, good-looking, you've got a great body. Why wouldn't anyone want to go out with you?"

"You're very flattering, Nostrils. Are you sure *you* don't want to go out with me?"

"Andy, be serious; why can't you ask her out?"

"It wouldn't work, mate."

"Simple question, are you seeing anyone else?"

"Oh, for God's sake, Nostrils, stop transmitting and start receiving."

It took a moment for my mind to process the instruction to shut up.

"Nostrils, I am homosexual."

Involuntarily, my mouth opened.

"No," I said, without even being aware I was speaking.

"Yes."

"No. You're kidding me, right?

"No, Nostrils, I'm not kidding you. I am homosexual."

"I didn't think they allowed people like you in," I said rather tactlessly, and almost immediately the tiniest hint of anger flashed across Andy's face. I wanted to explain.

"I mean, when I had my interview, you know up at Paddington, they said to us right at the beginning that homosexuals weren't welcome and that if anyone was queer, they should not return after the first tea break. In fact, they checked. They got you to bend over and pull your cheeks apart in front of three doctors. When I did that, one of them said 'Still tight, everything's alright'. I assumed they were checking to see if I was queer."

"Listen, Nostrils, they said and did the same things when I was interviewed but me, and a lot of other people like me, ignored the ignorant bastards and joined anyway."

"But you act so normal. When we first met, you even suggested I introduce you to Dawn."

"Nostrils, we're not an alien race. We are normal; we're just the same as you except we're attracted to people of the same sex. As for interacting with the women, I do just that; I put on an act. This job has real issues with *homosexuals* ..."

Once again, I noticed Andy emphasised the collective noun and assumed it was to indicate his preference for its use.

"Would they throw you out if they knew you were queer?"

"*Homosexual*, Nostrils. No, the job wouldn't get rid of me but life would be very difficult. There's a guy on A relief, Bill, who lives with his boyfriend in a job flat. Everyone knows, he's 'come out' as we say. There's nothing wrong with him but no one trusts him, no one wants to work with him. He's a really strong character and can cope with it but I'm not. I prefer to act straight, to put on a front and have an easy life. Nostrils, it's difficult enough that I'm black, if they knew I was ..." He waited for me to demonstrate that I was learning.

"Homosexual," I said.

"Yes, well done," Andy said patronisingly. "If they knew I was homosexual my work life would change completely, and I don't want that. Now I've trusted you with a big secret, don't tell anyone, please."

"What about Dawn? She really fancies you and hinted that she wanted me to set you up with her; how am I gonna explain this turn of events?"

Andy considered for a moment.

"Tell Dawn if you must, but ask her to keep the information to herself. If I've learnt one thing over the years, it's that plonks can be trusted much more than blokes."

"Really? I thought women liked to gossip."

"Nostrils, you're a nice bloke but you can be a bit of a dick."

"Are there many of you in the job?" I asked.

"Yes, there are plenty of us. In fact, we're everywhere." Andy rolled his eyes conspiratorially and asked, "What relief are you going onto?"

"C."

I thought he was just changing the subject; I was wrong.

"Well, let me think."

Andy paused momentarily.

"I've slept with three, no, four blokes on C relief."

"There are four queers, I mean homosexuals on C relief?" I asked disbelievingly.

"Well, I'm not sure they're fully qualified, card-carrying homosexuals, two of them are married with kids."

Chapter 63 – Obs commence

I'd discovered an off-street O P was an observation point located in a house or other permanent premises used by police officers to watch a particular area without themselves being seen. This was opposed to an on-street O P, which would be a van or other vehicle parked on the street with officers hidden inside it. I'd also learnt that a T K was a surveillance term for a telephone kiosk.

"It's a one-bedroom council flat overlooking the south entrance, it's a bit scabby, you know, the sort of place where you wipe your feet on the way out," DS Cotton said as he handed the keys to the off-street O P to Dawn.

"How come you have the keys, Sarge?" Dawn asked.

"There was a murder in there last year. This bloke had a fight with his girlfriend in the middle of the night, pushed her out of bed, stamped several times on her head and went back to sleep. Both of them were really drunk. When he woke, he noticed he couldn't walk because his right foot was unbelievably painful and so he took himself off to hospital. They did an X-ray and removed something from his heel; the surgeon who'd done some max fax work recognised the extraction as a piece of human cheekbone. The hospital called police and the bloke took them back to his flat. His girlfriend's body was discovered wedged by the bed. The post mortem showed she'd died from several stamps to the head. I later interviewed the guy and genuinely believed he had no recollection of what he'd done."

"What happened to the bloke?" I asked.

"He pleaded guilty to manslaughter and got five. The flat's been empty ever since and to be honest, I'd forgotten we still had the keys.

When you've finished with them, can you give them back to the council offices, they're only just down the road, and tell them we no longer require the premises?"

"Of course," Dawn said.

"What you doing for comms?"

"We've borrowed a couple of body sets from the Crime Squad, Sarge."

"Take spare batteries for the earpieces, guys, they don't last long."

By the time we'd got the keys, it was half past four, so we decided to begin the following day.

***

The living room window of the first-floor flat afforded an excellent view of the telephone box and Dawn placed a scabby looking armchair by the window. She then got us to do a practice run from the flat to the phone box, and before returning, she popped into Sainsbury's and collected a handful of carrier bags to spread out on the armchair so that we didn't have to sit directly on it.

"As soon as we see a schoolboy in the phone box, we'll be off. When we cross the road, we'll hold hands and act like a couple, that'll allow us to get closer to them. If we hear there's been a hoax call over the radio, nick whichever one we saw making the call. Don't wait for me to tell you, just do it."

"Yes, Dawn," I replied, my mind returning to that first day three months ago and the bus lane fiasco.

"We'll take It in turns to watch the phone box. It's harder than you think to maintain concentration on one thing when you're staring out of a window, so we'll do half an hour about. I'll start."

“Yes, boss,” I replied obediently.

At three o’clock we began our observations. The PR on the windowsill churned out call after call but for once, we felt no obligation to take any. Whilst Dawn watched, I used the toilet; it was absolutely disgusting. The bathroom, like the rest of the flat, hadn’t been cleaned in years and unless I was mistaken, the wall was adorned with dried crustations.

I wandered into the bedroom and examined the scene of the crime. I must confess to feeling a macabre fascination. I could see where the woman must have died: there was a dark brown stain on the carpet between the bed and the wall. The couple’s clothes were just where they had left them that night when they had undressed: a pair of red knickers were rolled up inside jeans like they are only when both garments are removed simultaneously. On the small bedside table were two half-full glasses, an empty plastic cider bottle and an astray overspilling like a volcano. Shoes littered the floor and a pair of abandoned red stilettos reminded me of Jessica Campbell. I was fascinated at the grisly scene, frozen in time probably only a few minutes before the woman met her violent death. I moved into the kitchen. The empty plates from their last supper sat on a sticky worktop amongst an array of encrusted pots and pans; in the corner, a bin cried out to be emptied.

I returned to the living room.

“You been having a gander?” Dawn asked.

“Yeah, I’m thinking of making an offer, I understand there’s no chain.”

“I wouldn’t go over twenty myself,” Dawn said.

“Pounds?”

“Pence.”

We laughed. I was acutely aware I would only be working with Dawn for another few days and knew I'd miss her. We hadn't got on at the start, but now it was like working with a really good friend.

At three thirty I took over watching the telephone box. Several people used the phone and at one point a queue formed, but none of them looked like possible hoax callers to me.

Dawn also took a look around the flat; I could hear, unlike me, she was looking through drawers and cupboards.

"What you looking for?" I asked, when she returned a few minutes later.

"I don't know really. I think it comes from doing this job for too long. It makes you really nosey."

"Oh, I remember what I've got to tell you," I said.

"Twice lately, I've been asked if we're seeing each other."

"By whom?"

"Sergeant Bellamy and Andy Welling."

"I hope you put them right, Chris. I'm not really bothered about Sergeant Bellamy, but Andy, that's a different story."

"I did put them right, of course, I said I never had, wasn't and never would be."

"Good. I wonder how that rumour started, this job's a nightmare."

"Apparently, someone saw me coming out of your house at a weekend. I said I occasionally have dinner there with you and your mum. That was all right to say, wasn't it?"

"Yeah, yeah. Who was it that saw you at mine then?"

"No idea. Do you live near any old bill?"

"Only Dean Campbell, as you well know. Is that where you were Saturday?"

"I did see them on Saturday, but please, Dawn, don't ask any more 'cos I'm really uncomfortable talking about it. I know you think I'm an idiot but I'm nineteen and as horny as hell."

"Your age is immaterial, Chris. You're a bloke so your brain is in your pants."

She smiled.

"I am going to change the subject. Will you let me take you out for a meal on Friday? To say thank you for ..."

I thought for a few moments.

"Well, so much really. Teaching me everything, putting me straight, putting me up."

"Yeah, okay, you can take me out. We'll go to the Berni Inn in Woodford Green; I haven't been there for years."

At five thirty the shopping centre closed, and the shutters were unrolled and placed across the entrance.

"Call it a day?" Dawn suggested.

I nodded.

We collected our things and headed towards the front door before I realised I'd left the PR on the windowsill. As I picked it up and set off back towards the hall, I made a casual remark.

"What a shit hole. How could anyone have lived like this?"

I had barely completed the sentence when there was the almightiest crash from the bedroom. Both Dawn and I froze exactly where we were.

"What the fuck was that?" I said.

"Something must have fallen over, best you check it out," Dawn replied.

"Suddenly you're not so nosey?"

"Go on, you are the man here."

"Suddenly you believe as a man I'm better than you at certain jobs?" I was enjoying this.

"Just check, please," she said sweetly.

The bedroom didn't seem any different; there was nothing obvious which could have made such a noise.

"That's weird," I said.

"I don't think she liked your comment about her housekeeping abilities."

"I think you might be right, Dawn. Sorry," I said, deliberately loudly as if speaking to someone who was in the room next door.

We made our way back to the nick.

"You know how I've very graciously agreed to go to dinner with you on Friday?" Dawn said.

"Yes."

"Can I ask you a favour in return?"

"Anything, partner, your wish is my command," I said.

"Speak to your mate Andy Welling, will you, see if he wants to ask me out? As you said, life's too short so as of today, I am declaring myself officially back on the market. And I'm not dating another married man as long as I live."

Chapter 64 – Dawn lays plans

The following day I reported to the Street Duties portacabin as usual, put the kettle on and knocked on the door of the sergeant's office to see if he wanted a brew, but there was no reply. Whilst I waited for it to boil, I sat at the desk and looked through one of Dawn's old magazines. I came across a do-it-yourself test entitled *'How much do you love your man?'* which someone, I assumed Dawn, had completed. She scored forty-two out of fifty, which qualified her as *'Head over heels in love'*. I remembered my brief encounter with Barry and how my perception of him had changed so dramatically over the evening; good-looking he wasn't, but personality he had in abundance.

I checked my watch; Dawn was late, even though she'd left the house ten minutes before I had. Even on our penultimate day, she still insisted on travelling to and from the nick in separate cars.

I stood up and opened the door leading to the back yard. Dawn was walking towards me and her face was serious.

"What's up, partner?"

"Sergeant Bellamy's in hospital. He had a heart attack last night."

"Oh, my God, is he going to be all right?"

"The ambulance crew managed to resuscitate him; he's still unconscious, he's in a coma, so it's possible he might have brain damage."

"Fuck me, Dawn, how old is he?"

"Someone in the front office reckons forty-four; that's why he was making the dash for cash."

"The dash for cash?"

"It's when people a few years from retirement try to get promoted so they get a better pension. Sergeant Bellamy would probably have been promoted to Inspector by Christmas; then in the five years he has left, he'll get to the top of the inspectors' pay scale and bingo, when he retires at fifty his pension is roughly equivalent to a PC's wage."

"God laughs ..." I said.

"What do you mean?" Dawn asked.

"It was one of my mum's favourite expressions. God laughs when people start making plans."

"How very true," Dawn replied.

"Is he going to die?" I asked.

"I don't know; you know everything the Chief Inspector has just told me. He wants me to act up and run the next Street Duties course and I said I'd think it over. I was due to go to Beat Crimes, but I could study for the skipper's exam instead."

"When does the next course start?"

"Two weeks. It might be interesting 'cos there's some Asian guy called Rik on it and we don't get many of them."

"If it's the same Rik I did my selection day at Paddington with, he's a really nice geezer."

Dawn had been carrying a folder which I hardly noticed, but when I told her about Rik, she opened it and removed an application form, attached to which was a small black and white photograph.

"That's him," I declared excitedly. "He seemed a really genuine bloke."

"Well, let's see, shall we?"

Dawn picked up the application form and studied it briefly.

"Where's he from?"

"London definitely, Manor something, is there a Manor Park?"

"Two points," she replied, as if we were doing a quiz.

"Height?"

"Six foot."

"Five eleven, one point."

"And what's his current occupation?"

"Shopkeeper."

"Retail manager, close enough; well done, three out of three."

"So, if you take the Street Duty route to promotion, won't that hamper your chances of getting into the CID?"

"That's one of the dilemmas. You can get a level transfer, that's a move from uniform to CID as a sergeant, but it's not easy. You have to find yourself an investigative role and then really shine at it. I'll think the whole thing over. It's a great opportunity and I ought to take it. That's what I like sometimes: everything can change in a flash in this job, you never know what's coming next."

"I'm not sure Sergeant Bellamy would share that sentiment this morning," I said.

"Fair point, poor sod," Dawn said.

"I think you'd make a great sergeant, Dawn," I said.

"Thank you."

"Oh, I've got something I need your advice on."

"Go on, Chris, but make the most of me, only two days left."

I told Dawn about the canteen lady and asked what I should do with the information.

"I wouldn't do or say anything, Chris," Dawn said conclusively.

"But it can't be right, can it?"

"No, it's not, but the job won't want to be told. The Chief Super's just sacked an Orthodox Jew; he can't arrest one of the black dinner ladies for theft. You've only got one more day of taking my advice, and my advice is to say nothing to anyone."

"Okay, I won't."

"What's more, I thought you were friends with the landlord of the Elephant. If you report this, he'll get done for receiving."

"Receiving?"

"Yes, Chris, receiving stolen goods."

"I never thought about that. But then sometimes I don't get you, Dawn. When I told you about Debbie and the drugs, you gave me the *'you're either a policeman or you're not'* lecture. Now you're taking exactly the opposite position."

"Chris, there's an enormous difference between a kilo of cocaine and a couple of tins of Fray Bentos."

"Fair point," I replied, mimicking a reply she occasionally used herself.

"So, where you taking me tomorrow, the Berni Inn?" Dawn asked.

"No, I drove over to Buckhurst Hill last night and found a nice little Italian down Queen's Road on the left."

Dawn's face fell.

"What?"

"Barry used to take me there."

"Oh, no problem. We'll go somewhere else."

"No, Chris; Ruberto's is fine. I'll have the Mediterranean Prawns followed by the Tornado Rossini. I need to move on, and besides, I saw you chatting to Andy yesterday, so I'm expecting to be asked out any day soon."

"Ah," I replied.

I'd considered telling Dawn that Andy was married or in a serious relationship, but I'd made that bloody promise about always telling her the truth.

"What? We had a deal, Chris, or are you jealous? I knew this relationship and you moving in and everything was a mistake."

Dawn was getting angry.

"No, Dawn, it's not that. In fact, I have asked him, but you're not his type."

"Not his type? Doesn't he like brunettes?"

"No, it's not that."

"Am I too old? I knew I'd wasted too long waiting for Barry. I'm on the bloody shelf and I'm only twenty-six."

I laughed. I couldn't help myself.

"Oh, so my life's a joke, is it? I'm glad you think it's funny."

"Stop transmitting and start receiving."

"You rude bastard," Dawn said.

"Andy agreed you were lovely but unfortunately, you lack that special something he desperately craves."

"What?"

"A penis."

"What? No."

"That's what he said."

"Really, are you sure he was being serious?"

"No, come to think about it, I think he was straight at the start of our conversation but the thought of taking you out so violently repulsed him that he decided, from that very moment on, he would only ever want arse sex with other men."

"You're not funny, Chris."

"Not even mildly amusing? I asked.

"Not vaguely."

"Mind you, even if Andy's homosexual, he's still got one thing you haven't," Dawn said.

I knew I was walking into a trap and smiled before asking the obvious question.

"And what, my partner, might that be?"

"More chance of sleeping with me than you." She laughed.

I laughed too, although it was put on. I knew Dawn didn't fancy me but if I was never told that again, that would be just fine with me.

Instead of doing the O P, that day was spent going through Sergeant Bellamy's work to find out what needed doing today and what could be put off until later. There were also several matters which had to be arranged in respect of the next Street Duties course. I was frustrated not to be doing the O P but when by five thirty no hoax bomb threats had been received, we knew we would have been unsuccessful anyway. We had just one day left to catch them; my chances of leaving Street Duties with a bang were starting to fade.

Chapter 65 – Loose ends

When we walked into the flat the next day, what we saw was a little disconcerting.

"What the hell?"

"Oh, my God, this is freaky."

"Seriously, what's going on?"

Between five thirty on the Wednesday and three o'clock that Friday afternoon, someone had done some serious cleaning and housework in our off-street O P. The blood stain was still on the bedroom carpet, but the bed had been made and the clothes which had been on the floor in a heap had been neatly folded and put away. The cider bottle and glasses had found their way to the kitchen, where the overspilling bin had been emptied and a fresh plastic liner inserted. The flat had definitely been vacuumed and dusted, although no trace could be found of a vacuum cleaner and there was a distinctly fresh smell in the air. Even the toilet and bath had been cleaned. The place was far from spotless, but someone had made a real effort to tidy up.

For ten minutes we walked around the small flat identifying everything that had changed.

"The council must have sent someone in. It must have been yesterday when we weren't here," I said, offering the only plausible explanation.

"But what about that loud noise when you said it was a ..."

Dawn mouthed rather than spoke her next word.

"Shit tip?"

"I don't believe in ghosts, Dawn, and even if I did, a cleaning ghost? Seriously?"

I was quite surprised by Dawn's attitude. From her facial expression and body language, she didn't like this at all.

"Dawn, if you're really that unsettled, go to the housing offices, they're only a couple of hundred yards away, or give DS Cotton a call and see if he's got any idea. I don't mind, I'm quite happy to sit and watch whilst you do what you've got to do."

"No, it's all right, I'll check later."

"I really don't mind," I said, hoping she'd just go if she felt that bothered.

"No. We've only done one day this week, which is rubbish and if you remember, more of the calls were made on a Friday afternoon than at any other time. Besides, I've got a really good feeling about today. Today, we'll catch these idiots."

Once again, we did thirty minutes about in the hot seat, but it seemed when we were off watch, we'd lost our inclination to go snooping, so instead we sat and chatted. The conversation was easy at first, but I had several things on my mind which I wished to clear up and now would be the perfect opportunity. I knew by bringing these matters up, I was sailing quite close to the wind and hoped Dawn wouldn't be too offended, particularly as we were going out for a meal later.

"Dawn, I'd really like to ask you about a couple of things but if you're not happy discussing them, just tell me and I'll shut up."

She was staring at the telephone box.

"That sounds ominous, are they about the job or are they personal."

"Three job related, one personal," I said, after a moment's hesitation gave me time to work it out.

"Have you been making a list? Go with the work ones first, we might leave the personal one for tonight."

"Okay. I've worked out what the DAC's wife is doing."

"Really? Go on then, what's your theory?"

"I think she buys say a leather coat in the sales, probably ones with a big discount. Let's say, for argument's sake, it cost one hundred quid. Then she removes the sale price tag and replaces the label with a pre-sale one; let's imagine that's one hundred and sixty-nine. She'll have cut the more expensive label out previously, like when we saw her doing it. Then she returns the leather jacket saying she's lost the receipt. The store will give her one hundred and sixty-nine quid and she'll have made a profit of sixty-nine quid."

"But the sixty-nine quid would be in vouchers. If you don't have a receipt, they give you vouchers. She'd only be able to spend them in one of their stores."

"Yeah, but they sell just about everything there, household, electrical, groceries. And she can use the vouchers to buy more clothes and do it all over again. Now if that is what she was doing, then she was doing it on a very large scale because she had loads of clothes, dozens of labels and details of all the stores around London and their sale dates. If she's got a car full, she might even have a house full? What do you think, partner?"

"You might be right," Dawn replied.

"What can we do about it?"

"I'll think that one over. One down, two to go. What's next, Chris?"

"I think this is trickier, but you decide."

I took the hot seat. There was no one anywhere near the phone box.

"You know the safe blower, Danny Daly?"

Dawn smiled immediately.

"What?" I said.

"Nothing," she replied.

"What? Tell me."

"I just wondered how long it would take for the penny to drop?"

"Don't you mean gold sovereign?" I asked.

"What's your theory about Danny Daly then?" she asked.

"Danny didn't have any sovereigns when I searched him on the street; I didn't miss them 'cos they weren't there. Then in the charge room, I know I counted out ten piles of ten, that's one hundred, right?"

"Was the last time I did maths," Dawn replied.

"My theory is that when the sergeant put the washbag away, he removed two of the coins, which he popped into Danny's jean's pocket before he threw the jeans to me to search. I'm so stupid. I didn't even realise when the sergeant told me to leave out from my notes the fact I'd searched him on the street. I didn't even realise when I added two coins to those in the washbag and still only had a hundred. God, I'm stupid."

"You're not stupid, Chris You're young and green, but you're on a really steep learning curve and riding it well. You'll get to blue, partner. Have you got any problems with what happened, Chris?"

Her voice was suddenly more serious.

I looked to my right to try to see any concern in her face.

"Keep looking at the phone box please, we're on obs, don't forget."

"Yeah, sorry. What was the question?"

"Have you got any problems with what happened with Danny Daly?"

I thought about the question for a few moments.

"How can I have? He admitted to me he'd done the burglary."

“And that’s the whole point, Chris. We only fit people up when they’re guilty. Don’t ever fit anyone up who’s innocent ’cos that’s the line you should never cross.”

“That’s interesting, partner, because it brings me on to my third ...”

I was going to use the word ‘issue’ but that sounded too challenging and that was not how I wanted to come across, so I substituted the word,

“... thing.”

“Go on? But keep looking ahead please, Chris, or I shall take over.”

I hadn’t realised I was doing it but it was natural to turn my head towards Dawn when I spoke to her.

“You told me a while ago now, that you backed William Rees up on an arrest and that you weren’t even there when it happened.”

“Yes,” Dawn replied cautiously.

“Didn’t you say the person he’d arrested was claiming to have been fitted up?”

“Yes?”

The tone in Dawn’s reply suggested she was less confident speaking on this subject than the others.

“I shouldn’t have told you that, I realise now, but I was panicking because of Barry’s bloody wife and everything. Well, what about it, Chris?”

“Are you aware William plants evidence – bags of cannabis, flick knives and off weapons – on prisoners?”

“No, not at all, and what makes you say that?”

“Because his locker is next to mine and he tools up every day before he goes out; he’s even offered me some ‘equipment’, so to speak. On some mornings his locker stinks so strongly of cannabis I'm surprised I don't stagger onto parade as high as a kite on High Beech hill."

Dawn said nothing for several minutes and I kept my eyes front and focused on the telephone box, so I couldn't gauge how she was reacting. Eventually, she broke what was slowly becoming a tense silence.

"OK. Thanks for telling me, I think. I still have to back him up in relation to that one particular case because that's the way it is, but I won't be doing it again."

"Go on then, what's this personal thing you want to bring up? Are you going to declare your undying love for me?"

"No, don't be silly; anyway, you already know that. Your mum says you're going to see your dad. I'm so pleased."

"Bloody hell. You and my mum. There's no bloody secrets any more."

"Well, tell me, where you going, what you doing, how do you feel?"

"We're going to meet on Saturday at the King's Head in Loughton, just for a few drinks, you know, see how we get along. I haven't seen him for twelve years and I feel really nervous. I've blocked out the memories of him leaving. I think it was just too painful, but I know I hated him for hurting Mum and for leaving me. I still don't understand how a man, or a woman for that matter, can just up and walk out on young kids."

I wanted to remind her that that is exactly what she wanted Barry to do, not because I wanted to score a point, or show her to be hypocritical, but because I thought she might better understand how and why her own father had done what he'd done.

I kept looking straight out of the window. There was a small queue for the phone now, but none of the people were schoolchildren, although just at that moment I saw my first schoolboy, in the uniform of the local comprehensive.

"The local school's turned out," I commented.

Dawn didn't reply.

"You okay, partner?" I asked gently, and glanced quickly across the room.

Dawn was crying. I think the irony of the situation that she'd been in for the last five years with Barry had just sunk in. I completely believe from her reaction at that moment, she'd never before compared her father's affair with his secretary with her own affair with Barry.

A good few minutes passed before she spoke again.

"I'm going to the bathroom to tidy myself up and when I come back, I'll take over."

And then the most amazing thing took place. The most amazing thing that had ever happened to me in the whole of my life. Dawn walked over. I thought she was going to reach by me, pick up the radio and ask for a signal check, but she didn't. She bent over and kissed me on my right cheek. I didn't respond, didn't turn my head to face her, I just continued looking forward. I think I was in shock.

"What was that for, partner?" I asked, as she stood up.

"Because I wanted to."

And with that she made her way to the bathroom.

I watched carefully, because several more schoolboys were milling about near the bus stop and phone box, but none had made a call. I sat up, more in hope than expectation.

I heard Dawn close the toilet door and imagined her pulling up her denim skirt and sliding down her knickers. I rebuked myself for allowing such indecent thoughts before muttering three words of poor mitigation to myself.

"I'm only human."

And then it happened.

"Golf November units, a coded message has been received stating there is an improvised explosive device in a shop at the Arndale Centre."

I immediately stood up. I hadn't taken my eyes off the schoolboys so I knew they hadn't made the call, but I remembered one of the hoax calls had been made from the other telephone box, the one at the west entrance. I was up and out in seconds.

"Dawn, there's been a coded message, I mean there's been a hoax call, it must be from the other telephone box. I'm making my way there now."

I didn't wait for her to reply, I'd given her all the information she needed, and time was now critical if I was to find anyone anywhere near the other box. I flew out the front door, down the stairs, across the busy road and sprinted through the shopping centre. At the square in the centre, I turned left and still running hard, made the western entrance no longer than ninety seconds after the call had come out. The box, however, was empty, no one was anywhere near it and I couldn't see any schoolchildren.

Nearby, an elderly white man was selling flowers from a stall.

"Excuse me."

I flashed my warrant card.

"Have you seen anyone making a call from that phone box in the last couple of minutes? It's very important."

"Unlikely, mate, it's not working. It was vandalised weeks ago. Some schoolkids smashed it up; I told them to stop but they ignored me. It's a shame you weren't around then."

A quick check confirmed the accuracy of what I'd been told. I turned and walked slowly back towards the square at the centre. This didn't seem to make any sense. The children by the other telephone box had definitely not made a call and the one at this end was inoperative. Was it possible, that for the first time in thirty-four calls and on the very afternoon we were waiting for them, they'd used a different phone? That seemed incredibly unlucky.

I felt and realised my earpiece had come out, which meant I'd temporarily lost communication with Dawn and the nick. It must have dislodged when I had been running through the shopping centre. I dropped my sight and started searching the floor.

"Chris, Chris."

I looked up to see Dawn walking quickly, almost running, towards me. She seemed concerned, but I couldn't think why. Then I noticed the strangest thing: as she passed people, they started to laugh at her. She looked normal enough to me in her light blue T-shirt under a darker blue denim jacket and a denim skirt, which fell below the knee; in fact, she looked quite attractive. It was as if someone had put a ridiculous sign on the back of her jacket. Now some shoppers were openly pointing out to others that whatever was on Dawn's back was worth a look.

"Chris, it's a coded message," Dawn said, as soon as she was just near enough for me to hear her properly.

"What?"

"It's a *coded* message. We've got to get everyone out of here."

I wasn't really listening; I was more intrigued as to what everyone was laughing at. When she reached me, I took her by the shoulders and turned her around. She resisted at first and we changed places through one hundred and eighty degrees as if in a dance. In her haste to catch me up, when she'd arisen from the toilet, she tucked her skirt into her knickers.

"Dawn, you need to sort your skirt out."

She grimaced as her hands cupped her exposed backside.

"Oh, no," she said, quickly pulling her skirt out and allowing it to drop down. "That's your fault, running off like that."

I looked up to see how many people were watching, but saw nothing but a sheet of brilliant white.

Chapter 66 – Dusk

The flash was definitely first, but only just. Then there was the thud, the low resinous thud, and I could physically *feel* the noise vibrate through my chest. Would it stop my heart? Accompanying the thud was a wind, a really strong rush of air and I was being carried backwards, quickly, uncontrollably. One second after the flash, there was nothing.

In my dream I could hear a monotonous buzzing and wanted it to stop. Surely, someone would turn it off soon? How could I sleep with that bloody racket going on? I wasn't comfortable at all. And then my head started throbbing too. I'd have to wake up, get up and take something for my headache; and then I could sort that bloody buzzing out too.

I opened my eyes but shut them immediately because there was dust everywhere. Not normal household dust but white plaster dust with bits in it. Where was I? I was lying on my back and next to a wall or something. I could smell an odour which was familiar, what was it? I became aware of my breathing, slow, heavy and deep. It was reassuring and the rhythm suggested I should go back to sleep; yes that seemed like a good idea, sleep. I'd deal with whatever when I wake up. My mind started shutting down.

I was dreaming now, standing next to a phone box, a TK, a TK, a TK, Telephone Kiosk. I need two pence to make a call, Chris. Two pence to make a call. Need somewhere to live. Chris, help. The phone's been vandalised, bloody vandalised. I really needed that phone to be working. Can't go back to Hackney, that's just not an option. I didn't like that bloke, Chris. Tommy said he was a nasty piece of work. Knickers, Dawn was wearing red knickers. Fancy that, seeing Dawn's red knickers. Chris, please. Poor Sergeant Bellamy, he's dead, you know, dead, dead, dead.

That bloody buzzing, really irritating, damned right annoying. Chris, go back to sleep now. Sort it out tomorrow. Fucking buzzing and now there's a voice too. There's no peace for the wicked.

Behind the buzzing was a voice; it tugged away at my consciousness and wouldn't let me go back to sleep. I started to feel guilty; I'd forgotten something, something important. I'd have to remember and get it done before I'd be allowed to sleep.

"Help me!"

Go away!

"Help me!"

For fuck's sake GO AWAY!

"Chris, I need you."

With all the effort I could muster, I moved my head ever so slightly and my eyes flickered open again. There was less dust now. Was this a dream? Where was I? I tilted my head forward and blinked. Everything I could see was broken, smashed to pieces, and glass was everywhere. And something was definitely burning, that was the smell, wood burning. My vision in my left eye was really blurred but I could make something out: perhaps ten feet away there was a pile of torn clothes covered in plaster and dust.

"Chris, help me."

Strange?

"Chris."

I needed to think, if I shut my eyes, I might be able to concentrate and work out what was going on. If it was too difficult, I'd just go back to sleep.

"Don't you dare leave me, Chris. I need you."

With less effort this time, I opened my eyes again. The words were coming from the pile of clothes.

Suddenly an unwelcome awareness started to dawn. This was no dream, this was real life. Something truly terrible had happened but I was alive and uninjured. Uninjured? Was I uninjured? I looked along the length of my body.

"Chris."

What a mess! My jeans, oh, my God, I'd definitely need new jeans. And I'd only just bought this pair. All my clothing was torn, stained and covered in white dust, one trainer was missing. Where the fuck had that gone?

I lifted my right hand: a thin splinter of glass had penetrated my palm and when I rotated my wrist I could see it protruding on both sides; a steady trickle of blood flowed. Why didn't it hurt?

"Chris, please!"

Then I realised the buzzing was coming from inside, inside my, inside my head; something was definitely wrong with my ears. Had my eardrums burst?

Cognizance brought pain, pure and undiluted.

"Chris, please, my God, you've got to help me."

My head wanted to explode, I moved my jaw and knew it was broken, my right hand screamed in agony and something was wrong with my face, not my jaw, the right side of my face. I touched my cheek but it wasn't there, my face just went inwards.

"Chris, you're bloody useless."

I started to tremble uncontrollably. Was I dying? Was I dead?

"You promised my mum, you promised, Chris."

I sat up and looked at the pile of clothes. The dust was clearing now and I could see several other bodies, all still, all in tatters. I was in what had been a shopping centre.

"Help."

Dawn!

I pulled myself up onto my knees. My right hand was useless; I didn't even want to look at it.

I considered crawling the ten yards or so between us, but the ground was covered in thousands of pieces of glass, so I pulled myself up, slowly, gingerly, tentatively. Blood started to run down my face, so I guessed my head was cut. I wiped my palm across my forehead.

"Chris."

I noticed the intonation in her voice had changed, she was watching me, she knew I was coming. I felt encouraged.

I stumbled, well fell, across the short but seemingly eternal distance between us, and slumped down by her side. I wanted to help her I really did but I was consumed by my own pain. It was all I could think about and I needed all my strength to deal with what was happening to me.

"Oh, Chris. I'm scared."

For the first time I looked at Dawn. She was lying on her side in the fetal position, almost curled up in a ball and by her tummy was a pool of thick dark red blood.

"Hello, partner," I said.

"Hello, partner," she replied; her voice was weak.

"Coded message," she whispered.

"I don't understand, Dawn?"

"It wasn't a hoax; I was trying to tell you."

Stupid though it may seem, I suddenly realised what had happened. A bomb, there'd been a bomb. And Dawn knew it was a bomb and yet she'd come to warn me."

"I think we're in a bit of a pickle," I said.

It was a daft thing to say but Dawn smiled, and it cracked the dust that was starting to crust on her face.

"Chris, I'm really scared."

"I'm here; I'll look after you now."

I wasn't at all sure I could, but I'd damn well try.

I repositioned myself, turning towards her. I noticed her right leg had been almost severed at the knee and the lower leg had turned at a most unnatural angle; but the pool of deep red blood by her tummy seemed to be growing. I knew I had somehow to stem the flow, or my partner would bleed to death. With my uninjured hand, I started to turn her on to her back.

"What are you doing?" she asked.

"I need to see what injuries you've got. First aid and all that."

Dawn relaxed a little and I rolled her back amongst an ocean of debris of glass, wood and plaster. Her jacket was open, and I lifted one side, her T-shirt was shredded, and I could see her stomach had been ripped open almost across the entire width of her body; her intestines hung loose in creased, white-blooded curls. They seemed to be growing before my very eyes. Blood was everywhere and running down into the pool. I couldn't do anything; the wound was too big; Dawn had been almost cut in half.

I looked up and around, desperately hoping to see someone who could help, an ambulance crew perhaps, but no one was there, just a few bodies here and there; where the fuck was everyone? I needed my radio, where was it?

"I think I've injured my stomach, there's such a terrible thumping pain in my guts."

She was panting every few words.

"Yes, you've got a nasty cut, but the ambulance will be on its way by now. You are going to need stitches."

"Oh, damn. I've never had stitches before."

"Nothing to worry about partner, they're a piece of cake."

"Is that all, a nasty cut?" she asked.

What could I say? I didn't want to tell her the truth but was afraid that if I hesitated or evaded the question, she'd know it was worse.

"I'm not going to lie, Dawn; your right leg is really badly broken."

"I can't feel it," she replied.

"It's probably just numb," I suggested.

She nodded.

I knew I couldn't do anything for her and that she needed proper medical help. But I could be there; I could comfort her and make sure she wasn't alone. I could reassure her and hold her. I put an arm around her and squeezed as tightly as my ever-ebbing strength would allow.

"I feel dizzy," she said. Her voice was definitely getting weaker.

"Am I going to die?" she asked quietly.

"Don't be so dramatic, Dawn. It's really not that bad."

"I'm so scared."

Her voice was no more than a whisper.

"I'm here, partner."

"I want my mum," she pleaded.

Suddenly, behind me I could hear movement, and turning slightly, I could see several uniform officers walking through the carnage and behind them I could just make out the uniforms of two ambulance crew.

"Help's here, Dawn," I said encouragingly, but she didn't reply.

I looked down; her chest was rising and falling but very slightly and her eyes had closed.

"Stay awake, Dawn. They're here."

Her mouth opened as if she was trying to speak.

"Stay awake, partner, don't go to sleep, they're going to need you awake so you can answer their questions."

I looked again at her chest and waited for it to move; it didn't. Panic gripped me; I shook her, gently at first and then more firmly. Still her chest didn't move.

"Help," I screamed, with every ounce of strength that I had.

"Help us!"

At ten past four, Police Constable Dawn Matthews, my Street Duties instructor and my best friend, died in my arms.

I dedicate this to the memory of the twenty-five Metropolitan Police officers killed in the line of duty during my service: Jane Arbuthnot, Martin Bell, Keith Blakelock, Laurence Brown, Stephen Dodd, Patrick Dunne, Yvonne Fletcher, John Fordham, Robert Gladwell, George Hammond, Stephen Jones, Alan King, Noel Lane, Ronald Leeuw: Nina Mackay, Ronan McCloskey, James Morrison, Philip Olds, Christopher Roberts, Derek Robertson, Kulwant Sidhu, Gary Sunnucks, Gary Toms, Stephen Walker and Phillip Walters. May you rest in peace.

From Black to Blue

It is eighteen months later. PC Christopher Pritchard has physically recovered from the bombing but remains mentally scarred. In the aftermath he spent carelessly and is now heavily in debt. During the search of a house, the hitherto honest officer steals six thousand pounds.

Delighted, at first, to be out of his dire financial situation, it soon dawns on Christopher the theft was an appalling act of dishonesty and he strives to atone for his mistake.

As his complicated personal life becomes ever more interwoven with the epidemic of police corruption at Stoke Newington police station, Christopher feels the noose of inevitable justice tightening around his neck.